ABOUT THE AUTHOR

Developing the imagination one might expect of a fantasy author, Guernsey writer Nicki Harrison has always loved creating stories. Alongside writing novels, Nicki found her ideal career in the travel industry and has been running her own business as a Travel Counsellor since 2017.

Her travels and experiences strengthened her love for creating immersive characters and unique worlds, hoping to take readers on the only type of journey she cannot create in her day job. Supported by her husband Shaun, family and friends (and of course the dogs), Nicki hopes that her writing will provide a fresh escapism for every fantasy lover with this sequel to her debut novel, *The Withering*.

DEDICATION

To Shaun,

Thank you for allowing me to use *her* name, helping me to embrace the destructive nature of a fire mage and for all your other brilliant suggestions.

ENCIA TRILOGY

N.K. Harrison

Reckoning

Book 2

Austin Macauley Publishers

London * Cambridge * New York * Sharjah

Copyright © N.K. Harrison 2025

The right of N.K. Harrison to be identified as author of this work has been asserted by the author in accordance with sections 77 and 78 of the Copyright, Designs and Patents Act 1988.

All rights reserved. No part of this publication may be reproduced, stored in a retrieval system, or transmitted in any form or by any means, electronic, mechanical, photocopying, recording, or otherwise, without the prior permission of the publishers.

Any person who commits any unauthorised act in relation to this publication may be liable to criminal prosecution and civil claims for damages.

This is a work of fiction. Names, characters, businesses, places, events, locales, and incidents are either the products of the author's imagination or used in a fictitious manner. Any resemblance to actual persons, living or dead, or actual events is purely coincidental.

A CIP catalogue record for this title is available from the British Library.

ISBN 9781035862832 (Paperback)
ISBN 9781035862849 (ePub e-book)

www.austinmacauley.com

First Published 2025
Austin Macauley Publishers Ltd®
1 Canada Square
Canary Wharf
London
E14 5AA

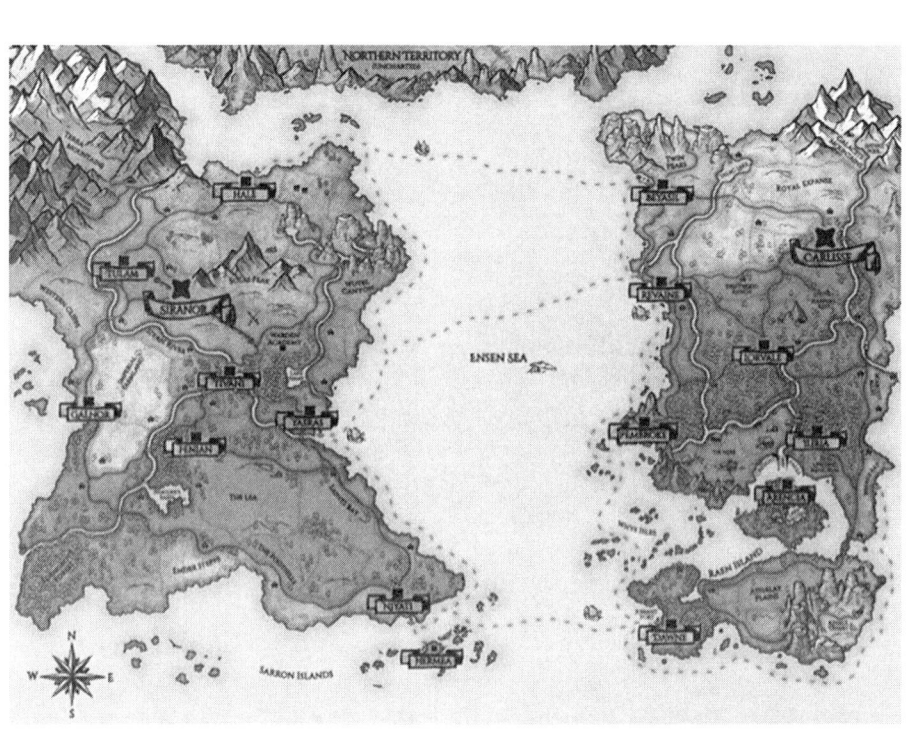

Acknowledgements

For being the pinnacle of support as I wrote this second novel, I wish to thank my husband, Shaun who has earned the dedication tenfold. I am also extremely grateful to my family, in particular my parents and my aunt, Sue. You have all delved into the world of dystopian fantasy just to support me on this journey. Words cannot express how much that means to me.

To my wonderful core beta readers and friends, thank you for everything! Every comment and conversation we had improved not only this story, but my writing. You also helped me to refine my writing style, a flair that is (slightly) more than just torturing your favourite characters.

I also would like to give extra thanks to a few special people. Firstly, James Angell for giving me the courage and connections at Austin Macauley to get published and Ryan de Haaff for once again giving my characters their faces. You can see his art and learn even more about the world of Encaris on the trilogy's dedicated website, *www.encia-trilogy.co.uk* which has been created and updated by Jess Wiper and the team at Third Aye Studio.

The journey to create this book would not have been possible without two more incredible people. Dominique Ogier-Keltie and Rachel Le Mesurier.

Meeting Dominique through my travel business and discovering her incredible talent for design resulted in us collaborating to create the cover. Her talent is undeniable, and I am so grateful to be able to call her a friend and credit Design by Dom.O for this artwork.

Chance made me lucky enough to meet a soul sister who just also happens to be an author in her own right and an editor. Lucky, right? Rachel, you really are one in a million and I'm so glad that our love of books brought us together. I couldn't imagine editing without your divine skill. Thank you for encouraging me to polish off the rough diamond that was my manuscript and guiding me as I turned it into this wonderful second book for the world to enjoy.

Table of Contents

Prologue	13
Chapter One: Retreat	21
Chapter Two: Intentions	37
Chapter Three: Declaration	51
Chapter Four: Creation	63
Chapter Five: Forewarn	80
Chapter Six: Stratagem	96
Chapter Seven: Resolve	113
Chapter Eight: Firestorm	134
Chapter Nine: Command	152
Chapter Ten: Assault	165
Chapter Eleven: Aftermath	181
Chapter Twelve: Reunited	195
Chapter Thirteen: Insight	208
Chapter Fourteen: Vigil	223
Chapter Fifteen: Ignoble	239
Chapter Sixteen: Coup De Grâce	254
Chapter Seventeen: Gambit	270
Chapter Eighteen: Peril	287
Chapter Nineteen: Tidings	301
Chapter Twenty: Breakthrough	315
Chapter Twenty-One: Lethal Cure	330
Chapter Twenty-Two: Atonement	348
Chapter Twenty-Three: Serendipity	366
Chapter Twenty-Four: Revealed	384
Chapter Twenty-Five: Incursion	397
Epilogue	418

Prologue

With a sunken heart and pounding head, Harrison Stone recalled the events of the past day. Despite not having properly slept since escaping Carlisse and returning to the safety of Arencia, he couldn't rest. Pacing outside the infirmary, his current concern was the welfare of his friend, Zack, who'd been blinded during the attack. Some of the most gifted healers among the Ar'encal had gathered to repair the damage to his eyes but no one had entered or left Zack's room for hours.

The painfully long wait was over when Maia Uriel, the leader of the Ar'encal, approached him.

"Finally, what are they doing in there?" Harrison asked, crossing and uncrossing his arms impatiently.

"What they can," Maia responded softly, trying to reassure him.

"Your people are supposed to be gifted, why is it taking so long?" he snapped, his frustration rooted in concern and a growing sense of dread.

Maia's magic had been enough to heal the bullet wound Harrison had endured during the ambush, a shot that otherwise would have been fatal, but now, his good fortune made waiting for an update on Zack's condition unbearable.

"Zack has been wounded by a poison unfamiliar to us. *My people* have never conceived such vile weaponry," she retorted, saddened by his choice to divide himself from the Ar'encal.

Harrison had just been initiated into the Aegis Guard, a group of warriors that were formed in Arencia as they sympathised with the plight of both mages and the Ar'encal, choosing to protect them despite the risks. Currently, however, his tone was lacking its usual compassion, making him sound more like a warrior than a sympathiser.

"I'm sorry, that came out wrong," he apologised, running his hands through his warm brown hair, the curls longer than he'd usually like. He didn't mean to blame Maia or the Ar'encal healers.

"You fear for your friend, that's understandable, but we share your concern. Zack is dear to us all," Maia began, turning her attention to Alex who was sitting near Harrison, his laced fingers pressed into his forehead. "You should both prepare for the possibility that the healers may not be able to cure him."

"So he could be blind forever?" Alex gasped, turning sharply to look at Maia. Her slender face was thinner than usual but there was no disguising her sorrow, even though she tried to use her dark, feathery fringe to conceal her eyes and defining nose ridges.

"I'm afraid so," she answered, casting her eyes to the floor. It took all her composure to hold back the tears she wanted to weep for the admirable young man.

Maia had befriended Zack's parents, Lucas and Cara Harper, over twenty-five years ago. Celebrated with them on the days he and his brother were born and mourned when Cara died. She'd seen the boys grow up, train diligently to become guardians and truly sympathised when Zack decided to leave Arencia. Her pride at discovering the lengths he went to when helping mages across the continent was second only to his father's. Knowing his condition was inflicted in the defence of the magically gifted, who may not be able to heal him in return, was heartbreaking.

Inside the infirmary, Lianna sat diligently at the end of Zack's bed, plaiting her thick, dark hair and then releasing it repeatedly while the healers attended to him. They'd tried several methods but after a while, Lianna's heart was filled with sadness, both her own and that of the Ar'encal present. She knew their attempts had failed. As the others left, a softly-spoken elder remained to speak with Zack.

"I'm sorry, the damage is too extensive. We've repaired the scars on your skin, but were too late to restore your sight," he explained, causing Zack to slowly sit up. As he reached out in the direction of the elder's voice, he took Zack's hand and gripped it firmly.

"Thank you for trying," Zack replied, giving the elder a grateful smile. "I know you did everything you could for me."

As he departed, the elder gave Lianna a sympathetic smile and she quickly moved to sit beside Zack.

"This is all—" she began, burying her face into her hands.

"Please don't say this is your fault," Zack interrupted, his tone kind. "The only person to blame is that hunter. She created the poison flask and threw it."

"At me!" Lianna wailed, her fingers shaking as she rapidly wiped away the tears from her reddened eyes. "If you hadn't pushed me out of the way, I'd be in that bed."

"And you'd prefer that? Because I know I wouldn't," Zack asserted, turning towards her voice with an expression of utter dismay. "Listen, Lianna... to my words or my feelings, whichever you are more inclined to believe. I don't blame you."

Even though his words and feelings resonated with pure honesty, Lianna couldn't stop berating herself. After a long silence, Zack's hand found her leg and she took hold, giving him a gentle squeeze.

"At least let me look after you," she pleaded. "You may be glad I wasn't injured, but I still feel your pain. Helping you will help me to feel better too."

"I won't argue with that," he replied with a shallow smile.

As she looked at him, the sight was agonising. He was clearly grateful to have her close but his eyes, which had once been a vibrant blue were now clouded and pale. Blind. He could hide his pain from the others, but not from her. Falling into a silent spiral of guilt, Lianna found herself trying to find new ways to apologise until Alex, Harrison and Maia entered the room.

"How are you feeling, bud?" Harrison asked, approaching Zack's bedside and placing a comforting hand on his shoulder.

"Harrison?" Zack paused.

"Yeah, it's me, Zack. Alex and Maia are here too."

"I'll be okay, although all that archery training seems a little redundant now," Zack responded, trying to make light of the situation. "Do you have any news on Rylie?"

Maia had briefly explained to Zack what happened to Harrison during the ambush and what she thought became of Rylie. He'd panicked when he first awoke in the infirmary to discover only Lianna nearby, the absence of his other friends setting his nerves on fire. While awaiting the healers, Zack had adamantly refused to let Lianna try to channel his fear away but calmed once Maia spoke to him. It was a small consolation, but anything was better than nothing.

"Not yet. Alistair is trying to conjure a vision but hasn't had any luck so far. Sadly, Nate and Paige's pleading doesn't help, not that I blame them for being worried," Harrison explained, quickly glancing out the door and shifting his weight impatiently, failing to hide his own desire to find Rylie. They'd been worried about her when she was lost in the woods after her date with Noah, but that situation paled in comparison to this.

"Harrison, you should be with them. You're the only familiar face here for Nate and Paige, apart from Evie. I can't imagine what they're going through," Zack suggested kindly, to which Harrison responded with a grateful squeeze of his friend's shoulder.

Lianna could sense that Zack didn't want him to leave, but wondered if his desire to hold that feeling back was driven by imaging Nate and Paige's faces and how distressed they must be. He was willing to sacrifice his own comfort, even now, for the benefit of others.

"I'll join you," Maia added, taking a deep breath and setting her shoulders back. "You all deserve to know about the Aeons, or at the very least, our beliefs of them."

Reading her body language, Harrison knew that he probably wouldn't like at least part of Maia's explanation, but if there was anything he could do, he needed to find out. Sitting idle was far worse than any task Maia could request of him. Promising to return later, Maia and Harrison left the infirmary and headed to Lake Baliten, where they knew they would find the Auren family.

The leaves that remained on the trees had turned deep, autumnal shades of red and brown but the chill in the air was enough to indicate the onset of winter. As they walked the forest path, Harrison's mind briefly wandered to thoughts of his hometown. It was much easier to feel the change of season in Tivani and he missed the cooler climate of the Western Continent, but despite the constant feeling of being a bit too warm, he had become very fond of Arencia and especially Lake Baliten.

Alistair had brought his son, Nate, and the rest of the Auren family to the area because it held positive memories of Rylie. It was where she'd first displayed control over her powers, and he was attempting to channel that energy to conjure a vision of her. As Harrison and Maia arrived, they could hear Nate and Paige arguing with Alistair, struggling to take in everything that had happened.

Their raised voices and heated words gave Harrison and Maia pause. It felt like a deeply personal, family argument that Harrison didn't want to interrupt, but Nate was demanding results. Maia knew, especially when it came to foresight, that was not easy to deliver. Each vision brought images to the seer, and while Alistair had worked for decades to control and expand what he saw, the level of concentration he needed to succeed would be impossible in this situation. It was Evie, the youngest among them who became the voice of reason.

"Arguing isn't going to bring my sister back," she interrupted, pressing her fingers into her temples.

"Neither is waiting while he stares at the back of his eyelids!" Nate shouted, pointing at Alistair. He quickly bit his tongue as his wife brushed past and caressed their daughter's long hair.

"My girl, when did you become so mature?" Paige asked, opening her arms to embrace Evie, who gratefully accepted while keeping a watchful eye on her father.

Nate exhaled a heavy breath and turned away, struggling to keep calm around Alistair. Despite wanting to believe his father had the best of intentions, learning he'd been tricked for twenty-five years was proving too much for Nate to simply accept. That deceit had fractured Nate's ability to rebuild a relationship with his father.

Joining them from behind, Maia sensed the opportunity to support her friend while Harrison looked towards Paige and Evie before approaching Nate. He stood in silence beside the man who had been a better father to him than his own, letting Nate speak first.

"You stayed with them. Through everything?" he asked, already knowing the answer.

"Yes," Harrison confirmed simply, wanting to reach out to him but deciding against it.

"Thank you," he replied, closing his eyes.

"I cannot begin to imagine how overwhelming all of this is for you, Nate, but can you please put aside this hostility until we find Rylie?" Harrison implored. The calm mention of his other daughter's name encouraged Nate to nod in agreement.

"What has happened to my daughter?" he asked, turning to face Maia and Alistair, dreading the answer.

"I believe she's transformed into an Aeon," Maia replied, indicating with a soft hand motion for Alistair to let her explain.

"And what is that exactly?"

"A state entered when the power and emotions of a person, mage or Ar'encal, become so unstable that they lose control," Maia answered. "Some tales even claim the caster embodies the deity they channel."

"How... and what does that mean for Rylie?" Nate pressed, struggling to remain calm.

"She is a gifted young woman, but harnessing elemental magic is challenging," Maia began. "Are you aware that magic is connected to emotion?"

"Yes, although we couldn't acquire much reading material without risking persecution," Paige said, looking over to her husband, knowing they'd tried their best.

"In a short space of time, Rylie discovered your imprisonment by Harrison's sister and then watched as she thought Harrison was killed, also by Siljanna's hand," Maia continued, encouraging Nate to sit down with his family.

Listening intently, Harrison placed a hand just below his heart, where the bullet Siljanna fired had punctured him. It was a miracle he'd survived.

"But Harrison didn't die," Evie stated, clearly grateful but looking around the room as if her unspoken question was obvious. "Why didn't his survival prevent Rylie's transformation?"

"Your sister doesn't know. She didn't see Maia save me."

"Rylie is now consumed by rage and a desire for justice. Something Harrison's sister is all too familiar with," Maia finished, glancing at each member of the Auren family.

"Is she still my daughter? Is Rylie still in there... even if she's not in control?" Nate questioned, his voice breaking.

"Rylie is acting instinctually, hunting the person who has wronged her and will continue to do so until her needs change. Deep down, she is still your daughter but if she acts upon her desire, I fear the power could consume her," Maia warned. "We must find and get through to Rylie before that happens."

"How?" Paige pleaded, grasping her husband's hand.

"The Ar'encal have runes powerful enough to repel and control Encia and therefore, magic," Maia said, engaging the entire group.

"Runes?" Nate asked with uncertainty.

"There are more? Like the one bestowed upon me when I joined the Aegis Guard?" Harrison added, his attention piqued.

"Yes," Maia replied confidently.

"You have one of these runes, Harrison?" Nate questioned, surprised at the revelation. "Can you be certain they'll work?"

"The rune protected me from Rylie's power and the Encia in the lake once," he explained, pulling the collar of his top down to reveal the mark.

"With some guidance from the artisans, we may be able to find something that will suppress the raw Aeon power in Rylie and present an opportunity for her to regain control," Maia concluded, allowing them all a moment to absorb that small grain of hope.

Harrison was the first to look towards Maia, his expression adamant. He didn't know how, but he wanted to help. She quickly acknowledged him with a graceful nod. The look she gave him spoke volumes. She had a plan but wasn't confident or prepared to give the Auren family false hope. Having been in captivity since the fire in Tivani, the last thing Nate and Paige probably expected upon regaining their freedom would've been to learn the traditions of the Ar'encal.

"Where do we begin?" Nate finally asked as Evie inhaled excitedly and hugged her mother again.

"Leave the runic challenge to me and Harrison, but any solution we discover is useless until we find Rylie," Maia replied, turning swiftly to face Alistair, who'd not said a word since the hostility with his son had been interrupted.

His eyes were closed but his eyelids flickered, and they all recognised it as the sign of a vision.

"Jumant Fort," he announced. "She isn't there now, but she will be."

Chapter One
Retreat

She'd never been one to run, never found a challenge to back away from. But what pursued her now was more than just a challenge; it was a death sentence, and Siljanna Stone was not ready to die. She had some vital mistakes to rectify.

Over the last few weeks, she'd been overcome by a single motivation, revenge. At the time, she felt justified by the events that had occurred, but her hatred of mages had blinded her to the truth. She'd instigated the manhunt for her brother, Harrison and close friend turned mage, Rylie Auren, blaming them for her father's death. Her first mistake.

She made a deal with Imperator Harlyn Rainer and the mage hunters, who took advantage of her rage for scientific and political gain. Her second mistake.

Her ultimate mistake, however, was hurting so many innocent people during that pursuit. Elijah Ashby, the innkeepers in Yasras, Queen Nadia and her supporters, even Samuel Fischer, who despite his glaring personality flaws, did not deserve to die in the way she permitted. Then there was her deep personal regret for the way she'd treated Nate and Paige Auren, putting them in horrendous captivity and using them as bait, just for the chance to make their daughter suffer.

In the moment of her perceived triumph, as she faced Rylie who had been captured by Cameron Weiss, with her favoured pistol in hand, she pulled the trigger but Harrison intercepted the shot. Then Siljanna's world and all she believed true began to unravel. After seeing him fall, Rylie erupted, her magic seeming to take control of the elements. A bolt of lightning struck Cameron, the Imperator's right hand, killing him outright while Rylie became engulfed by flames. Now, Siljanna was the hunted.

She fled Carlisse, but not before learning the true depth of Imperator Harlyn's deception. Under the cover of nightfall, she weaved her way to the northern town of Beyasil, hoping to put the large Ensen Sea between her and Rylie, if it was still possible to consider her the same person after that transformation.

Fumbling through town, Siljanna was surprised to see the streets full of people, even though it was early morning when she arrived. Beyasil felt like a town stuck in the past, with most of the wooden buildings largely held together with hope and some well-placed ropes. There were vendors selling wares on every street corner and labourers cursing at how the cobbled streets caused havoc on their joints while pulling at the stubborn donkeys who refused to drag their carts towards the docks.

Siljanna tucked herself down a side street to ponder the best way of gaining passage on one of the departing ships without any coin. Concealing herself from the nearby tavern, she succumbed to a nervous habit of letting her fingers glide over the partly shaved section of her hair, before letting them tangle in the thin, blond braid that made up the rest of her iconic style.

Pulling some strands out and shaking them quickly to the floor, she was wracked with concern, but before she could formulate a plan, she bumped into a familiar face. Her old friend turned mage hunter, Dylan Rose.

"Siljanna, what are you doing here?" Dylan asked, his pitiless voice intrigued.

"Dylan," Siljanna replied incredulously. She could hardly believe he was standing before her, his attractive features looking more tired than she'd ever seen. "I'm trying to get passage on a ship. The Imperator deceived me, our alliance was a farce. She wanted me to believe Harrison and Rylie killed my father, but everything she told me was a lie."

"I know," he confessed, dropping his head to avoid eye contact with her.

"What do you mean, you know?" she replied, her green eyes questioning him more intently.

Although Siljanna couldn't be certain, it smelled like he'd been drinking. It was difficult to tell whether the smell came from his breath or his shirt, however. She couldn't help but wonder if he'd been drinking all night into the early hours or just dealing with some shady individuals in the nearby tavern.

"I know Harlyn fabricated the report of your father's death," he explained, his tone laden with guilt. "Please understand, I was trained never to question the Imperator's motives. It was my duty to take Imperial secrets to the grave."

"Duty is all it takes to justify torture and murder?" she spat, her arms flying wildly to the sides.

"I don't recall you opposing, Siljanna," he fired back defiantly. He wasn't trying to diminish his guilt but wasn't about to let her claim that her actions were acceptable either. "Imperator Harlyn needed a mage alive; Juliette and I were to deliver one. You provided that opportunity."

With his excuse hanging between them, Dylan fell silent, looking shamefully towards the ground as he rifled through his pockets, pretending to search for something while anticipating Siljanna's counter. To his surprise, her tone changed.

"But you deserted our cause," she said softly.

"Because of Juliette," he admitted, answering her unspoken question. "You weren't the only one being manipulated."

Before Siljanna could give him the chance to explain, their conversation was interrupted by a shrill scream. Turning sharply towards the town gate and origin of the cry, Siljanna backed up into the shadows, panic written across her face. Her reaction in turn deeply worried Dylan. She was the fiercest woman he'd ever known so if she had a reason to fear, it was going to be a valid one.

"Siljanna, what's wrong?" Dylan asked, urgently grabbing her by the shoulders.

"Rylie," she muttered, her eyes fixed in the direction of the distant gate. She placed her hands on his arms without meeting his gaze, and that was when he felt her trembling.

"What's happened to Rylie?" he queried, gently shaking her to draw her focus back to him.

"Get me out of here and I'll tell you everything."

Taking her swiftly by the hand, Dylan led Siljanna through the side streets towards the harbour. As they crossed the market square, they could smell smoke and had to dodge several people who were panicked, desperately trying to flee something. They used the masses to conceal their hasty route towards the pier but only Siljanna knew the warm tones in the morning sky were not due to the sunrise.

Reaching the nearest passenger vessel, Dylan approached a sailor and thrust a coin pouch into his hand. Glancing at the contents and then at both Dylan and Siljanna, he nodded and allowed them down the gangplank to board. Standing on the deck, Dylan saw for the first time exactly what they were running from. A being of flame stalked the main street, heading directly for them and was screaming Siljanna's name. Although her face was recognisable, her features were changed. She didn't just look like fire, she was fire. Dylan almost found it difficult to believe the being before him was Rylie.

As the ship cast off and steadily moved through the low tide, away from the dock, Rylie's pace increased. Running, she launched a flaming projectile directly at Siljanna who threw herself backwards to avoid the blast. Where she'd stood seconds before was now just a scorched mark that darkened the wooden planks of the deck. Helping her up, Dylan instructed Siljanna to head below deck, but her legs wouldn't obey. Neither of them could take their eyes off the being stalking them.

As the ship gained some distance, Rylie bellowed Siljanna's name again and the sound reverberated menacingly. Motioning with her hands, the water below her and around the ship became turmoiled. As the ship struggled through the rising swell, the water adjacent to the dock rose to street level. Rylie placed her foot onto the water as if intending to walk across it and chase down the ship, but it evaporated on contact.

Unable to pursue, Rylie shrieked, the fire she exuded intensifying until the collected energy exploded. The windows of the harbour-side buildings shattered as she watched the ship carry Siljanna out of reach. Ignoring the structural devastation in her wake, Rylie stormed out of Beyasil and turned towards the coast, heading south. Siljanna could only assume that her former friend had succumbed to the power within and would find a way to cross the Ensen Sea and continue the hunt.

As the Eastern Continent receded from their sight, Siljanna and Dylan retreated below deck. Finding a private room, Dylan forcefully pushed Siljanna inside and barred the door.

"Explain, now!" he demanded.

"What do you want me to say? You saw what's after me, what Rylie has become. Her power is terrifying and it's my fault!" Siljanna cried, throwing herself onto the small cabin bed.

Dylan watched as she clenched her fists together, digging her nails into her palms until the pressure caused her to wince. Not wanting to see her harm herself, Dylan crouched before her and took her hands in his own.

"Fine, but please, will you tell me what happened in Carlisse?" he asked, his tone softening. He could see the woman who had been his friend at the academy surfacing while the vengeful warden commander faded away.

"I shot him," Siljanna began as a tear rolled down her cheek.

"Who?"

"Harrison. I couldn't control my rage and instead of capturing Rylie when I had the chance, I went to kill her, but Harrison got in the way," she explained. "Seeing him fall made Rylie change."

"Harrison's dead?" Dylan blurted out, his blue eyes wide with shock.

"No! I don't know how, but he survived," Siljanna quickly answered. "Rylie can't know. I doubt she'd be after me if she did."

"What exactly is your plan then? Return to Siranor and appeal to the Imperator?" Dylan assumed.

"I can't return to Siranor. If the Imperator's alive, she will declare me a traitor. I left her at the mercy of Harrison and his allies," she confirmed, showing no sympathy for the Imperial leader.

"Because she deceived you," Dylan acknowledged.

"Yes. She's corrupt and cannot be trusted. I just wish I'd known that from the beginning," Siljanna replied, critical of her earlier choices.

"What *is* your plan then?" he repeated.

"Return to the only hope of allies I have left," Siljanna answered. "The wardens in Tivani."

"May I join you?"

"You would do that?" she replied, genuinely surprised.

"The Imperator isn't the only corrupt person in the Imperium, but it may not be too late for me to make amends," he explained. "I want to put a stop to those that enjoy what they've become."

"The mage hunters?" Siljanna said, searching his eyes for confirmation.

"Yes," Dylan responded firmly.

"Then I'd be very grateful for your company," she confirmed, answering his original question.

As Juliette Lawrence arrived in Revaine, she was impressed at the sight of the Imperial warship anchored just offshore. The vessel had brought the Imperator and her entourage to the Eastern Continent and would soon return them home.

Juliette knew why they hadn't departed. The Imperator was awaiting the return of Cameron Weiss' body. He'd been struck by an unnatural bolt of lightning during the conflict at the castle and died instantly. No matter what most people thought about Imperator Harlyn Rainer, if there was one person she valued, it was Cameron Weiss. That was why Juliette had taken it upon herself to return him.

Reaching the dock, she saw a small boat surrounded by Imperial soldiers and an unfamiliar guardian.

"Miss Lawrence, I presume," greeted the unfamiliar but incredibly handsome guard.

"Yes, and you are?" she replied flirtatiously.

"Noah Harper, I'm a new acquaintance of Imperator Harlyn," he boasted.

"And where did you come from exactly? You're not from Carlisse or the Imperial Military," Juliette asked, her tone inquisitive.

"I cannot say," he replied enigmatically.

"You mean you will not say," she challenged, reaching for her satchel. "Clearly you know my name, but not who I am. If you did, you'd know people that defy me quickly regret it."

"A woman after my own heart," he replied assertively, bowing slightly and taking her hand, only to gently kiss it. Despite being suspicious, Juliette found herself aroused by this new warrior.

"Where is Imperator Harlyn?" she asked, adopting a more seductive posture.

"Aboard the warship. She's in a sombre mood and eager to return to Siranor," Noah advised. "Can I assume that large container holds Mr Weiss?"

"Indeed. Such a promising player, but in the end, just another casualty of the game," Juliette replied.

"You like to play games, Miss Lawrence?" Noah asked, a sly grin forming at the corners of his mouth.

She looked him up and down at that moment, taking in his every nuance. He was the first man in a long time she couldn't instantly read. Biting her nail momentarily then letting her finger hover over her lips, she nodded.

"Life is a game."

"Agreed. The rules have changed recently for me, but I'm a quick study," Noah remarked, unabashedly staring at her figure. He stepped aside to allow the Imperial soldiers to load Cameron's body onto the transport boat before turning back to Juliette. "Will you be joining us?"

As he spoke, Noah extended a hand towards her, his ocean-blue eyes enticing, but she hesitated. Much had changed since she left Siranor. Her partner, Dylan, had deserted her and she'd developed a favourable relationship with King Grayson. She could be a useful ally to the Imperator if she remained in Carlisse but with one more glance at Noah, she accepted he was too tempting to resist. As she took his hand, he lifted her aboard the small vessel, and they struck off towards the warship.

"You've piqued my curiosity, Mr Harper. Don't disappoint me," Juliette uttered, grazing her hand down his arm.

"I wouldn't dream of it," he replied alluringly.

After what felt like the longest day of their lives, Nate and Paige Auren found themselves wandering the crystalline walkways of Arencia at sunset. The recent weeks had seen them endure a lot while fearing for their family and despite their worries being far from over, the area did fill them with a sense of peace.

"Everything is so tranquil here," Paige whispered, her arm linked with Nate's as they walked.

"It's like a part of me remembers this place, but I convinced myself it was a dream," he replied quietly.

"Were you brought here as a child?"

"All I recall is growing up in Carlisse. My father was a researcher and advisor to the king so although we spent some time in Iliria and around these woods, I have no distinct memory of being here," Nate explained, exhaling deeply as he glanced at their beautiful surroundings.

"Don't blame yourself," Paige comforted, hearing the guilt in his unspoken confession.

"If I'd remembered this place, we could've brought the girls to safety years ago," he whispered, quietly scolding himself.

Stopping on one of the bridges overlooking the stilted homes that adorned the waterline, Paige turned to see Nate's eyes were glassy, their usual warmth fractured. Slipping herself in front of him she gently wrapped her arms around his neck.

"It is not your fault," she insisted, her voice soft. "We made a good home in Tivani and raised two wonderful girls, despite all the odds."

"I want to be a good father," he muttered, his gaze focusing on something in the far distance.

She tilted her head at the comment and read between the lines. He knew he was a good father, so his agitation was not because of recent events or his lacking memory, but because of his own father.

"So, it's Alistair getting to you," she asserted, her tone understanding.

Paige remembered what her husband went through after the war. When he received letters saying his parents had died, he was devastated. He left his home in Carlisse and had been travelling for years prior to the conflict, ending up in Yasras just before the military lockdown, which was when they met. He wrote to his family often but when he had the chance to return home, it was too late.

"I just can't understand why he lied. Why convince your only son that his parents are dead? They could've just instructed me to stay away."

"And would you have listened, stayed away at his request?" Paige probed, knowing her husband couldn't lie to her, even if he wanted to. "You can be so stubborn, my love."

Slumping his shoulders in submission, he knew she was right. He wouldn't have stayed away, and had he gone back, Paige was adamant to travel with him, proving she too could be stubborn. Had that happened, their lives would've been very different. The surviving Ar'encal and any mages that surrendered to Carlisse after the war became slaves of the royal family. If he'd announced who his parents were, he and Paige would've been forced into servitude.

Touching his chin, Paige gave him a long, comforting kiss and kept him in her arms until they heard footsteps.

"Good evening," Alistair greeted nervously.

When they'd first reunited, Nate had embraced him but as the truth of past events unravelled, Alistair had been more cautious around his son.

"Hello Alistair," Paige replied as Nate turned to face him. Glancing at his wife, he smiled and then extended a hand out to his father, who gratefully shook it.

"I'm sorry I've been so cold," Nate confessed.

"Please don't apologise. I cannot take back the mistakes of my past, but I can try to make up for lost time. Hopefully, I can get to know you all better, now we have the chance," he began but then recoiled, remembering they didn't *all* have the chance.

"Rylie..." Paige whispered, wishing desperately that her eldest daughter was safe with them.

"What did you see in your vision?" Nate asked, fidgeting nervously.

"I saw fire and felt Rylie's pain. She mourns a love she believes is lost and a family she believes is gone. Her desire to hunt the enemy that has escaped her grasp is intense," he stated, sensing the uncertainty in his son's voice, doubting that what he could tell him would help.

"You said she's going to Jumant Fort, why? What's there?" Paige enquired, praying for something positive to come from the revelation of Alistair's vision.

"Nothing," he answered. "The fortress was destroyed during the war. It's little more than rubble now. I don't know of any reason she'd head there but I'm determined to find out."

"Thank you," Nate replied. "I never realised you could trigger visions or control them so well."

"I've had over sixty years to learn a trick or two, and Evie will surpass me in no time," Alistair replied humbly.

"She's able to control her visions?" Paige questioned, looking deep into the eyes of the father-in-law she never expected to meet.

"She's getting better every day and Lianna is a good anchor for her, just as Nate's mother was for me," Alistair began, looking at his daughter-in-law who was every bit as beautiful as her children, his grandchildren. "Empathic abilities help sift through the fog created by emotion and allow seers like me and Evie to concentrate on the vision itself."

"Are you saying she hasn't had any seizures?" Nate added, equally as surprised as his wife.

"Not since arriving here. I'll continue training her in the hope that she'll never have to endure one again," Alistair replied, the absolute certainty in his cool eyes giving them a level of confidence they'd never previously imagined. "But for now, our focus is getting Rylie back."

After expressing their appreciation for his help, Alistair led Nate and Paige towards what would be their home while in Arencia, a neighbouring building to the house Evie currently shared with Harrison and the others. The chill made both Nate and Paige extremely grateful to be sleeping in a proper bed, instead of a prison cell, while the fading light reminded them of how tired they were.

None of them had slept the night before or really rested during the day and even if they didn't want to, the need for sleep beckoned.

That evening, Harrison left the house as quietly as he could, not wanting to disturb the others. They were all pleased that Zack would be transferred from the infirmary to their house in the morning but equally exhausted from the past two days. Before he could rest, Harrison had a meeting with Maia. Reaching the secluded garden behind the pavilion where the runes of the Ar'encal were forged, he found her. The wide space before him was surrounded by trees, but the central area was open to the night sky and the stars above, which reminded Harrison of the forge at Elijah's blacksmith.

The last time he'd seen Elijah, they were going for a drink at the Hawk Eye tavern, but their merriment had been short-lived by the conflict with Sampson and the following events stripped him of the chance to say goodbye. Harrison briefly imagined Elijah working at his forge and wondered how he was and if he'd ever see the gentle giant again. His current company was very different but diversely skilled, even more so than his crafting mentor. Although eighty-nine years old, Maia's delicate, youthful features masterfully concealed her age. Her undeniable wisdom and courage, however, came from her near century of life experience.

As he joined Maia beside the forge, Harrison greeted her politely, still feeling guilty for the way he'd spoken to her outside the infirmary.

"Hello Harrison, thank you for joining me at this late hour," she said, her attention on the pages of a tome she was studiously flicking through. Following her focus drew Harrison's gaze to both the weathered book and a large chest by her feet.

"Does that book detail the artisan runes you mentioned earlier?"

"And so much more," Maia began, her gaze momentarily leaving the pages at her fingertips. "This is the Tome of Arencia. It was written centuries ago by some of the earliest leaders of the Ar'encal. They passed down the artisan rune designs which have been studied by every generation since. It is my hope this tome will detail a way for us to contain the power of an Aeon."

"You hope?" Harrison repeated, concern surging through him.

"Please understand, in my lifetime, Aeons have been merely fables. My mother told me stories as a child but not even she encountered one," Maia continued, avoiding eye contact with him.

"How long can the Ar'encal live for?" he asked quietly, wondering if there was anyone alive who may have known or seen an Aeon first-hand.

"While mages have the same lifespan as humans, the Ar'encal can live for centuries. Even still, no one I know has witnessed an Aeon transformation," Maia regretfully advised. "If the tales written by our ancestors are correct, only a child born in the year of the deity whose power they triggered or were most gifted in, even could."

"No one transformed during the Uprising?" Harrison queried. He never had to live through a period of war, but his studies taught him that the Uprising was a brutal time in recent history and the Ar'encal's greatest defence had been magic. "Surely they would've tapped into whatever latent power they could during the conflict."

"Embodying such power intentionally is dangerous. That risk was deemed too great during the war and even more so when we were forced into hiding afterwards," she advised, trying to push back the harrowing memories.

"You did say that Rylie could be dangerous. Apart from the obvious, what did you mean by that?" Harrison wondered, hoping her explanation may lead to a solution as well.

"Magic is volatile because it is linked so closely to emotion. When a caster has the ability to enhance that power due to an affinity with the essence of a god, the reaction can be amplified beyond measure. Imagine trying to defend against an opponent that had become berserk," she explained, putting the situation into a familiar context for him. "Once in this state, the person may be unable to regain control. That is what I fear will happen to Rylie."

"She lost control because she thought Siljanna killed me," Harrison muttered, his hand hovering over the scar on his chest again without thinking.

"Indeed, that's why I believe seeing you alive is vital to our chances of saving her, but it may not be enough," Maia replied with renewed determination.

"And that's where the rune you are searching for comes in," Harrison added as Maia invited him to study the tome with her.

Looking over Maia's shoulder as she continued to read, he recognised the Arencian rune, the mark he'd received when becoming an Aegis Guardian. The simple but elegant rune protected him against the withering, made him resistant to Encia but also imposed a unique form of silence. Not that he would, but with the rune etched into his skin, he couldn't reveal the secrets of the Ar'encal or speak of Arencia to anyone who didn't know of its existence. The rune itself was known as a greater rune, for it combined two forces: resistance and silence. There were several more runes and great runes detailed in the tome, both offensive and defensive, which all stirred his creative curiosity.

"Why did your ancestors create these runes?" Harrison asked. "The entire race is gifted with magic, so what purpose do they serve?"

He could understand their uses for those without magical abilities, and to an extent, mages, but the runes had been created before the time when humans were invited into the Ar'encal lands.

"The Ar'encal are gifted, true, but just like any skill, some people are less talented than others. The runes provided a failsafe which, during the war were then adapted to aid mages, our human sympathisers and the Aegis Guard," Maia recalled, and she could see admiration in Harrison's eyes.

"If we need to place one or more of these runes on Rylie, do you have any idea how we can get close enough? When I received the Arencian rune, I was willing, but in her current state, I doubt Rylie is going to sit still while we brand her."

"That is where your crafting abilities come in," Maia began, turning the book to him. "Runes placed upon the flesh are permanent, enchanting the recipient's blood with Encia, but runes can also be placed upon items, clothing and weaponry."

Stunned by the adaptability of the runes, Harrison's professional curiosity was piqued. Quickly turning his attention to the tome, its pages going into detail about the varying types of runes and their applications, Harrison's mind wondered just how many possibilities lay before him. Some were recognisable, such as the varying elements but many of the other intricate designs were completely unfamiliar. Although he really wanted to scan the whole page, Maia tapped the passage she'd translated and intended for him to see.

"Items must first be branded and Encia moulded into the material. Encia is the essence of magic, so all it then takes is a person with powers to charge it," Maia explained.

"So, I could create an amulet, for example, engrave it with the runes needed and once infused, the chain reaction would suppress Rylie's power?" he asked, enthused at the potential.

"That is my hope," Maia admitted. "We haven't needed to craft runic items since the war, but I am far from talented in smithing. You on the other hand are."

"What if I misunderstand the tome?" Harrison queried.

"Don't worry, two of our best artisans have offered to guide you... if you're willing to try," Maia advised, turning her attention fully to Harrison.

"I'm willing and eager," he replied, looking at Maia with conviction. He'd finally told Rylie how he felt, and nothing would stop him from trying to get her back.

"Then I will summon Teagan and Freya, but remember Harrison, this is just the first step. Finding Rylie and getting the runic item onto her will be the greatest challenge," she cautioned.

"I understand, but I must try," Harrison asserted, knowing there wasn't a risk he wouldn't take to bring her safely back to her family, and to him.

As Maia departed to fetch the specialists she spoke of, Harrison's mind was flooded with thoughts of Rylie. He recalled the moment they were stargazing onboard the *Pilgrim* and how he'd recounted to her the tale of the Phoenix constellation. His thoughts quickly shifted to an image of her emanating the same power as the firebird but unable to control it. That was all the motivation he needed to begin. Lighting up the forge, he settled his mind on crafting an amulet. How they'd find Rylie and get close enough to put it on her was a problem for tomorrow. For now, his goal was to create protective gear so they could attempt to approach her and the runic amulet she needed to regain control. Sleep could wait.

Chapter Two
INTENTIONS

Departing the quaint lodge in Iliria, Caitlin, Spencer and Queen Nadia discussed their plan again before returning to Carlisse; a plan that Caitlin was still uncertain of.

"Are you sure, Nadia? Absolutely sure?" she asked for the umpteenth time.

"Caitlin, I understand your reservations, but really, I have no choice. We may not have planned it, but now Grayson believes I am with child. If I don't return, he will send people after me," Nadia asserted between slow, calming breaths.

"But he's a monster," Caitlin protested.

"I know but don't forget, he's also holding my parents captive."

"But you aren't actually pregnant!" Caitlin pushed back.

"That's why we need you, Caitlin. You can create the illusion that Nadia is pregnant, can't you?" Spencer asked calmly, redirecting her frustration.

"I suppose, but to maintain it, I'm going to have to remain by Nadia's side, even with the king," she replied, her argument slowly deflating. "Is that even possible?"

"We'll find a way to get around that," Nadia insisted.

"I can tell the king, given our previous experiences, that Nadia must remain in our care until she reaches full term. No exceptions and no conjugal visits," Spencer suggested, reaching out to hold Nadia's hand.

It sickened Caitlin to think of the times Nadia had sacrificed her body to appease King Grayson, and she knew Spencer hated it even more than she did. Each interlude had been against Nadia's better judgment and purely to spare the lives of her imprisoned parents. Now they had succumbed to their feelings and Nadia had decided it was worth risking everything for the chance to be with Spencer, she knew neither of them could bear the idea of the king laying a finger on her again.

"Fine, so we fake the pregnancy, then what?" Caitlin grumbled, still unconvinced that the risk they were taking had any justification.

"We have months to worry about that," Nadia said, reaching over to touch Caitlin's shoulder. She was always called an icy beauty and her demeanour seemed to be calming her feisty friend. "I know you fear for me, Caitlin, but for my parents' sake if nothing else, I have to go back."

Glancing over at Spencer, Nadia decided not to tell Caitlin of their plan to conceive a child together, at least not yet. Nadia truly believed that if her child were part mage and immune to the withering, she would genuinely be able to bring it to term.

"Okay fine, but how are we going to explain your escape from the dungeon?" Caitlin asked incredulously.

"I suggest we tell a half-truth. Say that Harrison's group freed us while rescuing Rylie's parents and we fled to protect the king's unborn child," Nadia answered, looking to Spencer to check he agreed with the suggestion.

"The king will likely have made an accord with Imperator Harlyn and that vile woman, Juliette," Caitlin opposed. "What if he doesn't believe that you were in any danger during the conflict?"

"Then we'll pretend that in the heat of the moment, we couldn't be certain," Spencer added, offering the woman he loved an affirmative nod. He thought the idea had merit. "The king never saw us with

Harrison and the others so should have no reason to suspect they were coming for us."

Racking her brain for any other way to argue against their plan, Caitlin came up empty-handed. Taking a deep breath, she nodded, not looking at either of her friends but agreeing to their crazy plan. Seeing her reaction, Nadia threw her arms around Caitlin and kissed her cheek.

"Thank you, Caitlin. You don't know how much this means to us," Nadia exclaimed, her smile pure.

"We better get going, before I can think of another reason we shouldn't do this," Caitlin replied, a faint smile creeping across her lips as she blushed.

Packing what little they'd accumulated since fleeing Carlisse, the three of them began the walk to Lorvale. From there, Caitlin was certain her parents' contacts would lend them horses to ride back to the ranch before taking the main road to Carlisse.

"Would you like to spend some time with your family before returning to the castle, Caitlin?" Nadia asked compassionately. "It's been too long since you spent some quality time with them."

"She's right, Caitlin. We're going to be lying anyway, so why don't we all take some time before returning?" Spencer added.

"It'll be a while before I need to show any signs of my pregnancy. I reckon we could stay with your family until the end of the week and even then, you don't have to return to Carlisse as quickly as we should."

"Won't the king question where I am? Surely your chambermaid would be there to attend to you now that you're uhh... with child," Caitlin queried, giving her friends a suspicious look but they could both sense her underlying hope.

"Grayson thinks little of anything that doesn't interest him, especially my welfare. If he does ask, we can say your parents sheltered us from the conflict and that I granted you the time off, knowing I'll need you more as the pregnancy progresses," Nadia replied without hesitation, proving she could be quite a convincing liar when required.

"I really appreciate that Nadia," Caitlin thanked. "In that case, I will stay at the ranch for an additional week or so after you depart."

Despite her growing concern for their dangerous plan, she couldn't deny spending quality time with her family would be a welcome reprieve and she trusted Spencer to protect Nadia with his life.

Imperator Harlyn Rainer's arrival back into Siranor was far from the success she expected. Travelling to Carlisse had presented the opportunity she'd sought for the last year, but the consequences of failure had been high. She believed the most important thing in her life was to capture a mage for her experiments with En-glycerol, but that hadn't happened. The trap they'd planned and even the failsafe she devised had both backfired, leaving her lucky to walk away from the encounter alive. Luckier than Cameron Weiss, whose remains were being transported back to Siranor in the vehicle tailing her own.

Losing him had taken quite a toll on Harlyn. Assigned as her protector eleven years ago by her father, Joseph Rainer while he was still Imperator, Cameron had been introduced as one of those employees who had been hired so that her father didn't need to invest his own time. When they'd first met, Harlyn was nineteen and had just begun studying at the Institute. She had adamantly opposed having a chaperone, but Cameron persisted. It took time, but over the years he became her friend, then confidant and for a short period, her lover. Leaning back heavily into the seat of her transport vehicle, the one she had often shared with Cameron, Harlyn found one of his old leather jackets tucked under the seat and could even smell traces of his cologne in the fabric.

"Why were you taken from me?" she muttered, holding the jacket tightly as she'd once been able to do with its owner.

They'd had so many conversations within the small confines of that car over the years, it had felt like their safe space. She'd confided in him about her difficult family situation and how it had only gotten worse since her father discovered his wife's affair with his brother. That situation had quickly led to the belief that Elias Rainer was in fact her biological father, a thought she'd only ever shared with Cameron until her outburst in Carlisse.

Whenever she'd needed to talk about her family history, he had always listened and never judged, letting her voice her hopes, frustrations or theories until she was content. Cameron knew there was no point trying to dissuade her and it was slowly sinking in that she'd never be able to talk to him again. Inhaling the lingering scent from his jacket, Harlyn closed her eyes and let her mind drift into a memory of the day she became Imperator.

"You look beautiful," Cameron whispered, bowing before her.

"But I don't want to look beautiful. I don't want to go out there and address those people. I don't want to be their Imperator," she argued, sounding like the stroppy teenager she'd been when they first met. *"I want to go back to my lab, I want to—"*

"Find your uncle," he suggested, finishing her sentence. *"You know he can't come back."*

"It's ridiculous! Why would he kill my father? Surely if he was going to, it would've been years ago," she protested, throwing the written speech she was meant to deliver on the floor.

The story of her mother, Miranda Rainer's affair with her uncle had become common knowledge within the Imperial circles, so to Harlyn, it seemed ridiculous for Elias to kill his brother over that infidelity. He admitted the affair lasted several years, but more importantly, it ended during the Uprising. Her mother had been exiled for the deception while he had been pardoned. Surely it was a poor motive for murder now.

That reasoning didn't stop the Shadow Council and their appointed scrutiny committee from suspecting Elias was to blame when Joseph

Rainer died. Her uncle was to be put on trial but quickly learnt the judge had been bribed into ruling against him. Unable to face imprisonment, he fled Siranor, leaving Harlyn with only her spoilt stepmother for family... and Cameron.

"I know you feel that way, Harlyn, and I wish I could change things for you... but I can't," Cameron said, adjusting the crest on her jacket so that it fell into the proper place. Standing so close to him, she couldn't resist running her fingers down his chiselled jawline. He closed his eyes, relishing her touch.

"If I go out there—" she began but stopped herself, hoping he'd look at her.

"You must go out there. The council has chosen you as the next Imperator, Harlyn. You should be honoured," he insisted, stopping her before she could build up an excuse. He knew if given the time to prepare a defensive argument, she wouldn't let it drop until she proved it true.

"An honour, how is it an honour to give up everything I love? My uncle, my work... you," she groaned, her argument growing despite his efforts. "I swear the council have chosen me out of nothing more than spite."

"Even if that's the case, they've chosen the most gifted and brilliant woman for the job," Cameron countered, piercing through her stony gaze in the way only he could.

They were very similar in height and as she took in his words, Harlyn leant in to kiss him, but Cameron turned away, the longer strands of his hair covering his eyes like a shield.

"Cameron, what's wrong?" she asked, trying to conceal the fear in her voice. This was their last chance to be together, as they both wanted.

"We can't, Harlyn. Not anymore. As protector of the Imperator and soon to be your military advisor, we cannot be romantically involved," he confessed, the pain in his voice audible.

"If you truly meant every word you just said, indulge me one last time," she replied defiantly, refusing to back away.

In a split second, he turned, his arms around her as he pushed her firmly into the nearby door. It ensured no one would interrupt their embrace. His kiss was deep, filled with passion and despair. As he pressed his lips against hers harder, their breathing became laboured while their bodies attempted to mould together, and she lost herself in him. The warmth of his hands, his tender caress and the fresh, citrusy scent on his jacket were innately familiar. They were just three of the reasons why she loved him. Then, as quickly as he began, he pulled away.

"That has to be the last time," he sighed, eyes closed as he turned away, collecting the pages of her speech from the floor. And it was.

After that moment, Harlyn stepped out of the room, accepted the role of Imperator and their relationship stayed professional, mostly at Cameron's insistence. And now, he was dead. She'd never feel his lips on hers again. Never hear his calming words of support or receive his encouragement to persevere with her studies. He always understood that the greatest discoveries often came at a high price, but in Carlisse, Cameron paid that price and now she had to endure the rest of her life without him.

Looking over to the papers on the seat beside her that, once signed, would release his body to be incinerated, Harlyn's reverie was interrupted by the dulcet tone of her driver's voice.

"Ma'am we have arrived at the Imperial Palace," he said softly, glancing over his shoulder with a concerned expression. He'd clearly anticipated that she'd be struggling to deal with Cameron's death.

"Thank you, James," Harlyn replied, collecting the documents and slowly reaching for a pen that she knew was stowed in the small compartment between the seats.

She had expected to feel despair when Juliette Lawrence and their new ally, Noah Harper delivered his remains, but in truth, losing Cameron had hardened her. All she felt was determination. She still wanted the mages and Ar'encal responsible for his death to suffer. She also vowed to make Siljanna Stone pay for abandoning her in enemy captivity, a situation she'd only narrowly escaped, but wouldn't allow anything to distract her from her true goals.

Initially, helping Siljanna to capture her brother and former friend, who'd become a mage, seemed poetic. A year earlier, the body of a murderer had been delivered to the Institute, the body of her uncle. He'd contracted the withering and killed a random person in Tivani to ensure his remains were taken to the Institute, and that random victim was Siljanna's mother.

No one dared challenge the Imperator's desire to examine the murderer alone, and while searching through her uncle's possessions, Harlyn found a journal hidden among his robes. It contained a letter addressed to her and explained everything he'd done in the years they'd been apart, including how he'd located an Encia spring and continued their research from an abandoned hut by Shauder's Basin. That discovery allowed him to progress their initial findings, but at a much greater risk. Without the resources of the Institute, he came into frequent contact with the raw substance and succumbed to the symptoms of the withering.

Elias' journal proved vital to Harlyn, both as motivation and guidance to complete their work manipulating Encia. She created Englycerol, a substance theoretically capable of absorbing raw Encia, and therefore, magic. Harlyn had intended to simply weaponize it, making the Imperial army impervious to magic, but to keep the favour of the people, Cameron encouraged her to devise another reason to test. Military dominance was Joseph Rainer's style, something he claimed didn't suit her. Science and facts suited her, and that suggestion got Harlyn thinking. *What if mages consumed her substance and the magic within them was absorbed and expelled? What if they could become normal people again?*

The theory gained momentum quickly, but she had no proof. She needed to test her substance on a mage, but the mage hunters never seemed capable of bringing one back alive. Joseph Rainer had decreed that hunters receive a bounty for a mage dead or alive, if they provided evidence of the kill. Harlyn knew that was the real reason a live captive was never delivered to her, until Siljanna provided a viable opportunity.

It all seemed to be going to plan, then at the moment of their victory, Siljanna succumbed to her fury and failed to apprehend the mage, Rylie Auren, attempting to kill her instead. Harlyn was the first to admit she'd taken advantage of Siljanna's hatred and even amplified it by twisting the facts of her father's autopsy, but the way Siljanna abandoned her in Carlisse was treason, an offence punishable by death.

The only consolation that came out of their disastrous mission in Carlisse was witnessing the fiery being that Harlyn believed was the mage they'd pursued, chasing Siljanna. She had transformed into something Noah described as an Aeon and seemed adamant to destroy Siljanna, something Harlyn wholly approved of. Even if Siljanna somehow eluded that thing, she wouldn't escape for long, not when Harlyn had the might of the entire Imperial Military at her disposal.

Realising that she'd hovered over Cameron's death certificate for an elongated period of time, and that her driver was still looking over his shoulder at her, Harlyn gripped the pen tightly and clamped her eyes shut.

"Ma'am… are you okay?" he asked hesitantly.

With a final loving thought of him, Harlyn signed the papers and rapidly exited the vehicle. Before heading inside, she turned back to James and handed him the wedge of documents and Cameron's old jacket.

"Please see to the necessary arrangements for Mr Weiss and ensure his apartment and office are cleared out," she instructed, to which James nodded courteously in response.

It had been five days since Cameron had been killed but she couldn't linger over his death or allow herself the time to mourn, not now. There was a more pressing announcement she needed to make; one her entire nation would hear.

The journey across the Ensen Sea on the merchant vessel made Siljanna feel even worse than her first experience aboard the Imperial warship. The size difference made a big impact on the motion sickness she felt and resulted in her spending most of the four sailing days in her cabin, consuming nothing but bread and water. Anything else was too much to bear. She couldn't wait to get back on dry land and was thrilled when the ship passed the welcoming yet imposing sight of the wardens' naval base. That solitary, stone castle would always be the most iconic feature in Yasras and meant they'd soon arrive in the harbour.

Stepping out onto the deck, the air was chilling but it didn't detract from her eagerness to disembark. Glancing over her shoulder towards Dylan, Siljanna found herself glad he would continue to travel with her. During the crossing, he'd listened to her version of events in Carlisse, how she'd learnt of Imperator Harlyn's deception and her guilt at almost killing Harrison. To her surprise, he was very sympathetic, which told Siljanna that he was also tormented by his past but was not ready to discuss it.

"Are you ready to go?" Siljanna asked as she shuffled down the gangplank behind the other passengers.

"I don't know. Is there even a place for me in decent society?" he replied, looking at his hands as if they were covered in blood. Siljanna couldn't help but reach out and take his hand, which made him look directly at her, his eyes questioning.

"Morgan will make a place for you in Tivani. With any luck, he'll help us both," she replied, hoping her confidence in their friend wasn't misplaced.

"He doesn't know what we've done."

Morgan had always been an honourable man, but Dylan didn't class himself that way anymore. He'd committed unspeakable atrocities since they trained together at the academy and that divide made him uneasy to approach Morgan for acceptance.

"No, he doesn't, but we'll tell him," Siljanna replied, the steely look in her eyes revealing the depth of her resolve.

"You're joking, right?" Dylan asked dubiously.

"I'm not and I won't lie to him. The only way we can hope for redemption is to earn it," Siljanna stated plainly.

"A bold plan. And if he rejects us?"

"Let's cross that bridge if we come to it," she answered, firmly believing it wouldn't come to that.

"You have a lot of faith in him," Dylan commented, chuckling lightly.

"He's earned it. Over the last year, even when we disagreed, he didn't let that stop him from doing his duty. He's one of the best of us," she replied honestly.

"Us?" Dylan questioned, his eyebrows lifting as he looked at her with an air of surprise.

"Wardens, Dylan. You and I may have gone astray, but we are still wardens. Harrison too. It's within us, title or not," Siljanna announced, making Dylan's smile grow.

"Wardens indeed," he replied quietly, closing his eyes and nodding with a soft smile.

"Does that mean you *will* come with me?"

"It does. Even if we cannot find redemption on this path, you always seem to find the best adversaries. If I'm going to go out, I'd prefer to do so in a blaze of glory rather than disappear into the shadows," he jested.

"I hope you mean a literal blaze. At some point, I may have to face what Rylie has become. What I turned her into," Siljanna admitted, her hands trembling at the thought. She crossed her arms in a futile attempt to hide the reaction, but Dylan saw through it.

"Let's go," he said, realising that if Siljanna was prepared to die to make amends, supporting her was the least he could do.

They decided against staying at the Crown and Anchor Inn after the way the innkeepers were treated and instead began the long walk straight to Tivani. It was nightfall by the time they crossed the eastern bridge meaning the streets were remarkably quiet and the fountain square deserted. As they made their way through what was usually the bustling market, they soon arrived at the guardhouse. Siljanna hesitated as they approached the main doors, doubt chipping away at her, but before she could overcome the uncertainty, Morgan exited the building and almost collided with her.

"Siljanna?" Morgan stammered, jolting with surprise. Her presence had been the last thing he'd expected.

"Hello Morgan, we all need to talk. Privately."

"All? Who's with you?" Morgan asked, his mind still trying to process the fact she was before him.

"Long-time old friend," Dylan greeted, stepping into view and causing Morgan to close his eyes, rubbing them with fervour.

"I'm sure you have a lot of questions," Siljanna began, her tone understanding but with a hint of urgency.

"I don't even know where to start! Wait for me in the guardhouse, I'm just on my way to check on Elijah and then we can talk," Morgan replied hastily.

"Is Elijah okay?" Dylan asked, recognising the name as the man Juliette had repetitively poisoned while they held him in captivity.

"He's getting better. Whatever virus he caught in Siranor really hit him hard, but it won't take me long to get there and back. Please, wait for me in my... in Siljanna's office," he replied, darting off before they had a chance to say otherwise.

"Still want to go with the honesty plan?" Dylan muttered under his breath as he opened the guardhouse door for Siljanna.

"We have to," she confirmed although he could tell she was more worried now than she had been at the dock in Yasras.

When Morgan returned, he entered the commander's office that had been his for the last few weeks and seemed both surprised and relieved to see them.

"I almost convinced myself I'd imagined seeing you. I've not had much sleep recently, so it was entirely possible," Morgan began as he offered for Siljanna to take the seat behind the desk. Her seat.

She politely refused, opting to take the guest chair next to Dylan, and Morgan would soon understand why. As he sat down, Siljanna and Dylan began to recount their tale, notwithstanding most of the unpleasant details. Surprisingly, Morgan didn't react until they'd finished and then was silent for a long time, trying to process all the information he'd received.

"Morgan, I understand it's a lot to take in, but please say something," Siljanna begged.

After another pause, Morgan looked between them, as if searching for something in their body language that their words hadn't conveyed.

"Why tell me this?" he asked bluntly.

"She didn't want to lie to you," Dylan responded before Siljanna had the chance.

"I couldn't bring myself to ask for your help if that plea was based on a lie," she added.

"What do you want from me?" Morgan probed, continuing to conceal his reaction to their tale.

"The chance to make things right," Siljanna answered, glancing over at Dylan, encouraging him to reinforce her claim.

"The things we've done are unforgivable. I've willingly ruined lives without question and caused countless people like Elijah to suffer needlessly," Dylan began, his tone unsettled but honest. "I cannot change that, but I can change what I do next. Imperator Harlyn will not let this defeat go. She will strike back, and I can help those she targets but not if I hide away or am put behind bars."

"Should I put you both behind bars, as penance for the pain you've caused?" Morgan challenged.

"Probably, and if you choose to, I won't resist," Dylan replied.

"Neither will I," Siljanna asserted, placing her hands on the desk and showing no resistance should he decide to arrest her.

Morgan looked at them both intently, considering everything he'd just learnt. During the silence, Siljanna couldn't help but reflect on how much he'd changed. From being the joker of their group at the academy, Morgan had matured into a true leader, someone more deserving of the warden commander position than she ever was.

"I want to believe you, but I need to think on this thoroughly. Will you remain in Tivani until morning?" Morgan asked, his tone stern. Siljanna was fairly sure if they declined, he wouldn't have hesitated to throw them into a holding cell.

"Of course, we can stay at my old home," Siljanna replied. "We won't leave until we've spoken to you again."

"Thank you, and good night," Morgan said gratefully, seeing them out of the guardhouse.

Chapter Three
DECLARATION

Arriving at her old home, Siljanna only remembered the state she'd left the place in once it was too late. The floor was still littered with empty alcohol bottles, the axes Harrison had lovingly made for her were lodged into the kitchen counter and wall, and all that remained of the hallway sideboard was splinters.

"Shit! This place is a wreck. Who did this?" Dylan asked glancing around the devasted dwelling in horror.

"Me," Siljanna admitted, shying away from him.

"*You* did this?" Dylan said, examining the carnage, kicking several bottles out of his way.

"There's a point when even the strongest will breaks. Mine broke here. This was where it began, where I decided to hunt Harrison and Rylie, no matter the cost. If only I'd known then, what I know now," she muttered, still unwilling to look him in the eye.

"I meant what I said to Morgan. We cannot change the past, but we can make better decisions from now on. You have the chance to rewrite your final memory of this place," Dylan replied, walking towards her and softly gripping her shoulder. Siljanna finally looked at Dylan and nodded before showing him to Harrison's old attic room to get some rest, as she retired to her old bedroom.

As morning came, so did a rapid knocking at Siljanna's front door. She'd barely slept, the memories, both good and bad from what seemed like a lifetime ago making her restless. She was already in the kitchen and could hear Dylan coming down the stairs behind her as she cautiously went to the door. She was expecting to see Morgan but couldn't help but inhale deeply in preparation to defend herself should it not be him. Opening the door, her concern was partially justified, as she was greeted by Téa Gray, her former subordinate.

"Siljanna, you need to come with me, now," she announced, more firmly than Siljanna ever recalled her capable of. "Arm yourself if possible."

Surprised by the request and Téa's demeanour, Siljanna turned to Dylan who revealed his favoured dagger and then looked at her own empty weapon belt. Her pistols were gone, likely still in the courtyard of the Carlisse castle but her gaze was soon drawn to Harrison's axes.

"Honour, justice and loyalty. Let's see if I can live up to those words this time," Siljanna whispered to herself.

"Let's go," Téa instructed in a way that made Siljanna pause. Téa had never been a strong or wilful person before, but Siljanna found herself unsure if she'd really changed so dramatically in the last few weeks or if it was all just an act.

"Where are we going?" Dylan questioned. "And who are you?"

"I am Téa Gray, Commander Morgan's lieutenant. He advised me of your return last night."

"He did?" Siljanna commented, trying to focus on the fact that Morgan confided in her rather than Téa being his choice for lieutenant. Both revelations were odd in her opinion.

"Yes, he did," she replied, offering her previous commander nothing whilst simultaneously ushering both her and Dylan through the door. "Imperator Harlyn is making a nationwide announcement and Morgan feels that you should hear it. We'll be tuning into the broadcast at the guardhouse."

"Do any of the other wardens know we are here?" Dylan asked, concerned that if too many people knew, they could be easily detected, or betrayed.

"No, I'm the only one. I'm... Morgan's partner," Téa stuttered, her boldness faltering.

"Partner?" Siljanna exhaled, unable to hide her surprise.

Morgan had been adamant not to take another partner after Harrison was banished, but the alternative meant he and Téa were romantically involved. Siljanna couldn't decide which was more unlikely.

"A lot has changed since you've been gone," Téa remarked, trying to regain her confident mannerism but was betrayed by her tone, leaving Siljanna confident it was all for show and contemplating what other truths she had embellished.

Entering through the back door of the guardhouse, they could hear several voices talking among themselves. Téa led them to a nearby concealed room, ensuring they remained out of sight but could hear everything before joining her comrades. When he noted her arrival, Morgan cleared his throat and gathered everyone's attention.

"Quiet! The Imperator's address is about to begin," he called out, ensuring everyone hushed as Harlyn's voice boomed through the radio:

"Imperial citizens, I speak to you today on a matter of national urgency. With great despair, I must inform you that while in Carlisse, I, Imperator Harlyn Rainer and King Grayson Brock were attacked by a force of Ar'encal, mages and their misguided sympathisers. This attack resulted in the death of Siranor's military councillor, Cameron Weiss. It proves our fear that the Ar'encal are far from the dormant enemy we believed them to be, and this rising threat must be stopped. The mage hunts alone are not enough so it is my duty today to inform you that we are once again at war."

The announcement sent a shockwave of chatter around the room, but Morgan quickly silenced them again with a loud series of strikes to the counter as the Imperator's address continued:

"Additionally, we face treachery from within. Commander Siljanna Stone of Tivani betrayed me and in doing so, each and every one of you. She is a traitor and should be apprehended on sight. Be vigilant. We face dark times, but we will emerge victorious, just as our parents did under my father's stewardship. Our great nation will prosper."

As the address ended, Dylan couldn't help but notice Morgan subtly look in their direction. He was expecting him to be furious, but Morgan's expression almost seemed concerned. As the other wardens dispersed from the common room to attend to their duties, reacting to the news amongst themselves, Morgan waited for the hallway to clear then ushered Siljanna and Dylan into his office where Téa was waiting for them.

"I suppose you saw this coming," Morgan began, speaking quietly as he closed the door behind them.

"I expected to be labelled as a traitor, but to renew the war… that comes as a shock," Siljanna replied, shaking her head in dismay at the course of action the Imperator was taking. "I won't ask you to risk yourself for me; Dylan and I will leave town as soon as we can do so unnoticed."

"Is this why we had to arm ourselves, in case a quick departure was required?" Dylan questioned.

"Precisely," Téa replied, looking towards him. "You should both go as soon as possible."

"No, I won't stand for this. It's already gone far enough," Morgan growled. "If there's any truth to your tale, and I believe there is, Imperator Harlyn has declared war on an already decimated race and the people protecting my friends, just to hide her desire to conduct questionable experiments on mages. I won't stand for it."

Genuinely surprised at just how much Morgan had changed since his days fooling around at the academy, Dylan surveyed the room and quickly realised that neither Siljanna nor Téa seemed to mirror his reaction. They'd seen how Morgan had grown over the recent years and it explained why they had so much faith in him.

"What do you want us to do?" Dylan asked, feeling hopeful that whatever they did next would bring him closer to the person he wanted to be.

"I don't know yet, but if we are to be at war, we will be on the right side of it," Morgan answered, and there was no doubt he meant it.

Turning away from the masses that had gathered in the Imperial Palace courtyard, Harlyn Rainer departed from the balcony intending to summon her Shadow Council. She took great satisfaction from knowing her words had just been broadcast on every radio frequency possible, and that although the public would be scared, she could now increase the mage hunts exponentially without repercussion. Her mood was finally lifting until she was stopped by her stepmother, Sabine Dumont who was blocking the doorway.

"So, you've finally returned," Sabine said, her tone flippant.

Harlyn's stepmother was only ten years older than her and possibly the most dislikeable person she'd ever known. Having been spoilt by Joseph Rainer and placed upon a pedestal like the trophy wife she was, Sabine was useful for very little. She looked incredible for her age with pale blonde hair falling below her shoulders and possessing an hourglass figure, but her flaky attitude was comparable to a lazy, over-demanding child.

"What do you want Sabine, I have no time for your antics," Harlyn replied defiantly as she placed her coat and gloves on a nearby peg.

"Antics? How can you speak to me like that? Your father would be appalled," she sneered, folding her arms in disgust.

"Just get to the point, Sabine. What must someone else do for you now?" Harlyn groaned, hoping she'd get rid of the woman quicker by giving her what she wanted.

"I want a bodyguard," Sabine announced, a look of pure indignation on her face. "With the soldiers going to war, I need protection. The young man that returned with you, Noah, he'd do nicely."

"You don't want protection, you want a toy. And no, you cannot have Noah Harper," Harlyn asserted, disregarding the hope of getting rid of her stepmother easily.

"Why not? I want him."

"He's *twenty-six,* Sabine and vital to the war effort. Go pick another puppet, one closer to your age that I don't need, and get out of my way," Harlyn scolded, frustrated at how selfish the dim woman was. It was clear Joseph Rainer was only looking skin deep when he married her.

"You rotten girl," Sabine retaliated as she marched up to her stepdaughter, raising her hand as if to slap her. Anticipating the blow, Harlyn reacted, turning her head, but when it didn't come, she looked at Sabine through the corner of her eye.

"Go on Sabine, strike me. Hitting the Imperator is an offence. Then I can give you the quarters you deserve, in prison."

The antagonising tactic didn't work, however, as Sabine, who was fully aware her stepdaughter was not bluffing, lowered her hand and left. Harlyn knew that Sabine could do little more than moan about how she'd just been treated. Seeking to have Harlyn impeached would require proactively approaching the council, and if she succeeded, would also lead to Sabine's privileges being revoked. That was something she would never risk. Committing herself to dealing with her stepmother later, Harlyn also departed. She had a military council to attend, a race to wipe out and a traitor to apprehend.

Awaiting Imperator Harlyn's arrival, Noah and Juliette were already in the war room on the lower level of the Imperial prison. With them were two others, a General from the Siranor military and a younger, olive-skinned man who looked like a seasoned recruit. With the Imperator still nowhere to be seen, Juliette became impatient.

"What's taking so long?" she huffed, sitting on a nearby table and swinging her legs impetuously.

"I'm sure the Imperator will be here soon," replied the General, whose name Juliette couldn't recall.

"You'd be correct General Owen," Imperator Harlyn announced as she entered the room, the heavy door shuddering the doorframe as it closed behind her. "Thank you for your patience."

Instinctively, Noah bowed slightly, a sign of respect he'd often over-emphasised to the last leader he followed, Maia Uriel of the Ar'encal. Witnessing his gesture, the young military man copied and General Owen saluted. Only Juliette failed to react courteously, but Harlyn didn't seem fazed.

"We came as soon as we received your missive," General Owen announced. "Please let me introduce Private Dorian Pesaro, the most promising recruit from the Imperial Military school."

"This is no place for trainees," Noah interjected, goading him intentionally.

"And you are?" General Owen questioned abruptly. He was not about to let some unknown informant talk to him with such disrespect.

"This is Noah Harper. He has invaluable knowledge of our enemy and has earned a place on this council," Harlyn advised, silencing the General's argument with a stern gesture before it began. "I assume you've trained at the Tulam facility, Private Pesaro."

"Briefly ma'am," Dorian replied, standing to attention, and giving Imperator Harlyn all due respect.

Hearing he'd been training in Tulam, the covert operations centre initially created for wardens that had evolved into a shadow training facility for individuals of particular interest, especially those with the skills required of mage hunters, piqued Juliette's curiosity.

"And what is your speciality, Dorian Pesaro?" Juliette asked, letting his name roll off her tongue. "I don't recall seeing you at the facility before."

"Anonymity and adaptability," Dorian responded, glancing at Juliette with disinterest. He'd heard all about her from his time in Tulam.

"Private Pesaro is particularly well versed at adjusting to any situation and is relatively unknown outside of Siranor," explained General Owen. "I believe he could be a valuable asset."

"I'm sure we can find a use for you," Juliette added seductively but received no reaction from Dorian. He remained stoic, his full attention given to his superior and the Imperator.

Quickly bored by the young recruit, Juliette turned her attention back to Noah who retained an air of secrecy that she was determined to breach. In her mind, he was everything she had wanted to make Dylan—dark, alluring and ambitious. Most importantly, when she fixed her gaze on him, he reciprocated.

"I have called you here today because we are at war, and I have every intention of defeating our enemy just as swiftly as my father did. Noah, what can you tell us about the Ar'encal?" Harlyn asked, making everyone in the room turn towards him.

"Nothing you don't already know," Noah answered, pulling his jacket collar down to reveal a curious-looking tattoo. "Do you remember what I told you about this mark?"

"It's some kind of silencing rune," Harlyn recalled. He'd told her about the mark, which he called a rune, on their journey back from Carlisse but the others were not aware.

"Indeed, I cannot reveal anything about the Ar'encal, where they are or who supports them. If I try to say—" Noah began but the words were ripped from his throat as his rune began to burn. He placed a hand over the mark as if to soothe it, but to no avail.

"Curious little thing," Juliette remarked, intrigued.

"If that rune prevents you from giving us any information about our enemy, how exactly are you an informant Mr Harper?" Argued General Owen, who looked at the Imperator's latest ally with contempt.

"It only prevents me from speaking, not showing. And even then, there are plenty of other insights I can provide that will prove my worth," Noah replied with confidence.

"Please enlighten us," Imperator Harlyn requested, waving her hand over a large-scale model map of both the Western and Eastern Continents.

Collecting a few different military figures, Noah reached across the map and indicated several points of interest, mostly in the area south of Carlisse.

"If you want to draw out your enemy, attack the town of Iliria. To learn more about Encia and magic, overthrow the Raen Isle capital of Dawne," Noah instructed.

As Imperator Harlyn observed each location, she wasn't convinced a full assault was a good plan, at least not yet. Joseph Rainer had been the totalitarian, with strong military advisors like Sampson Stone and allies among the Terrans to bolster his army's physical might, something her military lacked.

"We could be outmanoeuvred in unfamiliar territory, especially against an opponent with unknown strengths. A reckless plan," advised Dorian, his candour a surprise to everyone.

"And we cannot forget Siljanna," Juliette added.

"Siljanna Stone?" Dorian checked, looking at her with interest for the first time.

"Yes, have you had the pleasure?"

"It was some time ago, during my early military training days. A unit under my command was challenged to combat four wardens on their graduation trial. She was one of them and defeated almost half of my team single-handedly," Dorian replied, his muscles tensing at the recollection.

"So, you *have* had the pleasure," Juliette chimed, answering her own question as Dorian turned back to Imperator Harlyn.

"Is it Siljanna Stone we are pursuing?" he asked, his tone giving away a hint of dread.

"She's a traitor and will answer for her crimes," Imperator Harlyn confirmed.

"Where does she call home?" Noah asked the room, gently turning another military figurine in his palm.

"Tivani," Juliette replied, standing in front of him and leaning forward to point out the town's location while pushing herself against him provocatively. Noah smiled but made no other reaction to her advance, placing the military marker over Tivani.

"Then we have our targets," Noah suggested, looking to the General, then Dorian and finally Imperator Harlyn. "Use your alliance with Carlisse and instruct the Royal Military to attack Iliria and send your army to destroy Tivani."

"An aggressive manoeuvre," General Owen muttered, looking towards Dorian whose olive skin had gone notably pale. He knew that Dorian had been shaken by the way Siljanna defeated his team in the Wutel Canyon exercise, but also believed the training he'd undergone since had rebuilt that confidence.

"A foolish manoeuvre," Dorian whispered, but his words were just loud enough for General Owen to hear.

Knowing that Dorian was one of his most promising recruits, yet still feared the idea of a confrontation with Siljanna, gave him reason to pause. *Are the soldiers yet to experience combat ready?*

"How much time do you need to prepare the army, General?" Imperator Harlyn asked, picking up on his unspoken reservations.

"As much time as you can give me. The recruits who trained with Dorian and those who have joined more recently are still green. Before they engage our enemies, I want to personally assess them."

"What about the veterans?" Harlyn enquired, folding her arms.

"We shouldn't risk the veterans on a pre-emptive strike until a credible threat is established," General Owen admitted, receiving disgruntled looks from both Noah and Juliette while the Imperator turned her back on the room.

"Get them ready, General, and quickly. In the meantime, Noah, you and Juliette need to organise the mage hunters and return to Carlisse. Make sure King Grayson's soldiers attack Iliria," Harlyn commanded. "And Private Pesaro, I'm sending you to Tivani. As we need an established threat before we attack one of our own towns, ensure Siljanna Stone or another of our enemies is there. On this matter, you report directly to me."

As the Shadow Council disbanded, Harlyn took Noah by the arm and ensured he remained behind. Juliette raised her eyebrow in frustration, wanting to leave with him, but on the receiving end of a stern look from the Imperial leader, departed, allowing them to speak in private.

"Ma'am?" Noah questioned calmly, his bright blue eyes glancing at the hand that prevented his departure.

"You are certain that attacking Iliria will draw out the Ar'encal and the force you previously served?" she questioned.

"Without a doubt," Noah replied, his tone bordering cocky. He obviously couldn't say why the town was important to the Ar'encal people, but the hint was enough.

"And when the time comes, you will truly fight against your former allies?" Harlyn pressed, her grip on Noah's arm firm.

Something about Noah reminded her of Cameron. She wanted to trust him, but her better judgement wouldn't allow it. She needed convincing that he wasn't playing both sides. Caution was something Cameron had instilled in her and behaving in a way he'd approve of was the best way of keeping his memory alive.

"It will be my honour to cut down any Imperial enemy, especially Harrison Stone."

"So, Harrison Stone has gotten under your skin too, I see. Pray tell, what must one do to warrant such malcontent?" Harlyn mused, narrowing her eyes as she prepared to scrutinise his response.

"Exist. But he won't suffer from that condition too much longer," Noah hissed, meeting the Imperator's gaze. "Anyone that stands between my blade and him will suffer the consequences."

"You didn't answer my question," she replied, releasing him and crossing her arms. She was not about to let him leave until he did.

"He took away my power, my reputation... my life. I think it's only fair that I repay him in kind," Noah remarked, drawing his sword and brandishing it before the Imperator. Dropping to one knee, Noah turned the blade elegantly, pointing it towards the ground and looked up at her. "Would that please you?"

"I'm a scientist Mr Harper and put stock in results, not promises. Obtain a command position in the assault on Iliria and prove to me that your former alliances are just that, former. Then you'll earn my trust," Harlyn replied in a steady, yet sinister tone.

Nodding dutifully, Noah exited the room and headed down the corridor to find Juliette. Running his hand through his thick hair, he found himself smiling. The Imperator's demands aligned with his goals, leaving him confident he would impress and gain her favour. As he turned the corner, Juliette was resting against the wall, the slit in her dress revealing most of her slender leg and thigh.

"What did the boss want?" she asked, sounding mildly irked that she'd been made to leave.

"I'll tell you all the details on the way," he replied, allowing his hand to graze Juliette's hip, gently turning her in the direction he was walking. "Don't worry, I have a feeling you'll like the plan."

Chapter Four
CREATION

His morning had been the same as the last few, frustratingly uneventful. Sitting in his grandiose throne, its opulent detailing only outshone by his attire, Grayson Brock cracked his knuckles in between glances at the main entrance. He'd sent hunters to look for Nadia, and they were due to report in, but were late. She'd vanished during the mage assault on his castle, and as one of his possessions, he would not allow her to get away.

She was bound to be hiding somewhere with her freakishly loyal attendants, but he'd never invested any time to discover where they may have considered a safe place. Lost in thought, he closed his eyes until the sound of multiple approaching footsteps caught his attention. The distinct clatter of armour told him his guards had detained a person or persons of interest.

When he realised it was Nadia and her male servant being escorted towards him, he leant forward and studied her approach intently. The two of them were muttering something, but he couldn't make out what.

"You willingly return, Nadia? How surprising," he announced, his booming voice travelling through the empty hall. As they approached, the guards forced both Nadia and Spencer to kneel before the king. "You are with child?"

"I am. Spencer confirms it," Nadia replied. She may have been forced to kneel but was refusing to show him any reverence.

"How far along?" he queried suspiciously.

"It is very early days, my lord," Spencer answered, glancing at Nadia as he spoke, trying to mirror her confident demeanour.

"And how do you intend to ensure this one isn't lost like the others?" Grayson replied, turning his attention to Spencer, the jewels on his gilded waistcoat clinking lightly.

"The queen will require constant monitoring but by learning of the child this early on, I believe I can combat her condition to ensure the baby's health."

Glaring at them for a moment, he assessed their body language, hoping to see if it revealed any dishonesty. *If anyone is superior here, it's me.* Satisfied that they weren't lying, he stood and walked towards Nadia. As he did, the guards lifted both of them from the floor and applied restraints.

"What is this for?" Nadia hissed, tugging against the chains and trying to get away from the guards.

"You attempted to kill me, Nadia. Did you expect me to let that go?" Grayson replied, a sly smile twisting his lips. "Your fate and Spencer's are now tied to that baby. It dies, so do you. In the meantime, you will be confined to quarters."

"I did not make the attempt on your life, Grayson!" Nadia argued.

"Give up while you're behind, Nadia. It will take a lot more than words coming from your lips to convince me of your innocence," Grayson countered. "Besides, you tried to kill yourself once before so it's not that far-fetched to believe you'd try to take my life instead."

"My lord please, the queen had no involvement in that horrid affair. We only escaped the dungeon by chance and fled to protect your heir," Spencer added defensively, failing to avoid being cuffed too.

"If I had made the attempt on your life, why would I return?" Nadia challenged. "I was free and could've sent other assassins had that been my intention."

"Why return, you ask? For the love of your family, Nadia. Don't think I haven't learnt at least that about you. It's only because I've had your parents imprisoned all these years that you've obliged to our arrangement," Grayson answered, a sinister look spreading across his face. "But you need not worry about them anymore."

"What have you done?" Spencer asked, his question laced with dread.

Next to him, Nadia stood frozen, the only noticeable motion coming from her chest as she inhaled and exhaled heavily. Her piercing glare was locked on him and Grayson knew this was a perfect opportunity to hit her where it'd hurt.

"I ordered their execution," he declared with a deep rumble of laughter.

"*You bastard!*" Nadia screamed, launching herself towards him only to be held back. "How could you?"

The man holding Nadia was one of Grayson's most loyal soldiers. His frankly vile features and twisted expression showed that he enjoyed listening to Nadia's distress just as much as Grayson did.

"Because I wanted to!" he shouted back vindictively. "Someone had to pay for your crimes Nadia but once the guard told me of your condition, I couldn't take your life. Instead, I did what I knew would hurt you the most, and the cherry on top is that you've returned, so I still own you."

"I will never let you touch me again!" Nadia yelled, her body trembling with hatred. Suddenly a piercing pain seared through her and Nadia fell to the floor, unconscious. Terrified, Spencer thrashed against the shackles, landing on his knees beside her.

"Please, let me heal her!" he cried, hovering over Nadia's crippled figure.

"Take them away," Grayson commanded, before looking at Spencer with the dominance of a master. "Don't let my heir die."

Indicating for the guard to remove his restraints, Spencer picked up Nadia who trembled in his arms, and allowed the healing flow of energy to travel from his body to hers. The guard shoved him towards the exit but before leaving, Spencer turned back to the king, his verdant eyes adamant.

"I will need assistance, the queen's chambermaid at the very least."

"The little redhead bitch that delivered Nadia's poison?"

Grayson's instinct told him to decline the request, but then another ingenious thought came to mind. Although loyal to Nadia, the chambermaid was also one of his servants, his possessions and she was still yet to be apprehended. He could lure her back into the castle by agreeing to this request and then, should he need to assert further dominance over Nadia, could use the maid without having to endanger the mage keeping his heir alive.

"I told you, the queen had nothing to do with the attempt on your life. Neither did Caitlin," Spencer insisted.

"Fine. If she wishes to join you in captivity, she is welcome," Grayson replied, waving his hand to instruct the guard to take them away.

"No! She will need to be able to move through the castle and travel into town to get supplies for me. Without them, the child will die," Spencer said firmly, refusing to move as the guard prodded him again.

"I can send any old lackey to retrieve whatever you need," he countered.

"Nobody knows Nadia better than me and Caitlin, or cares about her welfare. Would you truly trust any old servant with the health of your unborn child?" Spencer insisted.

"No, but then I don't trust you or the red head either."

"But *we* would never hurt Nadia or the baby."

Considering the request, Grayson rubbed his chin while meeting Spencer's glare. He believed the man before him had no fear of his own death, but perhaps truly feared for Nadia. It was the only explanation for him continuing to care for her and the unborn child.

"I suppose. Just keep her out of my way... and my wine cellar. Although she may not be confined to quarters, her life will also be dependent on the life of my heir," he finally decided before lolling back on his throne.

Acknowledging his response, Spencer, simply nodded as the guard forced him towards the door. As they left, another soldier entered and approached the king. Spencer slowed just enough to overhear their conversation.

"Your Grace, I have news from Imperator Harlyn in Siranor," the soldier announced.

"Well, speak up you fool," Grayson responded, a hint of irritation in his tone.

The Imperator and her people had come to his castle, singed the wall of the banquet hall and destroyed one of his favourite lounge areas with some kind of acid. Then, Harlyn had the audacity to leave, throwing demands about while he was incapacitated. Although the alliance suited both nations, that didn't mean he liked the woman.

"Of course, my king," the soldier replied, his head dropping into a bow. "Imperator Harlyn has declared the recommencement of the war. She has identified mages in Iliria and instructed us to attack. Shall we comply?"

"She expects our support, and as it benefits me, she will receive it. Begin preparations to send some troops," King Grayson confirmed. "Capture any mages you can, they will all become subservient in the end. Kill the Ar'encal and anyone else who stands in your way."

"Sire, should we present any mage prisoners to the Imperator? I believe she is still seeking one," the soldier questioned.

"Absolutely not! They are my slaves. If she wants one, she can find her own," he spat, making it abundantly clear the alliance only remained in place because he willed it.

The soldier nodded briskly and rushed from the hall, overtaking Spencer, with Nadia still cradled in his arms and the guard escorting him to her chamber.

"Ha! So, the people that attacked the kingdom have been found. Now it doesn't matter that you'll be spending the rest of your days in confinement," the guard mocked. "We'll soon have new slaves to take over your former duties."

Spencer refrained from commenting and once they reached Nadia's chambers, the guard forced them inside, quickly bolting the door and leaving them trapped. Turning his attention to Nadia, Spencer noticed the blackening of her fingers spreading down her hand. Knowing the pain she felt was caused by discovering her parents' fate and amplified by the withering, he placed her gently on the bed and continued to heal her.

Leaving her to sleep once her symptoms had receded, Spencer realised how dark and gloomy the room was. Opening the heavy curtain, he glanced out the window and could just about see over the castle walls towards the Driftwood Ranch and wondered how Caitlin was doing. They'd agreed she'd join them in a week, but the events following their return had not gone how he and Nadia had hoped at all.

After a few moments, his attention was drawn back to Nadia, who began to stir.

"Spencer?" she mumbled, her hand softly reaching up to rub her blurry eyes.

"I'm here Nadia," he replied, kissing her on the forehead.

"I'm such a fool," she whispered, turning away from him and cradling her knees, "and I've damned you in the process."

"You were trying to save your parents, Nadia, don't blame yourself for underestimating the king's cruelty," Spencer comforted, turning her back towards him and into his embrace.

"If I'd known there was no saving them, I wouldn't have brought us back here," she whispered, her lips pressed against his ear as he gently kissed her neck. "I am truly sorry."

"Nadia, we were blessed to have the last few days at the Driftwood Ranch uninterrupted," Spencer insisted, keeping his tone compassionate as he gently placed his hand under her chin, her teary eyes locking onto his. "Grayson would've eventually found and dragged you back here if we hadn't returned."

"We don't know that," Nadia retorted weakly. "Perhaps we could've gone into hiding with the Ar'encal like Caitlin wanted. They were willing to help us."

"Nadia, he would've found a way to recapture you," Spencer countered, doing all he could to convince her. She'd only done what she thought was best, and he had agreed every step of the way. "Besides, he is still aiding the Imperator with her hunt for Harrison and the Ar'encal. If we'd stayed, it would've placed an even bigger target on their backs."

"What?" Nadia gasped.

"To support their continued alliance, the king just agreed to launch an attack on Iliria," Spencer advised, which made Nadia recoil.

"We have to warn them!"

"The doors are locked and the king will not let us leave. The guard didn't even attempt to prevent me from hearing about their plan," Spencer began, stepping away from her to search the nearby desk drawers.

"What are you looking for?" she asked curiously. Her body still ached but his healing had alleviated most of the pain. He turned back to her, pen and paper in hand.

"Like you just said, we need to get a warning to Harrison and the others. They need to know the Royal Military plan to attack," Spencer replied.

"How will we get the message to them?" Nadia questioned despondently. "I doubt the guards will send a letter for us, especially not without reading it first."

"Caitlin. After you collapsed, I negotiated for her to be able to assist me and travel freely into town to get supplies. She knows how to find the others, so we'll have to send her to deliver the warning," Spencer continued, beginning to write the note.

"But she doesn't plan to return for several days!" Nadia replied, her tone brimming with concern.

"It's our only chance," Spencer asserted, his attention still focused on the note. "As soon as she arrives, we'll implore her to make haste back to the others."

"I pray our warning doesn't arrive too late," Nadia muttered, clasping her hands together and wishing with all her heart for Caitlin to return earlier than they'd agreed.

Over a week passed and Harrison had worked tirelessly to enhance the Aegis Guard armour and weaponry. While enchanting them with various runes from the Arencian tome, he also created the elegant suppression amulet which they hoped would save Rylie. Working with raw Encia had been difficult, especially in its crystallised form but with his task complete, he was thoroughly relieved. Encia crystals were fragile but with the invaluable support from the Ar'encal artisans, Teagan and Freya, he was able to manipulate them into metal while also creating resistant leather armour. Leather was easier to work with because instead of holding the dainty Encia crystals, Harrison was able to recreate and improve on the elders' designs.

"This is remarkable," Maia commented as Harrison presented her with a leather chest piece that when touched, was freezing. "How did you achieve this?"

"Using the same branding method used on flesh. By debossing the gear, soaking it in liquid Encia and then enchanting it, the rune holds the power and channels it across the entire item. The exterior of that chest piece feels cold, right? Try it on," Harrison requested, and Maia obliged.

Slipping the item over her dress, she expected to shiver but didn't feel cold at all. She looked dubiously at Harrison who gave a subtle nod towards Freya. She summoned a burst of sleet and directed it at Maia, who anticipated the chill, but felt nothing. Looking down, the leather garment turned momentarily white before reverting to its natural colour.

"It absorbed the cold," Maia announced, impressed.

"The effects aren't permanent though. The Encia slowly dissipates and once gone, the garment doesn't retain any magic resistant properties," Harrison explained. "The process is much easier to duplicate though, as long as we can access liquid Encia and there is someone able to perform the enchantment."

"And what about the heavier armour and weapons?" She asked, running her fingers over a sword with a crystal placed elegantly in between the hilt and blade. "We knew the Encia crystals would retain the enchantment, but how did you mould them into the metal without fracturing them?"

"I made these receptacles for the crystallised Encia. They hold the substance in place within the metal and it doesn't seem to deplete. Or if it does, it's at a much slower rate compared to the liquid form," he answered, looking at her with enthusiasm. "Would you do the honours?"

As Harrison raised the sword which had the rune for fire engraved around the crystal, Maia cast the enchantment and embers immediately began to form and flicker around the edges. Taking a step back from her, Harrison made a series of practice swings, each slash trailing flames in its wake.

"What an incredible achievement, Harrison," Maia declared, genuinely proud of him.

"This success was only possible thanks to Freya and Teagan's guidance. My experience in smithing and battle were merely tools to make these creations more effective," Harrison replied with a meek smile.

Something Maia had noticed about Harrison was his humility. He never wanted to take credit for his achievements, but she wasn't sure if it was because he was humble or because he didn't believe in his own value.

"I'm sure they helped, but these adaptations are thanks to your ingenuity. Well done, Harrison," she congratulated again, even though it made him blush.

"Would you like me to show the other artisans the techniques I used? I'll happily enhance all the equipment for the Ar'encal and Aegis Guards, if you wish," Harrison added with pride.

"Already a saviour?" Came a cheery voice from behind them.

"Zack?" Harrison said, turning on his heel to greet his friend.

It had taken a few days before Zack had been able to confidently walk with a cane, but he was getting better. He'd probably never fully adjust to losing his sight but had taken the blow with dignity. His spikey, blond hair had flattened slightly while he'd been on enforced bed rest, but it was still his most recognisable feature.

During his recovery, Lianna had seldom left his side but as Zack approached now, he was accompanied by Evie and Paige Auren.

"Hello, Harrison," Evie greeted cheerfully. She had her arm wrapped around Zack who encouraged her to go up to Harrison. Feeling his gentle push, she jogged over and hugged Harrison who welcomed her embrace.

"How're you doing kiddo?" he asked. She'd been incredibly brave and mature since learning what happened in Carlisse and despite obviously missing her sister, tried to remain positive.

"I'm okay, I just wish we could find Rylie," she replied, looking over to her mother who remained by Zack's side.

"If anyone can sweetheart, it's you and your grandfather," Paige affirmed, smiling at her little girl. She too was obviously worried and wanted nothing more than to have her whole family together again but put on a brave face like the rest of them.

Evie had trained every day with Alistair to conjure visions of her sister and between them, they'd seen a few sporadic images, but nothing helpful. They knew Rylie was travelling south but they had no idea why, or what her true destination was. The only thing they were certain of was that she'd be in Jumant Fort at some point.

"To what do I owe the pleasure of this visit?" Harrison asked, walking towards Zack. His other senses seemed slightly heightened now and after hearing his approach, Zack extended a hand, which Harrison gladly took as he embraced his friend.

"Well, I haven't seen you in over a week," Zack joked, having likely planned that pun the entire walk over. He cracked a smile as both the girls groaned and scolded him playfully, but Harrison couldn't resist chuckling.

"That was terrible," he retorted, stifling another laugh as Paige gave him a look that said *don't encourage him.*

"We wanted to know how you were getting on. It sounds like you've made great progress!" Evie exclaimed, looking over Harrison's shoulder towards Maia and the others who were still examining his work.

Noticing her genuine interest, Harrison opened his jacket and took the amulet from his pocket, displaying it before both Evie and Paige.

"This is my most important creation," he admitted, holding the delicate piece with great care.

"Harrison, it's gorgeous!" Paige uttered through a deep breath, being very gentle as she took it from him to get a closer look.

It was made from silver and had various runes engraved around a choker-style band. At the centre, which would sit in the notch of the wearer's throat, was an Encia pendant delicately suspended in the hollow shape of another rune.

"What do all these runes mean?" Paige asked, handing the amulet to Evie who went wide-eyed at its beauty before giving it to Zack so he could run his fingers over it and visualise the intricate piece in his mind's eye.

"These runes are for more than just suppression. There's clarity, fire and resistance here. The only one I don't recognise is the centre one," Zack detailed, curious to discover the meaning of the hollow rune.

"The central one, according to all the records Maia and the others shared with me, is the mark of the goddess Talia, the Elementalist," Harrison explained.

"So, this will help Rylie break free of the magic controlling her?" Paige asked keenly.

"The magic isn't exactly controlling her. If the stories of Aeons are true, Rylie has embodied Talia's power because of her extreme emotional state," Zack answered.

"The Arencian tome details that transition as becoming an Aeon. The only way we'll be able to communicate with Rylie is to suppress that raw power so she can process her feelings," Harrison added.

"But we have to find her first," Evie muttered, her tone revealing that she felt locating Rylie was her responsibility but so far, she had failed.

"We don't expect you to force a vision, Evie. Don't forget the Aegis Guard are searching as well," Harrison replied, reading her guilt like a book. "Have we had any word from the patrols?"

"Not yet. The scouting parties have been out since we returned but on the last rotation, the reports said they'd only found signs of where she'd been," Zack advised, having likely heard as much from his father Lucas, the captain of the Aegis Guard.

"Has anyone been hurt?" Paige asked, twisting a lock of her hair with worry.

"No, not a single casualty. The reports I overheard claimed that Rylie appeared to chase Siljanna as far north as Beyasil and caused some damage to the docks there. We believe Siljanna made it onto a ship to escape though. She's probably back in Siranor by now," Zack replied.

"You were right Harrison, Siljanna did escape!" Evie exclaimed. Like many of the others, she thought that by now, his sister would be dead.

"But if she can't get to Siljanna, what is Rylie doing?" Paige continued, the conversation creating more questions than answers.

"I asked Maia about that. She assumes that in this form, Rylie can't cross the ocean, even though she was able to walk on water before. She's most likely trying to find another way across," Harrison replied, rubbing the back of his neck. The tension was manifesting and getting worse with each passing day.

"Let's hope we can find her before that happens," Paige prayed, her voice riddled with concern.

"Try not to dwell on it tonight. Let's just hope the guards find a clue or that Evie and Alistair get a clearer vision," Zack interjected. Hearing the tension in the room, he knew that everyone needed a reason to relax. They'd been through so much in a short space of time and the challenges to come required a clear head. Any distraction would do. "Until we receive more news, I've heard wonderful things about your piano-playing skills, Paige."

"You like music, Zack?"

"I love it! In fact, I used to play the piano, but haven't tried for years," he admitted, fidgeting bashfully with his cane.

"When I was your age, I tried to become a stage singer and pianist in Siranor. It wasn't meant to be but my love for music never faded, which is why I became a teacher. Would you like to play again, Zack? I could give you some lessons," Paige offered, swelling at the opportunity.

"I might struggle to see the keys," he teased, still making light of his condition. Paige knew it was just his coping mechanism, however, so she persisted.

"I'm sure Harrison could help me to indent the keys so that you could feel the difference," she suggested, glancing at Harrison who nodded, his eyebrows lifting with delight at the idea.

"Could you?" Zack wondered with intrigue.

"Sure," Harrison replied, pleased to have a less crucial task that would take his mind off the situation, even briefly.

"I'd love to hear you play, Zack, and my mum's the best teacher!" Evie added, linking her arm with Harrison's and encouraging him to leave the artisan grounds. He didn't resist, knowing it would do him good to finally get some rest.

As they left, he turned and gave a polite wave to Maia who was chatting with Freya while Teagan was placing the runic items in a nearby chest. He knew Maia also intended to head to the lodge in Iliria to see if they'd received any word from the current patrol or Caitlin and the others in Carlisse, so she wouldn't need him for a little while.

Although they were all on edge waiting for news, Zack had been right, they needed a break. The following days gave them a real chance to regroup and renew their determination. Nate and Alistair began to reconnect while Evie spent time at the library studying methods of controlling her visions. Alex threw himself into training, mostly with Harrison and Lucas, but also with the other Aegis Guards. He'd become a very admirable young man while trying to show he had a *warrior's heart*, so much so that Lucas rewarded him with the title of squire. Lianna also tried to keep herself busy, learning about the ecosystem of the area but mostly focused her time on aiding Zack. His sincerity was undeniable, and he often repeated that he didn't blame her for his condition, but she still felt guilty. His attitude only made her want to help more.

Although doing his best to get used to life without sight, Zack spent a lot of time with Paige who was enjoying teaching him to play the piano. He was grateful for the distraction, and one afternoon, Zack asked Lianna to meet him after a lesson.

"Hello, Zack, are you here?" Lianna called out, knocking on the front door of Nate and Paige's home. She could hear people inside, but it took a few minutes before Evie opened the door. She gave Lianna a quick hug and ushered her inside.

"Follow me, you need to see this," Evie instructed, her voice hushed but excited as she pulled Lianna by the arm. She was grinning widely, her joy completely infectious, leaving Lianna also smiling before long, but with no idea why.

Leading her towards the lounge, it didn't take long for the harmonious melodies to reach her ears. Hiding in the doorway, Lianna could see Paige sitting beside Zack at the piano. She assumed it was Paige playing but after a moment realised it wasn't.

"Well done, Zack. You're improving so quickly," Paige encouraged while flipping through a song book from the Ar'encal library.

"Thank you, Paige. I've tried very hard not to show it but it's easy to dwell on the things I've lost since the attack, the things I can no longer do because of my condition."

"It'll take time, but you're adjusting. I doubt I ever would've found the will to be as positive as you have over the last few days," Paige admitted, placing a reaffirming hand on his shoulder.

"These lessons have really helped. By learning to play again, you've given something back to me. That gives me hope that one day I may feel normal again," Zack explained, and his words made Paige smile. Her expression proved how much she loved teaching and that it felt good to know her efforts were helping his recovery too.

"When it comes to playing the piano, you've got a gift, Zack," she began, pausing when she noticed Evie and Lianna in the doorway. "Keep practising for a moment, I've just got to make sure my little stow-away daughter has finished her chores."

As Paige approached them, Evie gave her mother a big, innocent grin, but she didn't fall for it. Pointing towards the kitchen, Paige took her daughter lovingly by the shoulders and marched her to the sink, making her finish the dishes. Giggling lightly at the display, Lianna watched them leave before creeping closer to Zack, who had begun playing again as instructed. Pausing just behind him, Zack suddenly stopped.

"Lianna?" he asked, raising his head just enough that she could see him smile.

"How did you know it was me?" she asked, her joy audible as she took a seat beside him.

"You put almond oil in your hair. I could smell it," he answered, unaware of the tender gaze she gave him. "I'm glad you're here."

She quickly noticed how relaxed Zack appeared, his hands lightly resting on the keys and a soft smile on his face. His scars were almost unnoticeable thanks to the Ar'encal healers, but the distinctly faded colour of his eyes was a constant reminder of what he'd endured. The feeling she got from him was pure warmth and it almost counteracted the shivers that accompanied her guilt every time she looked at his eyes.

"The song you were playing was beautiful," Lianna admitted, breaking the short silence between them. "Hearing you play makes me wish I'd learnt how."

"Maybe there's something we can do about that," he replied, asking without words for her hands.

Giving them to him, he shuffled closer, placing her hands on top of his and then back over the piano keys. Slowly, he pressed a key, then another, the notes rising through the air as Lianna's fingers followed. She giggled softly, looking down at the appearance of her own hands causing the music and then felt his reaction to her joy.

Within a second, his hands began to glide across the piano, the same melody from before rising into the air. She closed her eyes and enjoyed the seamless feeling of their connected hands accompanied by the sound of the piano. The music slowed as the tune came to an end and when Zack played the final note, he stopped, turning one hand so that he held Lianna's in his own.

"Beautiful indeed," he declared, and for the first time, his words didn't make her cringe. In fact, she found herself uncertain whether he meant her or the music.

Ever since they'd reconciled at Harrison's celebration, Zack had toned down the flattery he used to fawn her with. At the same time, it was as though her empathic powers finally began to understand him. By knowing him better and then coming to care for him, especially after they went to Lorvale and he entrusted her with the story of his mother's death, her relationship with Zack had become something she truly cherished. Discovering his selflessness during the attack on Carlisse and then how genuine and kind-hearted he was in the aftermath, were unexpected blessings.

As she thought of him and the recent moments they'd shared, the warm feeling returned, followed by a slight pang in her heart. Being an empath, she was used to feeling emotions unexpectedly, but what she didn't expect was for the emotion to be her own. Realising that he'd spoken, and she'd been quiet for a little too long, Lianna buried the feeling and quickly grabbed her bag.

"I have something for you," she announced, retrieving a pair of shaded glasses. She touched his temple reassuringly before placing them on his face. "They'll protect your eyes while we search for a way to restore your sight."

"Thank you, but I'm getting used to other ways of seeing too. May I?" he asked, holding his hands up towards her face. She guided his hand to her cheek and allowed him to trace her features. "You're even lovelier when you smile like that."

She felt another pang in her heart as his fingers ran across her forehead and softly through her hair. His expression was kind but there was still a sadness behind his smile. She knew, although he tried incredibly hard to hide it, he was struggling to adjust to his disability.

"Zack…" she stuttered, realising she was lost for words.

"Your friendship means so much to me, Lianna," he expressed, lowering his hands from her face. "Thank you."

Lianna quickly realised that hearing him call her *a friend* truly upset her. She'd tried to lock down her heart after what happened with Spencer, but those efforts made this revelation come as a shock. Seeking the courage to say something, she froze and then their moment was interrupted by Paige re-entering the room.

"Zack, one of your colleagues from the Aegis Guard is at the door. There's some kind of commotion at the pavilion. I think you two better head up there."

Chapter Five
FOREWARN

Getting to the pavilion took longer than Zack wanted. Although he knew the way, he still needed to be led across the various bridges and stairways that connected their homes on the lower levels and the pavilion, located on the highest platform within the Crescent Falls. With Lianna's help, they eventually reached the main entrance and even from the stairway, Zack could hear raised voices, mainly his father's.

"These reports are damning, Maia! He's sent armed scouting parties through Lorvale and Iliria," Lucas shouted, his voice strained with frustration. "King Grayson is up to something."

"I'm sure he is, but my concern is Siranor. The Imperial Military almost wiped us out during the Uprising and Imperator Harlyn has every intention of doing so again," Maia argued. "We need the Aegis Guard posted along the shoreline. It's the only notice we'll get of an attack from the sea."

"That's not entirely true," Harrison mumbled, sounding distant compared to the others. Zack could imagine him standing in the far corner of the room with his arms folded, trying to bite his tongue while listening to his father and Maia bicker.

"Harrison, not now," Lucas bellowed, not wanting Maia's attention to be divided. He wasn't about to let her ignore his concerns.

"What's going on?" Zack called out, finally interrupting them.

He could picture the scene and his father and Maia arguing. They'd done so countless times in the past. Maia would undoubtedly be calm, collected and insistent while Lucas would be agitated but adamant. Harrison's contribution was the new factor.

"Your father is just stating his case rather loudly, as usual," Maia replied, acknowledging Zack's question while her tone still scolded Lucas.

"Maia, we have to bring some of the guards back. Spread so thinly, if Carlisse attacks, we will have no chance at defending ourselves," Lucas persisted, bashing his fist onto a nearby table.

"Why don't you listen to Harrison? He clearly has another idea," Lianna stated, her tone defiant as she unintentionally channelled the frustration of everyone in the area. Her outburst did the trick, silencing Lucas long enough for both he and Maia to turn their attention to Harrison.

"Maia's right. If Imperator Harlyn is anything like her father, she will use the Siranor navy and military to strike," Harrison began.

"Thank you, Harrison," Maia declared prematurely but Harrison spoke over her.

"But Lucas is right as well. With the Aegis Guard spread across the entire coastline and searching for Rylie, if Carlisse attacks, there will be casualties. We must seek aid," he concluded, walking to the centre of the room and appealing to both leaders.

"From whom? We have no allies," Lucas countered.

"I could reach out to the wardens," Harrison suggested.

"Siranor's elite guardians? I appreciate the offer Harrison but why would they help us?" Maia asked dubiously.

"We may not get the bulk force, but I truly believe Morgan and some of my old friends will help us," Harrison answered, trying to convince his new superiors it was worth a try.

"Friends like your sister, Siljanna and the one that wounded Zack?" Lianna spat in utter dismay.

"Lianna, that's uncalled for," Zack interrupted, placing a hand on her arm before turning back towards where he believed his father and Maia were standing. "Harrison told me about Morgan when we were in Carlisse. If Harrison trusts him, we should too."

After a short silence, Lucas approached Harrison. The older man's dark hair and beard showed signs of grey while his weary eyes tried to conceal the troubles coursing through his mind. Lucas would never admit it, but the recent events that led to his eldest son, Noah, betraying them, Zack's injury and their current predicament had taken a toll.

"All right Harrison, reach out to your friend. If there's any chance he will aid us, we must ask," he conceded.

"Thank you. I'll write to him and get a courier from Iliria to deliver the message as quickly as possible," Harrison replied.

Before leaving, he placed a friendly hand on Zack's shoulder and whispered his thanks. The result could have been very different if he hadn't spoken up.

"Do you really believe they will aid us... and can we trust them if they do?" Maia asked her peer, once ensuring Harrison was out of range.

"I have no choice but to hope so, unless you agree that we should recall some of the guards for defensive rotations," Lucas replied, turning to face Maia, who he deeply respected but genuinely believed was making the wrong call.

"You weren't on the front lines during the Uprising, Lucas," Maia stammered, her usual demeanour wavering. "The Imperial warships bombed our strongholds while their troops destroyed our settlements, and the mage hunters burned our sanctuaries. If they come for us again, we should have as much warning as possible to flee."

"I don't think dad is undermining the power of the Imperial Military, Maia. He's just more concerned about the enemy that is already on our doorstep, rather than one an ocean away," Zack said calmly, trying to articulate his father's argument without shouting.

"Exactly!" Lucas confirmed, signalling towards his son with pride because he'd understood the gravity of the situation.

"You know how much I value your opinion and experience, Lucas. Since becoming captain, you have evolved the Aegis Guard into real defenders for our people, but I cannot ignore the risk of history repeating itself," Maia replied, imploring Lucas to understand.

"As the leader of Arencia, I will defer to your judgement but know that I believe dividing our attention is a mistake."

"But Maia is right too. Having advanced warning of an attack could save hundreds, if not thousands of lives," Lianna added, trying to channel Zack's mannerism and amplifying their connection by taking his hand.

"Maybe it's time we cease the search for Rylie," Lucas muttered, expecting his son and Lianna to roar at the suggestion.

"You can't!" Lianna cried, reacting exactly how he'd expected.

"That would devastate the Auren family, and Harrison, but it may be the right thing to do," Zack replied, knowing how Lianna would feel about his comment.

"How can you say that?" she gasped, covering her mouth with both hands and stepping away from him.

"What if Rylie is moving sporadically because she knows the Aegis Guard are searching for her? Perhaps if we pull those scouts back, the reason she ends up at Jumant Fort may become clear," Zack explained rapidly.

It was obvious that not a single fibre of his being wanted to stop searching for Rylie, but he was beginning to understand they had to try something different. A change could result in Evie or Alistair uncovering why she ended up at Jumant Fort. After a short silence, Maia turned to Lucas and smiled softly.

"Let's hope Harrison's friend will send aid, but in the meantime, keep a few guards in Beyasil, Revaine and Pembroke," she began, reaching out and placing her hand on Lucas' arm. She knew his temper was just a reflection of how deeply he cared. "Then recall all the other guard units and distribute them as you see fit between Arencia, Iliria and Lorvale. I will instruct the elemental and psionic mages to assist you."

"Thank you," Lucas whispered, placing his own hand on top of hers and squeezing gently. An unspoken admiration passed between them until Lucas turned and headed towards the exit.

"May I come too?" Zack asked, feeling the swift motion of his father as he went to leave.

"Of course, I'd like nothing more than to have your council. Do you have any contacts or informants that might aid us?" Lucas replied, returning to his son's side.

"I believe I do," Zack answered with a faint smile.

Recalling that his son had spent years as the notorious mage smuggler and probably made several useful contacts in the process, Lucas wrapped his arm around his son's shoulder and ushered him towards the training centre.

"Can I do anything to help?" Lianna asked, sounding rather lost without Zack to care for.

"Please tell the Auren family our plan and continue to support them in any way you can," Maia requested, smiling softly at Lianna.

"Of course, I'll make sure they know we aren't giving up," she replied before rushing down the stairs and returning to the lakeside homes.

Since Imperator Harlyn's announcement, Tivani had become a ghost town. As Morgan patrolled the streets, people who once happily traded in the market and spoke to him about their day now silently rushed to the confines of their homes. The Uprising was still fresh in the minds of many, especially those who lived or fought through it, so the idea of its resurgence had created an aura of fear. During the week, the original propaganda detailing the 'ferocious powers' mages and the Ar'encal could wield had also re-emerged, which was far from helpful when trying to keep people calm.

Fear of the withering was difficult enough to manage, but now the locals seemed to be wary of an attack from those who were not only immune to Encia but enhanced by it. They would whisper about suffering the same fate as Anora Stone, a reference that would always cut Morgan to the core. With Siljanna and Dylan taking refuge in town, however, the townsfolk keeping themselves behind closed doors had made concealing them easier. In fact, Morgan had become so accustomed to not being spoken to, that he was surprised when a female courier called to him from across the street.

"Excuse me, are you Warden Commander Foster?"

"Yes, can I help you?" he replied, shaking off the surprise.

"I have an urgent message for hand delivery," she explained, reaching into her bag and retrieving a letter.

As he took it, Morgan recognised Harrison's scruffy handwriting instantly. Rushing to the guardhouse, he didn't stop to greet any of the other wardens, not even Téa, which raised more than a few eyebrows. Entering his office, Morgan shut the door forcefully before tearing open the letter. Whatever was on that page was going to be the first news he'd heard from his best friend in roughly a month. He was eager to read it, but before he was able to, a quiet knock alerted him to Téa's presence. He managed to quickly shove the letter into the desk drawer before she entered.

"Morgan, is everything okay?" she asked timidly, hanging by the doorway like a teenager waiting for her crush to notice her.

"I'm fine, Téa. I've just received some important news and wanted to read it privately," he replied, gesturing towards the door. He didn't mean to come across as unkind but really wanted her to leave.

"Is it from Siranor?" she probed. "We've been awaiting instructions on how to support the war effort."

"No, this is a personal matter. Will you please give me a moment?"

"Morgan, I'm your partner, or at least, I want to be. Don't you trust me?" she replied, sounding more than a little hurt.

"Téa, please… I know you want to be my partner but…" Morgan began then sighed heavily, trying to find the right way to articulate his feelings.

"But I'm not Harrison," she answered, finishing his sentence and looking away with disappointed eyes.

Téa had made it quite clear she was romantically interested in him and hoped that being his partner would allow them to bond, but Morgan just didn't want another partner or feel that way about her. He also didn't have the heart to tell her or know exactly how to, which was why he'd promoted her to lieutenant instead.

"Téa, I've trusted you with secrets no one else knows," Morgan countered. "Like how I helped Harrison to escape Tivani, my suspicions about Anora's murderer and that despite our differences, I'm helping Siljanna to hide from Imperator Harlyn. If anyone found out, any of those actions would see me accused of treason."

"You're an honourable man, Morgan Foster," Téa replied quietly, inhaling deeply as she failed to remain upset with him.

"To my detriment at times, and this letter could be another one of those times. Please, leave me be for a moment," he implored.

"I would never betray you," Téa began, but was halted by Morgan's desperate expression.

"Please, Téa," he repeated, fidgeting as he spoke.

"You won't do anything stupid?"

"No more stupid than usual," he replied with a smile.

"We're all doomed," she retorted, finally departing his office.

Knowing Téa would now give him the space he requested and likely keep the other wardens distracted, Morgan sat down and returned his attention to Harrison's letter. Written with a familiarity that only close friends could interpret, Morgan was easily able to imagine how Harrison said each paragraph, but that didn't make what he wrote any less jarring. He'd been through so much and now he and his new allies found themselves in dire need of aid. But the part that really put a fire in Morgan's belly was when he learnt that Harrison had almost died at Siljanna's hand. Tearing his katana from the wall bracket, Morgan marched straight to Siljanna's home.

Arriving at her front door, Morgan kicked it with such force one of the wooden panels split as it flung open. He didn't shout or call her name, but as soon as he made it into the kitchen, Siljanna was before him, armed with the axes Harrison had crafted for her.

"You shot him!" Morgan shouted, slashing the katana towards her. Siljanna quickly blocked the blow, knowing immediately what he was talking about.

"I told you we fought. That he fell but was okay," Siljanna argued. "Shooting him was an accident, I swear."

"Pulling the trigger of a gun is no accident Siljanna!" Morgan growled, his voice low but furious. The earlier belief he had in their tale waning.

"I wasn't aiming for Harrison! He stepped in the way," she cried as their blades locked.

"Who was your target then? Rylie, Evie, another innocent mage?" Morgan challenged, the look in his eyes unrelenting as he shook with rage. She had promised to tell him the truth. She lied.

"It was Rylie," Siljanna yelled, her tone strained as she used all her strength to resist Morgan's assault. She'd forgotten how physically strong he was. "But that was before I learnt the truth."

"Ah yes, this fabled truth and the reason you seek redemption. How can I possibly believe that? You deceived me!" Morgan countered, his loud entrance and rising voice having also drawn Dylan down from the attic bedroom.

"I didn't lie, Morgan, just omitted some details," she replied, her defensive stance faltering. Knowing she couldn't hold him off much longer, Siljanna twisted the axes in her hand, forcing Morgan to break contact.

"That's just as bad as lying and you know it," Morgan growled, the blue of his eyes cold as he stared her down, his katana still raised.

"How did you even learn more than what Siljanna told you?" Dylan interjected, making sure to raise his hands as he approached, so Morgan could see he was unarmed.

"Harrison wrote to me," Morgan announced, shocking Siljanna so much that her grip on the axes faulted.

Morgan took the opportunity to press his blade to her chest. With the point of the katana aimed at her heart, Siljanna released the axes, dropping them to the floor and met Morgan's gaze. He had every right to be angry, but she had to believe he wouldn't take the mortal blow.

"What did he say?" she asked softly, her hands trembling.

"Why would I tell you? Perhaps that's been your intention all along, to use me to get to Harrison and his allies. To finish what you started."

"I swear on my father's grave that's not true," Siljanna uttered, her voice barely a whisper. "Everything I did was for him, so I wouldn't say that if I didn't mean it. All I want is the chance to earn forgiveness."

Her words made Morgan pause and truly look at Siljanna. He didn't trust easily anymore, not since Anora's murder, but Siljanna stood before him, putting up no resistance as he pressed the point of his katana closer to her chest. She was at his mercy. At first, he thought it a bluff, but he soon realised what stood before him was a broken woman.

"I told Siljanna we should lie to you, but she was adamant to tell the truth," Dylan added calmly. "We are not here to deceive you… we just spared you some of the goriest details."

"Please, tell me what Harrison wrote," Siljanna pleaded, her gaze still locked on Morgan. He took another moment to consider his response but finally chose to lower his blade.

"He and his new allies need aid. They're under pressure from an increasing number of mage hunters, fear an attack from Siranor and have evidence that the Carlisse military is preparing to strike too. He's also still trying to save Rylie from her mystical affliction," Morgan informed, having only Siljanna's earlier description to go by when trying to get his head around what had become of Rylie.

"Save her, did he say how?" Siljanna asked, the guilt rising from her chest and escaping as words.

"Not precisely, but they have something that might help suppress her power. They believe she is heading to a place called Jumant Fort," Morgan explained, judging her reaction intently.

"That's all well and good, Morgan, but how can you help?" Dylan asked, his tone mildly dismissive.

"I can travel east with a retinue of wardens to help defend them. Our experience and combined forces could save lives," Morgan replied, raising an eyebrow at Dylan's attitude.

"When we last saw Rylie, she was only interested in burning Siljanna to cinders! Please don't be offended when I say no amount of teamwork is going to be enough to stop her," Dylan retorted.

"When did you become such a defeatist, Dylan?" Morgan challenged, his words mirrored by a provoking stare.

"I prefer realist," he remarked, his tone defiant. "When did you become such a white knight?"

"Is that meant to be ironic or just your attempt at being clever?" Morgan shot back, opening his arms as if needing to remind Dylan of his coppery skin tone.

"I'm always clever," Dylan began but then stopped himself from being too witty, recalling that Morgan was armed and moments ago had been ready to strike them down.

"The Imperator has instigated a second Uprising, but I refuse empower the aggressors. Instead, I will defend the innocent and I believe the wardens under my command will do the same," he asserted as Dylan shrugged flippantly.

"He's right, and we should go too," Siljanna announced, turning to Dylan. "You have insight into how the Imperator thinks, what Juliette is capable of, and I have a debt to repay."

"You would help them?" Morgan questioned suspiciously.

"What happened to Harrison and Rylie is my fault. If he has a way to save her, I presume all he needs is a way to reach her. I'm the perfect bait," she replied with conviction.

"You'd do that?" Morgan added curiously, looking at her very differently than he had a moment ago.

"Yes. I don't expect Harrison to forgive me, but that doesn't mean I shouldn't at least try," she replied honestly.

Just then, they heard a noise from beyond the kitchen window that sounded like bins clanging together. Rushing towards the window, Morgan looked out, scanning the main road and side alley for anyone, but saw nothing.

"What was that?" Dylan asked, wielding a dagger that Morgan hadn't even seen him equip.

"I'm not sure, but I think you've both been in town long enough. Harrison has asked me to meet him in Dawne. I'll send a reply to arrange the meeting and let him know you will both be travelling with me. Gather your things, we leave tomorrow," Morgan instructed, closing the shutters firmly.

After the shutters closed, Dorian Pesaro released the breath he'd been holding, almost unable to believe his luck. How Warden Commander Foster hadn't seen him after tripping by the trash cans was a miracle. Then, to top it off, he'd confirmed his target. Siljanna Stone was in Tivani as they'd theorised. He'd overheard enough, however, to know she'd depart before Siranor could launch an assault.

When he arrived in Tivani, the locals had all avoided him, being extra vigilant of strangers. Initially, it'd made blending in and locating Siljanna difficult but as he rushed to the train station to report back, it was a blessing that they kept out of his way. As he sat on the train with the countryside whipping past, Dorian couldn't help but recall the conversation he'd overheard. Not only was Siljanna hiding out in

Tivani but Dylan Rose, the defector, was with her and Warden Commander Foster intended to commit further treason.

Dorian didn't know these people well, but as the sun caught his arm, highlighting his natural olive complexion, he recalled the combat exercise in the Wutel Canyon. He'd led a team of military trainees against Siljanna, Harrison and Morgan during their final academy trial and although shaken at his team's defeat, he'd learnt a lot from the encounter. Siljanna, her brother and Morgan seemed to be decent people, not traitors and fugitives. Part of him still didn't want to believe it but he couldn't ignore what he'd just heard. After arriving back in the city, Dorian headed straight to the Imperial Palace to update Imperator Harlyn. She'd instructed him to report directly to her, which was against protocol, but he had no intention of disobeying a direct order from the Imperator. Waiting in the large marble foyer of the palace was nerve-racking and when Imperator Harlyn arrived, he immediately stood to attention.

"At ease Private Pesaro, I presume you've located our target?" Imperator Harlyn announced boldly as she glided down the grand staircase.

"I have ma'am, but that's not all I discovered," he replied.

"Out with it then. Do you have news that would prevent our assault?" Harlyn asked, crossing the floor swiftly to reach him.

"Yes ma'am. Siljanna is in town, Dylan Rose too," he began but paused as the Imperator reacted to the revelation.

"I'm sure Juliette would've relished the opportunity for another encounter with Dylan, if she hadn't already gone with Noah," Harlyn commented snidely.

"But tomorrow they'll be leaving, heading to Dawne ma'am, and they are not going alone," Dorian continued, ensuring he had her full attention.

"What do you mean, they aren't going alone?" Harlyn repeated impatiently.

"Ma'am, I overheard direct confirmation that Commander Foster is going to assist the mages and his friends against the interests of Siranor. He implied the wardens under his command would also support him," Dorian confirmed. "Siljanna and Dylan also plan to aid them against you."

As he explained the situation, Harlyn's mood darkened. She was a patient person but equally, had made a bold move by declaring the war renewed and needed viable reasons to justify it. She didn't want to go down in history as the Imperator who shamed humanity with defeat at the hands of the Ar'encal. She'd come too far and achieved too much for that to be the outcome.

"They leave tomorrow," she repeated, thinking aloud. After considering her options, she turned to Private Pesaro to deliver the order he was waiting for. "Fine, let them go."

"Ma'am," Dorian replied courteously as he bowed, assuming he was free to go but was quickly recalled by her.

"Private Pesaro, you are not dismissed. I have another task for you. General Owen said your speciality was to seamlessly integrate into unfamiliar places, and I want you to do just that. Return to Tivani in three days and make yourself known to whoever is in command once the traitors leave. Befriend them," she instructed.

"Of course, ma'am, but to what end?" Dorian questioned.

"I want to know everything that goes on in that town and when Siljanna or Dylan return. They will not avoid persecution," Harlyn replied, her voice seething. She didn't want to but would wait for the opportune time to strike.

Visiting Iliria on patrol, Harrison spent some time talking to the people in the market before heading to the lodge, hoping that Morgan's reply may have arrived. He'd become a familiar face with the landlady since joining the Aegis Guard and so when she spotted him, she handed over the letter with a smile. Tucking it into his pocket,

Harrison finished his rounds, checking on some of the other locals, most of whom were mage sympathisers, before departing.

Reaching the road out of town, Harrison pressed a hand to his inner pocket which held the letter. He desperately wanted to read Morgan's response but knew it was safer to return to Arencia first. Taking his attention off his surroundings for just a moment proved to be a mistake as a galloping horse and frantic rider almost collided with him. The horse reared in a desperate attempt to stop, throwing its rider to the ground. Quickly calming the creature, Harrison recognised the horse, and more importantly, the rider.

"Steady Cruise," he murmured, trying to calm the animal as he edged around him to the fallen rider, her bright red hair dishevelled as she rolled on the floor in pain.

"Ouch," Caitlin grumbled as Harrison reached out his hand.

"Caitlin, are you alright?" he asked as she slowly rose to her feet. "What are you doing here, shouldn't you be with Spencer and Queen Nadia?"

"They sent me, Harrison," Caitlin replied breathlessly. As she faced him, he could see the concern in her eyes.

"What's wrong? Are they in trouble again?" he asked nervously. They really couldn't risk attempting another rescue mission.

"They are, but you and your allies are in more imminent danger," Caitlin swiftly explained. "King Grayson is planning an attack on Iliria."

"Shit! Lucas suspected he was up to something. Looks like he was right. He's been debating with Maia about the best way to defend ourselves for days," Harrison replied, exhaling deeply.

"Do you have any way to defend the town?" Caitlin asked, looking over her shoulder towards Iliria while imagining all the innocent people living there.

"The Aegis Guard will do all we can. Some of the guards that were tracking Rylie were recalled last week, but we are still spread thin," Harrison replied before recalling Morgan's letter which was still tucked in his pocket. Making a silent prayer his dearest friend had responded with good news, he turned to Caitlin. "We should get to Arencia and warn the others, quickly!"

Turning to grab the reins while slowly stroking Cruise, who had now calmed, Harrison mounted and gave Caitlin a hand to jump up behind him. They rode swiftly to the concealed entrance of Arencia but had to stop when the poor horse spooked, determined not to walk over what appeared to be the crest of a waterfall. Although Harrison had learnt of the other concealed entrances, it'd take too long to reach the nearest alternative. Dismounting, the pair encouraged Cruise through the illusion, and reluctantly he followed.

After descending on the floating platform and tethering Cruise safely outside the pavilion, leaving him to nuzzle through the thin layer of snow and graze on the grass below, Harrison and Caitlin went in search of Maia. The curved wooden pillars in the entrance hall seemed lighter, reflecting the frost, while the leaves on the interwoven branches fell from their lofty heights to the chilled surface below. The daylight hours had become shorter too, but the evenings remained illuminated by the glowing Encia from the water that encased the city.

As they entered her study, Harrison and Caitlin were greeted by the sight of a worried-looking Maia speaking once again to Lucas, who was accompanied by another of the Aegis Guard. Seeing their arrival only seemed to add to her look of concern. The guard saluted and quickly left as they approached.

"Harrison, you've returned; good. Have you heard from your warden friend?" Lucas asked.

"His reply just came but I haven't had a chance to read it yet. Caitlin ran into me outside Iliria and has some disturbing news," Harrison explained, drawing their attention to her.

"We know King Grayson's soldiers are up to something. We just lost contact with a scouting party outside Carlisse," Lucas advised, pressing his fingers deeply into his temples. "Can you shed any more light on the situation, Caitlin?"

"Not as much as you are probably hoping, but I bring a letter from Queen Nadia and Spencer. The king has isolated them in the castle but in his hubris, revealed he intends to attack Iliria," Caitlin informed, handing the note to Lucas.

"It is as you suspected," Maia admitted gravely.

"We can't defend Iliria against the might of the Royal Military, even if we moved all the guards from the coastal watch points and Arencia. Their numbers are too great for us to defeat them alone," Lucas announced, his tone more alarmed than Harrison had ever heard before.

"You're right Lucas, while they may not send their full military force and I'm sure there are more Ar'encal that will join the fight, we need help. Harrison, please look at your friend's reply. We have to pray he is coming to our aid," Maia replied as both she and Lucas turned their attention to Harrison.

Reaching for the letter, Harrison ripped open the envelope and began to scan through Morgan's reply. His reaction was apparently not forthcoming enough as Lucas began to pace impatiently.

"Well, what does it say?" he pressed.

"Morgan is sailing to Dawne with a retinue of loyal wardens who will aid us," Harrison began, his eyes still running over the details in the message.

"Finally, some good news!" Maia exclaimed, her shoulders dropping with relief.

"There's more," Harrison continued, his tone uneasy. "Certain members of our group are not going to like it."

Chapter Six
STRATAGEM

Tivani's train station was eerily quiet when Dorian Pesaro returned. The recommencement of the war had set people on edge and their distress was noticeable. The handful of passengers that disembarked the train with him all did so silently, grabbing any luggage they had and briskly walking to their final destinations. After collecting his own case and heading outside, a shiver ran down his spine, but he convinced himself it was the chill and not the foreboding feeling in the back of his mind that caused it.

The cold spell that marked the beginning of Winter's Frost had really set in around Tivani, with snow covering the ground like a quilt. Luckily, the recent travellers that passed through had left distinct tracks on the main road. Without them to follow, Dorian would've gotten horribly lost when attempting to return to town. Crossing the northern bridge, he spotted the frozen river below and how the Encia-infused water still glistened when caught by the fading sunlight. Unable to resist the temptation, he scrambled under the bridge and stood on the frozen surface. It was the closest he'd ever come to the toxic water and somehow, being so close was exhilarating.

"What are you doing?" called out a voice that surprised Dorian enough that he jumped. He turned to see a female warden leaning over the bridge, staring at him inquisitively.

"Walking on water, of course. Why do you ask?" he replied, mustering all the charm he could.

The first day the rivers froze over each year was known as Temu's Shield and was celebrated by the religious folk. There were various songs and prayers written to thank the god for protecting them from the harmful water but for most people it was just the chance to spend the day at church with loved ones. Dorian had been raised by a religious family but since joining the army, didn't pray as often as his parents would've wanted.

"That's rather dangerous, you know. The ice could still be thin," the warden warned but there was an underlying playfulness in her tone.

Heeding the warden's words and preferring not to take the risk, Dorian removed himself from the frozen river and made his way back onto the bridge.

"I bet you can already tell I'm a city boy," he chuckled, extending his hand to the warden, who shook it. "Dorian Pesaro, Imperial Military Liaison."

"Nice to meet you, I'm Téa Gray, interim warden commander in Tivani," she replied politely.

"Ah, does that mean Commander Foster is out of town? I was sent here to meet with him by the Imperator," Dorian began, hoping that he came across as innocent as he intended.

"I'm afraid so. He took a retinue of wardens for training exercises in the Sarron Islands. They're expected back in about two weeks," she advised cautiously. "Can I help at all? I don't believe we were expecting an Imperial visit, otherwise Morgan... I mean Commander Foster, wouldn't have left."

"Not to worry, my visit was unscheduled. Imperator Harlyn understands the war announcement will have impacted every Imperial citizen, so liaisons like me are being sent to each major town to offer support," Dorian lied, using the most plausible excuse he could muster—and it worked.

"Your assistance is welcome. Being without Commander Foster during wartime is more challenging than I anticipated," Téa admitted, looking shyly towards the ground while clasping her hands behind her back.

"I'm glad to be here then," Dorian replied, taking notice of her subtle smile as she turned to escort him into town.

Chatting as they walked, Dorian quickly realised the interim commander had low self-esteem, seemed out of her comfort zone and therefore a strange choice for Commander Foster to place in charge. Befriending her as instructed should be simple.

As they travelled through the market towards the guardhouse, Dorian allowed Téa to show him places of interest, pretending he hadn't been to Tivani before. He turned on the charm whenever he could, causing her to blush, but at no point did she reprimand his flirtations either. When they arrived at the guardhouse, Téa led him into the commander's office, but rather than sitting down in the chair, she perched awkwardly on the edge of the desk.

"When did Commander Foster leave on the training drills you mentioned?" Dorian enquired, taking out a pocket notebook, to enhance his appearance as merely a liaison.

"They've only been gone a day, but I promise it's quite routine," she replied, sounding certain yet refraining from making eye contact with Dorian. If he didn't already know better, he would've believed her.

"And how many wardens went?" he probed, scribbling down notes while Téa tried to peek at the paper in his hand.

"Commander Foster took eighteen wardens with him on the training exercise. Why do you ask?"

"I just wondered if the reduced warden presence could be the reason the citizens seem so on edge," Dorian explained, curious to see how she would react to the suggestion.

"The Imperator's announcement has taken a toll. Many of the townsfolk hold Commander Foster in extremely high regard, so you're right, his absence is making a notable difference," she admitted.

Assessing her mannerisms was harder than Dorian thought, but that was only because he already knew the truth about Commander

Foster's actual whereabouts. He was struggling to tell if Téa knew everything and was just hiding it extremely well or whether she was genuinely in the dark and every time she broke eye contact was because she doubted her ability to lead while her commander was gone.

"It does seem like a strange time to take so many wardens on a routine training drill," Dorian replied rather bluntly, getting Téa's attention. "Surely it could've waited until the people felt more secure."

"Strange, or perfect," Téa insisted, speaking much faster than she had a moment ago. She truly believed what she was saying. "Commander Foster is only trying to ensure we are at our best should the war reach the Western Continent. Despite the reduced warden presence, he instructed those of us who remained to make periodic door-to-door checks on the locals during our patrols."

"He cares deeply for his charges," Dorian remarked, sounding more sincere than even he expected. It was refreshing to see such unwavering loyalty in a unit, even though they were a potential enemy. Imperator Harlyn wouldn't be pleased to know that the betrayer was such a strong and beloved leader.

"Indeed. I do not know of a more honourable man than Commander Foster," Téa replied, but while her words implied a fondness, her tone was undeniably sad.

"If you don't mind me saying, you seem to greatly undervalue yourself, why?" he asked softly.

"Do I really? I guess it's because before Commander Foster took charge, I was barely noticed. I'm certain I was little more than a hindrance to Commander Stone, despite my best efforts," Téa confided, mindlessly releasing her hair from the clip holding it back and letting the warm blonde strands fall around her shoulders. "Do you know what's become of her?"

"Siljanna Stone remains a wanted fugitive. Intel suggests she may return to Tivani, or has already been here," Dorian said, wondering what her reaction to that comment would be.

"What could incentivise her to come back here? As a traitor, she'd be arrested on sight," Téa asserted and once again, Dorian found himself wanting to believe her.

"That is reassuring to hear," he replied, watching as she fidgeted with a lock of her hair. She was a remarkably attractive woman, but he couldn't allow himself to be distracted. "We had wondered if Siljanna retained any support from within the Tivani wardens, but if she doesn't, the Imperator will be pleased."

"I'm glad. My colleagues and I only wish to protect and serve the Imperial citizens and would never support a traitor," Tea expressed, and for the first time, she came across relatively confident.

"I'll ensure to report that back to my superiors," Dorian began, looking around the office and spotting a rotation roster for the remaining guards on the wall. "With the commander and so many of the wardens away, do you feel able to secure the town?"

"I'm following Commander Foster's instructions as best I can," Téa replied, nervously shifting on the desk as she seemed to hold her breath.

"Can I be of some help to you in his absence? I have military experience and could always send written reports to the Imperator by courier if you'd like me to remain," Dorian offered, knowing this was the opportunity he needed to blend in.

"I would appreciate your assistance with the operational duties of being Commander," Téa replied with an impish smile before quickly shying away. "As long as that isn't a waste of your valuable time."

"Not at all. When not on assignment, we liaisons are treated like military errand boys. I'm sure I could be of much greater use here than back in Siranor," Dorian replied with a wink.

The relief on Téa's face was tangible as she hopped off the desk and extended her hand to shake his.

"Thank you," she replied courteously. "There are some bunks in the guest quarters, would you be happy to stay in the guardhouse for now? Unfortunately, the tavern is still being rebuilt."

"Of course, I'll take my things there now," Dorian accepted.

As he went to leave, he turned back to see Téa reaching awkwardly around the desk to retrieve something from the drawer. It was as if she wanted to avoid the commander's chair at all costs.

"Did you need something else?" she asked, freezing in place as her eyes locked onto his.

"No, it's just... if you regard Commander Foster as highly as you seem to, perhaps you should believe in the person he chose as his interim commander," Dorian announced, making her chuckle.

"Perhaps I should," she replied as her face and posture relaxed. Giving him a sincere look of gratitude, Dorian smiled back as he left. Achieving his primary goal had almost been too easy.

Gathering near the edge of Lake Baliten, Nate, Paige and Zack sat together to provide morale support for Lianna and Evie, who continued to combine their powers. Evie was still adamant to conjure a useful vision and lead them to Rylie while Alistair, who was also nearby, continued to stew over his own.

"I just don't understand," Alistair groaned, his face buried in his hands. "What could be so important about Jumant Fort?"

"You said it was an Ar'encal stronghold during the war. Could there be an Encia spring or something else that would enhance her power?" Nate suggested, turning towards his agitated father.

"The only Encia spring I know of is here in Arencia. There's not a single reason I can fathom that she'd go to an isolated fort on the edge of an island she's never been to," Alistair countered.

"You're probably right," Nate submitted, turning away and standing beside his wife, placing his arm casually around her waist.

Overhearing Alistair's frustration, Zack shifted the shades Lianna had given him and edged away. He wore the glasses regularly now and although they disguised his eyes, they had become a new reminder of his blindness. Thanks to his focused hearing and the recognisable thud of incoming boots, Zack was the first to be aware of Harrison's arrival. Clearing his throat and pointing, he alerted the others to their friend's approach.

Realising that Caitlin, Maia and Lucas were with him, Lianna broke contact with Evie and took a seat beside Zack, slipping her hand into his as she so often did while whispering in his ear to explain who had arrived with Harrison as Evie sat beside her parents.

"Caitlin, what are you doing here?" Lianna asked. "Is everything okay in Carlisse?"

"Far from it I'm afraid, but that's not why I'm here. Nadia and Spencer sent me to deliver a warning and help you this time," she advised, addressing the group nervously.

"Help us find Rylie?" Lianna assumed, gently squeezing Zack's hand with hope.

"I don't know where Rylie is, although Harrison filled me in on Alistair's vision as we came down from the pavilion. Is there any way I can help find her?" Caitlin offered supportively.

"No but thank you. If you ask me, the only person that could draw Rylie out is Siljanna," Nate cut in, becoming frustrated at just the thought of his former captor. "If I had Rylie's newfound power, I'd want to make Siljanna pay for the pain she's caused too."

Nate's anger was uncharacteristic and although rightfully aimed towards Siljanna, it provoked Harrison to break away from the group and confront him.

"I understand why you'd say that Nate, but can you imagine how Rylie would feel if she hurt Siljanna, or even worse, killed her and then discovered we're okay?"

"What are you saying, Harrison? She would've killed Rylie in Carlisse if you hadn't protected her, and that attack would've killed you if Maia hadn't been there," Nate challenged, startled that Harrison had started an argument about this. "Doesn't that bother you anymore?"

"Of course it does," Harrison countered. He rarely raised his voice, especially towards Nate, but there had been little time for any of them to process what could've happened.

"Nate please," Paige begged, placing a firm hand on her husband's shoulder.

"I know what Siljanna did was terrible, but I'll deal with those emotions later," Harrison replied, breathing deeply to calm himself.

"Can you really compartmentalise that easily?" Nate asked, his stare making it abundantly clear that he could not control his emotions so easily.

"I have to," Harrison affirmed. "My concern now is saving Rylie before she finds Siljanna. Killing a person, even an enemy, is a heavy burden. She already has to come to terms with killing Cameron Weiss. That's enough when we need her to regain control of her emotions."

After a tense pause, Nate's frustration deflated as he accepted it was not the time to dwell on unresolved grudges.

"You're right, I'm sorry. I almost lost everything dear to me because of Siljanna but I wouldn't want Rylie to carry that burden," Nate replied, sighing heavily as his tone softened.

"You have every right to be angry."

"I doubt I could ever find the strength to forgive Siljanna," Nate admitted quietly, turning to hold Paige's hand while Evie wrapped her arms around her father.

"But look at what we've gained," Paige gestured, indicating to the whole group.

They all fell silent for a moment as Nate looked towards his long-lost father and then at his youngest daughter. who was now seizure-free. What they now had once seemed like an impossible dream but became real because of Siljanna's actions. Nodding with a combination of submission and gratitude, Nate kissed his wife on the cheek before they returned their attention to Caitlin.

"Caitlin, you said you were here to deliver a warning... what warning?" Zack asked cautiously. Although they had enough problems to worry about, apparently, they were going to receive one more.

"King Grayson has issued an attack on Iliria," Caitlin informed them, watching her audience's faces fall with dread.

"Dad, can the Aegis Guard defend them?" Zack suggested, sitting upright sharply. During his years travelling the continent, before meeting Harrison and the others, Zack had aided several mages and their families, many of whom took refuge in Iliria.

"We can try, and our efforts will be easier thanks to Harrison's friend," Lucas advised. "Commander Foster is willing to aid us and travel to Dawne with a retinue of wardens. They'll hopefully arrive in the next few days."

"They're not travelling alone, however," Harrison added quickly. "Siljanna and Dylan are coming too."

"You've got to be joking!" Nate snarled, a look of disdain filling his eyes once more.

"Why would Morgan bring her here? Didn't you tell him everything she's done?" Evie cried, her lip quivering as she locked her wide eyes onto Harrison.

"Of course I told him, but Morgan's reply explained that Siljanna learnt of the Imperator's deceit. He truly believes she wants to make amends," Harrison answered, but there was something about his response that was unconvincing.

"There is nothing she can do to help us," Lianna growled, interlocking her fingers with Zack's and gripping tighter. Recognising her frustration as it boiled to the surface, he reciprocated the gesture while stroking her fingers with his thumb.

"That's not entirely true," Harrison began, looking at each of his friends but focusing mainly on the Auren family. "Nate just said that the best person to draw Rylie out is Siljanna and that is exactly what she is willing to do. Act as bait."

"That's it!" Evie exclaimed, her warm brown eyes glistening with comprehension. "Grandad, that's why you haven't been able to make sense of your vision and why I haven't been able to conjure one."

"You might be right, Evie," Alistair admitted, catching onto her train of thought. "We've been trying to discover why Rylie is going to Jumant Fort, but she's not. We need to lure her there."

"It would be the perfect place. Away from any settlements and unlikely to be searched by King Grayson's troops. Could we make that work?" Lucas asked eagerly.

"We can't, but she can," Alistair replied, pointing towards Lianna who glanced back with a look of shock.

"How can I do anything? I'm just an empath," she howled.

"No Lianna, this is what I've been teaching you. Your true power is that of a channeller," Alistair replied confidently. "Why do you think you've been able to help Evie? You've been channelling negative emotions like doubt, concern and fear away from her conscious mind."

"But it didn't work, Evie wasn't able to conjure a vision," Lianna argued, doubting her ability rather than power itself.

"Don't sell yourself short, Lianna. Rylie doesn't intend to go to Jumant Fort, that's why Evie's attempts failed. What she was trying to see hadn't been planned yet," Alistair explained.

"Then how did you see her in Jumant Fort?" Lianna countered irritably, "And how exactly am I supposed to get her there?"

"My vision must've triggered because I was angry at Siljanna. Listening to what she put my family through, the actions that resulted in Rylie's transformation," Alistair began, hesitating as he turned to Harrison, knowing that he had to reveal details he'd previously omitted. "In the vision, I recognised the fort because Rylie was chasing Siljanna over the battlements. She will catch and kill your sister."

"Precognition can be controlled, but it takes skill and practice. That vision wasn't conjured, was it Alistair? It came to you because you were angry," Nate added, recalling what his father had told him about controlling visions during one of Evie's recent training sessions.

"Angry and desperate," Alistair expressed with a sullen nod.

"You were seeing Siljanna's fate, not Rylie's whereabouts," Harrison realised, his voice laced with sadness. Although she'd hurt them in ways they never thought her capable of, Harrison didn't want his sister to die—but facing Rylie would apparently be a death sentence for her.

"I believe so," Alistair confirmed.

"So, to save the person I love, I must sacrifice my sister," Harrison muttered, clenching his fists.

"Not necessarily," Caitlin chimed in. "I'd have to be close by, but I could help protect Siljanna with an illusion."

"It's not Siljanna we should be trying to protect," Nate added hastily, fixing his glare on Harrison.

"But Caitlin's power could be useful," Harrison commented, turning to her while ignoring Nate. He wasn't willing to start that argument again. "Can you stay a while longer to help us?"

"Of course. Don't get me wrong, I want to get back to Nadia and Spencer, but returning with good news would be a nice change," Caitlin replied.

"Wait a minute! You're all still assuming that I can somehow channel a message to Rylie. And even if I can, are you really willing to trust Siljanna? I'm not!" Lianna cried, her voice ringing with doubt. "It's her fault Rylie became an Aeon!"

"We can't trust Siljanna," Nate agreed firmly.

"I don't trust Siljanna, but I do trust Morgan. He wouldn't lie or put us in danger," Harrison replied adamantly.

"Lianna, your power can get a message to Rylie. I can help you learn how," Maia asserted, channelling being one of her strongest talents. "Part of a channeller's power is to give or take away feelings of those near to us, but if the connection is strong, it can be projected outward too."

"What do you mean, projected?" Lianna asked, still looking highly sceptical.

"By channelling the energy of the people who care greatly for Rylie, and the threat of Siljanna's return, we can push those feelings into her mind. In her current state, Rylie's instinct will be to go wherever we tell her," Maia explained.

"And you'll tell her Jumant Fort," Alistair assumed.

"We may be able to do better than that, we could try and show her your vision, Alistair," Maia continued. "It'll prove to Rylie that she will encounter Siljanna there."

"Do you really think that could work, even with Rylie in her Aeon form?" Alistair enquired, looking towards Maia with an unconvinced expression.

There was so much they didn't know about the Aeon form that Alistair couldn't help but feel her confidence was unjustified. They all wanted her plan to work more than anything but Alistair's expression showed that he couldn't bear to see his family, especially Evie, heartbroken again should the attempt fail.

"With the whole family together, their strong bond should be enough to empower the channelling," Maia expressed. Hope was all they had and while she was willing to cling to it, her plan was soon disrupted.

"No, I'm going with Harrison," Nate declared, his tone sounding protective. "If your message reaches Rylie but something goes wrong… if Siljanna betrays us, I want to be there. I need to be there."

"You're worried, I understand that but…" Paige began, trying to reason with her husband.

"I don't doubt Harrison's abilities… I never will, and I want to believe in Morgan too, but I do not trust Siljanna. They are trying to save our daughter. I need to help and cannot do so from here."

"Of course you can join us, Nate," Harrison replied. They didn't always agree but he felt reassured at the thought of having Nate by his side.

"That's okay. Paige and Evie's influence should be enough to boost Lianna's connection to Rylie," Maia said, accepting that Nate needed to go. "I'll support the connection with my power too."

"Alright then, while the rest of you concentrate on your tasks, I'll focus on preparations to defend Iliria. Young Alex can assist me," Lucas added, marching off before anyone could say otherwise.

"What about me," Zack mumbled.

"I need you," Lianna replied almost instantly, causing Zack to shyly smile in response.

"Harrison, Nate, you must get that suppression amulet on Rylie. Regardless of whether Siljanna's desire for redemption is true or not, this may be the only chance to reach her," Maia informed as Harrison withdrew the amulet from his pocket.

"We'll get her back," Harrison replied before heading to the armoury, Caitlin and Nate following closely behind.

Since becoming squire for the Aegis Guard, Alex had worked incredibly hard to impress his superiors. From smartening up his messy blond hair, correcting his formerly notorious attitude and attending all the training drills he could, developing his lean, skinny frame into a slightly muscular one, Alex didn't look that different, but he was a different person now.

He realised that when Harrison had told him to show the quality of a *warrior's heart*, he was just protecting him from engaging in combat prematurely, but there was something about those words that still held great meaning for him. Squire was far from a flashy title and there was a lot of errand running, but Alex put his pride aside and did whatever was asked of him. He wanted to prove himself worthy of becoming a guardian and receiving the Arencian rune.

When Lucas arrived at the training centre, Alex expected it would be for another combat exercise or perhaps to send updates to the guard patrols, but he couldn't have been more wrong.

"Alex, come quickly, I need your help," Lucas commanded.

"What's happened?" Alex asked, rushing to keep pace with his captain.

"We must prepare for battle. King Grayson plans to attack Iliria and the townsfolk need us to defend them," Lucas explained briskly as they marched into his office.

"He's going to attack a town of innocent people, why?" Alex questioned, utterly baffled.

"To draw us out," Lucas replied bluntly, picking up the shield he displayed behind his desk and running a hand over it affectionately.

"So, it's a trap," Alex stated, reading between the lines as fear began to set in.

"Most likely," Lucas agreed, adjusting the straps on the shield so that he could carry it on his back.

"And we're going anyway?"

"Our duty is to defend those who are sympathetic to the Ar'encal and mage plight. The people of Iliria are good to us and they deserve to be protected," Lucas answered, placing a firm hand on Alex's shoulder.

"Are we going to survive?" Alex muttered, his tone barely more than a whisper as his knees gave way and he tumbled into a nearby chair.

Alex wasn't implying they shouldn't help, Lucas knew that but the danger they faced was terrifying. This would be his first taste of battle and it could easily be his last if he were to get injured, or worse.

"Some of us may fall, but it will be in the defence of innocent lives. An honourable death," Lucas replied as he knelt, placing himself at eye level with his young squire.

"But I'm only fifteen," Alex began, his breathing heavy. After a moment he dropped his head, disappointed with himself.

"Are you okay?" Lucas enquired softly, keeping a steady grip on his shoulder.

"I can't believe I'm only thinking of myself. Clearly, I'm not worthy of the Arencian rune, I don't have the heart of a true warrior," Alex whispered woefully.

"Don't be so hard on yourself. To be a true warrior is not to be without fear, but to fight on despite it," Lucas counselled, lifting the young man's head. "Will you fight with us?"

"You want me to fight?"

"I want you to be prepared to fight. Your main goal will be to protect any civilians and get them to safety should the battle reach the town centre," Lucas advised, pulling him to his feet and handing him a short sword that was perfectly balanced and sharp.

"I'd be honoured, thank you for believing in me," Alex replied, taking the sword while trying to stop his hand from trembling. The blade was engraved with the emblem of the Aegis Guard, a true warrior's weapon, not a training tool.

"Now go to the armoury and get some protective gear. You can see if Harrison needs any assistance before departing too," Lucas instructed.

"Where is he going? Will he not be defending Iliria with the rest of us?" Alex questioned, suddenly nervous that their best warrior was leaving them.

"Harrison will join us as soon as he can, but his request for aid from the wardens came through so he's going to meet them in Dawne," Lucas began. "They've also found a way to lure Rylie to Jumant Fort."

"That's excellent!" Alex exclaimed, imaging how pleased Evie and her parents must be. He missed Rylie too, but his longing to see her safely return was incomparable to the others.

"If you want to learn more, speak with your sister and Evie at Lake Baliten, but don't take too long, I need you here," Lucas instructed. Alex's responding energy made it clear that being needed by his captain had really impacted the young man.

"Of course, sir. I'll return as soon as possible!" Alex promised, turning on his heels and rushing towards the armoury.

As he arrived, his mind still spinning at how much he'd missed in just one morning, Alex found Harrison who was getting geared up and ready to go, with Nate and to his surprise, Caitlin also with them.

"Hello everyone, is there anything I can help you with?" Alex asked.

"I think we're okay thanks, Alex. Just preparing to head to Dawne and meet the wardens," Harrison advised, his tone less relieved than Alex had expected, but he didn't dwell on it.

"And not a moment too soon! Lucas just filled me in," he replied, grabbing one of the smallest leather chest pieces he could find and a sheathe for his new sword. "He also said you have a plan to save Rylie, is it true?"

"We have a chance, but it does mean relying on Siljanna," Harrison began.

"Siljanna, the woman that tried to kill us and is working with the Imperator… *that* Siljanna?" Alex asked dubiously, trying to conceal his surprise that Lucas hadn't mentioned that part of the plan.

"One and the same ironically," Nate muttered under his breath, tightening his leather armguards.

"Can you trust her?" Alex asked, knowing it was probably a stupid question and something they'd already considered.

"We can trust Morgan, he wouldn't bring her if she hadn't proven her intentions are pure," Harrison replied, reiterating the belief he had in his friend.

"Siljanna could have deceived him too," Nate commented as he picked up a crossbow to everyone's surprise. "I understand why we have to take this risk; I want my daughter back more than anyone, but we will be armed and ready for anything."

"Agreed," Harrison said with a short nod, watching Nate swiftly check, load and fire a practice shot of the crossbow at a nearby dummy, landing the bolt just off the centre of the target.

"Wow! I didn't know you could shoot," Alex blurted out.

"Not even I knew that," Harrison added, pleasantly surprised. Nate had travelled extensively before settling down with Paige in Tivani and picked up some survival skills along the way, but none of them expected him to be proficient with such a complex weapon.

"I haven't used one of these in a long time. My skill may be a little rusty, but Siljanna won't know that," Nate winked.

"Whether Siljanna is genuine or duplicitous, don't forget you've got me tagging along too. I can create an illusion in a pinch to distract her or save her, depending on the circumstances," Caitlin added with a smile, picking up a butterfly dagger and tucking it into her jacket.

"I hope it all works out. Are you sure I can't help you to get ready?" Alex checked.

"We'll be fine Alex, thank you. Carry on with any other duties you have for Lucas and if you get a moment, check in with your sister," Harrison hinted.

"That's my next stop," Alex confirmed as he hurried towards the door and made for Lake Baliten.

Chapter Seven
Resolve

Lianna was struggling to contain her anxiety as she paced the shore of Lake Baliten. The others were nervous too, so she was picking up on their concerns, but for once, most of the doubt she felt was her own. She had always believed her powers were passive but now Alistair and Maia were convinced she could actively push a message to Rylie. It was crazy!

As if sensing her distress, Zack took her hand as she passed and pulled her towards him. Placing both hands on her shoulders, he leant forward, allowing their foreheads to touch. He emanated a sense of belief in her and she tried to focus all her energy on that feeling.

"You can do this," Zack whispered, the warmth of his breath and sound of his voice equally soothing.

"How can you be so sure?" Lianna mumbled.

"I've seen Maia and the Ar'encal do some incredible things in my life. If she says you can do it, I believe you can," he replied without a second's hesitation.

"And if I fail?"

"Then we'll find another way," he answered reassuringly.

"I don't think Rylie will be picking up letters anytime soon," Lianna replied, raising her eyebrow sarcastically. Although Zack couldn't see the gesture, he heard it in her tone.

"Then we'll pin messages on every tree," he replied humorously, shaking her lightly for being so despondent.

Lianna couldn't resist his positivity for long and eventually allowed herself to smile.

"Now you're just being silly," she giggled.

"Not at all! A few simple posters that read 'Siljanna is at Jumant Fort, take the first right as you approach Dawne then justice is just five miles ahead' should do the trick," he continued, his voice becoming more and more spirited.

Certain he'd gotten through to her, Zack gave Lianna a hug before releasing her shoulders with a smile. Sitting down on a nearby log, they continued to wait for Maia and the others to arrive. Desperately wanting to remain in his embrace, Lianna winced as he stepped away. That small distance was enough to enable Paige and Evie's nervous excitement to flood back into her mind.

She was just about to start pacing again when Alex arrived. He gave his sister a friendly wave but beelined straight to Evie who embraced him instantly. They'd become close over the last few weeks, but this was the first time she'd seen them openly show such affection for each other. In fact, Lianna had never seen Alex openly show affection like that to anyone except her before.

"Hey, what's going on? Lucas told me to check in with you guys. Did you get a vision of Rylie?" he asked, wrapping his arms tightly around Evie.

"Not exactly, but we potentially know why and have a plan to reach out to her using Lianna's power," Evie advised, smiling sweetly as they parted.

"Lianna's empath power, how?" he questioned, the smile on his face warm and unwavering. "Consider me intrigued!"

Lianna could feel that similarly to Zack, her brother had absolutely no doubt in her ability, even though he had no idea what they expected her to do. Although he'd been a notorious troublemaker while they were living in Revaine, Lianna couldn't imagine life without her brother.

It was another few minutes before Maia and Alistair rejoined them and when they did, they came with several vials of Encia.

"Maia, can we please go over this again? I'm still not entirely sure how this is going to work?" Lianna grumbled as Maia gently took her hand and placed a vial in her palm.

"Of course, Lianna, I'm sorry for the delay," Maia apologised. It was easy for her to forget that Lianna was still learning the full extent of her powers. "Channelling is the true ability behind your empathic nature and harnessing it will enable you not only feel what others around you are feeling but manipulate their emotions and even communicate with them."

"I wish you all could've met my wife," Alistair chipped in. "Emilia was gifted. There were times during the war when we'd be apart for several weeks, but I knew she loved me because she channelled the knowledge into my mind."

"Emilia was Ar'encal, so she had a greater natural power, but that is why we have brought the Encia for you," Maia continued, keeping a steady gaze on Lianna.

"Should I take it now?" she asked, her hand shaking slightly.

"Not yet, let's practise first. Please, take a meditative stance," Maia instructed, so Lianna sat down, crossed her legs and placed her hands, palms up on her knees. With her eyes closed she inhaled and waited.

"That's good, Lianna," Alistair praised, crouching beside her but without getting too close, giving her space as she attempted to learn the technique.

"Focus all your energy on how you feel right now, and project that to anyone in the group," Maia continued. "Push your feelings, your thoughts to them. Let them know what you're thinking."

For a moment the entire group fell silent, with only the cool, gentle breeze creating a noise around them.

"I feel stupid," Alex announced abruptly. Evie turned and gave him a playful slap on the arm while stifling a giggle.

"Alex, stop it! Let Lianna try," she scolded, unable to hide the smile creeping across her face.

"I'm sorry, I don't know why I said that!" Alex replied, blushing at his sudden outburst.

"Oh my," Lianna gasped, opening her eyes and glancing at Alex.

"Lianna, is that what you were just thinking?" Maia questioned with a smirk.

"Yes," she admitted. The look on her face revealed that she genuinely hadn't expected it to work.

"Do you feel stupid now?" Maia asked, her smile spreading as she reached over and took Lianna's hand supportively.

"Not exactly," she replied sheepishly, "but Alex is only six feet away and my brother. How can I project a much more detailed message to Rylie when she's miles away?"

"That's a good question, we don't even know where Rylie is," Zack added curiously. Lianna knew he believed in her and that it was possible, so he was just probing for details on how the feat would be achieved.

"That's where Paige, Evie and I come in," Alistair replied. "Paige and Evie have the strongest connection to Rylie, and I had the premonition about her encounter with Siljanna at Jumant Fort."

"And Lianna can project all of that?" Evie queried, tugging a lock of her wavy hair. She was still amazed that her friend's power was so much more vast than they realised.

"You and your mum's bond will act like a pathway to Rylie and my vision is the message," Alistair explained. "All Lianna needs to do is deliver that message, just like she told Alex how she was feeling a moment ago."

"It's getting late though. Don't forget Harrison and the others need to meet the wardens in Dawne before heading to Jumant Fort," Alex interjected, looking up at the fading daylight. "Shouldn't we wait until tomorrow?"

"No, time is the one thing we cannot spare," Maia encouraged, not wanting to risk Lianna's doubts resurfacing.

"Okay then, let's do this," Alex accepted, giving his sister an approving nod before taking a seat next to Zack. He knew Lucas and the Aegis Guard were travelling to Iliria shortly but didn't want to miss this.

"Evie, Paige, please sit beside Lianna and place your hands on her. Focus all your energy on thoughts Rylie," Maia explained as the girls sat down.

As Evie touched Lianna, she shook briefly as a new premonition came to her. It was Rylie, still in Aeon form, moving swiftly towards a crumbling fortress. The flames on her skin burned intensely as she approached a large gate with a woman standing before it.

"Evie, are you okay?" Paige asked, noticing her daughter jolt.

"I think it's going to work! I've finally had a vision and could see Rylie approaching the fort. She must get our message!" Evie blurted out, her eyes flickering open as the vision receded.

Lianna instantly felt a surge of determination from Paige and Evie. With their connection strong, she took the vial of Encia and called out with her mind to Rylie. With the three of them connected, Maia then nodded at Alistair who drank his vial of Encia and knelt beside her. In seconds, his head lurched back and the earlier vision triggered. Once certain he was in control of the vision, Maia took Alistair by the hand and used her power to stabilise the images but remove the clutter of emotion before finally taking hold of Lianna. The moment all five of them were united, a gust of wind surged through the clearing and lifted the unanimous sound of their laboured breathing into the air. Pushing the limits of his vision to conjure more than just the original flashes of battle, Alistair felt his mind unravel as the premonition unfolded. Rylie would see exactly where to go and why.

As Alistair expanded the vision, observing more detail than he had before, Maia felt his earlier frustration towards Siljanna grow. Trying to channel it away and keep him calm, she soon realised that in doing so, she'd transferred the negative emotion towards Lianna, damaging her focus. As the young woman began to shake, Maia sensed she was about to hit a breaking point. If she didn't do something now, Rylie wouldn't receive their message and Lianna would be too exhausted to try again.

"Lianna, you must push past the images you can see and any anger or fear you feel," Maia whispered, leaning away from Alistair to focus her powers on aiding Lianna. Whatever images he'd revealed would have to be enough.

"I'm trying," Lianna stammered, her voice strained as if she were in physical pain.

"Think only of Rylie and how much you and your friends care about her," Maia continued, stroking Lianna's hand softly.

"You can do this Lianna. I believe in you," Evie added, and she truly meant it. Although she still held a great desire to be reunited with her sister in her heart, Evie was able to add a sense of deep admiration for her friend. That positivity gave Lianna the boost she needed.

"Evie's right. Even in this short amount of time, we have forged close bonds with one another. Draw on that for strength," Maia concluded, hearing Lianna's laboured breathing ease.

Soon, the distracting energy from Alistair was overridden by an empowering sense of belief from the people around her. Letting that emotion wash over her, Lianna clamped onto Maia's hand and pushed harder. She didn't need to analyse the vision, she just had to ensure Rylie received it.

"I will not fail," she said through gritted teeth.

Watching from the sidelines, Alex wanted to describe the sight before them for Zack, but instead he just wrapped his arm around his friend. After a few intense minutes, Lianna released her grip and collapsed backwards onto the floor. Hearing the thud, Zack jumped to his feet.

"What happened?" he called out, stumbling without his cane in hand. "Lianna... are you okay?"

"I'm fine," she replied giggling. "What a head rush!"

"Don't scare me like that," he exhaled, trying to sound grumpy but failing to do so. "Did it work?"

"I think so. The rest is up to Harrison and Siljanna," Lianna replied, staring at the sky as she enjoyed feeling the relief and excitement among the group.

Once they'd each gathered their weapons and some supplies and equipped the recently crafted rune armour, Harrison, Nate and Caitlin departed Arencia on horseback via the concealed southern bridge into the woodland rim of the Athalay Plains. Nate vaguely remembered the area from his years travelling and was startled by how close he'd been to Arencia even then. Shelving the desire to reprimand his memory further, he focused on the ride to Dawne and confirmed to the others they'd reach the town before nightfall.

When they arrived, the first thing Harrison noticed was just how similar Dawne was to Tivani, only on a smaller scale. There was a rustic feel to all the buildings, many with strong wooden frameworks and thatched roofs. His thoughts then shifted to just how devastating it'd be if Rylie confronted Siljanna here. In her current form, she would incinerate hundreds of homes and shops with very little effort.

Walking through the dusty streets, Harrison noticed a smithy and large workshop making up the corner, with a tack shop and stable where they could leave their horses. Slightly further down the road looked like the main shopping street and in the centre was a wooden crossroad sign indicating the way down to the harbour. Following the road, Nate pointed out the inn and spotted a run-down tavern nearby, its windows and doors boarded up.

"This place looks just like Tivani did twenty-five years ago," Nate muttered, somewhat astonished at the resemblance.

"I was just thinking that. Tempted to renovate another tavern?" Harrison joked, playfully punching Nate's arm.

"Well, the last time I checked, my tavern had seen better days," Nate replied with a smirk. "And that little place has potential."

Nate allowed the prospect to distract him from the severity of their situation for just a moment before continuing with Harrison and Caitlin to the harbour. Although there were only three proper docks, the surrounding streets were bustling with traders sorting through cargo and fishermen calling out to passers-by, aiming to sell what remained of their daily catch. At the end of the harbour was a notice board that confirmed the next passenger ferry was due to arrive first thing in the morning. With time on their side, the trio decided to head back to the inn.

The innkeeper greeted them politely before sliding the sign-in book and two keys towards Caitlin.

"They've only got two rooms available. I hope you boys don't mind bunking up," she teased, handing Harrison the second key.

"No problem, Caitlin. We'll meet you here in the morning," Harrison replied, knowing that she wasn't really giving them a choice. Waving cheerfully, she jogged up the nearby staircase to find her room, leaving him and Nate alone in the lobby.

"Come on Harrison, join me for a quick drink, we need to talk," Nate said, indicating a small lounge bar opposite the reception.

The lounge was a dive, but the barman gave them a friendly smile and after Nate's signalled for two drinks, whipped the beers down to them.

"I think I know what you're going to say," Harrison began, taking a gulp of the bitter yet refreshing drink. "You're worried."

"I am worried, but not for the reason you're probably expecting. I'm worried that I've disappointed you."

"What?" Harrison replied, his eyes wide with shock. "Why would you think that?"

"Because on more than one occasion, I've let my anger towards your sister get the better of me and you've often been on the receiving end of that," Nate began, staring down at the amber liquid in his glass.

"Siljanna's put us all through a lot," Harrison acknowledged, speaking through a deep sigh. "You've barely spoken about what happened after the fire and during your time in captivity. Do you want to talk about it?"

Nate paused for a moment, unsure whether or not he wanted to speak, but decided that Harrison deserved to know what he'd experienced, and that speaking to someone other than his wife would be good for him.

"During the tavern fire, Paige and I were trapped and eventually passed out from the heat. When I awoke, we were already in an Imperial holding cell. Someone transferred us, Elijah and another young man to Siranor, but we weren't given any explanation as to why," Nate recalled, turning the glass in his hand and mustering the strength to continue.

"Elijah was with you, was he okay?" Harrison asked, a foreboding feeling setting in. The thought of yet another of his friends suffering just to help him made him feel uneasy.

"We were chained to the walls and interrogated. I tried to resist but one of the Imperator's thugs beat me until I lost consciousness. I later learnt that Elijah was poisoned while in captivity," Nate continued without looking up from his glass.

"I'm so sorry, Nate," Harrison muttered, his brow furrowing at just the thought of what they'd endured.

"When I came to, Elijah was gone, and the young man was dead. Paige was catatonic from fear, but the restraints stopped me from being able to hold her. I've rarely felt as helpless as I did in that prison," Nate admitted, finally taking several, long gulps of his drink as if hoping to wash away the memories.

"I'm glad you and Paige are both safe now," Harrison offered quietly, glancing guiltily at Nate through the corner of his eye. He couldn't help but wonder how different things would've been had he made different choices.

"As am I," Nate replied swiftly, not assigning any blame towards Harrison. "I'm not entirely sure how long I was unconscious, but it wasn't long before I discovered Siljanna's involvement. When she entered our cell, Paige just froze so she turned her rage on me."

"But you couldn't have known anything that happened after the fire."

"Siljanna was eager to fill me in. She revealed how she was hunting my girls, accusing them of being mages and both you and Rylie of murder. Of course, I refused to believe it. For days she tortured me, but I refused to speak. I forced myself to endure whatever she attempted in silence," Nate began but paused, closing his eyes as he took a deep breath, the words he intended to say causing him pain.

"She hurt Paige, didn't she?" Harrison asked, reading the dread on Nate's face.

"Yes, she began to strangle her... and I couldn't bear to watch so I told Siljanna everything," Nate recalled, sounding ashamed. "In return, she injected Paige with some kind of solution and separated us. At the time, I didn't know if she was dead or alive."

"I can't even begin to imagine what was going through your mind," Harrison sympathised, pressing a fist into his stomach and pushing back the sickening feeling that arose from the revelation.

"I'd lost all hope. Siljanna had me moved to the Institute where the Imperator began running tests on me. I think she was trying to forcefully trigger magical abilities within me, but nothing worked. Then again, magic is linked to emotion and by that point, I was numb," Nate explained, his eyes reflecting just a portion of the hopelessness he felt at the time.

"Nate..." Harrison began but genuinely didn't know what to say so instead, fell silent to allow him to continue.

"It was several days before they took me to another holding cell and I discovered Paige was alive. That's when they took us to Carlisse, where your friends found us," Nate concluded, finishing his drink shortly afterwards.

"They intended to use you as bait no doubt, but we were already there trying to save our other friends when we discovered they had you," Harrison recalled, abandoning his drink and turning his full attention to Nate.

"Despite everything Siljanna put me through, she did equally terrible things to you. You were dying in that courtyard when Maia and I found you. Can you truly forgive her?" Nate questioned, turning on the stool so that he faced Harrison.

"I don't know, and I honestly won't until I see her again. But I do understand her," Harrison replied honestly, leaning forward as he spoke.

"What do you mean by that?" Nate asked, taken aback by Harrison's admission.

"I don't condone anything she's done, but if the situation had been reversed, if you'd died in that fire and I believed Siljanna were to blame, I cannot say I wouldn't have reacted in the same way she did. The darkness that consumed her is within me too," Harrison answered, expecting Nate to recoil, but he didn't.

Harrison's confession, although quite touching when he thought about the underlying bond they'd developed, was also revealing. Nate couldn't deny that if he were in Siljanna's position, he wouldn't have reacted any better either.

Sat together in silence, the barman wandered over and topped up both of their glasses before quickly making himself scarce again. They'd all but forgotten he was there, but Nate took the refill and raised his glass, clinking the side of Harrison's. With an appreciative smile, a gesture that Harrison gladly returned they drank until both glasses were empty.

"You're an incredible young man, Harrison," Nate declared as they rose from the barstools. "Know that no matter what happens tomorrow, I'm on your side and I trust your judgement."

"I'm glad you're with me Nate," Harrison replied sincerely, wishing he could articulate just how much their relationship meant to him.

"Let's get some rest. I think tomorrow is going to be the hardest trial we've faced yet," Nate suggested, leaving some coins on the table to pay for the drinks before they headed to their room to get some sleep.

At first light, Harrison and Nate were awake and waiting for Caitlin in the lobby. They could see the harbour through the front window and a boat was just coming into port.

"I'll wait for Caitlin, you go," Nate offered, unable to ignore Harrison's impatient fidgeting. It was a combination of nerves and excitement, but Harrison quickly accepted the offer and dashed outside towards the harbour.

The main street was quieter than it had been the day before. It was too early for many of the shops to be open, but the dock was busy with sailors helping to secure the ship while the rest of the crew offloaded the cargo. When Harrison saw the gangplank lower, his heart skipped a beat. He watched several people disembark but quickly spotted one of the faces he was looking for.

"Morgan!" he called out, striding decisively towards his friend. He didn't even give a thought to how Morgan might react; he just knew his friend would feel the same relief and joy he did.

"Harrison! You look bloody awful my friend," Morgan replied, a smirk spreading across his face. As the pair gripped one another's shoulders, they embraced like long-lost brothers.

"It's good to see you."

"Did you really think I'd let you down?" Morgan asked, the cheeky undertone he was renowned for dominant in his voice. "I can't allow you to save all these people without me."

"Well, I almost died without you watching my back, so clearly I still need my partner," Harrison chuckled, mirroring Morgan's light-hearted tone.

"Yeah, I've got to say, your letter was a heavy hitter," Morgan admitted and then looked over his shoulder with an air of concern. "I guess my reply came as a shock too."

"You mean the part about Sil joining you? You're right, we didn't expect that," Harrison confirmed, reaching to touch the strap of his broadsword which was resting in its usual place. It was a subtle gesture, but Morgan noticed.

"But you still came," he remarked, an unspoken question in the air between them. *Are you okay with this?*

Harrison didn't reply with words. He simply winked at his friend. He knew that Morgan wouldn't endanger him or the people he was asking for help protecting.

"He didn't come alone though," called out another deeply familiar voice that instantly grabbed Morgan's attention.

"Nate?" Morgan stammered as the other man joined them.

"Hi Morgan, thanks for coming," Nate replied, shaking the young commander's hand.

"I'm so glad to see you well. Siljanna explained that she held you and Paige captive in Siranor. At the time, we all genuinely thought you were dead," Morgan explained, an apology forming in his mind.

"You had no way of knowing the truth, Morgan. Please don't feel bad," Nate insisted, raising his hand softly to stop him before turning and calling Caitlin over.

"Are you going to introduce me to your friend?" Morgan asked charmingly, offering his hand to the bright red-haired woman who came and stood alongside Nate.

"Morgan Foster, this is Caitlin Mason. She and her family are good friends who helped us when we first arrived. Caitlin is also close to Queen Nadia of Carlisse," Harrison introduced.

"That's an impressive repertoire," Morgan exclaimed. "It's good to meet you, Caitlin."

"And you, Morgan. Harrison speaks very highly of you," she replied. "I am rather anxious to meet your company, however."

"You're referring to Siljanna," Morgan acknowledged, not even considering that his warden companions could give anyone reason to fear.

"We are all somewhat dubious of Siljanna's sudden desire for redemption," Nate muttered but kept his tone as light as possible.

"She obviously said something to convince you that she's genuine. Where is she?" Harrison asked with a subtle tension in his tone.

Looking over his friend's shoulder as the remaining passengers and wardens disembarked the ship, Harrison waited with bated breath to catch a glimpse of his twin. As the passengers milled around the pier, searching for luggage or making onward travel plans, Harrison turned his back on the vessel, glancing at Nate before resting his eyes on Morgan. Another unspoken question hung in the air. *Had Siljanna already gone back on her word?*

Morgan didn't need to answer, however. While Harrison's back had been turned, Siljanna descended the gangplank and approached her twin.

"Hello Harrison," she greeted quietly, touching her brother on the shoulder. Jumping slightly, Harrison whipped around to take in the sight of her.

She was noticeably unarmed but that did little to reassure Harrison; he knew she was a skilled fighter, with or without a weapon.

"You came," he uttered, unable to express the other thoughts running through his mind. Seeing her for the first time since they'd clashed in Carlisse silenced him.

Siljanna looked the same and entirely different all at once. Her blonde hair was still partly shaved but the rest was longer, almost ragged, and mirrored her expression. She looked equal parts nervous and determined to be there, but also as if she'd just been terribly sick.

"I made a vow, to myself and to you," she replied quietly. She clearly wanted to say more but her own emotions had created a lump in her throat too.

The silence soon ended when the rowdy crew from the boat began to descend. They were laughing among themselves while carrying heavy boxes that clinked with each step. It didn't matter whether they'd been sampling the alcoholic goods or were just cheerful people, as their comradery interrupted the awkwardness between Harrison and Siljanna.

It wasn't until after the dock had gone quiet that a final figure approached them. Dropping a bag of supplies near Siljanna's feet and touching her shoulder supportively, Dylan was about to introduce himself to the group when instead he was faced with the tip of a crossbow bolt.

"You!" Nate growled, his entire body rigid with aggression.

"Nate, what's wrong?" Harrison questioned, raising a hand and imploring Nate not to fire. "How do you know Dylan?"

"I beat him while he was in captivity," Dylan admitted, recognising Nate instantly then looking down at his hands. "I did a lot of things in Siranor that I am not proud of."

"Under my orders," Siljanna added defensively, stepping in front of Dylan, and using herself as a barrier should Nate fire.

"This situation is becoming alarming familiar," Harrison muttered, watching his sister put herself in the same danger he had when protecting Rylie from her.

"Siljanna, step aside. This is not the time or place for altruism," Morgan instructed, slowly directing her to one side while taking her place and turning towards Nate. "Please Nate, lower your weapon. I swear they are here to help."

"No one needs to get hurt here," Siljanna added, her gaze fixed on Nate's weapon and gesturing for him to lower it.

"It must be nice not to be on the receiving end of a lethal firearm," Harrison retorted, touching the area beneath his armour that was scarred from Siljanna's shot. "Imagine if Nate had pulled the trigger."

"Harrison, I..." Siljanna stammered, covering her lips with her hands. She didn't know how to make him believe anything she could possibly say next.

"Save your excuses, Sil. Neither of us can change what's been said and done," Harrison replied, his tone abrupt yet somehow not malicious.

"I don't expect words to convince you, but I am not the same person that hunted you. Those actions from a few weeks ago seem utterly alien to me now," Siljanna vowed, regardless of her brother's attempt to end the conversation. "I will prove to all of you that I've changed."

Studying his twin carefully, Harrison noticed several more uncharacteristic qualities. When he'd last seen her, Siljanna embodied the same aura as their father. Strong and determined yet borderline callous. Now, her posture was utterly deflated. Dark circles encased her eyes, distorting that reflection of their father and adding to her ragged look. It was as though she'd not slept since their last encounter.

"What brought about your sudden change of heart?" Caitlin asked, inching towards Siljanna, unable to contain her curiosity.

"I overheard the Imperator's confession when Harrison's group had her cornered in Carlisse," Siljanna began, glancing back at her brother as he recalled the moment.

"So, you finally believe that Mum was killed by Elias Rainer, a human suffering from the withering?" Harrison challenged, his eyes narrowed into slits.

"Yes."

"And that Sampson started the tavern fire?" he added quickly.

"Yes. I know that I wrongly accused you and Rylie of what happened that night. The Imperator lied, telling me Dad had been incapacitated by the injuries you gave him and couldn't escape the fire that, at the time, I believed Rylie started. Harlyn fuelled my rage, but I was wrong," Siljanna continued, her voice breaking as she spoke.

"That doesn't erase the pain you've caused, Siljanna," Nate said, his crossbow still firmly aimed through Morgan at Dylan.

"I wish I'd believed Harrison from the beginning, but Dad was my hero," Siljanna tried to explain, registering the disapproving looks from both Nate and Harrison.

"Wishes are as useful as excuses, Siljanna," Harrison added. He was about to say more but her response burst through.

"You'll never understand, because you hated him," she cried, but there was no malice in her tone, only devastation.

"I know he meant a lot to you, Sil and despite everything, I also understand why you reacted the way you did," Harrison announced, surprising everyone but Nate.

"You do?" she asked dubiously, wiping away a tear that threatened to roll down her cheek.

"I do, because had I been in your position, I don't think I would've reacted any differently," Harrison answered.

"I didn't expect you to say that," Siljanna admitted, her green eyes focused on her brother. "Thank you."

"Understanding isn't the same as forgiveness," Harrison clarified but he could see her cling to that glimmer of hope regardless.

"It's a start," Siljanna replied softly.

"Did she tell you all of this Morgan? Is that why you believed her and Dylan?" Harrison asked, still acutely aware that he was standing in a precarious position.

"She told me, and her claim was backed up when the Imperator labelled Siljanna and Dylan as Imperial traitors," Morgan advised.

"We are targets too, just as you, the mages and the Ar'encal are," Siljanna confirmed.

"Will you both fight for the mages and Ar'encal now?" Caitlin asked, her head tilted sideways as she examined their mannerisms curiously.

"We will," Dylan replied, his hands still raised despite Nate slowly lowering the crossbow. "If they'll accept our support."

"Prove your worth first by helping us save Rylie," Nate suggested, looking passed the harbour to where Jumant Fort could be seen poking out on the headland.

"Of course, whatever it takes," Siljanna replied as Caitlin inched closer.

"You could get hurt, even die," Caitlin hinted, wanting to see Siljanna's reaction to the prospect of death. "We are dealing with a mage who has tapped into god-like power."

Processing the warning, Siljanna didn't respond with words but took a moment to breathe. With her eyes closed, she nodded firmly then looked back at the group to let them see her resolve.

"You have a plan to defeat a super-powered being of flame," Dylan scoffed, assuming no such plan existed.

"Unlike orchestrating an ambush, our situation cannot be planned with absolute certainty, but we do have a plan," Nate replied firmly. "See that fort on the outskirts of town? The others in our group are luring Rylie there and in case they succeed, we must arrive first."

It was obvious that Nate didn't like or trust Dylan, for understandable reasons, and his antagonistic behaviour only added to that doubt. Slinging the crossbow over his shoulder, Nate noticed that Dylan's left hand was tucked into his belt. Although Siljanna was clearly unarmed, Nate grew certain that Dylan was concealing a small blade and silently alerted Harrison to his suspicion as well.

"Let's go, we'll fill you in on the way," Harrison suggested.

"What about the wardens?" Morgan asked, quickly noticing that the warriors were patiently waiting just out of earshot. "I rallied three units so there are eighteen of us, as well as Siljanna and Dylan, prepared to defend you and your allies."

"Thank you, Morgan. Please can you send them onwards to Iliria?" Harrison asked, pulling a pouch from his jacket pocket. "There should be enough coin here to rent some horses from the stable in Dawne. The owner is tending to ours and expecting you."

"It's a long ride through the Athalay Plains and around Bremer Bay to reach Iliria, but if they head straight there, they should reach the town by dusk," Caitlin explained, pointing at a nearby map to highlight the route they should take.

"We'll join them as soon as we can," Harrison added.

"How about I travel with them, so the rest of you can focus on saving Rylie?" Dylan suggested, having noticed Nate's increasingly suspicious glare.

"Alright," Morgan replied, handing over the coin pouch Harrison had just given him.

"Ask for Captain Lucas Harper when you arrive," Harrison instructed, knowing that Lucas and the Aegis Guard would be there long before the wardens arrived.

As Dylan departed with the other wardens, Siljanna steeled herself for what was to come. Since learning the truth, Dylan had been her only constant ally and secretly, she wished he would stay, but also understood why he chose to leave. They'd only narrowly escaped Rylie in Beyasil and facing her again was daunting.

Siljanna always defined herself as an expert tactician, usually able to read her opponents with ease, but she'd never faced anything like what Rylie had become. She believed in Harrison and that he'd soon divulge whatever plan they had devised but knowing very little about magic put her on edge. Having become an Aeon also made Rylie decidedly more dangerous and unpredictable. Just thinking about what was to come made a deep shiver course down Siljanna's spine. Trying to push the anxiety aside, she looked towards her hands and realised they were shaking. To her surprise, Caitlin stayed beside her while Morgan, Harrison and Nate saw Dylan and the wardens off.

"Are you okay?" Caitlin asked, gently touching Siljanna's hand.

"I'll be fine," Siljanna replied, clasping her hands behind her back to mask her fear.

"Can I be blunt?" Caitlin continued with a directness Siljanna seldom received but secretly admired.

"I get the distinct feeling I couldn't stop you even if I wanted to," Siljanna teased, letting a faint smile raise the corners of her lips.

"Why come back? I've always believed that for everyone, there's a point of no return. When a decision sets the course of our future. But you're different. You came back to face the people you hurt most. Why?"

"How could I not? My actions were based on twisted tales and misguided beliefs," Siljanna admitted, her tone frank.

"But surely over the weeks you hunted Harrison and the others, you had time to contemplate the situation," Caitlin probed, her curiosity growing.

"It's easy to be blind when you don't want to see the light," Siljanna answered, looking straight at Caitlin with an expression that conveyed her regret.

"An interesting choice of words," Caitlin commented, taking a few steps forward and looking towards Harrison.

"What do you mean?"

"The trap that you intended to lure us into left Harrison's friend, Zack, blind," Caitlin explained, only to be met by a look of horror on Siljanna's face.

"Blind, but how?" she blurted out.

"You didn't know? It was that vile mage hunter, Juliette. The one you sent to enthral King Grayson. She threw some concoction at his feet and the vapours left him blind," Caitlin answered, pausing briefly to take in Siljanna's reaction. There was nothing about it that seemed fake.

Since learning of her imminent return, Caitlin had created a mental image of what Siljanna would be like. She expected her to have a commanding presence, exude confidence and be stubborn to a fault, but the woman before her was none of those things. In fact, had Caitlin not seen Siljanna in Carlisse, she would have found it difficult to believe the person before her had orchestrated all the atrocities she knew Siljanna was responsible for.

"I have so much to atone for," Siljanna whispered.

"So that's why you came back, to make amends?"

"That was my hope, but I fear it's too much to ask," Siljanna replied, letting Caitlin see that she was shaking. "No matter how I feel, I must face the consequences of my actions."

"You're afraid?" she asked, already knowing the answer.

"Yes, but not just for myself," Siljanna began, casting her eyes to the ground.

"What do you mean?" she questioned softly.

"I fear for Harrison. He's already dealt with so much, he shouldn't have to lose Rylie too."

"Or you," Caitlin added firmly. "He may be distant now, but you can't atone for anything if you're dead."

At that, Siljanna stifled a laugh. Although she was afraid and very aware that facing Rylie was life-threatening, Caitlin's words resonated deeply within her. She did want to earn Harrison's forgiveness and to do that, she had to survive.

"You're a difficult person to argue with," Siljanna replied, running her hands through her hair, giving them something to do other than tremble.

"And you're a difficult person to defeat," Caitlin retorted cheekily. "But as long as you're on our side, I'm glad."

"Of that, I can assure you."

"The part about being difficult to beat or being on our side?" Caitlin checked, raising her eyebrow wickedly.

"Both," Siljanna replied, her lips softly curling into a smile, causing Caitlin to mirror her expression as her eyes glistened with intrigue.

The only person Caitlin knew who had shown such resolve in the face of adversity, although perhaps not with as much flair, was Nadia. She hadn't expected to find similarities to a person she cared so greatly for, in someone like Siljanna. It was a pleasant surprise.

Chapter Eight
FIRESTORM

Located five miles from Dawne, the group made haste to reach Jumant Fort. Siljanna had been bracing herself for the next confrontation with Rylie ever since departing Tivani, but as they made their way towards the dilapidated fortress, she needed to distract her mind from thoughts of impending doom.

"So... what is the plan exactly?" she asked, nervously adjusting the straps on her leather corset as they walked, the fort getting closer with every stride.

"That's a good question. I'm struggling to imagine what we are truly facing," Morgan added, his gaze shifting from Siljanna to Harrison, in hopes that he might be able to expand on her frightful description.

"It's probably not to the tactical standard you would've hoped for, but the idea is to get this amulet on Rylie," Harrison replied, pulling the intricate piece from his pocket.

"And how do you hope to get close enough without being reduced to ashes?" Siljanna challenged, her eyebrows furrowed as she stopped sharply and glared at her brother.

"She won't hurt us," Nate remarked with a surprising level of confidence, but it did little to reassure Siljanna. She knew his statement excluded her.

"How can you be so sure?" Morgan queried, scratching the growing stubble on the side of his face anxiously.

"Rylie only became an Aeon after witnessing what she thought was Harrison's death, combined with the belief that her mother and I were imprisoned," Nate explained, recalling Maia's theory. "Her magic has been amplified by these negative emotions, so we aim to counter them."

"We're hoping when she sees me alive and her father free that she'll pause long enough that I can get this on her," Harrison concluded, running his finger absent-mindedly over the amulet.

"But Rylie isn't herself anymore. This god-like power has consumed her. What if seeing you isn't enough?" Siljanna challenged, her nerves intensifying.

"That's where the amulet comes in. It's engraved with a suppression rune. It should reduce her power to a level she can control," Nate added as Morgan encouraged Siljanna to press on.

Looking more than a little unconvinced, the entire group could see how edgy Siljanna felt, but despite that, she didn't attempt to retreat.

"In the last few generations of Ar'encal and mages, Aeons have been little more than a myth. We are working mostly on hearsay and hope I'm afraid," Harrison admitted, his tone determined although his words were tinged with doubt.

"Easy for you to say, you're not the bait," Caitlin chimed in, willing to say what Siljanna wouldn't.

"You don't need to defend me, but thank you," Siljanna replied, her tone unconvincing.

"If anyone knows that, it's me," Harrison replied. "But that doesn't mean I expect you to be defenceless during the encounter."

As his words caught Siljanna's attention, he pulled some leather greaves, shoulder guards and bracers from his backpack and handed them to her. After another search, he presented a pair for Morgan too while Nate handed over a shield to him.

"What are these?" Morgan asked, simultaneously admiring the armour and replacing his own with it.

"Thanks to the Ar'encal, I've learnt to craft runic armour. These pieces are specifically resistant to fire," Harrison explained.

"We are all wearing enhanced gear," Nate added, revealing his own chest armour while Caitlin flashed her cloak and boots, all of which bore the same symbols that were engraved on the armour Harrison and Nate had just given them.

"No tactician but also no fool, my friend," Morgan declared, winking at Harrison who couldn't help but smile.

"I also have... an added defence," Harrison began, softly touching the Arencian rune that was concealed by his clothes. "So, although she'll be after you Sil, what you need to do is lure Rylie to me."

"An *added defence*?" Siljanna questioned.

"I can't explain it now, you'll just have to trust me," Harrison replied firmly and Siljanna knew not to push further.

"What about you, Caitlin? What's your part in this?" Siljanna asked, turning her attention to the person who seemingly had no reason to be there.

"My job is to make it harder for Rylie to kill you," Caitlin answered cheerfully, her stride more like a skip. She definitely was not a warrior.

"I'm sorry... I don't follow," Siljanna replied quizzically.

"Caitlin is a mage, one gifted with the ability to create illusions," Harrison explained, glancing curiously at his sister to see her reaction.

"You're a mage? I didn't realise," Siljanna stuttered before subtly turning her face away and biting her tongue.

She'd held such hatred towards mages since her mother's death, meeting one who seemed so normal and kind came as quite a shock.

"Is that a problem?" Caitlin asked, intentionally turning so that Siljanna couldn't avoid eye contact.

"No, I've just never allied with a mage before. I guess I expected to sense your power somehow. To know you were different," Siljanna confessed, trying to explain but feeling like she was only making things worse.

"We aren't all that different you know. We just have different abilities," Caitlin began.

"I don't think our abilities are comparable," Siljanna replied, meaning it to be a compliment but realising that it didn't come across that way.

"Okay, so you can single-handedly take on dozens of armed fighters… but you can't do this," Caitlin said before vanishing.

"Wait, what?" Siljanna exhaled, turning sharply in every direction but unable to locate Caitlin. She didn't feel threatened by her trick, however, which was a welcome change. In fact, she found herself quietly impressed.

"Over here," Caitlin whispered in her left ear, making Siljanna turn on her heel, only to be faced with thin air. Then finally, Caitlin reappeared behind Siljanna, tapping her right shoulder.

"How did you do that?" Siljanna asked, spinning to face her.

"I can manipulate the space around me, altering what you perceive. I didn't actually go anywhere, but my illusion made you believe I'd vanished."

"Does your magic only affect you?" Siljanna asked, a look of marvel on her face.

"My illusions can affect anything as long as I'm close enough and focus on what I want the outside world to see," she replied.

"And you're planning to use this power to help us against Rylie… somehow?" Siljanna continued, deeply inquisitive.

"That's the plan, but ironically, it tends to work better when I don't plan too much and allow my needs or emotions to control the outcome," Caitlin confessed, biting her lip awkwardly.

"Filling me with confidence there," Siljanna replied sarcastically, causing Caitlin to burst out laughing.

"Better to be here and possibly help than at home and not help at all, don't you think?" she retaliated playfully.

"I'll give you that one," Siljanna admitted, a weary smile forming on her lips.

"You can depend on Caitlin. Her power could provide the distraction we need in a dire situation," Harrison added with a smile, not only at Caitlin's playful antics but at the fact Siljanna was smiling too. It was the first time he'd ever seen her guard down around a mage.

It was mid-morning when Fort Jumant came into view. The crumbling stone structure must've been a magnificent sight to behold in its prime. Perched on the cliff edge overlooking the gently lapping Ensen Sea, and the uninhabited rocky isles that connected Dawne to the mainland, the fortress walls seemed to glisten, as if the Encia in the sea below had infused in the stone.

The remains of the site were larger than they expected with tall walls that would've offered good concealment for any archers or mages during the Uprising. With only one side undamaged by cannon fire, however, it was clear the Imperial Navy had devastated the Ar'encal. Only one tower remained standing, looking proudly out to sea while guarding the small collection of buildings below it and the adjacent courtyard. As the party drew near, Morgan spotted something amiss in the panoramic view.

"Look at the clouds overhead! What could cause such a deep red hue?" he asked apprehensively.

Noticing the clouds track unnaturally towards the fort and swirl ominously, Siljanna felt herself pale as dread set in. She knew nature wasn't responsible for that skyline.

"Get to the fort, now!" she cried, urgently pointing to the large gate and encouraging the group to run forwards.

Morgan and Harrison were the first to reach the gate but quickly discovered it was sealed. As they thrashed at the woodwork to find a weakness, they called back to Siljanna.

"What is it?" Morgan shouted.

"Rylie," she called out in response, looking over her shoulder to see their former friend at the end of the opposite path while dark, rumbling clouds made the sky even more foreboding.

Rylie's burning gaze pierced through Siljanna like a spear. Emitting a ferocity that was emphasised by the flames dancing on her skin, she was every bit as terrifying as Siljanna remembered. Without conscious intent, Siljanna took a step back, then another and another before turning on her heel and breaking into a sprint towards the fort. At the same time, Rylie lunged after her.

As Siljanna approached the gate, Harrison and Morgan had broken through, but only enough to squeeze in one person at a time… and she didn't have time to wait. Noticing some steps leading up to the parapets, Siljanna threw herself towards them and clambered to the top at speed. She refused to look back but spared a glance down to see Nate and Morgan make it into the courtyard below, with Harrison just behind them. It was only when she realised Caitlin wasn't with them, that Siljanna skidded to a stop.

Having seen her change direction, Caitlin had instinctively followed Siljanna, but in doing so, put herself in harm's way. With relief, Siljanna saw her breach the top of the stairs but within a split second, her relief became dread as fire erupted from the steps below, catapulting Caitlin off her feet. As she collided with the stone floor, Caitlin landed on a rusty iron grate, which immediately gave way.

"No!" Siljanna screamed, rushing to the edge of the grate even though Caitlin had already fallen through. Looking down into the dark catacombs, Siljanna caught a glimpse of Caitlin who was gripping onto her arm in agony, but alive.

"Siljanna, *go!*" she urged, just as more flames crashed into Siljanna's shoulder. Her armour shielded her from the worst of the blast, but it was a stark reminder that she needed to keep moving.

Watching the horror unfold above them but unable to help, Harrison, Morgan and Nate tried to assess their surroundings. They'd had no chance to plan really how, but they couldn't let this opportunity to save Rylie slip through their fingers.

"We have to get to them," Harrison called out, his voice filled with urgency. "Nate, did Alistair tell you anything more about this fortress?"

"He didn't know much, only that it used to be an Ar'encal stronghold during the Uprising," Nate began, frantically recalling his prior discussions with Alistair. "It was bombarded by the Siranor fleet, reducing it to the rubble around us. He did mention a network of catacombs that held equipment, but that'll be below us and we need to get up there!"

"What about Caitlin? It looked like she fell beneath the walls. We should find her. She may be hurt," Morgan added.

"This courtyard must be a convergence point. There should be internal passageways leading up to the battlements and the rooms below," Harrison assessed aloud, scanning for access points.

"I'd be willing to bet that leads down to the catacombs," Morgan predicted, pointing to an almost imperceptible door.

Without words, Harrison nodded, and Morgan rushed towards the concealed door. Although Morgan wanted to help them save Rylie, they'd heard Siljanna's cry and seen Caitlin fall. As only Harrison or Nate stood a real chance of getting the amulet on Rylie and suppressing her power, he was the best person to go in search of Caitlin.

As Morgan disappeared, Harrison and Nate turned their attention back to the upper level, just in time to see Rylie stalking her target.

"Rylie!" Nate cried, but his voice didn't reach her and before he could call out again, she was gone.

"Let's go. She's headed towards the tower. Siljanna must be trying to find a way down," Harrison explained hastily, hoping that if they headed in the same direction, their paths would eventually cross.

Reaching the base of the tower, they found an open door and headed inside. After a mere few strides along the corridor, Harrison realised they were adjacent to the cliff and scarily close to the destroyed section of the fort. The walls and even parts of the floor had begun to crumble into the sea below and it wouldn't take much for the beams they walked on to do the same. Harrison knew that if the fall didn't kill them, contact with Encia would spell certain death for Siljanna, Morgan and potentially, Nate too. The last thing he wanted was to watch any of them succumb to the withering, but he had to push those fears to the back of his mind.

"Be careful, the floor is falling apart," Harrison called out, turning back to Nate while progressing forward cautiously.

"We have to keep going, I'm not leaving this place without my daughter," Nate responded. He clearly wanted to rush ahead but his self-preservation stopped him from moving recklessly.

Harrison nodded with a soft smile. Nate really was a good father and someone he genuinely respected. Although he would never deny the way he felt for Rylie and his own desire to have her back, Harrison also wanted to save her so that he could reunite the Auren family. They deserved it after all the hardship they'd endured. The day Sampson caused the fire at the Hawk Eye tavern felt like a lifetime ago but was the catalyst that started everything.

Letting the door fall shut behind him, Morgan marched through the catacombs in search of Caitlin. Now below ground, it would've been pitch black if not for the slitted grates overhead allowing in tendrils of light.

"Caitlin, can you hear me?" he shouted as he followed the snaking pathways deeper underground.

"Morgan, is that you? I'm over here," she called back, her voice emphasising how much pain she was in.

"Stay put, I'm coming," he instructed in a sympathetic tone, relieved she was alive.

After becoming warden commander, even though he'd believed the role temporary, he'd developed an authority that he never foresaw in himself, especially during those lazy days in the academy library. He was still himself but being in command had made him a better man; someone that was acutely aware of the people that relied on him. People like Caitlin. Before long, he found her, leaning against one of the cold walls, cradling her arm.

"I think it's broken," she explained with a wince, "and my ankle is throbbing too."

"Lucky for you, I'm a gentleman," he replied with a cheeky smile as he whipped his arm behind her back and scooped Caitlin into his arms. She was so light, he almost found it hard to believe her weight had been enough to break the grate in the first place.

"My hero!" Caitlin swooned playfully, allowing him to carry her.

"We better get out of here. Our heroic duties may not be over yet," Morgan added, reminding Caitlin that Siljanna was still in extreme danger.

Before Morgan could head back in the direction he'd come from, they heard an almighty crash. Dust billowed through the catacombs, and they knew it was likely caused by Siljanna or Rylie. Looking at her for confirmation, Morgan was met with a solid expression from Caitlin. She was not going to be the damsel of this encounter, even if she couldn't walk, so they pressed ahead, towards the destruction.

Running as evasively as she could, Siljanna desperately searched for a way off the parapets. She needed to reach Harrison and the others, but her heart thumped so loudly in her chest, it clouded her ability to think. The deafening sound of her heartbeat was soon penetrated by a ball of fire that came hurtling in her direction. She ducked just in time but fell to her knees in the process and had to scrabble around the corner for protection. She couldn't help but watch as the attacking element collided with the wall, the force causing the stone to break away and crash into the ocean below. Knowing that with every pause, Rylie would be getting closer, Siljanna forced herself up and broke into a sprint again.

Still looking for a stairway to get back to the ground level but seeing nothing, Siljanna began to fret. Her only hope was within the tower. The parapets didn't directly connect to the structure, but it had a large glass window that somehow hadn't shattered. Calculating the trajectory in her head, she concluded that she could reach it with a strong enough leap. The lower level of the building appeared to lead to an antechamber between the courtyard and whatever was left of the inner fortress and that was where she hoped she'd find Harrison and the others.

Grinding to a halt opposite the window, Siljanna turned back to face Rylie for the briefest moment. Her fiery hair grew more intense as she reached her hands towards the sky, where the clouds rumbled ominously. Dread filling her soul, Siljanna couldn't help but recall the lightning bolt that killed Cameron Weiss. Refusing to succumb to the same fate, she propelled herself off the edge just as a streak of electrical energy crashed into the spot where she'd stood. The impact launched her forward even faster, meaning all she could do was curl up her body as she hurtled through the glass.

Crashing with the wall on the other side before falling to the floor below, pain shot through Siljanna's shoulders and neck, leaving her dazed. She tried to stand, knowing she needed to keep moving but her knees buckled. Slumped against the wall, she gazed at her hands. They were shaking uncontrollably, and she knew it was fear. She'd done all she could, but this would be her end. She could run no further and had no strength to fight. Her eyes, still blurry from the impact, turned to the window above to see Rylie. Her landing was sharp but controlled, the air itself guiding her descent.

Staring at the cause of her rage, tendrils of fire began to whip around Rylie's arms and body. To Siljanna's distorted vision, it was almost beautiful. Then she felt the heat. It wouldn't be long before her skin would blister and burn. She just prayed it would be over quickly. Closing her eyes and awaiting the blast, Siljanna was stunned to suddenly hear Rylie growl with frustration and rush through the archway beside her. Rubbing her eyes and trying to comprehend what'd happened, Siljanna finally noticed Caitlin through the window. Still cradled in Morgan's arms, with one hand gently touching her temple and the other pointing towards the archway, she realised Caitlin had created an illusion of Siljanna escaping, but only Rylie had seen it.

Carefully, Morgan released Caitlin and moved to help Siljanna stand. They each took an arm, using Morgan for support and although he couldn't use the shield he'd been given, he ensured both women were guarded by his body. If Rylie came back, she would have to go through him to harm them, but he sincerely hoped that would not be the case.

Charging forward and through a door, almost smashing it off its hinges and burning the splinters on contact, Rylie scanned the room in search of Siljanna. The door hit something with a loud crash but whatever it struck was not enough to break her gaze from the sight ahead; a sight she had not expected. Her father, crossbow raised and loaded.

"Rylie, stop! It's me…" Nate declared, his voice low and calm but firm. Staring at his eldest daughter, he could see her through the flames, but it took every ounce of strength to contain his fear.

"No!" Rylie hissed, disbelief evident in her wild expression.

"I know you thought Siljanna captured me, and you're right, she did. She had your mother too, but we're free now. This isn't a trick, Rylie. Please, don't make me pull this trigger," Nate begged, his tired eyes imploring her to believe him.

Cocking her head, a jerking motion that somehow looked fluid, she seemed to search his expression for signs of deceit. Noticing his eyes flick to something or someone behind her, Rylie's power reacted to the second presence before she attempted to turn. Summoning a supernova of blistering energy that lashed out in every direction,

Rylie intended to incinerate whoever dared approach, but a hand took her by the shoulder and pulled her close anyway.

Holding her tightly in his arms, Harrison felt the searing force of her attack travel through his protective garments and ignite the rune on his collarbone. While it throbbed, doubt began to eat at him. Rylie was more powerful than they'd even guessed. *Would his armour endure?*

"Rylie, stop! Look at who you are attacking," Nate screamed, begging for his daughter to cast her eyes backwards, but she didn't hear him over the crackling sound of the blast.

As the intense heat continued to barrage his body, Harrison realised that without the protective power of his rune, he'd already be dead. That knowledge was enough to reinforce his determination. He had to persevere. Reaching into his pocket, Harrison grabbed the amulet and wrapped it around Rylie's throat, connecting the clasp swiftly so that the suppression rune met her skin. As the amulet began to glow, the energy around her dissipated and everything went still.

Once the flames on her skin receded, Harrison could smell charred leather. Knowing it was the remnants of his armour, which had just about withstood the overwhelming heat Rylie exuded, he smiled with relief, grateful it had protected him for long enough. Turning Rylie in his arms, Harrison looked into her eyes. The ferocious blue flames were extinguished, leaving behind her natural, greyish-blue irises which stared back at him in disbelief.

"How can this be?" Rylie whispered, a tear rolling down her cheek as her vision locked onto Harrison. Placing her now cool hands on his chest and face, she began to tremble.

Harrison wanted to tell her everything, but finding the right words was never his forte. Instead, he leant in, giving her a deep, reassuring kiss. At first, she tried to recoil but his grip around her back was too steady. Feeling the familiarity of his touch, Rylie relaxed, returning his kiss with fervour. He knew then that they didn't need words. As their lips parted, Harrison gently stroked her cheek, wiping away the tear before Nate cautiously approached.

Smiling softly, Rylie turned towards her father who dropped his crossbow and rushed forward as soon as he realised she was herself again. Her clothes were in tatters, having been thoroughly singed by her Aeon form, but nothing was going to stop him from embracing her. His eyes closed for a moment, all the tension escaping from his body as he rejoiced at having his daughter in his arms. What remained of her clothes turned to ash while she was in his arms, so before letting her go, Nate dropped his knapsack and whipped the cloak from around his shoulders over her, to spare her blushes.

When he finally released her, Harrison passed Rylie a small bag, containing a basic outfit and some boots they'd packed for her, just in case, and then stood beside Nate. They both turned away respectfully to allow her to change. In that brief moment, Harrison placed his hand on Nate's shoulder, and they shared a silent moment of joint delight. They'd done it. They saved her.

"I still don't understand. How is this possible?" Rylie asked as she rejoined them, even though her smile revealed that she didn't care, as long as the sight before her was real.

"It's a long story, but we'll tell you everything when we get back to the others," Nate promised, stroking her hair lovingly.

"What about Siljanna? If she's here, isn't she after us?" Rylie continued, quickly spinning to check the doorway behind them. As she did, Morgan came through, still using his body to protect both Siljanna and Caitlin. While Caitlin had a noticeable limp and leant on him, Siljanna was doing her best to stand tall.

"Is it over, are you back with us, Rylie?" Morgan enquired hesitantly.

"Morgan, why are you here… and guarding Siljanna?" Rylie questioned, her brow furrowing with confusion.

"I swear, I am no longer a threat to you or anyone you hold dear," Siljanna declared, her eyes gleaming with sincerity.

"She helped us lure you here," Caitlin added. "Siljanna was willing to die if it meant making amends."

"You arranged this?" Rylie asked, her expression becoming lighter as the news sank in.

"I only helped," Siljanna replied quietly. "After you transformed, I discovered the Imperator's trickery. Everything I did was to avenge my father. I believed he was a victim, but the Imperator took advantage of that and fuelled my anger with lies."

After a brief silence, Rylie stepped closer, giving a quick glance at Morgan who instinctively stood between them. Silently confirming she wouldn't attack, his stance relaxed and Siljanna stepped forward to face her former friend.

"I doubt I'll ever understand how you can justify the things you did," Rylie began, taking in the injured, filthy appearance of the once fiercely proud warden before her. "But I'll listen."

"Thank you. I won't ask for your forgiveness, but I will try to earn it," Siljanna replied, bowing her head slightly before returning to the supportive shoulder offered by Morgan.

Giving her a nod in response, Rylie turned back to Harrison and gave him another hug. She didn't know how he extinguished her power, but looked immensely grateful that he had. Although it was still her underneath the rage, it was as if the power was in control of her actions, rather than Rylie deciding of her own free will.

"I hate to cut this reunion short, but we shouldn't linger here. Your friends in Iliria are still facing an imminent attack. Even with Dylan and the wardens on their way to aid them, we should go," Morgan hasted to remind the group.

"Wait, Iliria is under attack?" Rylie asked, turning in a panic towards her father and then back at Harrison for answers, but the voices that spoke came from behind her.

"The Carlisse Royal Military marches on the town, at King Grayson's command," Caitlin advised, handing Rylie the letter Spencer wrote so that she could quickly understand what the others knew.

"It's safe to assume his accord with the Imperator remains intact," Siljanna added.

"While you weren't yourself, Imperator Rainer declared the war renewed. She claims Harrison and your friends instigated the attack in Carlisse and has labelled Siljanna a traitor," Morgan said, emphasising Siljanna's statement.

"We believe she intends to wipe out all mages, the Ar'encal and anyone that supports the mage community," Harrison revealed in a softer tone as he reached out and took her by the hand. He knew she'd blame herself for distracting them from protecting the innocent townspeople, but they could still get there in time.

"Where are the others, are they safe?" Rylie continued, her questions coming out rapidly.

"They're at our new home," Harrison answered reassuringly. "Lucas and Alex will already be enroute with some guards to help defend the town."

"Lianna is allowing Alex to go with them? I'm surprised she or Zack would support that," Rylie exclaimed.

"I almost forgot, you don't know…" Nate muttered, placing a hand over his mouth.

"Know what?"

"Zack was blinded during the ambush in Carlisse," Nate answered, glancing apologetically at Harrison as Rylie shuddered in his arms.

"He's going to be okay, don't worry. And Alex has been training daily, mostly with Lucas but is really proving he has what it takes to be a guardian," Harrison explained, a hint of pride in his tone. "He was given the rank of squire and although I doubt Lucas will put him in battle, Alex will likely be a big help in Iliria."

Seeing that she was lost for words, Harrison gave Rylie a comforting squeeze. She was blinking rapidly to process all the information she'd just been given when Caitlin hobbled forward.

"I'm in no shape for another battleground," she whimpered, keeping the weight off her injured ankle and cradling her potentially broken arm. "Besides, I need to head back to Carlisse."

"You can't go back there alone, it's too dangerous and you're wounded," Siljanna protested.

"I'll be okay. I can visit the healer in Dawne and travel by sea rather than attempting to ride. Sneaking into the library and finding Nadia and Spencer should be easy enough. No one knows that castle better than I do," Caitlin replied, wincing through the pain but trying very hard to hide her discomfort.

Siljanna wanted to argue further but decided against it, biting her tongue and looking away abruptly. Glancing between them, Harrison could tell Siljanna's reaction was out of concern. Caitlin seemed to realise that too but also accepted she'd only be a hindrance in Iliria. They had to go on without her.

"How will you get there on your own?" Nate asked, also concerned for the young lady.

"There's a regular trade ship that sails between Dawne and Revaine. After I've been healed up, I'm sure I could hop onboard and then catch a ride onwards to Carlisse," Caitlin answered, and they couldn't deny her resourcefulness.

"You still shouldn't go back alone," Siljanna groaned.

"Is there anywhere else you could go? Could you wait in Revaine until we send word from Iliria?" Morgan asked.

"I could stay with my parents again for a day or two," Caitlin offered. "They'll have me moving back in if I stay too long though."

Although Caitlin clearly wanted to go straight back to her friends, with the king's attention and forces fixated on Iliria, she could spare a day or two. In fact, Spencer's letter had detailed that they'd been confined to Nadia's quarters, so Harrison couldn't help but wonder if they'd prefer to be alone.

After hearing Caitlin's suggestion, Siljanna turned to face her with eyes that implored her to head to the safety of her parents' home. With a smile, Caitlin acknowledged her request and agreed.

"All right, that's settled," Harrison smirked, registering Siljanna's reaction. It had been a long time since he saw the guardian in her surface, and it was a pleasant reminder of their academy days.

"We'll escort you back to Dawne, make sure you're healed up and then be on our way. We need to collect the horses from town anyway," Nate advised, sounding just like a typical parent.

"Nate, will you take Rylie back to—" Harrison began to ask, only to have his words cut short as the rune beneath his collar pulsated. "Will you take Rylie home?"

"No, he will not," Rylie insisted, stamping her foot on the ground in protest. "I'm not letting you all charge off into battle and leave me behind."

"Rylie, we've just got you back and don't want to see you injured or worse within hours of saving you!" Nate argued, clearly supporting Harrison's idea of taking her to the concealed safety of Arencia.

"Besides, that amulet is suppressing your power," Harrison added, hoping the excuse would be enough.

"Suppressed, not extinguished," Rylie exclaimed, turning sharply to face Harrison as the natural curls of her hair flicked out wildly. "I'm not keen on the idea of taking this amulet off yet, but you have to believe that I can help… that I can fight."

Although he wanted nothing more than to keep her safe, Harrison did believe she could fight. Her untamed power was more than just formidable, it was terrifying but even with it subdued, her skill at wielding twin blades had been impressive for a beginner.

"She should come with us, Harrison. I can vouch for her tenacity first-hand," Siljanna added with a chuckle, showing off her blistered shoulder guard to the rest of the group.

Her comment made Harrison let out a short burst of laughter. There was no way he was going to win this debate now.

"Fine, we all go to defend Iliria and protect one another," he dutifully conceded, despite his and Nate's continued concern.

As they headed towards the main gate of the fortress, Harrison offered to aid Siljanna so that Morgan could carry Caitlin once again. As his sister draped her arm over his shoulders, he leant in, speaking to Siljanna in a hushed tone.

"You were supposed to take my side," he whispered, a single raised eyebrow framing his sceptical expression.

"I didn't mean to go against you," Siljanna stuttered. "I thought you'd approve of me siding with Rylie."

"Well, your choices were to side with your brother or a woman with the power to become a fiery Aeon, so it's pretty suicidal to go against the latter," Harrison replied with a playful energy.

Laughing nervously at his comment, Siljanna turned to face her brother in earnest.

"I am on your side," she promised.

"Are you now?"

"I can't fathom how to repair the damage I've caused," she added, wondering if it was even possible to do so.

Hearing her words and the remorse in her tone, Harrison just shook his head and smiled.

"Sometimes things need to be broken, so they can come back stronger," he mused, supporting her effortlessly.

"Does that mean... can I repair what's broken?" Siljanna began, an incredulous look on her face.

"You've already started to," he replied simply.

At that Siljanna stared at him, desperately searching his warm brown eyes for any hint of insincerity but found nothing. She began to shake ever so slightly as tears rolled down her face. Finally, she crumbled into him, allowing him to take all her meagre weight as she quietly sobbed with relief. Holding her steadily in his arms, Harrison felt a part of himself restored. He had his sister back.

Chapter Nine
COMMAND

Piercing through the choppy waves, the *Pilgrim* carried her crew and passengers towards Revaine. Among them was a very bored Juliette Lawrence. She'd spent over a week coordinating the mage hunters before Noah had been ready to depart and thought that dull, but sitting in the confines of the small cabin was much worse. Throwing herself onto the bed, she turned to her new partner.

"This journey takes too long. Why couldn't we use the Imperial warship? We are supposed to be at war," she grumbled.

"The ship is in Yasras for maintenance, Juliette, you know that," Noah chided, looking at her out of the corner of his eye. "Besides, with traitors infesting the warden ranks, would you really trust that crew? We'll utilise the warship once Private Pesaro has reported back to the Imperator and flushed out the rats."

"Private Pesaro... the things I could do to him," Juliette muttered seductively, letting her head drape backwards as she nibbled her lip.

"He's barely old enough to be called a man. Surely you can aim your sights a little higher," Noah taunted, his back to her as he unsheathed his sword.

"Is that an invitation?" she replied, flipping onto her stomach and locking her dark eyes on him. Sword in hand, he faced her, raising the blade so that it rested under the point of her delicate chin.

"Romance is a distraction and therefore a tool," Noah answered, his tone cool and calculated. Pressing the blade lightly upwards, Juliette rose to her knees. Her eyes darted from his blade to the buckles on his armour and back again.

"We have three more days on this accursed boat to be as distracted as we like," she hinted, her body slowly writhing.

Resting the blade next to the bed, Noah placed his cold fingers on her shoulders and slowly brushed down the straps of her dress. Breathing heavily, she wriggled her arms free, trapping the delicate material just above her chest before letting it fall, rippling down her body to her knees. She expected Noah to ravish her, but he didn't. Instead, he just took in the sight of her, like an artist would a canvas. She enjoyed his admiration but with a shiver, grew impatient and pulled him close.

"Don't let me get cold," she insisted, tugging at the buckles on his armour, discarding anything that stood between her hands and his flesh.

"I'm still deciding what to do with you," he revealed, slowing her hands as she reached the final layer of his clothing.

"You like getting your way, don't you?"

"Dominance is power and there is little I covet more than that," Noah confirmed, finally allowing her hands to explore his chest.

Once he too was completely disrobed, Juliette lingered on the edge of the bed, waiting for Noah to make a move. That simple pause, accepting his dominance, was all the encouragement he needed. Kissing her neck, he wrapped his arms around her back and lowered her into the sheets. Juliette's anticipation grew as he continued to explore her body with his hands and lips, her body reacting to each icy touch. She could feel Noah's intensity with every motion, but he was too clinical.

Manipulating his body subtly, Juliette used his vigour to make their intimacy sublime. Discovering how to satisfy her, Noah became relentless. She'd never felt anything quite like it. He took ownership of her body in ways Dylan never would and the satisfaction was unparalleled. With sweat gleaming off their bodies, Juliette clawed Noah's back, wanting more and he couldn't help but laugh at her unabating desire for passion. With a roguish smile, Noah fulfilled her every whim until Juliette released a cry that was undoubtedly heard by the neighbouring cabins.

A few hours later, Juliette awoke, swaddled in bed linen but without Noah beside her. Sitting up, she looked around the room, finding him standing naked before the mirror.

"I like the view," she mused, biting her lip provocatively.

"What exactly do you see when you look at me, Juliette?" Noah asked, the gravitas in his tone slowly manifesting.

Standing up from the bed, she joined him and examined his reflection. Lean muscles framed his strong bone structure and determined features. Running her fingers over his skin, she continued to look at him through the mirror as she replied.

"I see strength and desire... but for what, or whom?" she asked curiously.

"Where you see strength, I see weakness. This body was bested twice... by Harrison," Noah responded, hissing the name of his nemesis. He cast a glance at Juliette, expecting her to say something but she remained silent. "My deepest desire is to see him ruined."

"Such hatred," Juliette muttered. "You'll beat him eventually."

"I am not a patient man," Noah retorted, pushing her away as he began to dress.

While he focused on the belt that held up his trousers, Juliette examined the rune on his collarbone. It looked like a stain on his near-perfect form. He'd been particularly vague about it too, but she understood whatever magic it possessed, prevented him from speaking about the place he once called home.

"How did he defeat you?" she asked, her gaze steady and voice serious. Even she knew this was no time for frivolity.

"I don't rightly know. Prior to him, I was untouchable and could've had any partner I sought. No one dared to challenge me, but Harrison took away any respect I had among—" Noah began, only to have the rune glow and stifle his words.

"Among your comrades?" Juliette offered.

"My subordinates," Noah corrected, pressing the rune firmly until it stopped aching. "They all wished to befriend me, but none were worthy. I was destined to be their superior, until they betrayed me by siding with Harrison after he joined our ranks."

"Their ranks," Juliette suggested, looking at him defiantly. "You are one of us now, a mage hunter."

"Indeed. And I will lead the infiltration into Iliria and ensure the destruction of—" he continued, becoming irate as his words were once again abruptly cut off by the rune. Clawing at the intricate design seared into his skin, Noah made himself bleed.

"That little thing sure is a nuisance. If only you could tell us where those annoying mages and Ar'encal are hiding," Juliette began, creeping towards him. "We could root out the core problem with this world, gain the Imperator's favour and fulfil your desire all in one targeted attack."

"Trust me, attacking Iliria will draw them out. The more pressing need is to ensure that King Grayson is a true ally or enlist his soldiers by force."

"Ooh, I like the second option," Juliette enthused, turning from him and rifling through her satchel. After picking out a vial, she turned back to him, raising the transparent container so that he could see the discoloured liquid inside.

"I know I probably shouldn't be, but I am surprised you favour aggression. I thought you'd grown fond of King Grayson," Noah replied, glancing over his shoulder at her.

"I may have enjoyed playing with him, but I made my choice. I chose the Imperator. I chose you," Juliette answered, watching his gaze flick between her body and the vial.

"What is that?" he asked, gesturing at the solution with deep intrigue.

"The same thing I used on Harrison's spiky-haired friend last time. It's a potent little concoction that's designed to mutilate anything soft it comes into contact with... like human skin," she replied, a wicked smile curling her lips.

"Spiky-haired friend? Tell me, was this friend blonde, holding a bow and remarkably similar in appearance to me?" Noah asked, reaching out and taking the vial between his fingers.

"Why do you ask?" Juliette replied, her posture becoming rigid as her whole body stiffened.

"Because if you took out my pathetic little brother, I'll distract you in whatever ways you wish for the remainder of this voyage," he replied, his tone and smile a combination of menace and lust.

Relaxing, Juliette sauntered up to him, snatched the vial and placed it on the side table.

"This is going to be fun," she vowed, answering his question with a simple smirk before indicating for Noah to discard his clothes once again. He wasn't going to need them for some time.

Once the *Pilgrim* docked in Revaine, Juliette and Noah forcefully appropriated two horses from the vendor outside town and rode straight to Carlisse. Arriving at the gates of the walled city was a strangely comforting experience for Juliette. She had meant it when telling Noah that she enjoyed enthralling King Grayson during her last visit and secretly expected to be a welcome sight for the monarch now.

Leaving their exhausted mounts in the palace courtyard, expecting one of the nearby servants to tend to them, Juliette and Noah made their way through the main hall towards the throne room. Entering, they could see King Grayson addressing a select portion of the assault force, his booming voice travelling all the way to the back of the room.

"As servants, they pose no threat, but the free mages and Ar'encal now mean to end our coexistence," he declared, standing in front of the throne, elevated from the soldiers below. "The queen's efforts to poison me proved to be part of a greater insurgent plot. During a stealth attack on my great palace, those renegades intended to gather intel on me and discover our weaknesses, but of course, I have none, so all they achieved was the start of a conflict that will lead to their destruction."

"How motivational," Juliette whispered sarcastically to Noah, who stood with his arms folded, obviously unimpressed.

"This impertinent attempt on my city cannot go unpunished," King Grayson insisted, focusing on the officers at the front of the room before noticing Juliette and Noah's presence. "Our scouting parties report minimal defences, meaning they are unprepared for a frontal assault, so that is your charge. Go, defend my honour and do not return until every enemy before you lies captured or killed."

With a hand motion, the king indicated for Juliette to join him upstairs before turning his back on the gathered soldiers and departing through a door behind the throne.

"Your presence is required," Noah commented abrasively.

"Jealous?" she mocked, which only garnered her a look of utter distaste. Her interest in him was purely physical but now she couldn't help but wonder if he cared or wanted something more.

"Make him wait, I want you here for this," Noah replied, marching to the front of the room.

Noticing his brash approach, a bulky officer with untrusting eyes blocked his path.

"Who are you?" the officer asked bluntly.

Noah glanced at the man, disregarding his attempt at a threatening demeanour almost instantly. The weapon in his hand, an elegant royal halberd, garnered more attention. Its serrated steel tip was fastened to the wooden shaft and adorned with a silver-plated motif of the kingdom, but it was difficult to tell at a glance if it was a deadly weapon or simply decorative.

"Are you here for posture or a purpose I wonder?" Noah asked rhetorically, meeting the older, taller man's gaze with confidence. Juliette assumed he was the ranking officer in the room but Noah brushed past him and stood before the other soldiers, just as the king had.

"I won't ask again. Who are you?" shouted the officer, following Noah onto the elevated platform. He began to perspire as his eyes darted to the steps leading down. Clearly even senior officers were not meant to stand on the regal platform without invitation.

"I am no fool, unlike your king," Noah declared while all the other soldiers looked on in disbelief.

"Watch your insolent tongue," the officer threatened angrily, brandishing the tip of the halberd towards Noah.

"Put that thing down before you hurt yourself," Noah instructed, his commanding tone making the other man falter.

"What do you mean, a fool?" called a voice from among the soldiers crowded in the room.

"Your king sends you into battle without knowing your enemy, expecting you will face no resistance, but he is wrong. I know your enemy; I know what you will face," Noah called out and paused for a moment, listening to the reaction of the soldiers. Their uncertain chatter was undeniable. "Follow your orders and face death or follow my command and be victorious."

"You would ally yourselves with this stranger without approval from our king?" challenged the officer, speaking past Noah to his peers.

"Your king cares only for the spoils of war. Dead men can deliver no spoils," Noah retaliated, glancing back at the officer. "Who are you anyway?"

"I'm the man leading the charge," the officer declared, puffing his chest in a feeble attempt to look intimidating.

"If this man represents the best leader you have in the field, you are absolutely doomed without me," Noah mocked.

A stifled rumble of laughter travelled around the room, revealing some dissent among the ranks. Taking advantage of the opportunity, Noah smiled and encouraged Juliette to approach.

Her skin-tight trousers emphasised every curve and she knew all the soldiers, including the officer were looking at her, not at what she held. Reaching the self-proclaimed leader who clearly expected her touch to be sensual, she shocked him by forcefully grabbing his chin. Slapping her hand away, he watched as she tumbled backwards theatrically, but then in a swift retaliation, uncorked the vial and threw the contents in his face.

For the slightest moment, those close enough could hear the pain in his scream, but within seconds, there was nothing but silence as the officer dropped to the floor. Dead. With his face blistered and almost unrecognisable, even to his peers, Juliette relished in the horrified gasps from the men around her. Collecting the halberd from its former wielder, she joined Noah in front of the soldiers.

"For you," she postured, handing the weapon to Noah. Gripping it tightly, he thrust the spear outwards, letting the tip hover in the faces of the remaining soldiers that had amassed at the front of the room. One by one, they each stood to attention and saluted, signalling their allegiance to him.

"Good," Noah remarked, smiling at Juliette as she blew him a kiss and slipped through the rear door towards the king's chamber. She could have her fun now while he focused on properly organising the assault force.

As King Grayson had sent scouts, Noah expected his father would've sent troops to defend Iliria by now. He explained that they'd focus on guarding the temple and town hall but would certainly barricade the main road and set up vantage points to keep watch. Individually, the soldiers they'd usurped were pathetic, but if combined with the mage hunters in the city, they had decent numbers—something the Aegis Guard did not.

While their attention was affixed on the descending military on the northern road, their eyes would be averted from the secondary river access that ran behind the town. Juliette and Noah could travel with the mage hunters, using the shadows for cover, and strike straight into the heart of town. The only thing they had to leave to chance was whether or not Harrison would be there.

Knowing that Lucas and the guards that had already returned couldn't wait long, Alex rushed back to the training grounds to help them prepare for battle. There were still dozens of guards travelling back from their various posts but waiting was not an option, so while Zack was better off staying behind to instruct the missing guards where to go, Lucas and Alex journeyed to Iliria with those present.

By dusk, they'd set up an operations base using an old barn that was conveniently just outside the town square. Its location was out of the way but provided a good view of the main road. Sitting inside, Alex listened intently to Captain Harper as he addressed the squads.

"Grayson's troops will likely attack from the northern road. It's the most direct approach to the town square," Lucas began pointing to a map he'd pinned on the wall. "His army will not be expecting any real resistance. We must capitalise on this naivety."

"We could set up a watch post by the river bend," suggested Parker Cole, a senior guard. "There's decent cover in the treeline for our archers."

"Do it. Have Uriah's team set up as an advanced watch point and then your team on the river bend. Take Alana with you too. She can act as a runner to get updates from your teams to those of us remaining here," Lucas instructed. "The more notice we have of the enemy's approach, the better."

"Are we going to tell the townspeople?" Alex enquired, his question disrupting Lucas and Parker, who had begun muttering between themselves, marking the map with tactical locations and vulnerable spots.

"I've informed the town alderman. He's going to ensure the elderly and vulnerable remain in the temple of Ceris, but everyone else has just been told to stay in their homes while we sweep the area," Lucas replied, trying to sound reassuring.

"But why aren't we telling them the truth?" Alex asked, his eyes widening with surprise at the revelation.

"We don't know when the Carlisse army will attack. This could all be a ruse or diversion, although I doubt it," Lucas explained before giving a solid nod towards Parker, who rallied two teams and headed to their advanced positions. "If the people knew, they could panic and try to flee. We cannot protect them if they scatter."

Just as the archer teams left the barn, four cloaked figures entered. It was Maia and with her were Teagan, Freya and a young mage boy. Alex had seen him a couple of times before and knew he was Freya's son but couldn't recall his name.

"Maia, what are you doing here? You must get back to Arencia," Lucas ordered.

"These are my people too, Lucas. It's me that the townsfolk welcome, feed and provide rest to or conceal if under threat. I won't abandon them," she argued, taking in his dominant demeanour and responding in kind.

With her youthful appearance and tender features, it was easy to forget that Maia was the most wizened and experienced of the Ar'encal and the leader of their race.

"Fine, we'll be erecting a barricade around the town square, make sure you and the healers stay within it," Lucas grumbled.

The people left behind would need her leadership and resourcefulness if the battle went badly. Although her powers would be a welcome aid, the Ar'encal would not survive without their leader.

"We'll provide whatever aid we can," Maia confirmed before turning to her companions. "Teagan, take the casters that volunteered to come and reinforce the barricade. Freya, you and Sebastian head to the town hall and set up a triage base. It's unlikely we'll get through this unscathed."

Peering outside, Alex noticed that dozens of Ar'encal and mages had accompanied Maia. Most were speaking with the amassed Aegis Guards, whose numbers were also growing, but there was a clear divide between the older and skilled casters compared to youthful mages who, despite being brave had no experience in combat.

As Teagan strode out, he began directing the mages to vantage points where their skills would amplify the town's defences while allowing the more experienced casters to join the front line. With a defensive force of this size gathering, Alex couldn't help but wonder how the townsfolk could be oblivious to the imminent threat but conceded that Lucas' point was valid. If the people fled, they would be defenceless. Once the healers also departed, Alex hopped off his barrel seat and approached Lucas.

"How can I serve, sir?" he asked politely.

"I need you to be my eyes and ears, Alex. Keep the people safe and alert me of anything untoward in town," Lucas replied, placing a proud hand on his shoulder while glancing at Maia.

"A warrior at heart indeed," Maia noted whimsically, gracing him with an equally proud smile. Hearing the comment filled Alex with determination. He would not let them down.

As evening drew in, Lucas found himself getting anxious. The Aegis Guard had established a defensive perimeter around Iliria, but there had been no sign of the kingdom's forces. He'd received word hours ago that Uriah's team had moved higher up the road, but they hadn't reported in since.

The town of Pembroke lay to the southwest of Carlisse, so he began wondering if King Grayson would've chosen to deploy his soldiers and strike from that direction but then disregarded the notion. To send his troops through the mire between the two towns seemed unnecessarily dangerous. Consumed by his own thoughts, Lucas barely noticed Alana approach him.

"Sir, pardon my intrusion. I have news," she announced, saluting as she stood before him.

"What is it, Alana?" he replied, hungry for any kind of update.

"A well-organised and heavily armed force is upon the southern road, sir. They make no attempt to conceal their approach," she advised.

"Wardens," Lucas whispered, relief piercing his earlier concern for the lives of his men and the townspeople.

Nodding his thanks to Alana, Lucas made haste to greet them. He had hoped that Harrison would've arrived before them and made the formal introductions but wasn't about to refuse their aid or send them away.

As the rider of the lead horse dismounted and strode towards Lucas, he couldn't help but inspect the man. He didn't wear the same armour as the others but his lean muscles and stern face proved he was a fighter. "Morgan Foster?" Lucas asked, extending a firm hand towards the stranger.

"Captain Harper, I presume? My name is Dylan Rose, a friend of Commander Foster," Dylan replied, taking the older man's hand and shaking it respectfully. "I come on his behalf with the warden force promised."

"Where is Commander Foster?" Lucas questioned, hailing Alana and two other guards over to receive the welcome addition of warriors to their ranks.

"He stayed with Harrison to help rescue Rylie. If there's a way to get her back, they'll find it," Dylan answered, his tone exuding more confidence than he expected to hear from himself.

Their conversation was soon interrupted by the distinct sound of a war horn, shortly followed by raised voices.

"Well, let's hope they do so and get here fast," Lucas said urgently, rushing towards the blockade on the main, northern road with Dylan following closely behind. "Take your warriors and help reinforce the barricade. In particular, defend Teagan of the Ar'encal. His psionic powers could be the difference between victory and defeat in this fight."

"Consider it done… but what about you?" Dylan asked.

"I'll join you shortly but must check the guard rotation protecting the town hall. We've set up medical provisions inside, but should the Carlisse army breach the barricade, they'll be an easy target," Lucas explained, concern engraved in the furrows of his brow.

Watching Captain Harper depart, Dylan instructed his fellow wardens to bolster the defences around the barricade. Some of them knew that he'd trained in Tulam and become a mage hunter, but so far, none of them had treated him unfairly for it and followed his lead without question. He wasn't proud of what he'd become, and this was his chance to atone. *I'm not proud of the things I've done before, but this is my first chance to atone. I will not let this opportunity slip by.*

Chapter Ten
Assault

Since taking command of the Carlisse soldiers, Noah split the assault force into smaller groups and instructed them to travel just south of Lorvale, to minimise the chances of any scouts discovering just how many warriors would be part of the attack. Reconvening at the bend in the river, less than an hour's march from Iliria, Noah addressed the soldiers.

"Your task is simple, follow the main road until you hit the northern entrance to the town," he began, the confidence in his voice capturing the attention of every warrior. "Be watchful of the treeline. There will be archers intending to ambush you, so ensure the shield bearers are positioned on the outer edge."

"What should we do if they attack before we reach the town?" asked the officer Noah had selected to signal the charge after Juliette relieved his predecessor of the responsibility.

"Strike back," Noah instructed blatantly. He had assumed that objective was obvious. "Leave no guards alive. Our numbers give us the advantage, but only turn your attention to taking prisoners after we have established a foothold in town."

"Where will you and the mage hunters be?" the officer asked, looking behind him at the huddled group of mage hunters, with the notable Juliette standing amongst them.

"I have covered this... we will be travelling downriver from here on," Noah snapped, not liking to repeat himself. "As leader of the main assault force, you will distract the eyes of the enemy scouting parties, meaning we can reach the western edge of town and sneak in through some old mining tunnels."

"Will the defenders not expect that?" A second warrior questioned, not wanting to fail as Noah had suggested they would by going for a direct attack.

"They may post a small patrol, but it'll be nothing we can't handle," Noah insisted. "The risk is worth it. The tunnels have an exit near the temple, which is in the heart of town. Exiting there will allow us to attack from behind while you press from the front."

"Of course, Mr. Harper. We will keep the enemy attention away from the river to safeguard your passage and attack the resistance with all our might," the officer promised, saluting him.

"Good man. Don't let me down," Noah replied, clapping the officer on the shoulder before letting him repeat the plan to all the other soldiers who may not have heard.

He still felt that the Carlisse soldiers were poorly trained but was beginning to believe that now they were following a decent plan, his plan, the attack would succeed. All he needed was a chance to get behind the front-line and Noah knew he could cause some serious damage to the Aegis Guard. He expected some of his old comrades would pause upon seeing him, a delay he would take full advantage of. The more guardians he and the mage hunters could take out before he confronted Harrison, the more sure he could be that their combat would not be interfered with.

The mage hunters also knew to defer to Juliette's command if he located and engaged Harrison. He didn't want or need any help to take him out. Their secondary goal was to secure prisoners once the defensive line fell, an easy enough task even for the most dim-witted soldier. He had stressed for them to focus on the mages, however, as any Ar'encal that chose to fight would likely fight to the bitter end rather than submit. They'd lost their freedom after the Uprising, and having been in hiding ever since, would not sacrifice what little they had by becoming slaves.

As night fell, the warden forces had integrated themselves with the other guardians and bolstered the defensive line as instructed. Reports from the scouting parties had diminished, however, which created a greater tension among the guardians. Locating the man he assumed to be Teagan, Dylan hoped to receive some kind of update on the situation. He'd never met an Ar'encal before and was immediately shocked by how young he looked. His warm red hair was long but had been loosely pulled back, away from his narrow face. He was muttering something under his breath with one hand outstretched towards the barricade while a guardian, covered in sweat and grime spoke rapidly to him.

"Uriah and his entire team are dead, Teagan. They sacrificed themselves to ensure we had time to reach you," said the guard through laboured breaths.

"I'm sorry, Parker," Teagan replied without looking up from the barricade. The soldier named Parker sunk his head, taking a moment to collect himself while Teagan finished his incantation.

The steady fall of sleet dampened the cold ground. It wouldn't take much to make the entire area icy, but the increasing sound of clattering steel boots told them the weather was not slowing down the Carlisse assault force.

"Where is Captain Harper?" Parker finally asked, speaking to the Ar'encal like an elder rather than an equal.

"I'm not sure," Teagan replied, concern evident in his voice.

"I've just seen him," Dylan announced, striding towards them.

"And you are?" Parker asked, his voice suspicious while he retained a steady grip on the bow in his hand.

"Dylan Rose, I am with the wardens and here to aid you," he explained politely.

"I've heard your name before, Dylan Rose. Not as a warden, but as a mage hunter," declared Parker, raising the bow and notching an arrow at lightning speed. Instantly, Dylan raised his hands in submission.

"I am a proud defector," Dylan began, his tone steady while he fixed his gaze not on the guardian, but on Teagan. "I've come to atone for the transgressions of my past but will leave in peace if you prefer."

"Lower your weapon, Parker," instructed Teagan as he crossed the short distance between them while Dylan took the opportunity to examine the Ar'encal further.

Despite his youthful appearance, there was a sense of wisdom in his cool, grey eyes. He also had a pale scar on the left side of his nose, just below the subtle ridges that defined his race which told Dylan he'd seen battle before, likely during the original Uprising.

"Captain Harper is checking the defences near the healers, but will join us shortly," Dylan confirmed, finally able to explain why he intruded on their conversation in the first place.

"Well then, let's make sure there's someone here for him to join," Teagan replied with authority. "Parker, take your squad to the roof of that barn and give us whatever ranged support you can. We'll focus our efforts on defending the barricade."

With a nod, Parker rallied what was left of his unit and was gone just in time for Dylan and Teagan to turn their attention to the emerging military. Their vast numbers soon swamped the northern road, but it was impossible to tell how far back the line went. Even combined with the wardens, the defenders of Iliria were outnumbered five to one. The kind of odds only Siljanna liked.

Taking a deep breath, Dylan drew his sword and joined the front line. Looking to the wardens on either side of him, the pallor of their armour distinct against the darker garb worn by their allies and his own hunter gear, Dylan considered just how different his life would've been had he not gone to Tulam in his final year of training. *Would I be a proud warrior like the others? Could I still become one?*

The clatter of armour and steel in his vicinity was soon interrupted by another blast of the war horn. Their enemy had halted approximately twenty metres ahead of the barricade. As his skin prickled, Dylan saw the army leader raise his sword and pause. The building tension was almost unbearable until, with a loud battle cry that was echoed by the enemy soldiers, the leader signalled the charge. Then, all other thoughts in Dylan's mind evaporated as his trained body took over.

In just minutes, the scene went from anticipation to action and Dylan was in the thick of the fight. He didn't even recall collecting the shield in his hand, but as he used it to block the onslaught of two royalists, he was grateful to have it. The Carlisse soldiers were not taking any prisoners and Dylan's instincts told him the same. Although he wasn't proud of becoming a mage hunter, training in Tulam had made him a resilient, resourceful killer. In this situation, those skills would save his life.

Colliding with another soldier seconds after the last two fell, Dylan risked a glance over his shoulder, only to see the rare sight of a warden fall. He'd never properly met the young man or learnt his name and now he never would. Kicking out sharply against his assailant with renewed determination, Dylan struck back, launching forward with tremendous force. The momentum took both him and the royal soldier to the ground, but only one of them stood back up. Rising, Dylan noticed the ground becoming littered with bodies from both sides, but the Carlisse soldiers kept coming. They were quickly being overwhelmed.

"Pull back," he cried, wiping the grime from his face as he repeated the command to everyone nearby. "The barricade is lost."

"We must hold this position!" Teagan shouted back while fending off three soldiers with a telekinetically controlled spear.

"If we stay, we die. Pull back and regroup with Parker's squad," Dylan argued firmly.

As the remaining defenders and wardens overheard their argument, several of them began to pull back while trying to keep the enemy forces at bay. Helping those in his immediate vicinity, Dylan put an end to another royalist, but in doing so realised that Teagan had stood fast, refusing to retreat. Standing on an elevated platform, Dylan watched him create a wall of psionic energy that spread from behind the barricade all the way around town.

"Get out of here!" Teagan yelled.

"What are you doing?" Dylan challenged, pushing back all the soldiers on their side of the line.

Calling out an incantation. Teagan flashed a determined look at Dylan and then, he was gone, enveloped by a large explosion. The shockwave spread rapidly in every direction, cracking the barrier until it shattered like glass, blowing Dylan off his feet and into an old shed. He raised his arms to protect his head, but nothing would cushion the impact.

Several bits of broken wood crashed on top of him but once the dust settled, he crawled out from the rubble and looked back towards the barricade where now, only death remained. In the centre of a circle of destruction was Teagan's body, his red hair noticeable amongst the sea of metal-clad soldiers.

"Fool," Dylan muttered under his breath, shaking his head while putting pressure against his ribs.

He wasn't sure if he'd sustained an injury from an attacking soldier or his impact with the wooden structure, but his entire left side was in agony. A young mage rushed to his aid, grabbing Dylan by the arm and encouraging him to retreat.

"Let his sacrifice not be in vain," said the woman while seeming to cast some kind of incantation.

Dylan just nodded in response and followed her towards the second line of defence, where Parker's team were providing cover fire. Although he strongly felt that had Teagan retreated, they would've all been able to regroup, his display of force had stopped hundreds of the enemy soldiers and bought them the precious commodity of time.

Not only hearing but feeling the rumble from the shockwave, Alex glanced in the direction of the barricade and steeled himself. He wanted to help the Aegis Guard, but his orders were to protect the civilians. Glancing through the window to the temple of Ceris, he could see several people and families cowering in prayer.

On the other side of the square, Alex saw Maia rush out of the town hall, but Lucas forcefully pushed her back, pointing towards the doors she'd just burst through. He couldn't make out what they were saying, but it was clear she wanted to help the soldiers at the barricade, and he wanted her to stay. Whatever he said proved to be enough as Maia slumped her shoulders and stood still while Lucas ran in the direction of the barricade. She was just about to turn back inside when out of nowhere, several cloaked figures ambushed her from behind. Among them was a slender woman with short dark hair in skin-tight clothing that Alex didn't recognise, followed by a face he absolutely did, Noah.

Casting a wave of elemental magic which broke up the ground around them, Maia attempted to defend herself, but Alex feared she couldn't face that many alone, no matter how powerful she was. His feet were already in motion as he drew his sword and lunged at one of the cloaked figures. As he pulled the sword back, his hand shaking, Alex watched the cloaked figure fall to the floor. He'd never killed anyone before but couldn't allow himself to overthink what he had to do; Maia needed aid.

Alex reached her just in time to see the slender woman throw something at her and whatever it was made Maia collapse. Rushing to her side, Alex skidded to his knees, using his body to protect her. She was gasping for breath as her body violently contorted, her eyes wild with panic. She glanced towards the barricade and then to Alex and he understood her plea.

"Lucas!" he cried, projecting his voice as loudly as he could while scrabbling to his feet and grabbing Maia by the arm.

Trying to drag her to safety, he heard a crack and saw the slender woman draw a devilish whip from her belt. She pressed forward while Noah watched, arms folded and a sinister smile spreading across his face. Fears of death polluted Alex's mind until Lucas charged in and with a shoulder barrage, knocking his son to the floor.

"Stay down," he ordered before turning his attention to the woman who'd injured Maia.

"I know you... but do you know me?" asked the woman, her tone somehow playful.

"You're Juliette Lawrence, the wretch that crippled my son!" Lucas growled, the anger in his voice undeniable.

As his captain charged, sword brandished in her direction, Alex threw his body weight against the heavy town hall doors and dragged Maia inside. He heard the clang of swords colliding and presumed that someone had saved Juliette but when he turned back to the scene in the square, she had vanished. Noah, however, was still on the ground staring at his father with a venomous look on his face, while Lucas was ordering the Aegis Guard to combat the mage hunters as best they could.

Drawing his sword again, Alex intended to return to the fight but froze as he witnessed the unimaginable unfold. Juliette broke away from the guardians and hunters fighting only to lash out at Lucas with her whip. As the weapon coiled around his captain's neck, she yanked backwards, forcing Lucas to his knees. Dropping his weapon, Lucas gripped the whip with both hands, trying to free himself but despite his best efforts, he ended up restrained before his eldest son. Juliette then seemed to slither around her prey, wrapping even more of the whip around his neck.

"Stay very still," Juliette whispered, her breath grazing his ear as her gaze shifted to Noah, who slowly approached his father.

"You picked the wrong son, Captain Harper," Noah spat, subtly nodding at Juliette.

Staring at the scene in disbelief, Alex watched as the foul woman behind Lucas pulled at the whip with all her strength. The asphyxiating pressure wrung his throat and his body quickly became starved for air. He continued to claw at the whip until his fingers refused to obey and his arms went limp. His final sight before the end was of his eldest son, grinning.

Pausing briefly, relishing in the surge of power from victory over his father, Noah awarded Juliette with a menacing look of approval. Recoiling her weapon, she returned his admiration before sauntering towards the town hall.

As Lucas dropped to the floor, Alex felt himself scream even though he heard no sound. Finally unfrozen, he rushed towards Lucas' body only to be met by a boot, which kicked him to the ground.

"Where's your hero then? Where is Harrison?" Noah asked arrogantly. Just as he finished asking the question, they both heard the clatter of hooves coming from the southern road.

"Ask and you shall receive," Alex hissed, having no way of knowing but certain it was Harrison and the others.

Having ridden as fast as their mounts could take them, Harrison and Rylie were the first to reach the town square in Iliria and clearly it wasn't a moment too soon. The Aegis Guards were deep in combat with the mage hunters, and they assumed Noah would also be nearby. Nate, Siljanna and Morgan came up behind them shortly afterwards and they each swiftly drew weapons from their saddle bags. Harrison's particularly large broadsword had been wrapped and firmly placed lengthways behind the saddle, but he freed it with ease as they dismounted before grabbing more weapons from another bag.

"Take these," Harrison offered, presenting a simple, slim pair of knives to Rylie which he'd bought in Dawne while the others ensured Caitlin was seen by the healer. "Promise me you'll be careful."

"I will. Thank you, Harrison."

Turning to see Nate strap a handmade quiver filled with crossbow bolts over his shoulder, then Morgan with his favoured katana in hand, Harrison steeled himself for battle. Looking towards Siljanna, he noticed her wielding a beautifully crafted pair of axes. The axes he'd made for her.

"Morgan, Sil... follow that path. It'll take you to the northern road. The main conflict will have started there, so that's where Dylan and the wardens will be," Harrison instructed, and they both dashed off at speed.

"We'll help you take care of these mage hunters," Nate affirmed as Harrison turned his attention to them.

"Good. Nate, find a vantage point. You'll be able to provide better cover from up high," Harrison suggested, wielding his trusty blade expertly, its weight and motion as familiar to him as breathing.

"Over there," Rylie indicated, pointing to the inn which had a small balcony on the second floor.

With a nod, her father jogged over and clambered up a trellis to reach the upper level. From the elevated position, he could see the entire square and the Aegis Guard in battle. Letting loose a shot and taking out one of the cloaked mage hunters, Nate scanned the rest of the square. His gaze soon found the fallen remains of Lucas and noticed a soldier towering over Alex.

"That way, quickly!" he cried to Harrison, who launched from still to sprint in a heartbeat. Rylie couldn't keep up but ran as fast as she could in the same direction.

Reaching the scene, Rylie paused in horror, but Harrison immediately set his sights on Noah. He didn't even notice it was Alex on the ground until he got closer, but that only fuelled Harrison's strike more. His sword collided with Noah's blade which he'd somehow managed to raise while twisting to face Harrison.

"Just who I was looking for," Noah sneered.

"What have you done, Noah?" Harrison yelled, taking a step back, his blade and body ready for battle. His eyes flicked to Lucas and sorrowfully accepted he was too late to save him.

"Just relieving myself of some baggage. The old man only held me back," Noah spat.

"I see your fall from grace has done nothing to slight your arrogance," Harrison retorted before lunging at Noah. Their blades clashed again, and it was clear, although still under the influence of his own hubris, Noah was prepared for a real fight.

"The time has come for the world to see just how inferior you are compared to me," Noah hissed, striking ferociously at Harrison.

Sparks flew between their blades as they circled one another, both trying to find an opening. When a crossbow bolt whistled past them, Noah didn't flinch, and Harrison knew Nate was telling him there wasn't a clear shot. He would have to defeat Noah alone.

With the opportunity to flee, Alex scrabbled to his feet and found Rylie. She combed a hand through his matted hair and was about to ask a question when she spotted Juliette targeting the town hall.

"We must stop her. She's going after Maia!" Alex called out. The urgency in his voice spurred Rylie to run as fast as she could to intercept her.

Barely recognising the woman she'd once studied medicine with, only seeing the hunter from the opposite balcony in Carlisse the day Siljanna and the Imperator tried to trap them, Rylie shook the memories of that fateful day aside and focused just in time to see the whip as it slithered through the air towards her face. It nicked her cheek before recoiling to its mistress who looked at her with a smug expression.

"It's been a while, Rylie. Last I heard, you were a fiery monster with devastating power… but you seem to have let that slip through your fingers," Juliette taunted. "Just like your career in medicine and your home. Is there anything you haven't lost?"

Refusing to rise to the bait, Rylie recalled the bullish young Juliette. Even before she became a mage hunter, she'd been cruel. Back then, Rylie often wondered if a person could get much worse. Standing before her now, Juliette proved it was indeed possible. When she didn't reply, Juliette released the whip again, lashing out with the intent to strike and disarm her. Instead, Rylie used one of her blades to catch the whip. As it looped around the long slim metal of her knife, she turned sharply, pulling Juliette off balance and with a graceful twist, used her second blade to sever the whip in two.

With her weapon destroyed, Juliette hissed at Rylie before turning on her heels and running towards the town hall. Noticing her flight, Alex grabbed his sword and joined Rylie in pursuit. Juliette was incredibly quick, however, and reached the building before they could. When they caught up to her, she had a young mage boy held in a chokehold and another vial in her free hand.

"This little treat is called En-glycerol. You won't have heard of it, but it's Imperator Harlyn's favoured concoction. But rather than tell you how it works, how about I just show you?" she declared, her tone sinister.

Before they could respond, she launched the vial at Maia who was still unconscious on the floor. As the vial broke and the liquid connected with her skin, Maia's eyes wrenched open and she released a piercing scream. The strange substance seemed to drain the very life from Maia, making her skin turn grey and the tips of her fingers blacken. Reacting to her cries of pain, both Rylie and Alex rushed to Maia's side but within that short window, Juliette was gone, and she'd taken the mage boy with her.

Kneeling beside her after wiping away the liquid, Alex pressed his head against Maia's chest. She'd collapsed again, but he and Rylie both relaxed when they heard her ragged breathing.

"She's alive," he confirmed.

"Thank goodness," Rylie exhaled in relief. "But who was that young boy?"

"Oh no! That's Freya's son, Sebastian. We must help him!"

"Go, Alex! Juliette is unarmed now and you're faster than me. I'll head back out there and help Harrison if I can," Rylie replied, quickly looking over her shoulder to the closed doors that led to the town square.

With a glance back at Maia, Alex nodded and then ran through the rear exit of the town hall in pursuit of Juliette. As soon as he was gone, Rylie took a deep breath and returned the way they'd come. Although she'd never considered herself religious, she made a silent prayer to the gods that Harrison was okay.

Deflecting another series of blows, Harrison could hardly believe how different it was fighting Noah this time. He was still arrogant, but his rage had turned him from an opponent who was easy to disarm into the relentless and proficient warrior the Aegis Guard had known him to be.

"How did I let a pathetic excuse for a warrior like you defeat me?" Noah snarled, pausing his onslaught even though it allowed Harrison to shift into a more defensive stance.

"You under-estimated me and you continue to do so," Harrison replied, not allowing Noah's words to rile him.

"A mistake I won't repeat. And now I know how to truly destroy you," Noah countered, his hubris reaching a whole new level.

"Enlighten me," Harrison retorted sharply as they circled one another, looking for an opportunity to strike.

"It's all those people you care for. Your destiny is to die defending them and I'm going to make sure it's me delivering the killing blow," Noah answered and to Harrison's frustration, he wasn't wrong. He had and would always put his life on the line to save another, especially someone he loved.

"So, you'd hurt countless people just to defeat me?" Harrison questioned in disgust.

"Without hesitation or remorse," Noah growled.

"Then you're nothing more than a callous bully!" Harrison proclaimed, staggered by Noah's admission.

"Thank you," he smirked, taking pride in what any other would consider an insult.

"Every bully I've ever known was a coward," Harrison added, and his words had the desired effect. As Noah roared, he charged at Harrison, swinging his sword wildly.

Defending against a multitude of blows, Harrison shifted his weight in an attempt to disarm Noah, just as he'd done against Morgan in their academy trial. Before he could, Noah kicked out, catching the back of Harrison's foot and he dropped to the floor. With an almighty scream, Noah raised his blade and plunged it towards Harrison's chest, but his blade connected with the empty ground as Harrison flipped backwards and was on his feet again.

"You'll have to do better than that," Harrison taunted, collecting his blade and provoking Noah to attack again.

Breathing heavily, Noah realised he was beginning to tire. He couldn't continue at this pace for long.

"You may have saved most of these people tonight, but what about all the townsfolk in Tivani?" Noah replied insidiously.

"More empty threats, Noah?" Harrison scolded but was unable to disguise how on edge the implication made him feel.

"Far from it. The Imperator plans to attack Tivani next and flush out that treacherous sister of yours. But, if I'm not mistaken, she arrived with you. I wonder who will defend those people if you are all here?" Noah replied, enjoying that his comment hit a nerve.

"You can't keep attacking innocent people!" Harrison shouted, losing his composure as he struck back, but his frantic strikes were easily blocked.

"Is Siljanna truly on your side now? How quickly you absolve even the most heinous of deeds against you," Noah sneered before launching his counter-attack. "I'll never forgive the person that ruined my life. You!"

"You believe that? Fine. How, how did I ruin your life, Noah?" Harrison questioned as their blades collided again, leaving their faces mere inches apart.

"I had power and respect in Arencia," he hissed, able to name the place with only Harrison in range. "You humiliated me, taking that away. Then, knowing I wanted Rylie, you took her as well."

"You speak of Rylie like a possession! She was never yours to own," Harrison spat back, recalling what had really happened between them and not even bothering to bring up the fact he'd cared about her long before Noah even met them.

"When I want something, I take it, and I wanted her. But then you took her, and they all expected *me* to be okay with it!" Noah screamed, breaking the stalemate with a strong kick before attempting a vicious upward swing.

Dodging swiftly, Harrison retaliated with three precise blows that ended with them staring down each other's blades again. Pushing his rival away and calculating his next attack, Noah's advance was halted when he heard the war horn, this time declaring retreat.

"Those useless grunts!" Noah hissed, glancing around to notice the Aegis Guards rout the last of his mage hunters and that Juliette was long gone.

"Looks like you'll have to fight your own battles, Noah," Harrison scoffed, enjoying the chance to antagonise his opponent.

"This is not the last you've seen of me," Noah declared as he pulled a small spherical object from his pocket. Throwing it at the ground towards Harrison, the object exploded and released a large cloud of thick, heavy smoke.

With his vision shrouded, Harrison covered his face until the smoke began to dissipate. Once clear, Harrison knew Noah would be gone. He glanced up at Nate who answered his questioning glance with a shrug. The smoke cloud had been large enough to conceal Noah's escape. Accepting he was gone, Harrison's next thought was to find the others. To his relief, Rylie emerged moments later from the town hall and ran towards him. She threw her arms around him on contact and Harrison returned her embrace as they stood for just a moment, reassured by each other's well-being.

"Juliette?" Harrison finally asked.

"She got away, kidnapping a young mage boy in the process," Rylie answered, her eyes dropping to the ground with sadness. "Alex is trying to catch up to them, but I fear she's already gone."

"Any others wounded?" he questioned, cupping her face reassuringly in his hand.

"Maia's inside the town hall and in bad shape. We need to get her back to Arencia," Rylie informed, glancing back to where she knew the Ar'encal leader was lying.

"Get your dad and do what you can for Maia. I need to check on Morgan and the others," Harrison replied.

"Be quick," Rylie insisted, eager to get help for Maia.

Chapter Eleven
Aftermath

The northern road had been decimated by the blast, a large crater surrounded by debris from the barricade being all that remained when Harrison arrived. He stood motionless, shocked to see the number of dead bodies and wounded fighters. He couldn't imagine what had happened, but the result was devastating. The Aegis Guards were respectfully pulling both their comrades' and enemies' bodies from the dirt, laying them along the roadside and covering them with sheets. Even after all he'd endured, Harrison shivered, the sight before him immensely sad.

Noticing his arrival, Morgan waved Harrison over to where he and Siljanna were talking with Dylan. Silently, they shared looks of pure relief to see each other alive and well before refocusing their attention on the conversation.

"Once Teagan caused the explosion, the fight was all but over," Dylan explained, his voice a little shaky. "Some of the Carlisse soldiers attempted to continue the assault but they couldn't breach the ranged fire from Parker's squad."

"And all the other warriors deserted?" Siljanna asked, examining their surroundings as if expecting to be ambushed.

"Yeah. A handful ran west but the majority headed back north, presumably for Carlisse," Dylan said nodding.

"Pembroke is the nearest town west of here," Harrison recalled, joining the conversation. "The land between us is called 'The Mire'. It's mostly bog and swampland which will be seeping with raw Encia. Those soldiers must've been desperate to flee that way."

"Harrison, you weren't here. Everything happened so fast. The royalists weren't taking any prisoners but when Teagan sacrificed himself to take them out with some kind of psionic blast, all their bravado vanished, as did their leader," Dylan explained, wiping his brow as sweat trickled down his forehead into his eyes.

"It's hard to believe that Teagan's gone," Harrison muttered, remembering all the time they'd spent together creating the runic armour.

"What are you saying?" Dylan countered, his tone defensive. "His death isn't my fault."

"I'm not blaming you, Dylan," Harrison promised. "I just spent a lot of time with Teagan recently and it's hard to accept that he's just... gone."

"Are all those soldiers risking exposure to Encia by crossing the swamp?" Morgan asked, keen to change the subject and give Dylan a chance to regain his composure.

"Yes, they will be. The mire is rich in Encia-infused water. Should any of those soldiers spend too much time wading through it, they will become sick," Harrison confirmed, glancing at his sister and then over to the guardians who were busily trying to recover the wounded and dead from the crater.

"We could send the wardens to help safeguard the people," Morgan suggested, looking over to the men and women who had helped protect the town.

They had willingly committed treason to follow their commander. Harrison believed that the wardens were loyal to Morgan and would continue to do so, regardless of the risk.

"I appreciate the offer, Morgan, but the locals in Pembroke won't know the wardens. It must be the… us," Harrison replied as his rune tingled.

"But the withering will only make them sick, not dangerous," Siljanna remarked. "I don't understand… why would we send warriors instead of healers?"

"Your mother would disagree," Morgan retorted, his tone ominous.

At the mention of their mother, Harrison mind was flooded by the series of events that led to her death, and Siljanna's silence led him to believe that she too was recalling that fateful day. She'd disbelieved Morgan and Harrison for so long about Anora's killer but now, seemed to believe their version of events. That's when Harrison noticed his sister rubbing her eyes fiercely, refusing to let tears fall. It was as though she felt she had no right to weep.

"You're right, the prospect of death can make even a normal person more dangerous than a trained soldier," Dylan submitted, his comment laden with misery.

Harrison didn't know where or when Dylan had experienced such hardship. It was a personal experience they were not privy to, but whatever happened had impacted him deeply, just like Anora's death had affected Harrison, Morgan and Siljanna.

Hushed by the sombre tone their conversation had taken, the four warden graduates realised just how much their lives had changed since their training days at the academy. Looking at each of them, Harrison noticed for the first time how much older they seemed. Older but stronger.

"If only we could access the Imperator's research. She was working on some kind of formula to extract Encia and believed it capable of helping people with the withering," Siljanna began, breaking their silence.

"You mean the Imperator has a cure?" Harrison asked, his warm eyes growing wide in disbelief.

"Not exactly. She aims to strip mages of their abilities so they can rejoin society," Siljanna explained, recalling what now felt like a sales pitch used by Imperator to convince her they were her allies.

"If they weaponize it, could it strip mages by force?" Harrison questioned, his initial surprise quickly replaced with concern.

"Knowing the Imperator, that was probably her true intention all along," Siljanna agreed, looking over to Dylan, certain he knew more but he didn't comment.

"Regardless, if the principal effect is to strip the body of Encia, it could cure the withering and that would be a game changer," Morgan insisted, thinking purely about protecting the people in Pembroke by ensuring any afflicted soldiers were treated.

Looking between themselves, they had to admit, En-glycerol doubling up as a cure was plausible. In their hands, it could be used solely as a curative for people like Queen Nadia, but with no way of infiltrating Siranor to obtain the formula, that was little more than wishful thinking. After a moment, they all turned to Dylan, hopeful he might know something considering all the time he spent as one of the Imperator's private wardens.

"Good luck trying to get your hands on her research," Dylan replied, answering their unspoken question with a despondent tone. "Even as her private guard, I never caught a glimpse of the En-glycerol formula. The only person to ever get that close was Cameron Weiss."

"And he won't be able to help us," Siljanna affirmed.

"Why not?" Dylan asked. "I saw enough subtle looks of admiration to get the impression he cared for Imperator Harlyn in a greater capacity than as just her advisor. Cameron would never betray her but giving the people a cure would make Harlyn a hero. That's something he'd value and would want for her, even if she didn't care for the political benefit."

"Cameron Weiss is dead," Siljanna advised with a shudder. Aeon Rylie had conjured a bolt of lightning, which killed him and she almost suffered the same fate in Jumant Fort.

"I can't believe you forgot to mention that!" Dylan began, exhaling loudly as he processed Cameron's fate and considered the repercussions. "It explains the Imperator's haste to declare war. There were only two people in this world she truly cared for, her uncle Elias and Cameron Weiss."

"Elias Rainer is the man that killed our mother. Good riddance I say," Harrison remarked, his low voice tinged with bitterness.

Siljanna reached out and put a hand on her twin's shoulder. Harrison rarely allowed his emotions to surface, but their mother's murder would always affect him.

"And he had the withering," Morgan added, without any doubt of what he'd witnessed that day.

"Let's tackle one problem at a time, shall we?" Dylan suggested, more calmly than Harrison had expected. "We have soldiers fleeing west that pose a threat to Pembroke and others north, likely returning to Carlisse. They could regroup and send another, even larger strike force."

"And we mustn't forget Caitlin, she is awaiting our word to return to the castle and help her friends," Siljanna reminded. "She saved my life in Jumant Fort, the least I can do is offer her my assistance in her endeavours."

"Then there's the fallen… and the people of Iliria. A lot of good guardians lost their lives tonight and our friend Maia is severely wounded," Harrison added. "Noah also implied that he and the Imperator have offensive plans that we should discuss, Morgan."

"One problem at a time," Morgan repeated lightly, receiving a grateful look from Harrison. "I can instruct the wardens to focus their efforts on helping the Ilirian townsfolk to rebuild. The locals will have seen us defending them so will hopefully welcome our aid. While they do that, we can take some time to talk."

"I'll travel north to find Caitlin and let her know what happened here. Where is her family home?" Siljanna asked, trying to play down her affection for Caitlin, which still came as a welcome surprise to Harrison.

"Her parents own the Driftwood Ranch. I could show it to you on the map," Harrison offered, knowing that the Aegis Guard would likely have one in the base of operations they established.

"I vaguely remember passing it when I first arrived," Dylan confirmed, brushing the longer strands of his hair away from his face. "Let me go with you."

"Thank you, Dylan," Siljanna replied gratefully. They both felt relaxed in each other's company and at the idea of travelling together again. Although the tell was subtle, Harrison noticed.

Once the group headed to the barn that had been converted into a command post, they quickly found a map pinned to the wall. After highlighting the route from Iliria to Revaine, then onwards to the Driftwood Ranch for them, Siljanna and Dylan made some rough sketches and noted the locations where they could stop for supplies. Grabbing a few essentials, they prepared to say their goodbyes to Harrison and Morgan.

"All right then, I'll speak with Alana and ask her to keep watch in Pembroke. She can be our eyes to the west," Harrison continued, passing a flask of water to Siljanna as he always used to during the academy training days. "After that, I'll help the remaining guards take our wounded and dead back... home."

Siljanna cocked her head at the hesitation in Harrison's speech and he could imagine exactly what she was thinking. *Did he stutter because he considered the Ar'encal sanctuary his home now, or was there another reason?* She also examined the new tattoo under his collar and noted that he didn't mention the name of the guardians he now served. He may have openly forgiven her, but she silently accepted that regaining his full trust was going to take more time.

Ready as they could be to go, Siljanna instinctively pulled her brother into a familial embrace.

"Stay safe," she whispered, her voice almost pleading.

"You too. I will see you again," he replied warmly, wrapping his long arms around her easily, his hold steady. He truly believed they would see each other again.

After speaking with Alana, Harrison returned to the town hall to find Nate, Alex, Maia and Rylie. The long rectangular building looked plain but very solid, with heavy doors and a reinforced roof. Once inside, he spotted a small ginger cat on a table under the window. It hissed as he arrived, but Harrison knew the poor thing must've been terrified during the fighting. Crouching down and allowing the cautious creature to investigate him, Harrison chuckled when it decided he was wholly uninteresting and walked away, curling up on a nearby pillow.

Wishing he too could just curl up and forget the world, Harrison left the cat in peace and strode towards the makeshift medical area where he found Rylie and Nate. There were several Aegis Guards in the room too, all with injuries and Maia, who was wrapped in a blanket and sleeping on a small cot. As he approached, he could see she was shivering even though her skin glistened with sweat. Even more concerning was the way her fingertips had turned dark, almost black.

"It's like she has the withering," Rylie pondered aloud as Harrison arrived beside her, placing his arm around her waist. Resting her worried head on his shoulder, she relaxed into him and allowed his sturdy presence to comfort her.

"Is that even possible for an Ar'encal?" Harrison asked, his voice soft, addressing his question to either Rylie or Nate, who looked like a concerned parent as he sat beside Maia.

"I don't know, but whatever's happened is serious," Nate answered quietly, ensuring not to wake Maia. "You were mortally wounded in Carlisse and yet Maia was able to heal you, but when Freya applied equally powerful healing magic to Maia, her symptoms shifted for a minute but then returned as severe as they were before she'd been healed."

At the mention of her name, Harrison noticed the artisan, Freya, who also helped him to create Rylie's amulet was tending to the wounded. Every so often, she glanced towards the door, waiting for someone. A moment later her prayers were answered as the heavy doors opened and Alex entered, but he was alone and wore an expression of deep sorrow. Breaking away from the group, Rylie went over to him and offered a friendly embrace, which he tentatively accepted.

"I couldn't find them," he admitted, his voice muffled as he buried his face into Rylie's shoulder.

"Don't blame yourself, Alex," she replied. Although she was worried about the young boy Juliette had kidnapped, Rylie wanted to reassure Alex too. He really had done all he could.

"Freya is going to be devastated," he continued, turning his gaze to the Ar'encal who was trying to focus on the triage situation.

"Do you want me to tell her?" Rylie asked, brushing Alex's messy hair, just like she would for her sister whenever Evie felt distressed. She didn't know Freya but at just fifteen, delivering such news was a heavy burden for Alex to bear.

"No, I'll tell her," he replied, moving out from her embrace and towards the Ar'encal healer.

Reaching Freya, Alex spoke softly, delivering the devastating news while placing a comforting hand on her arm. Freya cried out, falling to her knees as the confirmation that her son was gone sunk in. Rylie shivered with pride and sorrow as she watched Alex embrace the woman and allow her to cry. *When had he become so mature?*

Shortly afterwards, Freya released Alex and encouraged him to leave. She clearly needed time to process her grief, so he rejoined Rylie, Harrison and Nate around Maia's cot. Nate stood, allowing Alex to take his chair, which he gratefully accepted. With a deep breath,

Alex let his head slump into his hands. Facing them again, he forced a steady smile and tried to act as though they believed he was okay.

"We need to get these people back to Arencia," he began, trying to suppress the flood of emotions threatening to overwhelm him.

"Let's start by finding transport for the wounded," Harrison replied, reading exactly how Alex felt and knowing that focusing on a task would help more than any counselling.

"When I was outside, I spotted several carts and a carriage full of supplies. I think Zack must've sent them for us. We can leave the supplies here and use the carts to carry the wounded. There should be some extra tack for the horses in the barn we occupied before the fighting began too," Alex suggested.

"Great idea," Harrison acknowledged, immensely proud of Alex's resilience.

"I'll help get everything ready," Nate offered and strode purposefully from the hall. Deep down, he probably wanted to escape the smell of blood and the sound of tears. Although he'd proven himself an able arbalist, he was a passive man at heart.

"Did either of you see what happened to Maia? It could help the Ar'encal to heal her," Harrison enquired, his expression gentle as he looked between Rylie and Alex.

"Juliette… she threw something at her when the mage hunters attacked. Maia was defending herself with magic but then suddenly she collapsed. I managed to get her inside but only because—" Alex stuttered, but then choked on his words.

"Lucas died defending you," Harrison said, finishing his sentence before crouching down before the young man. He didn't touch him, but showed Alex that he could lean into him if he needed to.

"Oh Alex, I'm so sorry," Rylie whispered, tugging at a loose curl that had escaped her half-plaited hairstyle. She couldn't help but wonder if things would've turned out differently had Harrison and the others not needed to rescue her. "If only…"

As if reading her mind, Harrison reached up and squeezed her hand, shaking his head ever so slightly.

"If things had unfolded differently, they may have never reached out to the wardens and the Aegis Guard would have risked being overwhelmed while defending Iliria."

Taking solace in his gesture, Rylie then recalled something Juliette had said.

"Before throwing a second vial at poor Maia, Juliette called the solution 'En-glycerol' and boasted that the Imperator created it," she explained while Alex nodded in agreement.

"The Imperator did create it," Harrison began, but his words trailed off.

"Harrison?" Rylie probed, looking at him curiously.

"Siljanna was just telling me of a formula the Imperator created. It's designed to strip Encia from mages and we theorised that it could be a cure for the withering," he began, before turning sharply to Maia and truly assessing her condition. She really did appear to have all the typical symptoms of the fatal illness.

"You think the same substance could do this to Maia?" Alex asked, his voice brimming with concern.

"Perhaps. Encia is part of the Ar'encal and if this En-glycerol is meant to destroy it, this could be the side effect for them," Harrison conceived, his brows deeply furrowed as he inched towards Maia and placed a hand on her leg. Although she was not conscious, the simple gesture stopped her body from trembling momentarily.

"So, Imperator Harlyn's manufactured a weapon that can strip mages of their abilities and weaken the Ar'encal all while acting as a cure for the withering?" Rylie repeated in disbelief. It was impressive and terrifying to think that anyone could create something powerful enough to contend with the planet's natural essence.

"It's just a theory, but it's possible," Harrison confirmed. "The Imperator may not even be fully aware of its effectiveness."

"Where are Morgan and Siljanna now?" Rylie asked, realising that she hadn't seen them since they arrived in Iliria.

"Morgan's over with the wardens by the barricade and Siljanna's gone to the Driftwood Ranch to find Caitlin. They really seemed to connect when we came searching for you. She and Dylan are going to try and protect her and will likely report back to us on anything they see happening around Carlisse," Harrison explained.

"Dylan… he's here?" Rylie asked and Harrison realised that she probably hadn't seen him this whole time.

He'd never mentioned to her that Dylan had joined up with Siljanna and supported her ever since they evaded Rylie in Beyasil. Her emotional state and Aeon powers meant her focus was purely on Siljanna and as a result, she hadn't registered his presence back then or expected he'd return with Siljanna to aid them now. Last she knew, he was still a mage hunter.

"Yes, he's changed a lot recently, but I believe he means to help us now," Harrison affirmed.

"Will they come to Arencia after finding Caitlin?" she asked, worrying at her lower lip.

"No, they aren't aware of Arencia. If they send word, they know to send it to the lodge in Iliria."

Trying to hide her relief, Rylie nodded and gave him a faint smile. She knew as a member of the Aegis Guard, he couldn't tell Siljanna of Arencia but wondered if perhaps he'd told her to meet them at the Crescent Falls or hinted in some other way to the location of their sanctuary, but he hadn't, and she was extremely grateful for that.

Throughout the night, Rylie found herself wishing she believed Siljanna wouldn't betray them again, especially for Harrison's sake, but there was a niggling doubt she couldn't ignore. That feeling did not extend to Morgan, however, who had proven twice now that in their hour of need, he was a true friend and ally.

It was the early hours of the morning by the time they'd treated the wounded as best they could, placed the fallen into transport carts with as much reverence as possible and were ready for the journey back to Arencia. Approaching Harrison with the last bag of supplies for the cart he was loading, Rylie decided to suggest they extend Morgan a special invitation.

"We should bring Morgan with us to Arencia," she whispered.

"Really?" Harrison replied, surprised by how confident Rylie sounded. "Do you think the others would approve?"

"I do. Although only a small number came, the people I've spoken to have all said that the added warden presence gave us hope, and their skill ensured that more of the Aegis Guard, mages and Ar'encal survived," Rylie replied, but quickly noticed that Harrison seemed to have unspoken doubts. "Would you like me to ask the others first? I'm sure Freya could decide on Maia's behalf."

"No, you're right. I don't think anyone would oppose," Harrison muttered, securing the final bag of supplies in the cart without looking at her.

"What's wrong? You're worried about something," Rylie probed. She knew better than anyone that Harrison wasn't great with words, but she could also tell when he needed to get something off his chest.

"Arencia is a haven for us, but knowing about it could become a burden for Morgan," Harrison began, struggling to find the right way to express his concern. "Morgan came here for me but must eventually return to Tivani."

"I know, but why would knowing he has a safe place among us be a burden?" Rylie asked, turning him to face her. She had no doubt his reason would be justified but couldn't comprehend what it might be.

"If the Imperator learns that he aided us, Morgan could be targeted. Without the Arencian rune, if they capture him... if they break him—" Harrison began, but the words cut off in his throat.

"He could reveal our location," Rylie said softly, realising what Harrison was thinking. Pausing for a moment, she contemplated the best way to answer him. Meeting his worried, brown eyes with a look of steady confidence, she continued. "He came here for you despite the danger and I'm certain he always would. I think this knowledge is a burden he'd welcome."

Exhaling a chuckle, Harrison nodded in defeat. Rylie was right. Since meeting at the Warden Academy, he and Morgan had been there for one another. They'd developed a level of trust few friends achieve. Although these were dangerous times, any number of people without the Arencian rune could reveal the Ar'encal's secret location and he agreed that Morgan deserved to know he had a safe place among them.

"He would be thrilled to see Evie and your parents again," Harrison commented, a subtle smile warming the corner of his lips.

That simple expression was enough to tell Rylie she'd alleviated his concern, and he knew it. At the mention of her mother and sister, Rylie's heart skipped a beat.

"I can't wait to get back to them either," she replied, hugging her arms as if the motion would contain her growing anticipation.

"I'm not sure if I'm ready for him to meet Zack though," Harrison said playfully.

"Why?" Rylie asked, her head tilting with innocent curiosity.

"Because Morgan knows too much!" Harrison replied, unable to prevent his grin from widening.

"Oh, and their humour... the jokes will be unbearable! Perhaps we shouldn't invite him," Rylie revoked with a giggle that revealed the dimple on her cheek.

It may have only lasted for a few seconds, but in that time, their greatest concern was enduring a few embarrassing stories shared by an old friend to their newest friends. They knew deep down they would cherish those moments and instantly agreed that Morgan should be allowed to join them.

"I'll finish loading these supplies and meet you by the horses. Will you go and invite *the black diamond* along?" Harrison asked, saying Morgan's old nickname in a humorous tone.

Sputtering out another laugh, Rylie nodded and headed towards their friend to make the offer.

"Hey Morgan, can I borrow you for a minute?"

"Sure, is everything okay?" he replied.

"Oh yes, I just wanted to ask if you wouldn't mind leaving the wardens in Iliria for a while and joining us. There's a place we feel you should see," she began, curling her finger playfully and encouraging him to follow her to the transport wagons.

"A place I should see?" he queried, raising his eyebrows curiously, his eyes gleaming with intrigue.

"You've proven yourself a true ally to the mages, Ar'encal and Aegis Guard. Although we cannot invite all the wardens back with us, as their commander, we'd like to invite you to the place we now call home," Rylie explained, her smile sincere.

"Rylie... I don't know what to say," Morgan stuttered, humbled by the gesture.

"Say yes and join us," Rylie replied, her smile growing.

Returning her expression with a definitive nod, Morgan gratefully accepted and quickly advised the wardens remaining in Iliria that he'd return in a few days.

Chapter Twelve
Reunited

Travelling at a pace best described as a crawl, mainly to keep the wounded comfortable, it took longer than usual to reach the Crescent Falls from Iliria. Morgan was grateful for the steady journey, however, as it allowed him to take in the vivid surroundings they'd rushed past on the way up from Dawne. While relatively dormant around town, the river they followed grew increasingly turbulent as they progressed, and the vegetation became more verdant than he'd ever seen before.

"It's because of the Encia," Freya explained softly, reading his amazed expression easily as she sat in the cart he followed, healing an unconscious guardian.

"I'm sorry?" Morgan stuttered, his focus so absorbed in the beauty of the flora that he barely heard her.

"The Encia causes the trees around here to grow stronger and healthier than anything you're used to seeing. All nature is made stronger when infused with the planet's natural essence," she replied, speaking more clearly as she tucked a blanket over her patient, allowing them to rest as she shifted towards the edge of the cart, closer to Morgan.

He couldn't help but feel a distinct wisdom radiating from the woman before him, even though she looked remarkably young. Her wavy blond hair and light complexion reminded him of Téa, but unlike his friend, Freya's unmistakable nose ridges highlighted her race while her hazel eyes were raw, which Morgan assumed had been caused by so much more than just a sleepless night.

"I've always thought of Encia as toxic. I've seen its effect first-hand," Morgan began, closing his eyes momentarily and grimacing as he pictured the withered face of Anora Stone's murderer. "But these plants are clearly thriving."

"Do you believe in the gods?" Freya asked, her question confusing him.

"What has that got to do with the nature around us?" Morgan queried, remembering only after it was too late that it was rude to answer a question with a question. His mother would've been horrified. Luckily, Freya just laughed and gave him a sweet smile.

"You remind me so very much of a young Zack Harper," she announced, resting her weary head in one hand that she propped up on the edge of the cart. "Have you met him?"

"Who is he?" Morgan asked, making the same mistake again and internally scolding himself.

"As a boy, he was curious. I've never known a kid to ask so many questions or be as easily distracted by shiny things. Now, he's an honourable young man who became a friend to your friends. He led them to Arencia, just as we now lead you," she answered, fondly recalling the memories.

"Arencia... that's the first time I've heard the name of the Ar'encal home. You are understandably secretive though. Thank you for inviting me to your sanctuary," Morgan replied respectfully.

"The Aegis Guard cannot tell you about our home. They are magically sworn to silence," Freya explained, making Morgan feel better about why Harrison hadn't said anything specific. "In return for their sacrifice, our runes protect them from the harmful effects of Encia and therefore, magic."

"Are the Ar'encal all religious?" he wondered aloud, returning to her earlier question.

"Many of us put our faith in the goddess Ceris, mother of the planet," Freya answered, bowing her head in a subtle sign of respect to the goddess she worshipped. "Others devote themselves to one of her seven children, whom we call our deities. Some remain agnostic."

"If the Ar'encal all benefit from Encia, why would any choose not to believe in your goddess?" Morgan pondered, his flurry of questions continuing.

"When we welcomed the human scholars into our home, before the war, we hoped to gain knowledge, and we did. But with knowledge comes scepticism and the thirst for more knowledge," Freya replied, a hint of regret in her tone.

"Were you there when the scholars were welcomed into Arencia?" Morgan asked, his mind reeling at the thought. If she was, it meant she must be at least fifty years old and she barely looked half that.

"I lived during the time we co-existed peacefully. Then the war happened. I lost many friends, both human and Ar'encal," she confirmed as Morgan tried to conceal the shock of her age.

"I'm sorry you lost so many dear to you," he stuttered. Although his words were far from eloquent, they did convey his genuine sympathy.

"Towards the end of the war, I even fell in love with one of the human scholars who supported us. He gave me my beautiful son, Sebastian," she answered, tears welling in her reddened eyes.

"What happened to your son?" Morgan wondered, assuming the worst by her reaction.

"He was taken during the assault last night."

"That's awful," Morgan began, wishing he could say something to console her.

"Luckily his father has already passed, otherwise he would've recklessly gone to find him and likely died in the process," Freya replied, filling Morgan with an even greater sense of sorrow.

"When did your husband pass?" he asked, worrying only after he'd spoken that it could be another recent trauma.

"When Sebastian was very young. He was in Revaine during the mage hunter attack that devastated the town," she began. "Anton was a wonderful man and remarkable intellect, but he couldn't harm a flea. He would never have stood against warriors like the ones who attacked us last night."

"Please extend your faith and place it in Harrison. He is the most honourable man I know and if there's a way to save your son, he'll find it," Morgan replied, filled with certainty and a determination to help find the kind Ar'encal's son. Freya replied with the same sweet smile she had before.

"Said just like Zack would. Honestly, the similarities between your personalities are undeniable," she began, turning her attention back to the guard groaning at the absence of her healing touch. "I am sorry to burden you with my grief."

"Please don't apologise, you are taking me to your home and introducing me to this incredible part of the world," Morgan replied kindly as his horse shook its head a little, aiming to nibble on a nearby bush.

"This is just a glimpse of the beauty you'll find in Arencia. I look forward to seeing your reaction if this simple forest impresses you," Freya chuckled, forgetting her troubles for just a moment.

Finally, their convoy arrived at the magnificent Crescent Falls. The path veered away from the river, but only to end at a grand observation platform at the edge of the waterfall. Morgan dismounted and dashed to the nearest edge. Looking down, he couldn't resist gripping the stone barrier. The water plummeted so far down that the bottom was completely out of sight, disguised by mist. He glanced back at Harrison and Rylie as they joined him on the platform.

"What do you think?" Harrison asked, a wicked smile on his face.

"It's incredible and terrifying," he gulped, glimpsing down the sheer edge of the waterfall again.

"I remember seeing this place for the first time, and I reckon my expression mirrored your current one," Harrison laughed.

"Our friend Zack brought us here after we escaped Carlisse," Rylie added, giving Harrison a playful look that told him to stop laughing, but only because she'd soon join him if he didn't.

"I just heard about this Zack fellow. Sounds like he and I are equally wonderful people," Morgan mused, making Harrison's laughter increase. "So, he brought you here, is this Arencia?"

"Ah so you've learnt the name of this place," Harrison replied.

"I have friends in high places," Morgan jested as he glanced towards Freya.

"You haven't exactly found it though… not yet," Harrison teased.

"It was actually Alex, the young squire over there that discovered the true entrance for us," Rylie noted, looking at Alex who gave them a thumbs up.

Morgan had no idea what silent conversation just happened between them but figured he was about to find out. Before he could ask, Harrison started walking slowly backwards, away from him and towards the open edge of the platform. He smiled as Morgan looked on, his eyes wide as Harrison appeared to step off the edge and disappear.

Blinking rapidly, he tried to process what he'd just seen. His best friend had either just died, or there was some other magic at work.

"I swear he never used to be this theatrical," Rylie commented, rolling her eyes as she headed in the same direction.

"Wait!" Morgan called out, shaking his head but in the blink of an eye, she was gone too.

Peering back over the edge while holding onto the barrier even tighter, Morgan realised that he didn't see Rylie fall, nor did he hear her or Harrison scream. Surely they would've screamed with a drop like that. It was a natural, human instinct when in peril.

"Are you coming? We haven't got all day," called out the distinctly familiar voice of Harrison, seemingly from nowhere.

"You're either incredibly good at throwing your voice or I'm in some delusional form of grief and hearing your voice from beyond the grave," Morgan shouted back, moving very cautiously towards the opening. Spray from the waterfall bounced all around him but somehow, not a single drop landed on his skin.

"Perhaps I've been a ghost this whole time," Harrison mocked, and Morgan could hear his smile.

"You're an ass, you know that?" he replied jovially, creeping ever closer to the edge.

"A dead ass?" Harrison asked, ridicule still lacing his every word.

"If you aren't dead, I can rectify that," Morgan replied wittily, his eyes narrowing into slits as he sceptically tried to make sense of the bizarre situation.

He was able to peer over the edge and just as he'd seen from the safety of the barrier, all that was within his sight was the sheer vertical drop of the waterfall. The power and noise coming from the rushing water beneath his feet was almost deafening but made him wonder, *how can I still hear Harrison so clearly?*

The area around him seemed distorted, which he assumed was caused by the spray and mist from the falls, but no matter how hard he searched, he couldn't find anything that would explain hearing Harrison as if he were mere feet away, when he wasn't there.

"You're so close, Morgan!" Rylie called, her tone encouraging. "Just take another two steps."

"That'd mean walking off the edge of the waterfall… are you serious?" Morgan replied, taking in a deep breath as he found himself amazed he was even considering such a thing.

"Just jump, you'll find something to grab onto," Harrison encouraged, repeating the words Morgan had said to him during their graduation trial in the Wutel Canyon.

Morgan couldn't stifle the laugh and knew he had to trust his former partner. Trying not to overthink it, he closed his eyes and jumped forward with both feet, his arms outstretched hoping to grab onto something while still anticipating a great fall.

Instead, his feet connected with the ground, and he felt a hand reach out to steady him. As his eyes crept open, Harrison shook his hand, still laughing while Rylie rushed forward and hugged him.

"Welcome to Arencia," Harrison announced and then motioned for him to look around.

The first thing Morgan noticed was Harrison's expression. He'd enjoyed that far too much. Next, he turned back to the convoy and saw Alex, the young man they'd mentioned earlier join them with Nate not far behind. Both of them looked at him with joyful expressions while over in the cart, Freya was clapping.

"How is this possible?" Morgan asked, his voice barely audible, but Rylie caught the question.

"It's an illusion. Now that you've passed through it, the magic fades and you can see the truth," she explained. "Look down now and you'll see what I mean."

Releasing him from her embrace, Rylie allowed Morgan to step towards the real edge of the platform and take in the true sight of Arencia. Its graceful buildings dotted along platforms that jutted out from the waterfall were simply breathtaking. As Morgan's eyes went wide, Harrison triggered the rune which made the platform descend and continued to enjoy Morgan's reaction.

Lowering into the waterfall, Morgan was first amazed by the way the water continued to splash around them, but at no point did the harmful liquid land on him. There must have been powerful magic at work because he refused to believe it was merely luck. Turning his focus to the city, Morgan could see the striking architecture of the buildings, the sweeping rooftops and delicate crystalline bridges connecting each platform. Behind one of the higher platforms and its grandiose building, he could see more of the trees he'd seen on the path coming down from Iliria, but these were even taller, their bark glistening with more than just frost. Rubbing his eyes, Morgan could hardly believe that most people would never witness this place and its remarkable beauty.

"This place—" he began but quickly fell speechless.

"Quite something, isn't it?" Harrison acknowledged, knowing exactly how Morgan felt.

"How do you get horses into the city?" he asked, making Harrison chuckle.

"That's your first question?" he replied incredulously, only to receive a shrug and a wonky smile from his friend. With a roll of his eyes, Harrison answered. "Some of the horses will descend on the platform but most are too fearful. They'll be led to another entrance to the southeast… we actually passed it on the way to Iliria. It is concealed but not in quite as stylish a manner."

"Alex and my dad will join us shortly but there should be guards at the base of the platform that can help Maia and the others," Rylie explained, her hands fidgeting as she looked towards the city. Both Morgan and Harrison could tell she was nervous and excited to see her friends and family again.

As the platform came to a halt, just as Rylie had expected, Aegis Guards were patrolling the landing area. Harrison quickly explained Maia's situation and that several other people were injured so they rushed to assist, but not before letting them know that Alister and Evie were in the pavilion. Inhaling deeply, Rylie turned to Harrison and Morgan, the anticipation bubbling out.

"Come with me?" she asked, twisting a lock of her hair anxiously.

"Of course," Morgan replied, but as they followed Rylie towards the pavilion, he leaned over and whispered to Harrison, "who's Alistair?"

"Rylie's grandfather… long story," Harrison whispered back, smirking at Morgan's shocked response.

Sitting on the floor in the pavilion, Evie pulled a disgruntled face as her grandfather approached with yet another random object. He'd been trying to help her conjure specific visions by letting her hold objects that held significance but so far, she'd only seen the inside of her eyelids.

This time, however, Alistair approached her with something instantly familiar, Rylie's favourite dress. The last time she'd seen it was the night she and Harrison finally became a couple, the night which began as her horrific date with Noah.

"But I've already seen that vision, Grandad," Evie protested.

"Which vision are you expecting, my girl?" Alistair countered, holding the dress out to her.

"The moment Harrison and Rylie kissed," Evie replied, still dutifully taking the dress from him.

"Do you remember how she felt at that moment?" Alistair asked, looking at her intently.

"Happy…" Evie answered, although deep down she wasn't sure if that was how Rylie felt in the moment or how she felt when witnessing the vision.

"Come on Evie, you can do better than that," Alistair replied in a tone only a parent and scholar could obtain. "Focus on the dress and uncover how Rylie felt while wearing it."

Doing as instructed, Evie held the dress in both hands and was suddenly washed with the images, but not what she had seen before. This time, she saw Noah screaming at Rylie, followed by her rushing through the forest. The vision showed Rylie catch the dress on a branch and without realising it, Evie ran her finger over the ripped fabric.

"She was angry… mortified."

"Keep going, sweetheart. Chase the vision and discover more," Alistair encouraged, placing a supportive hand on her knee.

Gripping onto the material tighter, Evie followed the images and saw the moment Harrison arrived. Although she couldn't hear what was said, Evie felt how he lifted Rylie's spirit and then saw their dance.

"Now she feels relief and gratitude," she added, a tear of joy rolling down her cheek while she continued to immerse herself in the vision.

"Well done, Evie, that's fantastic. Now focus on that feeling and take yourself away from what you are seeing and search for another moment where Rylie felt that emotion," Alistair instructed.

"Is that possible?" Evie asked with uncertainty, her eyes remaining closed as her mind remained in the vision even though she could hear the real world around her.

"We'll find out together," he replied, placing a small vial of Encia in her free hand, which she assertively drank.

Holding onto those earlier emotions, Evie let the sights and sounds around her slip away. She knew that trying to force visions of specific moments never seemed to work so kept her mind open. Slowly, an image came into focus. It was Rylie standing in a doorway, relief apparent on her face as she looked at a petite girl sitting cross-legged on the floor, her long, wavy hair swaying gently in the breeze.

In an instant, Evie's eyes shot open. It wasn't a moment from the past or the future, it was the present! Scrambling to her feet, Evie turned and there she was, standing just a few feet in front of her. No flames or uncontrolled power, just Rylie, her big sister. Unable to contain herself, Evie launched forward.

"You're here, you're really here!" she cried, tears of joy racing down her cheeks as she collided with her sister.

"And you're all right," Rylie exclaimed as she returned Evie's embrace. "I'm so relieved."

"I know!"

"What?" Rylie replied, bemused but Evie couldn't explain. She was too overjoyed to make coherent sentences but was apparently capable of sobbing and laughing at the same time. Seeing her fumble over her words, Harrison, who was standing with Morgan just behind them couldn't help but laugh.

"Are you tongue-tied, Evie?" he asked, a wide grin on his face.

She stuck her tongue out at him playfully but had to admit that after all the times she'd moaned at him for not telling Rylie how he felt, finding herself lost for words was rather funny.

After another squeeze, Evie released her sister and transferred her embrace to Harrison while Alistair made his way over to his eldest grandchild. Kissing her lightly on the forehead, he closed his eyes and thanked the gods they were able to save her. He'd given up his family once and refused to do so again.

When Nate and Alex joined them, Evie could barely contain her excitement. She rushed over to Alex first, running into his arms so quickly that she almost knocked him over.

"You're back!" she blurted out, her rosy cheeks glowing almost as much as her dampened eyes.

Her joyous expression illuminated her face as she muttered incoherent praise for the safe return of her loved ones. Accepting her into his arms, Alex smiled softly but Evie quickly realised he was not himself. He felt heavier somehow but rather than pulling away, she took his weight and let him rest on her shoulder.

"Evie…" Alex muttered, burying his head into her shoulder.

"What happened?" she whispered, but when Alex remained silent, Evie just continued to hold him.

"Do I get a hug, kiddo?" Nate asked, coming towards his daughter but doing nothing to break her contact with Alex.

Reaching a hand out to her father, Nate linked fingers with his youngest daughter and instinctively brushed his free hand over her hair, the reassuring gesture he'd always done when she used to have her seizures.

"What happened in Iliria?" Alistair asked, looking for anyone to respond to Evie's last question.

"The people are fine, we got there in time," Morgan began.

"The wardens really helped us to fight back the attackers from Carlisse," Harrison continued, placing a grateful hand on Morgan's shoulder.

"But?" Evie asked, knowing there had to be a 'but'.

"Where are Maia and Lucas?" Alistair added, concern filling his chest. "What about Teagan and Freya too? I assumed they'd return with you."

"Teagan sacrificed himself to protect the town and Maia was hurt during the attack," Harrison began, knowing that what they had to say next would be even more upsetting.

"Freya is tending to Maia now, but her son, Sebastian was kidnapped as Noah and Juliette fled," Rylie continued, not wanting Alex to feel responsible for breaking the news.

Alistair reacted instantly and was clearly distraught. He'd been living among the Ar'encal for decades and in that time, had become close friends with many of them.

"I can't believe Teagan's gone… and poor Freya," he began, but let his words trail off as he registered that Maia was injured and quickly became distressed. "What happened to Maia, is she going to be okay?"

"Freya mentioned that her condition shifts but currently she's stable. They're heading to the infirmary now," Nate replied, trying to reassure his father who nodded in gratitude.

Maia had been extremely close to Alistair's wife, Emilia and a good friend when she died. When he'd struggled to mourn her loss, Maia helped him through that difficult time, becoming one of his most valued friends in the process.

"How did she get hurt? Where was Lucas?" Alistair challenged, folding his arms in mild frustration that the guard captain hadn't done a better job of protecting his primary charge.

"Lucas…" Alex mumbled, his voice cracking.

"Yes, Captain Harper. Where is he? Why didn't he protect Maia?" Alistair pressed, his frustration growing.

"He did!" Alex cried, the tremble in his voice travelling down his entire body.

Standing with his arms loosely wrapped around Evie, allowing her to hold him upright, Alex turned away from Alistair. He'd been able to stay strong in front of the wounded and other guardians, but now, in the safety of Arencia and supported by his closest friends, he crumbled.

"Where is he, Alex?" Alistair asked again, his voice significantly softer than it had been a moment ago.

"Captain Harper is—"

As Alex choked on his mentor's name, Alistair and Evie both knew something awful had happened. With a surge of worry for her friend, Evie cuddled Alex even tighter. She wanted him to know it was okay not to speak.

"Lucas was killed during the skirmish," Harrison explained, taking the burden away from Alex.

"He died saving Maia and Alex," Rylie added, her eyes falling to the floor as she spoke.

"Where's Zack?" Harrison asked, knowing that somehow, they had to break the news to him too.

Harrison told Evie when she was younger and struggling to deal with what she claimed were nightmares that he believed that when bad things happen to good people, it's because they can grow after suffering from adversity. Zack had suffered far more than his fair share though, and this loss would hit him hard. She knew he'd need the support of all his friends to get through it.

"I'll get him," Alistair offered, looking ashamed about his earlier outburst. He should've known he would've protected Maia with his life. "I believe he's having another piano lesson with Paige. Lianna will almost certainly be with them."

Chapter Thirteen
Insight

As they waited for the others, Nate remained with his daughters and Alex inside the pavilion. Keeping one arm wrapped around the small of Rylie's back, her father's touch seemed to be the only thing keeping her anticipation in check while Evie was still consoling Alex.

Paige was the first to arrive and as soon as she laid eyes on her children and husband together, she couldn't hold back the tears. Covering her face with her hands, she exhaled deeply before running over, taking her eldest daughter tightly in her arms, then extending one arm out for Evie to join the embrace. Finally, Nate wrapped his much larger arms around all of them and they took a moment just to be a family for the first time since the fire in Tivani.

Shortly behind Paige were Alistair, Zack and Lianna. As soon as Rylie noticed them, she rushed over and hugged Lianna who squeaked in a combination of excitement and relief. How she was able to process all the emotions going through the room right now, Rylie would never know. Finally, Rylie turned to Zack. The cane in his hand and dark glasses covering his eyes confirmed what Harrison had told her.

"Oh Zack," she murmured, reaching out but unsure if she should touch him.

"Rylie, unless you're on fire, get over here and give me a hug!" Zack insisted, his arms open wide. Unable to resist, she went straight to him but carefully placed her arms around his neck.

"I'm not on fire," she replied playfully, and he chuckled at the comment, pulling her in tighter as she scruffled his spiky hair.

"Oh, it's so good *not* to see you!" Zack exclaimed, and although his eyes were shielded, she just knew that he winked cheekily while delivering the comment.

"A blind joke already?" Lianna chided but was unable to maintain a serious expression.

"He can tease to his heart's content," Rylie said, knowing that deflecting concern with humour helped him to relax.

"I'd rather we all laugh than cry any day," Zack added honestly, shrugging his shoulders innocently.

"And we wouldn't have you any other way," Rylie affirmed.

After a brief spell of light banter, Harrison and Morgan, who had stepped outside, returned. Proving how quickly their friendship had solidified, Harrison didn't need to say anything as he approached. Reaching out to place a sturdy hand on his shoulder, Zack mirrored his greeting perfectly.

"Welcome home my friend. Does that mean everyone else is back… where's my father?"

Alex took in a sharp breath at the mention of Captain Harper and the whole room seemed to go perfectly still, Zack's question hanging in the air.

"Such sadness and dread," Lianna whispered, looking around her friends.

"What happened?" Zack pleaded, his tone dire compared to the moment before. "Please, someone talk to me."

With his disability, Zack couldn't read his companions' faces as he always used to be able to do so well. He could, however, hear their breaths catch on words they needed to say.

"Zack, your father was killed in Iliria," Harrison replied, keeping hold of Zack's shoulder as the news made his friend's entire body go rigid. "I'm so sorry."

"He died saving me and Maia," Alex blurted out. Rylie knew how bad Alex felt but couldn't take her eyes off Zack. Dipping his head, he leant into Harrison's sturdy touch and trembled ever so slightly.

"How did it happen?" Zack muttered, his question mechanical. He didn't want to know, but he needed to know.

Harrison sucked in a deep breath, about to inform his friend that he wasn't there when Lucas was struck down but before he could, Alex approached. Zack heard the footsteps across the stone floor and turned towards the sound.

"Maia was hurt in the battle by the mage hunters, who were being led by Noah. I called Captain Harper over to protect us," Alex began, trying his best to keep his voice steady. "I'm so sorry! If I hadn't called him over, he'd still be alive."

"But then you and Maia could've died," Zack replied, surprised at the way Alex seemed to blame himself.

"Captain Harper protected us while I took Maia back to the shelter but when I went back to help him, I froze. I couldn't move until after I saw him fall," Alex recalled, finally expressing why he felt so guilty.

"Noah is a ruthless fighter and will torment your body *and* mind given the chance. He spent years convincing me I was inferior... a failure. Don't blame yourself for his cruelty."

"He instructed that wretched mage hunter women to kill Captain Harper. He wanted her to strike him down and as she did, he just watched with the most sickening grin on his face," Alex continued.

"Are you talking about Juliette, the one we chased to the town hall?" Rylie asked, recalling the way she severed the whip Juliette wielded and then imagined how she must've used it to kill Lucas just moments before they arrived.

"Yes, *her*," Alex hissed.

"She's the one that attacked Lianna in Carlisse, the one that did this to me," Zack revealed, his voice growling.

"She has a lot to answer for," Rylie asserted, her frustration equally notable. *If only I'd tried to use magic when we fought. I could've rid the world of Juliette's evil.*

"She will," Zack responded, his tone steadying as he took in several, long breaths. "Noah killed my father… Juliette was just his weapon. I refuse to let him break your spirit again. Don't let him break yours either."

"Do you want to know how he died?" Alex asked nervously.

"I'd rather remember him as the strong and proud warrior he became, rather than what my brother reduced him to in his final moments," Zack replied, in between laboured breaths.

"Like the wardens, the Aegis Guard swear to protect people. But that promise may come at a price," Harrison added solemnly. "Lucas Harper died a hero, and we'll all remember him that way."

"Sometimes surviving is the hardest part," Lianna said quietly, reaching her brother and putting an arm around him.

Hearing Zack say 'inferior' reminded Harrison of his own confrontation with Noah. He'd used that exact term which proved that despite hating him, Zack knew his brother to the core. It also alerted him to the fact he hadn't spoken to Morgan about Noah's threat against Tivani. Deciding it wasn't the right time to raise the subject, he told himself to bring it up after they'd had time to decompress.

"Will there be a funeral?" he asked.

"There's an Ar'encal tradition. A vigil to honour the fallen as we send their souls to the Idyll Sanctuary," Zack replied softly.

"Where?" Alex questioned, his brows raising curiously.

"It's where we believe the souls of the fallen go after death," Zack began, a sad smile forming on his lips. "If there's any truth to the fables, the Idyll Sanctuary is the true heart of the planet and where the goddess Ceris retreated to after leaving the world to her descendants. Many of the Ar'encal deities returned there after their lives were complete too. Knowing there is a haven for people with good souls remains a comfort to the rest of us."

"Do you believe your mother is there?" Lianna asked, a tear running down her cheek.

"Yes. The very least I can do is reunite my parents by honouring my father with a vigil."

"Many guardians lost their lives defending against the Royal Military... Tegan too," Harrison advised, remembering the sight of all the dead soldiers on the roadside after the battle. "We'll honour them all."

"I've only ever seen one vigil before, the one for my mother... if only I could see this one too," Zack mumbled, his heart heavy with grief.

"There might be..." Evie began, her eyes turning to a dark honey shade as an idea struck her. Glancing at Lianna, a wide smile soon spread across her petite face.

"Oh, that could work," Lianna quickly replied, proving she had caught on to Evie's idea.

"We'll need to get some things," Evie hinted as she and Lianna receded into a private conversation.

"Okay... while those two concoct their ingenious plan, isn't there someone we need to introduce?" Rylie asked rhetorically, looking at Harrison with her eyebrows raised.

Morgan had been there the whole time, standing quietly in the background and just smiled as Harrison turned, remembering him for the first time since the reunion began.

"Oh right, of course! Everyone, I'd like you to meet warden commander, Morgan Foster," Harrison introduced, managing to say Morgan's title with a perfect balance of reverence and ridicule.

"Best friend and former partner, Morgan Foster?" Zack asked, recalling his name from the stories Harrison had shared with him during their travels.

"For my sins," Morgan replied, chuckling wickedly.

"If it wasn't for Morgan, we may never have escaped Tivani. He's the unsung hero of our tale," Rylie explained, her expression conveying the deep gratitude she felt.

"Oh, so he's the hero now?" Harrison retorted humorously, looking over his shoulder to Rylie who tried to innocently deflect his comment.

"Of course not, everyone knows that's me," Zack butted in, causing the entire group to laugh for the first time.

"I was informed you and I would get on, Zack," Morgan announced, striding over and taking Zack's hand, shaking it in a firm but friendly manner. "My informant was clearly correct."

"Oh gods, spare me," Harrison muttered in jest, covering his face with his hands.

After a few moments of mutual teasing, Harrison quickly suggested that they continue to show Morgan around Arencia. Together, they visited the rest of the pavilion, the artisan's forge where Harrison had helped to create the magically infused armour they all wore and Lake Baliten before crossing the series of crystalline bridges to reach the base of the waterfall and the area they now called home.

Along the way, Evie pointed out the path towards the Maiden Falls, making sure to inform Morgan that her premonition helped Harrison to find Rylie there and led to him finally telling her how he felt. She was rewarded with a playful embrace and hair ruffling, which wasn't quite the praise she wanted. Their final stop was the Aegis Guard training grounds and infirmary. Alistair broke off from the group early to go and check in on Maia while the rest of them enjoyed Morgan's reaction to the impressive facilities.

"This place is unbelievable. No wonder the Ar'encal want to keep it a secret," Morgan uttered, his expectations completely blown away.

"It's more of a need than a want. When being chased by military forces and mage hunters, this place is quite the safe haven," Harrison replied.

"And this is where you bested Zack's brother and earned the right to become an Aegis Guard?" Morgan asked.

"Best moment of my life," Zack hastened to add.

"Sounds like you put on a good show," Morgan chuckled, remembering their trials at the academy and his own sparring sessions with Harrison.

"Not even close. Noah's hubris defeated him before I even raised my weapon," Harrison replied, his original duel with Noah not being anywhere near as honourable or challenging as the sparring sessions he and Morgan used to have.

"Morgan, have you ever defeated Harrison?" Alex asked.

"Yes, I have!" Morgan declared, his pearly white teeth shining as he shot a wicked grin towards Harrison.

"Once," Harrison opposed with a grin, folding his arms in a highly defensive posture.

"That's still a defeat," Morgan countered, his smile broadening.

"No way!" Alex gasped, his eyes twinkling as he looked towards Morgan with newfound admiration. "Will you stay and become an Aegis Guard too?"

"I can't stay, but I can promise that the Aegis Guards have my support, and that of all the wardens under my command," Morgan replied earnestly. "Together, we'll be a force to be reckoned with."

"Thank you, Morgan. I have no doubt your support will make all the difference," Rylie added sincerely.

Doubling back to the infirmary, Harrison opened the door and let the others enter ahead of him.

"And that my friend, ends your tour," he said to Morgan. "Our last stop is the infirmary, as I'd like to introduce you to Maia Uriel. She's the leader of the Ar'encal but was badly wounded in Iliria. We can all check on her and ask about the vigil at the same time."

The infirmary was noisier than usual with healers rushing between the scattered beds, aiding the wounded. Only a few of the survivors had serious injuries so the group quickly gathered the commotion around one particular room was where they'd find Maia. Their suspicions were quickly confirmed when they saw Alistair leaning on the curved door frame and looking into the room, biting his nails anxiously.

"Alistair, what's going on?" Alex asked, trying to peer past all the healers hurrying to and fro.

"Freya and some of the others are trying to heal Maia again. It's their fourth attempt," he mumbled in response.

"What happened to her?" Zack asked, quietly hoping that someone could explain what she was going through.

"She was cornered by the mage hunters and that Juliette woman threw something at her," Alex explained. "Rylie, what did she call the solution?"

"En-glycerol. Apparently, the Imperator created it to strip mages of their powers," Rylie answered, her tone filled with contempt.

"Well, its effect on the Ar'encal is quite different. Maia still has her powers but she's incredibly weak. As soon as they stop healing her, the fatigue comes back, then the shadows and blackened fingertips," Alistair replied, his concern undeniable.

"It's just like the withering," Morgan replied, using his height advantage to peer over the others and see Maia being tended to in the room beyond.

"You're right," Alistair replied, his eyes not wavering from Maia. "She can survive this condition but will need daily healing."

"Just like Queen Nadia," Lianna added, looking around the group as they all remembered her situation and the way Spencer would regularly heal her, not just from the abuse of the king, but from her self-inflicted condition.

"You said there is no cure, right?" Harrison asked, aiming the question at Alistair and recalling the queen's hope for salvation.

"When I was a royal advisor in Carlisse, I read theories on the withering and Encia's toxicity to humans, but even with my years among the Ar'encal, I've never found a cure," Alistair confirmed, repeating his earlier confession that he did not know of a way to help Nadia.

"That's so heartbreaking," Lianna said, dropping her head in disappointment. "The exhaustion I felt from her and Spencer in just that brief encounter was crippling, yet they've endured it for years."

"With everything else going on, the thought of finding a cure slipped my mind," Harrison admitted.

"Mine too," Lianna replied, a tear running down her cheek as the bombardment of emotions from around the room impacted her.

Falling silent, the group watched on, Freya and the other Ar'encal finished their healing chants over Maia, who slowly sat herself up in the bed, allowing her back and head to rest against the sturdy wooden headboard. Her feathered hair was ragged, but she looked better than before.

"Thank you, all of you," she whispered to the healers.

"It's the least we can do, Maia. Do you feel strong enough to continue healing yourself? This ailment is persistent, it's going to take some study to find out if and how we can cure you fully," Freya explained, her extreme tiredness evident in her tone.

"I believe so, but I know you aren't far if I need help," Maia replied gratefully. "Please, get some rest my friend."

"I will, and in the meantime, you have visitors," Freya announced, dipping her head in the direction of the door and the group huddled around it.

With a soft smile that was still laden with worry for her own son, Freya and the other Ar'encal departed, allowing the rest of the group to enter. Lianna pulled up some chairs and led Zack to a seat beside Maia. Alistair and Alex grabbed the other seats while the rest of the group stood huddled around the end of Maia's bed. The first person she noticed, however, was Rylie, who she reached out to instantly. Although her fingertips were grey and she had the slightest tremble, Rylie didn't hesitate to take Maia's outstretched hand in her own.

"It's so good to have you back with us, Rylie. I see the amulet worked," Maia greeted warmly.

"Harrison mentioned how you and the artisans helped him to create this amulet for me. I don't even know how I can truly thank you," Rylie replied sincerely, squeezing ever so gently.

"All I ask is for you to make me a promise," Maia began.

"Anything."

"Take some time to study your elemental powers and the deity, Talia. Your Aeon form took hold when you were overly emotional, but that power is still within you. Just imagine what you could do if you learnt to control it," she hinted.

Maia had quickly proven with the water display on Lake Baliten that Rylie could control her magic and clearly believed she could achieve so much more.

"If you'll help me, I'll try," Rylie promised with a resolute nod. Giving her hand another squeeze, Maia silently told Rylie she had a deal before turning her attention towards Alex.

"Alex, I'm so glad to see you safe. The last thing I remember before falling in Iliria was you rushing to my aid," Maia admitted, causing Alex to blush.

"I didn't get hurt, but others did. Teagan and Lucas are both…" Alex began, a lump catching in his throat.

"Gone," Maia whispered, her empathic traits telling her what Alex failed to say. Somehow sensing that she was reaching for him, Zack edged closer and smiled wearily as her hands covered his. "I'm so sorry."

"Thank you. Will there be a vigil for them and all the other fallen?" Zack asked quietly.

"Of course, I'll make the arrangements," Maia affirmed, attempting to get out of her bed.

"Absolutely not. You'll rest Maia. I can handle the arrangements for the vigil," Alistair instructed. Although his tone was stern, his expression was kind.

"Thank you, Alistair."

For a moment, her eyes clamped shut as a shooting pain seemed to travel through her arm. Once it passed, she glanced at the only face among them she didn't recognise and then at Harrison.

"Are you going to introduce me?" she asked, not giving them a chance to fuss over her condition.

"Oh, of course! Maia Uriel, this is my good friend Morgan Foster, warden commander from Tivani," Harrison replied.

"It's an honour to be welcomed into your home," Morgan added politely.

"You came to save us in a very dark hour, the honour is mine," Maia insisted in a soft tone. "How did the wardens' fare in the battle?"

"They supported the Aegis Guard at the barricade," Morgan explained. "Sadly, we lost one warden, a young man called Quinn, but most only had minor injuries. They all offered to stay and help repair the damages around town."

"Is that Elijah's nephew?" Harrison asked, to which Morgan confirmed with a sombre nod.

"I'll be sure to inform his family when I return to Tivani."

"We can honour Quinn in the vigil tonight, if you'd like to," Maia offered.

"That's very kind. He was one of the first to volunteer for this mission and I think being remembered during your memorial is something he would've wanted," Morgan confirmed, his eyes lowering as he thought of the eager young man whose life had been cut tragically short.

"It's settled then. The vigil will begin after sunset on Lake Baliten," Alistair said. "Please excuse me, I had better start making the arrangements."

As Alistair departed, Evie quickly turned towards Lianna, the earlier mischievous smile returning to her face.

"Can I borrow you now?" she asked, grabbing her friend by the hand and whisking her from the room without giving her any chance to oppose.

With a look of curiosity, Rylie waved a swift goodbye to Maia and the others, chasing after her sister and friend.

"They're your children," Nate teased, aiming the comment at his wife, a wide grin on his face.

"Ha! They take after you more than me, Mr Auren," Paige replied in jest, slapping his arm, and Nate couldn't deny it.

"You guys haven't changed a bit," Morgan laughed, enjoying how familiar it was to be with both Harrison and the Auren family again.

Harrison almost forgot that when Morgan decided to move to Tivani, he rented a room at the Hawk Eye tavern for a while, until he found an affordable home of his own, but in that short time had become quite close to Nate and Paige Auren.

"I'm sure our lives used to be more normal," Nate commented.

"I definitely don't recall you guys being normal," Harrison added with a wicked grin.

"The cheek!" Nate cried, pretending to be insulted.

"How about we all go and make ourselves useful for the vigil tonight and let Maia get some rest?" Paige suggested, cheerfully hustling the remaining members of the group out of her room.

With an almost imperceptible sigh, Maia allowed her tired body to slink into the bed. With her fingers above the quilt, she gave a gentle wave to each of them as they departed, and then allowed herself to get some rest.

Harrison still struggled to believe how a woman who looked younger than him could be as mature and resilient as Maia had proven to be, but even with all her supernatural powers, she needed rest to withstand the twisted form of the withering coursing through her system.

"Please don't let me miss the vigil," Maia requested, her voice hushed as she drifted off.

"Of course not, we'll send someone for you at sundown," Harrison replied softly, closing the door behind him.

Having rushed from the infirmary to the pavilion and now on their way to Lake Baliten, Rylie was almost out of breath trying to keep up with Evie and Lianna.

"Are you two going to tell me what you're plotting and why we needed these vials of Encia from Maia's office?" she asked in between heavy breaths.

"It's for Zack!" Lianna called back with a giggle, her hand still locked with Evie's as the younger girl strode with purpose towards the lake.

"We have to get there before the others," Evie insisted, her pace quickening further.

"But why?" Rylie questioned, her pitch rising in confusion.

"I can't be distracted if I'm going to see it," Evie replied, her words providing absolutely no explanation.

"See what?" Rylie shouted back, not feeling frustrated in any way, but her curiosity reaching a whole new level.

"You'll see," Evie answered enigmatically.

As they made it to the shore of Lake Baliten, there was no wind circling within the sheltered glen, which in turn made the water so still it could've been mistaken for a sheet of glass. In the distance, Rylie caught a glimpse of the Ar'encal bringing the bodies of the fallen and placing them in ceremonial caskets. They were too far away to recognise anyone, but she could instantly spot the garb of the fallen warden, the pale grey armour with its steaks of black and gold unique among the dead.

By the time Rylie looked back towards her sister, Evie was standing in the water, wiggling her bare toes under the surface. With a shiver, she steadied her breathing, and a premonition came. She wanted it, welcomed it, and allowed the images to wash over her while the water itself rippled around her feet.

"I've never seen her so in control," Rylie whispered aloud, a pang of pride swelling her heart.

"She's incredibly determined," Lianna agreed, placing a hand over her heart. "If her idea works, it'll mean so much to Zack."

"What exactly is this grand idea?" Rylie asked again, keeping her voice low. She glanced at her sister who, despite having gentle tears running down her cheeks, did nothing to break contact with the water.

"She wanted to conjure a vision of tonight's ceremony. We don't know what's involved but it was clearly important to Zack," Lianna began, her warm skin tone masking the blush in her cheeks as she mentioned Zack.

"Okay, but why is one of her visions going to mean a lot to Zack?" Rylie asked, still confused.

"If she can see what will happen tonight, I channel her vision to Zack when the ceremony starts, so it'll be as if he were watching it too," Lianna explained.

"You can do that?" Rylie asked, her eyes wide in amazement.

"It's how I got the message to you about Siljanna," Lianna advised, her expression determined.

"That was you two?"

"The vision was technically Alistair's, but the process inspired Evie, and I truly believe she can do this," Lianna replied, her smile pure as she glanced at the Encia vials that Rylie still held. "The challenge with connecting to you was the distance whereas this time, it'll be the length of time. That's why we grabbed the Encia, just in case I need a boost to stabilise the connection with Zack during the channelling."

"You and Zack already seem a lot closer than before."

"It's strange but ever since he lost his sight, I've been able to see who he really is," Lianna admitted sheepishly.

"I'm glad… he really fell hard for you," Rylie replied, fondly recalling her conversation with Zack in the barn at Driftwood.

"He's so much more genuine than I ever realised," Lianna professed, knowing it'd taken her far too long to notice.

"And she finally gets it!" Rylie declared, throwing her arms up in celebration. "Better late than never."

As Lianna hid her face in her hands, they both laughed at the situation. Everyone knew how oblivious Rylie could be when it came to romantic matters, but Lianna didn't have that excuse, especially not with her empathic powers. Granted, Zack had come on too strong when they first met, but if Rylie could tell his feelings for her were genuine, she had every right to tease Lianna for not realising sooner.

"It may be too late for me and Zack to be anything more than friends though," Lianna mumbled, peering out from between her fingers.

"Do you want to be more than friends?" Rylie asked, the anticipation behind her words palpable.

"I don't know… maybe," Lianna mumbled, biting on her nails as she spoke and trying not to laugh at Rylie's dramatic eye roll.

Just as Lianna was about to continue revealing her uncertain feelings, Evie gasped, pulling both of their attention back to the present. She stumbled backwards out of the water before landing softly on the grass bank. When Evie's eyes opened, tears ran down her face, but her expression was sheer amazement.

"What did you see?" Rylie asked, kneeling beside her sister, Lianna not far behind.

"The vigil tonight, I've never seen anything like it. We have to make this plan work. Zack needs to see this," Evie replied, wiping away the tears.

"He will, we'll make sure of it," Lianna replied.

Chapter Fourteen
Vigil

Once the sky turned dark, it was time for everyone to gather at Lake Baliten. Crossing over the meandering bridges from their homes, guided by the soft glow of crystalline lights and luminescent water, the group approached the shoreline. A crowd of mourners had already gathered, openly weeping for lost loved ones, friends and comrades while on the far side of the lake, Maia and Alistair could be seen coordinating dozens of caskets, each being placed into simple wooden boats.

The boats were each wrapped in vines that had begun to flower, flourishing thanks to the infusion of Encia. Dressed in the same traditional garb they wore when Harrison and the others first arrived, Maia, Alistair and the Ar'encal seemed to blend into the surrounding nature. Their robes were unique, tailored to suit the wearer, but there was an undeniable synergy between them and the forest.

Taking Zack by the hand, Evie softly pulled him towards the shoreline, knowing Lianna and the others would not be far behind.

"Why are you taking me lakeside?" Zack enquired earnestly. "I don't need to be in front of everyone else."

"Trust us," Lianna whispered cryptically, gently pushing him forward.

Once the last casket was ready, Evie removed her shoes, slipping her bare feet into the chilly water, one hand still interlocked with Zack's and reaching out the other to Lianna.

"It's about to begin," Evie announced excitedly. As she spoke, she could feel Zack tense up slightly.

"Zack, close your eyes," Lianna instructed, gently brushing her hand over his face before taking hold of his other hand, connecting them in a small triangle.

Although he didn't understand, Zack obeyed and tried to steady his breathing. Within a few seconds, an image began to flicker, like a dream trying to pierce through the subconscious and eventually filled his mind's eye. The image of Lake Baliten, the mourners and the burial boats took Zack's breath away. Not only because of the emotional significance but the simple fact he could see the sight that would be before him now, had he not been blind. His other senses were still heightened, and he could hear the sobbing of a nearby family, but it was *seeing it* that meant the most.

He tried to focus his attention on the caskets, one of which held the body of his father, but the vision panned towards Maia. Watching as she pressed her hands together and began softly chanting, Zack was engulfed by the moment. As the onlookers around him fell silent, the Ar'encal beside Maia telekinetically pushed the boats into the water. Gliding to the centre of the lake, Encia trailing gracefully in their wake, Zack caught a glimpse of a group of Aegis Guards, including Parker, who stood on the opposite shoreline.

Each of them held bows, and once the boats were in place, they fired. In mid-air, the arrows erupted into flame and connected with their intended targets. Struck by the fiery smell as the caskets burned, Zack heard more of the Ar'encal mirror Maia's chant, allowing her to call out the names of the fallen. She notably paused before saying *Lucas Harper,* and when she did, it was as though his name lingered in the air. During his time as captain, Lucas had helped hundreds of people, so his loss was felt not just by Zack and those who called Lucas a friend, but by everyone in Arencia.

After reading each name aloud, including the young warden, Quinn Ashby, the collective voices of the chanting Ar'encal grew louder. When the flames reached the purified Encia scattered along the rim of each burial boat, the heat reacted with the water which evaporated while the glistening bioluminescent Encia remained. The vapours then turned into wisps of light and rose into the sky.

"Let their souls ascend," Zack muttered, as a tear escaped down his cheek. Instinctively, he squeezed Lianna's hand ever so slightly, and she felt that even such a simple touch gave him comfort, but it wasn't enough to mask the grief as he mourned.

As dozens of wisps swirled around the boats, Lianna did everything she could to focus on Zack. Only Zack. It would be so easy to be overwhelmed by the sadness surrounding her, but Lianna knew if she lost her concentration, Zack would lose this chance to see and feel the vigil as it happened, and she wouldn't take that from him. Breathing deeply, Lianna recalled their trip to Lorvale. It was during that trip she realised just how caring a person Zack is. It took years of enduring hostility from his brother before he finally abandoned his home, but even then, he did everything he could to honour his parents under the guise of the mage smuggler.

Sparing a glance over her shoulder, Lianna could see the wisps of energy intertwining with one another, illuminating the dark sky before cascading like snowflakes onto the surface of the lake. When the scene went quiet, Zack released Lianna and Evie's hands and opened his clouded eyes.

"Thank you, both of you," he breathed, the utter sincerity of his words palpable.

As Zack released her, Lianna turned to find her brother. He'd also developed a strong bond with Lucas, and she knew the vigil would've been difficult for him too. When she spotted Alex, she was grateful to see that Harrison had placed an arm around her brother and supported him during the ceremony, with Rylie tucked under his other arm and her parents close behind.

When Harrison turned and saw her looking on, Lianna mouthed a *thank you* to him before returning to Zack's side.

"I think it's over," she said quietly, linking her arm with his to guide him away from the lake.

"Oh, the ceremony is over, but the vigil tradition is to stay up until dawn, celebrating the lives of those we've lost. I'd like to do that for Dad… will you and the others join me?" Zack asked, his tone hopeful.

Rather than responding, Lianna placed Zack's hand on her cheek so he could feel her expression and the joy his request brought her. As his fingers traced her smile, which travelled from her eyes all the way to her lips, his grateful nod confirmed he knew they'd all share this time with him.

Arriving back at the landing of their stilted homes, everyone gathered at Nate and Paige's house. To no one's surprise, Paige had prepared some nibbles and Nate was behind the breakfast bar offering drinks. He didn't have the same array that used to be available at the Hawk Eye tavern, but the scene was both familiar and comforting, especially to Harrison.

Moving from the kitchen into the living room, Zack made his way to the piano and started playing a soft but joyful tune while Harrison took a seat beside him, seeming to enjoy how much better this approach was compared to his mother's funeral, where everyone cried for the entire day and barely spoke about her or to each other.

With everyone together and music playing, Nate reached out to Rylie and took her hand, leading her into a dance and making her laugh as he whisked her around the room. With the scene becoming more familiar, Harrison glanced over to Evie, half expecting her to pull out a sketchbook and start drawing. Instead, she asked Alex to dance and although he was nervous, after an encouraging shove from his sister, he stumbled closer to Evie and reluctantly took her hand. Harrison couldn't help but recall the rebellious thief he was when they first met in Revaine and how much he'd changed since. He was growing into such a genuine, young man.

The last time Harrison recalled feeling this relaxed was during his graduation, although his Aegis Guard celebration was a close contender. Having all the people he loved together again meant everything to him, although there really was no replacement for Tutor Anderson falling off a bench while rescuing his obscenely large pint of ale. There was only one thing Harrison hadn't done during the night of his graduation, and he wasn't about to repeat that mistake. Standing up, he approached Nate and asked to cut in.

"Think you've got the skills, young man?" Nate teased with a wicked smile as he twirled Rylie away from Harrison.

"Oh, it's going to be like that, is it?" Harrison replied, his grin widening as he slipped between Nate and Rylie, taking her hand. Spinning her behind his back and away from Nate, then back into his arms, Harrison taunted his partner's father again by dramatically dipping Rylie, her head passing him by just a few inches. Her laughter said it all and Nate playfully bowed in defeat, allowing Harrison to take over.

"You two crack me up," Rylie chuckled as she continued to follow Harrison's lead with grace.

"And you mean everything to me," Harrison replied, turning her again, but much slower this time. As their bodies reconnected, he leaned in and gave her a soft kiss, their lips meeting effortlessly as she kissed him back.

"Thank you for bringing me back, I don't know where, or what I'd be without this amulet… without you," she admitted, touching the enchanted item briefly, not wanting to break hold with him.

"Well, you'd probably still be a flaming hot mess hunting Siljanna to the edge of the world," he replied humorously.

"If you hadn't been so careless and died, I never would've transformed in the first place, would I?" she countered, one eyebrow raised as she playfully scolded him.

"So, the moral of the story is, I can never die," Harrison confirmed as his grin widened.

"Pretty much," she replied, her tone so chipper it caused them both to laugh.

As they continued to dance, Rylie couldn't help but notice Harrison's posture. She hadn't seen him relax like this for the longest time. Glancing into his eyes, which were a molten combination of brown and gold, a warmth radiated from him and seemed to travel through his entire body. The familiar curls he'd had in his teenage years were being kept at bay by his cropped haircut but physically, his muscles were leaner, just as they had been while training at the Warden Academy. The Arencian rune embellished below his collarbone was a pleasant reminder of his return to the lifestyle that suited him. The life of a guardian.

As she lowered a hand to touch the mark, her breath caught. When Harrison noticed, he slowed the pace of their dance until she looked at him.

"Rylie, is everything okay?" he asked, using the hand placed on her back to gently stroke her.

"You've done so much just to protect me," she whispered, resting her head on his shoulder, adjusting effortlessly to their new speed.

"And I'd do it all again in a heartbeat," he replied, kissing her forehead.

"Really?" she mumbled, knowing she didn't need to ask but wanting to. This dance felt almost as special as their night on the lake, and she wanted to savour every moment.

"Why wouldn't I? I love you," he answered and as his words registered, Rylie stopped dancing to look at him directly.

Although deep down, she knew how he felt, it was the first time Harrison had ever said his feelings aloud with such ease and for a moment, Rylie was stunned.

"I... you just..." she stammered, a soft smile forming across her face as her eyes glistened with tears of joy.

"Lost for words?" he quipped, turning her smile into a laugh. Having been friends for so long, teasing her felt natural and would always be a playful part of their relationship. He also knew exactly how she'd react.

"I love you too," she finally announced before planting several small kisses on his lips. "I can't believe how easily you just said that, Harrison Stone."

With their dance having slowed to little more than a waddle, Rylie rested her head on Harrison's shoulder, allowing him to glance around the room and notice Maia arrive and head straight towards Zack. He couldn't hear what they were saying, but Zack instantly stopped playing the piano and walked into the corner of the room with the Ar'encal leader.

"Oh, the music stopped," Rylie said, slowly pulling away from Harrison.

"Looks like Maia is having a word with Zack. Maybe go ask your mum to take his place at the keys," Harrison suggested.

"Sure thing," Rylie agreed, heading towards her family and indicating for her mother to continue playing while Harrison picked up a drink and found Morgan.

"I wonder what that's about," Harrison pondered, nudging Morgan who turned his attention to the secretive conversation between Maia and Zack.

"Zack looks rather unsettled, must be serious," he replied, becoming equally curious.

After a few minutes, Maia gently touched Zack's shoulder as he nodded and then left him to contemplate whatever it was she'd asked.

Although both were eager to know, neither Harrison nor Morgan intended to enquire until Maia approached them.

"I think he'll want to speak with you," she advised gently. Everything she did seemed more careful now as it took a great amount of energy to keep her condition at bay, but despite that, she remained ever graceful.

Heading over to Zack, who was now using the wall to support his full weight, Morgan was the first to question his new friend.

"Is everything all right?" he wondered, passing Zack as he spoke while Harrison placed a hand on his shoulder, confirming they now stood either side of him.

"I'm not sure if I'm totally honest," Zack stammered, grasping one hand with the other firmly to stop them both from shaking.

"What's wrong?" Harrison added, noticing Zack's distress and becoming concerned.

"Maia just told me that she doesn't feel anyone in the guard is ready to take on the mantle of captain. In the interim, she's decided that Parker will manage the guard rotation and training schedule but wants me to work with him as an advisor and to handle any liaison duties," Zack replied, his tone hollow. "We'd both report to her, effectively sharing the captain role."

"You don't seem very pleased," Morgan observed, Zack's scrunched body language showing how greatly concerned he was.

"A blind man with limited combat skills shouldn't be an advisor," he insisted, continuing to strain his clenched fist with his open hand.

"Why can't Parker take on the role fully?" Harrison asked, hoping that answering his question would calm Zack down.

"My dad was a travelling merchant before he came to Arencia. He made contacts and friends that continued to help him and the mage sympathisers after the war," Zack explained, without realising how much admiration he showed for his father as he spoke. "Parker, however, doesn't have many contacts. In fact, he doesn't easily trust anyone outside of Arencia. He's a brilliant soldier but would put an arrow in between the eyes of any potential threat. That's helpful in combat, but not when seeking allies or information."

"But you have trusted contacts from your mage smuggler days," Harrison added, putting the pieces together.

"Yes, but I could tell Parker who they are," Zack babbled, trying to form his excuse.

"But would he trust them?" Morgan questioned softly, beginning to understand Maia's reasoning. "Would they trust him?"

"I don't know."

"Did you give Maia your answer?" Harrison asked, trying to reassure Zack with a steady pressure on his shoulder.

"I said no, obviously! But she made me promise to think about it overnight. She claims I have the same quality my dad did when it comes to dealing with people," Zack answered, worrying at his lower lip. "You're a commander, Morgan. Would you want someone like me as an advisor?"

"I only became warden commander by default. When Siljanna left to… well, hunt down you guys, I was the only one she trusted to fill her shoes. Then, when she betrayed the Imperator, the role just stayed with me," Morgan explained. "And to answer your question, I'd always accept help from reliable people."

"You didn't want the responsibility?" Zack asked, seemingly surprised at his lack of ambition, a trait he mirrored.

"Not really, but now that it's mine… I wouldn't want to relinquish it either," Morgan confirmed, not having really thought about it until Zack asked.

"I just don't think I'm the man for the job. In fact, if Maia had asked me who the next captain should be, I would've said you, Harrison," Zack stated, turning towards his closest friend.

"Me?" Harrison remarked, frankly shocked.

"Your combat and leadership skills are undeniable, plus you've got friends on both continents now. You'd literally be the perfect fit," Zack countered. "Can I put your name forward to Maia instead?"

"Zack, just stop for a second. Take a deep breath. I know what you've been through and can only imagine how your confidence has been knocked by losing your sight, but your help will be invaluable to Maia, Parker and the Aegis Guard," Harrison began.

"How do you figure that?" Zack fired back dubiously.

"Because every member of the Aegis Guard trusts you," Harrison replied, his words sincere.

"Says the guy who held his giant sword to my throat for several minutes when we first met," Zack replied, the memory of their first encounter at the Crown and Anchor Inn causing a slight smile to breach his doubt.

"That I did, but I didn't know you then. Look at us now," Harrison opposed, looking confidently at his friend. "We've relied on you pretty much every day since leaving Yasras and wouldn't be here without you. You saved us, Zack."

"No amount of sword skill can ever replace genuine trust and intuition," Morgan added, suddenly even more grateful for the support of his wardens.

Zack may have come across like a fool, especially when they first met, but he always acted in the best interest of others, which was probably the quality Maia had referred to.

"I don't know guys. I mean I know it'd make my dad proud, but my handicaps, they're barriers I can't ignore when it's regarding the safety of everyone in Arencia and our allies," Zack replied, doubt continuing to plague him.

"Take the position, Zack. It sounds like Maia and Parker will not only value but need your aid," Harrison pressed, encouraging Zack to stand tall.

"Will you stay too? I'd feel a lot better knowing we have you as a backup to rely on too," Zack asked, which resulted in Morgan failing to stifle a deep rumble of laughter.

"Second fiddle again and Sil isn't even around this time," Morgan teased, remembering how they used to joke about Siljanna always being the favoured twin in their training days.

"Yeah, all right smart ass," Harrison retorted, punching Morgan playfully before turning back to Zack who was laughing, albeit half-heartedly at the sound of their scuffle. "Think about it overnight, Zack, and have a chat with Lianna too."

"If it's the thought of becoming an active guardian again that's making you nervous, Harrison and I can teach you some of the self-defence techniques we learnt at the academy. Your condition doesn't make you defenceless. Think of it as a challenge to overcome rather than a handicap," Morgan asserted in a kind and reaffirming way that proved he was a true leader in his own right. "And if there's one piece of advice I can give you, when you accept the advisor role, pour yourself into it and give it your all."

"When?" Zack scoffed, raising his eyebrows at the remark. "Don't you mean if?"

"We'll see in the morning," Morgan replied.

"What my esteemed yet gormless comrade is trying to say is, take the time you need to decide," Harrison commented, getting one back at his friend for the earlier jab. "We will support whatever you choose."

"Thank you, both of you," Zack replied, taking all their comments in. Finally, with a firm grasp on Harrison's shoulder, mirroring his friend's earlier reassurance, Zack collected his cane and headed across the room in search of Lianna.

Sitting on the sideline, Lianna enjoyed watching the merriment in the room. It lifted her spirits in a way that was almost indescribable. Before long, Alex pleaded with Evie for a break from dancing and took a seat by the food. With a giggle, Evie met up with Rylie and they both came over and joined Lianna.

"This is nice," Evie began, the smile on her face showing how much she preferred the Ar'encal vigil custom to a traditional funeral.

"Celebrating the lives of lost loved ones is much better than mourning their loss," Rylie concurred.

"Speaking of loved ones, did I see you and Harrison share a little moment on the dance floor," Evie probed, poking her sister playfully.

"Yeah," she giggled, glancing between her sister and Lianna. "He said he loves me, and for a guy who's not great with words, it came so easily."

"Is that all?" Evie teased, a wide grin spreading across her face as she wound up her sister.

"That's pretty big, Evie. Don't burst their bubble," Lianna said, unable to scold her as the wicked intentions of the youngster filled her heart.

"Yeah but, it's been obvious for so long that he loves you," Evie continued, the glint in her eyes emphasising her taunts. "Besides, I have a confession. Harrison told me he loved me way back on the Pilgrim, so you're not the first Auren to hear him say that."

"What?" Rylie replied, gobsmacked.

"Do you reckon that means he loves me more, because he told me first?"

Listening to Evie and her light-hearted mocking made Lianna laugh, which only encouraged Rylie to retaliate playfully.

"Well now, that just won't do," she declared just before darting towards her sister. "I'll have to take out the competition."

"No!" Evie wailed, but it was too late. Her sister grabbed her around her waist and began relentlessly tickling her. Falling to the floor in a fit of giggles, Lianna stepped away from the siblings, still laughing while Nate attempted to intervene and referee the situation. His efforts didn't go as planned and he was quickly dragged into the scuffle, just as Morgan and Harrison approached.

"Help... Warden... Commander," Nate whimpered theatrically, overdramatising his plea.

"Not my jurisdiction," Morgan jested, raising his glass with a wink and tilting his head towards Harrison. "Try asking an Aegis Guardian."

"I'm off duty!" Harrison smirked, matching Morgan's motion and taking a swig of his own drink.

Their united gesture told Nate his peril did not compare to the vital task of consuming the delicious contents in their glasses and the scene before Lianna soon unravelled into a hilarious combination of sibling rivalry and over-dramatic parenting, but it was so much better for her than a typical funeral. The playfighting didn't last long but the smiles created by the foolishness were worth it. Just as Rylie claimed victory over her little sister, Zack appeared beside her.

"Dance?" he asked, offering his arm out to her.

"Sure," she replied sweetly. Lianna had never really danced before but luckily, it was clear Zack intended more of a waddle than an actual dance.

"I need to talk to you about something," Zack explained, speaking in a hushed tone, his lips close to her ear. She could feel the chill of his breath and it tickled, making her shiver ever so slightly.

"Do tell," Lianna replied, encouraging him to speak while wrapping her arms around him. She cherished the moments when they could be this close.

"Maia has decided that no one in the Aegis Guard is ready to step up and be the next captain yet. In the meantime, she wants Parker to share the role… with me," Zack began, embracing Lianna tightly.

"Are you serious?" Lianna replied, reacting a little too loudly, but quickly quieting herself. "Zack, that's fantastic! That means you'll be staying here in Arencia too, with me… I mean, us."

"Harrison and Morgan think it's a good idea too," Zack began, his tone revealing his concern. "If I accept, I'll be working alongside Parker daily with anything concerning the people of Arencia, our allies or informants. Harrison has offered to support too in a secondary capacity. Both he and Morgan say they can train me in self-defence so that I'm not a total hindrance, but I just don't know."

"Don't know what?" Lianna probed, feeling the self-doubt seep from him.

"If I'm good enough."

"Do you want my honest answer?" Lianna asked, knowing that she hadn't always been kind to him but equally, had never lied to make him feel better.

"I value your opinion a lot, Lianna and right now, I need some brutal honesty. I hope you can sense that," Zack confessed, his body tensing slightly as he anticipated her response.

"If you'd asked me that question when we first met, I would've given you a different answer, but I was wrong back then. I can say without a shadow of a doubt, you are the most genuine, loyal and determined person I've ever met," Lianna replied. "Not only are you good enough, you'll be the best advisor any leader could ask for."

"That's a pretty good speech to cripple low self-esteem," Zack replied, softly placing a hand on her face, feeling her expression. As he did, she leaned into his touch and felt her chest rise and fall sharply, her heartbeat thudding in her ears.

"Zack, can I ask you something now?" Lianna murmured, placing her hand on top of his.

"Anything," he replied simply, without hesitation.

"Can you ever forgive me?"

"For what?" he questioned, honestly perplexed.

"For treating you the way I did. For dismissing your affection so bluntly when we first met," Lianna explained. "If I could take it all back—"

"There is nothing to forgive," Zack announced, his fingers tracing her face, attempting to read her body language as he once could. "I'm just glad you gave me a second chance."

"Will you give me a second chance? Could you ever feel that way about me again?" she asked, her voice barely audible.

As a tear dropped down her cheek, it met with Zack's thumb, and he caressed it away. His touch was soft, but Lianna couldn't help but dread his response. She'd been so insistent that they only be friends, and now here she was, just a few weeks later asking for more.

"Well, that's easy… because I never stopped loving you," he replied, caressing her face as his heart swelled.

"That can't be true. I would've felt it," she replied, jerking away from him in surprise but quickly taking his hand in hers.

"I told myself every day that I could only love you as a friend, because that's what you wanted. I was lying to myself and to you because I wanted to make you happy," Zack explained, being honest about his feelings for the first time since they rekindled their friendship. "Don't try to process my words, just embrace the truth behind them."

At his encouragement, rather than clinging to her desire for control over her power, Lianna let her guard down and every ounce of Zack's affection washed over her. This time, she knew it was more than just attraction. He did desire her but alongside it was a feeling of wholeness, as if the thought of being with her completed him. Each emotion was like ecstasy and finally, once she'd let each one touch her heart, Lianna ran her fingers through Zack's bright blond hair, the spikes flicking through her fingers as she pressed her lips against his.

The kiss was awkward at first with Lianna pressing her lips against him too hard, hoping that would prove she returned his feelings. Gently, Zack placed his fingers under her chin, shifting her face slightly so that when he kissed her back, their interlocking lips fit together seamlessly.

For the briefest moment, Lianna felt as though they'd disappeared into a world of their own, until the cheering and applause from around the room brought her back to the reality of everyone at the vigil watching them.

"So… we aren't keeping this a secret then," Lianna whispered, letting herself giggle at the situation.

"Yeah, that was never going to happen anyway," he replied, mirroring her laughter, implying that he would've shouted the news to the world at every opportunity.

"It's about time you guys got together!" Rylie called out while clapping enthusiastically at their public display of heavily overdue affection.

"Better late than never," Harrison added, joining the rest of the group as they applauded.

"Hey, you guys can't talk!" Lianna protested with a smirk.

"Ahhh no… I'm oblivious, you were just stubborn," Rylie countered, her smile beaming.

As Lianna chuckled in defeat, she threw both her arms around Zack and buried her head into his shoulder.

"At least I don't owe you that kiss anymore," she muttered, her voice muffled as she pressed her face into him. Zack responded by holding her tighter, letting the joy of having her in his arms do all the talking.

Chapter Fifteen
Ignoble

Although they left Iliria ahead of Harrison and the others, Siljanna and Dylan had gotten hopelessly lost in the winding trails around Lorvale. Finally giving up and sticking to the main road leading west, they walked for hours before finding the rocky coastline and veering north to Revaine. It was getting late by the time the welcoming shanty town came into view.

"Finally, I know where we are," Dylan exclaimed, his feet aching from the long day.

"How much longer until we reach Caitlin?" Siljanna asked, her determination supressing whatever aches and pains she also felt.

"Not long, but it'll be dark by the time we reach Revaine. We should stop overnight and gather some supplies," Dylan advised. "I think there's a little market just past the main gate."

"We can't stop. I need to make sure Caitlin's okay," Siljanna insisted, folding her arms and dismissing his suggestion.

"I'm sure she's fine. Why are you so worried about her?" Dylan asked, his curiosity piqued.

"She was kind to me, even when Harrison and the others were still suspicious. I never expected that, especially from a mage," Siljanna confessed, fidgeting with the braided portion of her ashen blonde hair.

"I get it. Kindness has been somewhat of a stranger in my life too," Dylan replied, touching her shoulder empathetically until she relaxed and dropped her hands down. "The only person I had for over two years was Juliette, and that relationship was—"

"Toxic?" Siljanna offered, unable to deny the opportunity to speak bluntly.

"I never really loved her, if that's what you were wondering, but I wanted to," Dylan began, his head sinking as he looked sheepishly at the floor. "I allowed Juliette to control me because I was clinging to the person I thought she could be."

"I can't imagine someone like her ever being more than a manipulative siren," Siljanna muttered.

"Training changed both of us, but not for the better. I found myself in a situation where I had to make a choice and I chose to spare Juliette. In hindsight, maybe I shouldn't have," Dylan began, his voice filled with regret.

"Do you want to talk about it?" Siljanna asked, encouraging him to face her. She was not going to judge him, but she wouldn't force him to speak either, unless he was ready to do so.

"Not really," Dylan replied honestly, but Siljanna could sense the conversation wasn't over. "Allowing someone to control you is debilitating. At first, I convinced myself it wasn't too bad, I wanted to love her… and she is incredibly desirable, but by the time we reached Carlisse, her attitude was intolerable. I had to walk away."

"We've both made some pretty horrendous mistakes, but for the record, I'm glad you're with me now," Siljanna advised with a warmth Dylan didn't expect.

"Thank you. I promise we'll reach Caitlin in the morning. If I recall, the Driftwood Ranch is only an hour or so outside of Revaine."

Just as he'd expected, it was dark by the time they reached Revaine, but there was still a hustle and bustle amidst the streets. Vendors in the market were only just closing their stalls and lamp lighters were patrolling the streets, giving the oil lanterns the spark they needed to flicker into life. The town was exactly how Dylan remembered, a collection of shack houses and patchwork buildings that, in any other city, would've been condemned. Even though they lived in near poverty, the people of Revaine seemed mostly cheerful. There was a sense of community here that was lost, especially in bigger cities like Siranor or Carlisse, but sadly, the concept was also lost on Dylan.

After finding a small inn near the main gate, Dylan and Siljanna brought a few basic supplies before turning in for the night. Tossing under his bedsheet, sleep came but rest did not. Dylan's dreams were harassed by images of Juliette. They became so vivid, it was as though he were reliving each moment, starting from the day they met. Juliette was introduced to him as an unconventional recruit and alchemist with great potential, but that description didn't do her justice.

His unconscious mind flickered between their encounters, he recalled her incredible ability to create lethal toxins and despite never receiving formal training prior to joining the covert academy in Tulam, her willingness to enter combat. She was fearless, gorgeous and deadly. A prized student who quickly earned the admiration and infatuation of her peers, including Dylan. She seemed unstoppable but before long, her addiction to *the hunt* saw her killing mercilessly, often without consent and even disobeying orders. Her impertinence soon became a concern among the tutors and beyond, reaching the political hierarchy in Siranor. Mage hunters were weapons created to serve the Imperator, not their own ambition, but Juliette frequently crossed that line.

As the dream bounded forward, Dylan's skin erupted into a cold sweat as he relived his graduation trial. His instructions were clear. To graduate, Dylan had to teach Juliette that her actions came at a price. She either had to submit to their superior's command or the consequence would be her life, which Dylan had been ordered to take. After hours of desperate research, he discovered a saving grace in her old school friend, Ava Willan. It had been reported that Ava was a mage and now threatened the people in Galnor, her former hometown before moving to Tivani.

Deceiving Juliette into joining him on the hunt for a rogue mage, they travelled to the farming town and quickly located Ava. Seeing her old friend for the first time in nearly two years, Juliette was initially confused, a feeling that was amplified when the other girl panicked. Recognising their mage hunter attire, Ava tried to run but her action also told Juliette she was their target.

Thrashing in his sleep, the words he and Juliette exchanged that day came alive in the dream, as did the actions he took to get through to her, which started with catching Ava by the arm and throwing her to the ground.

"You bastard! Why didn't you tell me she was the target?" Juliette hissed, slapping him violently.

"We have orders, Juliette. She is our target," he insisted, imploring her to do as instructed... as expected. "Knowing wouldn't have changed that."

As Ava writhed on the floor between them, Dylan noticed Juliette slowly backing away. The only person she'd considered a friend was now the thing she enjoyed hunting most, a mage. That quandary was enough to give even Juliette reason to pause.

"I won't do it, and I won't let you either."

Looking into her eyes, Dylan was startled by her empty expression. It was as if Juliette felt nothing, but her memories with Ava combined with sheer stubbornness prevented her from striking. Knowing what she did not, the real consequence should she disobey orders again, Dylan knew he had to act. Kicking Ava hard to ensure she stayed on the ground, he rushed towards Juliette, forcing her against a nearby wall. Pressing his dagger against her throat, Dylan cried out for her to see sense, even though he knew she was going to resist.

"Juliette, we are mage hunters. This is what we do," he shouted, nicking her skin with the blade just enough that a droplet of blood escaped.

"We are mage hunters, and as such, I'll do whatever I want!" she retaliated, pushing forward despite the blade.

Realising he would not break her, Dylan reached down with his free hand and took a vial from her satchel, knowing that any one of them would be fatal. Slamming her into the wall, he turned his back on her and paced towards Ava. As he poured the substance down her throat, the young woman gurgled momentarily... and then she was gone.

"It had to be done, Juliette," he whispered, feeling her approach him from behind at speed.

Punching him as hard as she could while they stood over the corpse of her former friend, Juliette flung a verbal assault at him that was as visceral in his sleep as it had been at the time.

"You had no right to do that! Those concoctions are mine and now everyone will think I killed her," she spat, hitting him again.

"I'm going to tell the tutors that you did do this, as instructed," Dylan replied, ignoring her strikes and tossing the empty poison vial on the floor.

"Why would I ever go along with your lies?" she growled, stamping on the vial in frustration.

The broken glass crunched under her heeled boot as she looked down at Ava's corpse and then back to Dylan. He was expecting her to be furious, but for a moment he wasn't certain whether it was the death of her friend or the fact he used her toxin that had made her angry.

"Because it's in your best interests to do so," Dylan shouted, struggling to keep his composure.

"What are you talking about? I choose which orders I follow," Juliette declared arrogantly.

"You don't have a choice this time," Dylan insisted, crossing his arms to show that he was not going to back down.

"And why is that?" Juliette challenged.

"Because if you don't, they'll make me kill you. Don't force my hand again. Please."

As she registered the truth behind his actions, Juliette's entire demeanour changed. Relaxing, she adopted her classic, seductive stance and sauntered towards him.

"They were going to make you kill me if I disobeyed, is that it?" she purred, seeming to enjoy the potential threat.

"Yes. Don't make me hurt you, Juliette," Dylan muttered in response, letting his arms go limp as she trailed her fingers over him.

Coiling her arms around him like a snake would its prey, she pressed herself into him and grazed his ear with her lips.

"You want me to follow their command, fine. But in return… you will follow mine," she whispered, her tone flirtatious as she encouraged Dylan to run his fingers through her raven hair.

He never imagined what the true consequences of agreeing to her demand would be, but soon found out. She made being enthralled enjoyable at first, even addictive but in truth, it was as mentally destructive as her concoctions were toxic.

Luckily, Siljanna knocking on his door spared Dylan from recalling more of his sordid past. Rubbing his blurry eyes, he realised it was dawn so began to get up. After collecting their belongings, he and Siljanna continued towards the Driftwood Ranch. Passing the open fields and quaint farmland was peaceful, almost surreal in comparison to what they'd witnessed in Iliria.

Strangely, news of the attack had spread but the people they could overhear talking on the streets seemed to consider it little more than gossip and hearsay.

"Do you think King Grayson sent messengers to discredit any word of the attack?" Siljanna asked in a hushed tone.

"Without a doubt," Dylan replied, knowing that's exactly what the Imperator would've done in the same situation.

"Did you ever meet him, King Grayson? I thought you abandoned Juliette before entering the city," Siljanna added with mild curiosity.

"No, I never met him, but I did enough research to know that he was about as pompous as a man can be. Juliette couldn't wait to meet him," Dylan replied, rolling his eyes as a smirk crept over his lips.

"I never had the privilege either. He was *indisposed* by Juliette's poison when I arrived in Carlisse," Siljanna recalled, shuddering at the memory.

"Was it that bad?"

"I can only assume its potency was severe. King Grayson remained unwell for the duration of our time in the city, and you've heard in more graphic detail than anyone what happened while I was there," Siljanna began, wincing as she spoke.

"From what I recall, it was rather uneventful," Dylan quipped, trying to conceal a smile at the almost unbelievable series of events that had truly occurred.

Nudging Siljanna's shoulder, his humorous approach forced her to relax. He didn't judge her past transgressions and had helped her to see that while the past cannot be changed, what they did from now on was what truly mattered.

"I don't remember you being so funny, Dylan... Thank you."

At first, she just chuckled softly, but before long, Siljanna broke out in a full burst of laughter. Hearing her laugh so heartily, Dylan just wrapped his arm around her shoulders and squeezed. It was good to have a real friend again, someone who wanted him around for who he was and felt better by his presence.

After a few more miles of walking down the dusty roads, they were relieved to come across the large wooden archway with the words *Driftwood Ranch* inscribed into a hanging sign. Following the tree-lined path, they only stopped when a dark-haired man riding a chestnut horse approached them.

"Please tell me your name is Siljanna," the rider requested as he steadied the horse with ease. His tone was warm, matching his healthy tan and welcoming smile.

"I am, and this is my companion, Dylan. May I ask who's asking?" Siljanna replied.

"My daughter mostly, she's been fretting about you ever since she got home. I'm Drew Mason, Caitlin's father," he answered.

"Is Caitlin here?" Siljanna asked, her relief instantaneous.

"Yes, she apparently promised you she'd stay out of trouble until you arrived here or sent word. I can only wonder how you obtained such an agreement from Caitlin. She's usually so impulsive," Drew muttered amicably. "Follow me, I'll lead you to the house."

Arriving at the ranch house after cutting through the fields, Siljanna's growing smile became even brighter as a burst of energy with trailing red hair flung the front door open and came pelting towards her.

"You're okay!" Caitlin cried, gingerly wrapping her still-aching arms around Siljanna. The healer in Dawne had been able to reset her ankle, but the injury to her arm was going to take longer to fully heal. Pleasantly surprised by her embrace, Siljanna placed a cautious hand on Caitlin's back and patted her. The awkward reaction made Caitlin break away, a sheepish smile on her face before speaking again. "How is everyone?"

"There were a few losses during the battle," Dylan began, intending to continue their honesty streak but he was quickly interrupted.

"But Harrison and the others are all okay," Siljanna said, knowing that Caitlin was already worried enough about her friends in Carlisse.

"So, the Royal Military really did attack Iliria?" Drew asked, sounding quite shocked as he dismounted the horse.

"What have you heard?" Dylan asked curiously.

"Mostly just gossip after the troops were seen heading south towards Lorvale. Then Caitlin arrived claiming a battle was imminent in Iliria, supporting the rumours we heard in town," Drew began, clasping the back of his neck with one hand.

"The rumours were true for a change, which of course I tried to tell you," Caitlin added hastily.

"Yes, okay darling, I'm sorry I didn't believe you. However, it was only because the next morning, messengers were sent to every household proclaiming it was all just a training exercise."

"And people believed that?" Dylan asked dubiously.

"Most of the townsfolk did. Better to believe the lies of a tyrannical king than face up to him," Caitlin chided.

"Caitlin!" her father cried, warning evident in his tone. "Get inside if you wish to speak so candidly."

Following Caitlin indoors, Siljanna and Dylan were introduced to her mother, Elissa, briefly and then hustled into a small side room that they assumed was used as an office. Shutting the door firmly, Caitlin turned to both Siljanna and Dylan, concern evident across her face. Despite obviously still wanting to reach her friends in Carlisse, Caitlin's first question was to ask what happened in Iliria.

Siljanna was surprised that Caitlin wanted to hear more details, but assumed that deep down, she needed to know. She and Dylan filled her in as briefly as they could but finding out about Lucas was her breaking point.

"Oh no, poor Zack," she whimpered.

"You mentioned that name before, who is he again?" Siljanna asked, genuinely trying to remember their earlier conversation.

"He's the one that helped Harrison as they fled the Western Continent and Lucas is… was his father," Caitlin replied, filling in the gaps for Siljanna.

"Is he a warrior? Why wasn't he there with the other guards and Ar'encal to defend Iliria?" Dylan queried, wondering why such a valuable ally wouldn't have been present.

"Because he's blind," Siljanna recalled.

"It was your former associate that attacked him," Caitlin added.

It was well within Juliette's capability to mutilate a person as well as kill them. She truly was beyond redemption. Momentarily, the room fell silent until Siljanna pushed their focus onto Caitlin's other pressing concern.

"Have you heard anything from your friends in the castle?" Siljanna enquired, hoping for some good news.

"Nothing since the letter advising about the attack on Iliria. I sent a reply explaining my absence was due to injury and that I hoped to return in a day or two, but I've had no response," Caitlin replied, worrying at her lip.

"I doubt the Royal Guard will accept any correspondence now their army has been defeated and scattered," Dylan suggested, trying to make her feel better.

"Try not to be too worried," Siljanna added.

"I wish I knew how. When Nadia chose to go back, I was against it," Caitlin exclaimed, throwing her hands upwards in frustration. "She insisted the king wouldn't hurt her now that he believes she's pregnant, but we were finally free. It was insane to go back."

"People in Queen Nadia's position are never truly free," Dylan interjected, looking at Caitlin sombrely, "but what do you mean, the king believes she's pregnant?"

"It's all a ruse. Nadia has the withering and would die without daily treatment from Spencer. He's a mage with healing abilities. Every time she's been pregnant before, she's lost the child within the first eight weeks," Caitlin explained, her tone filling with sorrow.

"What would make King Grayson believe she can maintain the pregnancy now?" Dylan probed. "From what I learnt about the king, he's arrogant and brash, but not a fool."

"The king was about to have Nadia executed when Spencer blurted out that she was pregnant to protect her. While in captivity, they concocted a plan," Caitlin began.

"The queen was going to be executed?" Siljanna interjected, trying to process all the information she was feeding them as quickly as possible.

"The king had been poisoned and he blamed Nadia. Her detest for him was no secret," Caitlin explained and Siljanna almost admitted that she instructed Juliette to provide her and the Imperator with an advantageous position in Carlisse but decided against it.

"So they are doing what, exactly?" Siljanna coaxed, allowing Caitlin to focus on answering Dylan's question.

"Spencer's lie saved the woman he loves, and I was to create the illusion she was pregnant to continue the ruse. We had time before Nadia would be showing signs, but what they intended to do once she supposedly reached the final trimester was… a work in progress," Caitlin admitted, shuffling her feet awkwardly.

"Could they not try for a child together? A mage baby would be resistant to the withering," Dylan suggested, leaving Caitlin stunned.

"They could then claim it's the king's heir," Siljanna added, agreeing and expanding on Dylan's thought process instantly.

"That must be their plan," Caitlin whispered, realising the truth.

"Spencer can't be the only healer in the castle, though. Why would King Grayson allow them to stay together?" Dylan queried, finding more holes in their convoluted plan. "If they're in love, surely he knows that."

"The king doesn't care about the depth of their affections for one another, as long as he gets what he wants. An heir," Caitlin confirmed. "Spencer sent a letter to me ahead of the attack. Its contents were jarring to say the least. I only showed Harrison and the others one page, the page about the attack."

"What else did the letter say?" Siljanna asked, noticing that Caitlin was trying to hold back tears.

"Spencer managed to convince the king to let him remain with Nadia, insisting he could keep the keep the baby alive but they are locked together in Nadia's quarters and will be kept there until the baby is born."

"She chose imprisonment over a lifetime of being hunted," Siljanna commented, closing her eyes and wondering what she would choose in that position. She'd been both the hunter and the hunted now and knew the consequences of both.

"It's safe to say King Grayson would never let her escape with his unborn child," Dylan added. "If she hadn't returned, the attack on Iliria and anywhere else King Grayson claimed she'd been sighted would've been justified."

"You're right," Caitlin admitted. "I can't believe I didn't even think about all the people that may have been caught in the crossfire had Nadia and Spencer listened to my protests and decided against returning."

"It may have seemed dangerous at first, but Nadia saved countless lives by going back," Siljanna confirmed.

"That's not the worst of it though," Caitlin said, her lower lip trembling.

"Caitlin, tell us... please," Siljanna implored, Touching her very gently on the shoulder.

"The king had her parents executed, by way as a punishment for her transgressions."

"So although she saved countless lives by returning, the ones that meant the most to her were taken anyway," Siljanna whispered, feeling a pang in her heart for the queen. She could empathise with anyone who had suffered the loss of their parents.

"Please, will you help me set them free, truly free?" Caitlin pleaded, turning sharply to face both Siljanna and Dylan. "I cannot use my illusion magic without staying close by, and don't want to be trapped in the castle alone after they escape. A more conventional approach, however, could work."

"You mean, overthrow the king?" Dylan asked sceptically. "We may be talented warriors, but we can't go against squadrons of guards."

"I helped Harrison and the others sneak in before, I could get you in undetected too," Caitlin informed, her voice resolute.

"Then what, kill the king? We're already fugitives in one continent, you want us to commit regicide too?" Dylan protested.

"The king is a threat. He's allied with the Imperator and could launch a counterstrike on Iliria, but we wouldn't need to kill him. We could capture and use him to find out the Imperator's plans," Siljanna suggested with a glint in her eyes. Her tactical confidence was shining through for what felt like the first time since her training days.

"No, he should die!" Caitlin argued, her enraged expression as vivid as her hair. "After everything he's done, he doesn't deserve mercy."

"The same could be said about me. Yet you chose to befriend me without question," Siljanna countered.

"That's different. You reacted to a traumatic situation badly and granted, did some awful things for what... maybe a month?" Caitlin shouted back. Biting her tongue, she took a deep breath and lowered her voice to a growl, not wanting her parents to overhear what she needed to say. "King Grayson Brock has been a cruel man his entire life and a tyrant since taking the throne. For seven years we have endured his abuse. He turned mages into slaves throughout the kingdom, harassed us while we served him and took whatever... whoever he wanted, whenever he wanted."

"Did he force himself on you?" Siljanna whispered, an incredulous look on her face as she stepped closer to Caitlin, intending to reach out to her.

Caitlin didn't answer her question and closed herself off to Siljanna's touch. Wiping away her own tears, Caitlin regained her composure with a slow, long inhale before continuing her tale.

"The king possesses everything he touches and if you don't submit, you die. Or worse, someone you love dies. Why do you think Nadia stayed all those years, let him impregnate her several times?" Caitlin asked brazenly.

"I don't know," Siljanna replied, nausea building in the depths of her throat.

"He imprisoned her parents all those years and said they'd never see the light of day unless she submitted to him. It was only after she slept with him that the king would command his guards to take food to them."

"And then he killed them to punish her," Dylan added.

"More like torment her!" Caitlin replied, her voice filled with loathing. "King Grayson should die for the things he's done."

"Caitlin, of course we can understand your hatred, but even if he deserves it, we'll only make things worse by assassinating him," Dylan insisted.

"Why, Dylan?" she challenged, pushing past Siljanna who was still recoiling from the insinuation that King Grayson had dominated women, including Caitlin, against their will.

"Because it would cause anarchy in the kingdom," Dylan explained, knowing more about political comings and goings than Caitlin realised.

"That is why we should challenge his reign. By capturing King Grayson, he could be made to face charges of war crimes against Iliria among any other crimes we can prove," Siljanna proposed, shaking off Caitlin's horrifying revelation for now. "It was Nadia that discovered his plot with Imperator Harlyn wasn't it?"

"If we free them and find evidence that her parents were held in captivity until their execution, that would be sufficient proof to explain Nadia's initial silence," Dylan commented, catching on quickly to Siljanna's idea.

"Caitlin…" Siljanna said softly, looking at the first mage she'd ever befriended with hope. "Will you agree to this plan? Overthrow the king and have him imprisoned for his crimes."

It took a long time before Caitlin responded and even when she did, her expression showed them that she wasn't pleased.

"Fine. We'll go through the old smuggler tunnels. I can get you into the castle undetected, but we'll need to free Nadia and her family and capture the king simultaneously," Caitlin replied, her voice quiet but firm.

"Then it's decided," Siljanna replied, gently turning Caitlin to face her again. Looking deeply into her emerald eyes and realising how similar they were to her own, Siljanna finally embraced Caitlin properly, as she should've done outside.

"I'm trusting you," Caitlin whispered, before burying her head into Siljanna's shoulder, her hair covering her face as she imperceptibly sobbed.

When Siljanna felt the dampness on her skin from Caitlin's tears, she waited until her new ally was ready to pull away from her embrace. As she did, Caitlin kissed Siljanna on the cheek, a gesture that took Siljanna completely by surprise. It was just a peck, but was it just a harmless gesture between friends or was there a deeper meaning behind it?

Although Siljanna felt her heart skip a beat, now wasn't the time to ask. There was a lot at stake, but if she and Dylan could succeed in overthrowing Kind Grayson, it would make life better for a lot of people in the kingdom and severely set back the Imperator's war effort. It was too good an opportunity to miss. Making Carlisse a safe place for them would also provide Siljanna the opportunity to talk with Caitlin about whatever that kiss meant.

Chapter Sixteen
COUP DE GRÂCE

They waited until dark before making their way through the smuggler tunnel to Carlisse. With most of the Royal Military still absent and the market stalls closed for the evening, the streets were quiet, allowing them to slip through the servant's gate and into the library with ease.

"Nadia's room is down the hall, but I expect she'll be heavily guarded. The king's chambers are in the other direction, up the gallery stairs," Caitlin advised in a hushed tone. "He has a trio of personal guards led by Liam Kane. You'll easily recognise him for he's a brute with a face only a mother could love."

"Dylan, you capture the king. I'll protect Caitlin and get the keys so we can free the queen and Spencer," Siljanna instructed without hesitation or doubt.

"By any means necessary?" Dylan asked, his tone reminiscent of her own in Siranor when she ordered him and Juliette to torture Rylie's parents.

"Lethal force only if required," Siljanna replied cautiously, adamant not to repeat her earlier mistakes. Dylan quickly smiled back at her, indicating that he too had learnt from his past.

Creeping through the main library door, Caitlin went to check the way ahead but was quickly grabbed by a patrolling guard. Clasping his hand over Caitlin's mouth to silence her cry, he whispered in her ear from behind.

"Silly little mouse. Didn't you think we'd increase patrols after your last infiltration?" the guard hissed.

As Siljanna realised what was happening, she pulled her axes free, preparing to strike but Dylan beat her to it. Pulling the guard's head backwards then wrapping his hand and lower arm around the man's throat, Dylan tensed his muscles and twisted sharply, snapping the guard's neck. As the body fell into Dylan, Caitlin wriggled from his limp grasp and stepped swiftly out of the way.

"I figured that was required," Dylan offered quietly, glancing at Siljanna while lowering the dead guard to the floor. As Siljanna nodded with silent gratitude, she focused her attention on their assailant and an idea settled in her mind.

"Change of plan," Siljanna began, the wheels of her mind visibly turning as a new plan formed. "Dylan, take the guard's attire and attempt to get the keys to release Spencer and the queen. Caitlin, be prepared to use your power and steal them if needed."

"All right," Caitlin muttered, still a little shaken.

"Once you have the keys, wait for my signal," Siljanna continued.

"You'll be okay taking on the king and his guards alone?" Caitlin asked apprehensively.

"I can handle them," Siljanna replied, the steely look on her face.

"Be careful," Caitlin insisted. "Grayson Brock can be aggressive when he wants to be."

"He's never had to deal with a woman that fights back before."

Once Dylan slipped the deceased guard's armour over his clothes, he and Caitlin looked back briefly towards Siljanna as she gave them a firm nod, turned on her heel and headed directly for the king's chamber.

Finding the gallery staircase Caitlin mentioned wasn't difficult; Siljanna just followed the increasingly garish decor. The more jewels and gold trim, the closer she was. Reaching the top of the stairs, she began to feel the anger boiling beneath her skin. Caitlin may not have answered her question back at the ranch, but Siljanna couldn't get past the disgusting thought of the king forcing himself upon her. He'd probably victimised countless other women too, including his unwilling wife. King Grayson was little more than a predator, Siljanna knew that but now she cared for someone he'd assaulted, she struggled to find the will to follow through with her own plan of capturing him. Before she could decide, her thoughts were interrupted by the trio of soldiers Caitlin had warned her about. They were all that stood between her and the king's opulent chamber door.

"Intruder," shouted the first guard, charging towards her as he drew a short sword.

"Protect the king," demanded the second, instructing the third guard to remain by the door as he too approached Siljanna.

The second guard was brutish, with a hideous nose that must've been broken more than once. She concluded that he was Liam Kane, King Grayson's stalwart defender and leader of the trio. Gracefully drawing her axes, Siljanna's mind instantly registered their encumbered movement, restricted by too much plate armour. That didn't excuse the sloppy way they showboated with their blades, however, allowing her to surmise a child could've evaded these guards.

Letting them come to her, Siljanna reacted with cat-like agility to the first guard's swing, deflecting it with ease. Propelling herself backwards with a cartwheel kick, her boot connected with Kane's chin and knocked him down. Landing firmly, she launched another powerful kick, striking his comrade in the back. As he tumbled to the floor, Siljanna struck him sharply in the temple with the haft of her axe, rendering him free of consciousness.

She turned back towards Kane just in time to dodge the blade he thrust at her from the ground. As his sword sunk into the wall inches from her body, Siljanna felt herself grin, almost impressed he'd gotten so close. Acknowledging he was now unarmed, Siljanna sheathed her weapons and challenged him to a brawl. She was not afraid of him and figured another beating could only improve his visage.

Hindered by his gear, Kane was slow and his strikes laboured, but he was more skilled than Siljanna first assumed. As they fought, she evaded his first strike, only to have her counter blocked, allowing him to land a strong series of blows. Winded, Siljanna fell back a few paces, cradling her sternum as Kane aggressively pressed his advantage. Attempting to connect a strong haymaker, Siljanna ducked, causing his fist to collide with the wall. She heard several fingers crack as he cried out in pain, which encouraged the third guard to abandon the king's door and join the fight. Brandishing a spear, he pointed the tip towards Siljanna.

"Surrender now," he cried but his uncertainty was glaringly obvious.

He held the spear at the end of the shaft, keeping the largest space possible between himself and Siljanna, but in doing so made the weapon flimsy. Seizing it for herself, Siljanna thrust the spear backwards, the wooden pole catching the guard in the throat. Crippled and coughing, he dropped to his knees, allowing Siljanna to slide the weapon over her shoulders, shrinking its length considerably, but increasing her manoeuvrability in the narrow corridor. The king clearly only dressed his guards to look intimidating rather than training them to truly be so.

Cradling his now broken hand, she heard Kane's groans recede and become a frustrated growl. Spinning rapidly, Siljanna ensured the blunt handle of the spear collided with his face. The loud crack and resulting thump as he crashed to the floor was all Siljanna needed to hear to know he was no longer a threat. Discarding the spear, she approached the door they'd attempted to protect, wiped a droplet of sweat from her brow and forced it open.

Inside, the grandiose room was quiet, too quiet. Siljanna couldn't bring herself to believe that the king hadn't heard the commotion outside but wondered if he was a true coward or, like a cornered rat, preparing to strike from the shadows. She found herself in a parlour at first, which was covered with plush pillows and flowing drapes but from that central room, Siljanna could see three doors that led to interconnecting rooms. Between the sofas, a small table was set with a decanter of wine and two glasses, meaning the king had been expecting company, but she was definitely not the person he had in mind.

Softly, she pushed the far-left door open to reveal a bathing room, luxurious by normal terms but rudimentary compared to what she had experienced in Siranor. The second door led to a walk-in closet, brimming with regal cloaks, tunics, breeches and a variety of shoes, much more than any person would need, but it wasn't the range of attire that captured her attention. A very young, very scared slave girl was huddled in the corner, sobbing quietly.

"Please don't hurt me," she whimpered, her trembling arms wrapped around her knees.

"I promise, I mean you no harm," Siljanna replied, noticing the girl's dress was torn and her hair dishevelled.

"Are you going to kill him?" she muttered, her eyes glistening with tears and now, hope.

"Just go… get somewhere safe," Siljanna instructed, ushering her out of the room.

By process of elimination, Siljanna assumed the final door had to lead to the king's bedchamber and where he'd chosen to hide. Pushing the door open, Siljanna cautiously entered, alert for an attack but found King Grayson standing defiantly before her, armed with nothing more than a glare. Barefooted, he was dressed in a satin tunic and trouser set that slightly concealed his overweight frame. There was an attractive quality to his face, but it was quickly diminished by his arrogance. He was naturally bald, with just the crown framing his thick, furrowed eyebrows.

"You attacked my guards?" he asked, his tone disgruntled and mildly perplexed. He clearly hadn't been expecting a female assailant.

"I defeated your guards," Siljanna asserted.

"You should be arrested for assaulting my men and entering the king's chambers uninvited," he declared in a tone that made her skin crawl and was matched by the calculating look in his eyes. "But I can think of a dozen better things to do with a woman like you."

"Oh, can you?" Siljanna said, masking her utter disgust. "I can think of better things to do with you too."

Closing the gap between them with two strides, Siljanna faced King Grayson and punched him as hard as she could in the face.

As Dylan and Caitlin approached Queen Nadia's room, they could hear talking up ahead. Placing a finger to her lips, Caitlin pressed herself against the wall and closed her eyes.

"What are you doing?" Dylan asked.

"Eavesdropping, how about you?" she mocked, assuming it was obvious.

"We're supposed to be getting the keys, does it matter what they're chatting about?"

"How can a former Imperial spy have no curiosity?" Caitlin whispered, hushing him a moment later. Rolling his eyes, Dylan leaned against the wall and listened to the banter.

"This whole situation doesn't make sense," remarked a flustered male guard. "First, Queen Nadia is a traitor who attempted to poison the king, then she's pregnant and must be spared. Next, she's abducted by rebel mages, but then somehow involved in the rebel conspiracy against the monarchy. Then, after the queen returns of her own free will, King Grayson punishes her with the knowledge that her parents were executed, claiming it was recent when in fact, it happened years ago. You cannot tell me you believe this tale. It smells worse than rotten eggs dropped in vinegar!"

When they heard the truth of Nadia's parents' execution, Dylan had to quickly place his hand over Caitlin's mouth to stifle her anguished cry. Even from the little she'd said, Dylan knew the situation was deeply personal for her, Spencer and especially the queen. This revelation proved a lot of what they'd endured had been for nothing.

"Finn, I admit it sounds strange, but what are you going to do, challenge the word of the king?" argued his comrade.

"Oh, because he's the epitome of honesty," Finn countered in a deeply sarcastic tone.

"Lower your voice, dammit. You'll be accused of treason if you express those thoughts in the wrong company," warned the second guard. "I know you've always felt for the queen's plight, but while King Grayson sits on the throne, he won't let anyone contest him."

Glancing at Caitlin, whose eyes had welled up with tears, Dylan knew he had to proceed with the plan. Getting the keys to the queen's chamber was vital but rather than needing evidence of her parent's imprisonment, Dylan wondered whether these guards, especially the one called Finn, who seemed more than aware of King Grayson's antics, would speak up in support of the queen.

Without a word, Dylan marched around the corner before the guards. Thanks to his disguise, they paused as he approached, their hands readied over their weapons.

"Excuse me, I'm new to the guard and was hoping for some insight," Dylan announced, clearing his throat and then bowing slightly, hoping it came across as respectful.

"There haven't been any inductions to the Royal Guard for months," Finn challenged. "Who are you?"

"I was trained in Siranor as a warden. I moved to Carlisse a few weeks ago and offered to join the Royal Guard just yesterday," he replied, fabricating half-truths to support the lie.

"What brings you to us, rookie?" questioned the second guard.

"I couldn't help but overhear you just now. Rumour has it that the queen is in confinement because she has evidence against the king. Is it true?" Dylan asked, hoping to exacerbate their doubts.

"It's true," Caitlin announced, charging around the corner to join them.

"You're the queen's chambermaid, aren't you?" Finn queried, recognising Caitlin remarkably quickly.

"Yes, my name is Caitlin Mason," she confirmed. "Release Queen Nadia and I guarantee you'll discover the truth. The time has come for King Grayson to answer for his crimes."

"You're more naive than you look if you think the king will stand trial at the queen's command," Finn countered, and although his words said otherwise, both Dylan and Caitlin could see a curiosity in his expression. He wanted to know the truth.

"She never said he'd face the trial willingly," Dylan added, noticing through a nearby window that a red drape had been released from a balcony on the opposite side of the castle, which he assumed was Siljanna's signal.

Reassessing both Dylan and Caitlin in silence for a moment, Finn's expression slowly went from suspicion to acceptance as he reached into his pocket for the key to Nadia's chamber. Offering it to Caitlin, she gratefully snatched the delicate object and lunged for the door.

"If this proves to be a ruse, you'll both be arrested," Finn warned, but his voice wasn't threatening. He seemed to believe them, and Dylan was certain he wouldn't be disappointed.

As she flung the door open, Caitlin was greeted by the sight of Nadia laying with her head cradled in Spencer's lap while he gently caressed her, using his healing touch to alleviate her withering symptoms. When they realised who had entered, Nadia sat up, her crisp blue eyes wide with relief while Spencer got up and strode towards the door, embracing Caitlin with both arms.

"You're okay," he whispered, holding his friend tightly.

"I could say the same about you," she replied. "Come on, we need to go."

"What's going on?" he asked, looking briefly at the guard who had apparently opened the way for Caitlin to enter and was allowing them to leave.

"King Grayson is about to be de-throned," Caitlin answered with an intensity she rarely displayed.

"Are you serious?" Nadia stammered. "How?"

"Come with us and you'll soon find out," Caitlin smirked, surprising both Spencer and Nadia equally. "That bastard is about to get exactly what he deserves."

Gathering her thoughts as she exited her chamber for the first time in several days, Nadia could hardly believe what was going on. Even though Spencer had his arm wrapped tightly around her waist for support, she was adamant about standing tall as they entered the throne room. Usually, Grayson would be sitting on the throne, and she would be made to kneel before him, but this time was very different. Instead of sitting proudly above the rest, Grayson was on his knees, chained in front of the Royal Guards by a woman. His three elite defenders were also beside him, looking like well-trained dogs glaring in silence at the woman holding the chain that restrained their master.

Caitlin then strode onto the platform and stood between her and the female warrior holding Grayson captive. Nadia could tell her friend knew the mysterious warrior, but wasn't certain how or when they met. Nearby stood another man, who was not a Royal Guard, but was wearing the same heavy armour. Rather than focusing on him, Nadia looked around the gathered soldiers. She recognised Finn Thoran, the kind guard who had been assigned as one of her watchers for years, but many of the other faces were unknown to her.

"Queen Nadia, please let me introduce you to Siljanna Stone and Dylan Rose. They are former wardens that have chosen to no longer serve the Imperator," Caitlin explained as Nadia ascended the stairs towards her friend, glancing briefly at the spouse she despised.

"You'll pay for this you bitch," Grayson hissed, assuming the entire plot had been contrived by Nadia. Rather than rising to his bait, Nadia turned her attention to Royal Guards looking on in muted anticipation.

"What's going on here?" she asked inquisitively.

"My lady, we in the Royal Guard wish to know the truth. Have war crimes been committed against the people of Iliria?" Finn asked, his unsettled gaze shifting to one of disapproval as he glanced at the king.

"Why would you believe my answer?" she questioned. "The king will just refute any claim I make."

"It has taken outsiders to present the opportunity for a fair trial. The king's word is under scrutiny, but if you wish to remain silent, despite knowing about your parents..." Finn continued, faltering at the realisation that she didn't know everything, yet.

"You mean because they're dead," Nadia clarified, her tone harsh. Even though she knew the Royal Guards didn't order her parents' deaths, she couldn't help but wonder if the executioner was present.

"Not just dead. They were executed years ago," Finn confessed, glancing at the king whose eyes were bulging out of their sockets with rage.

"Years ago?" Nadia whispered, her voice trembling as she staggered back into Spencer's supporting arm. This truth was yet another blow and although it crushed Nadia to think of all they'd endured in the false attempt to keep her parents alive, she found the new level of hatred towards Grayson was all the motivation she needed.

"My lady, I cannot fathom your heartache, but if you give us no alternative, we will defend the king against these intruders," Finn finished, his expression pleading.

Nadia took a second to assess each of the faces of the nearby guards; most of them genuinely seemed to want her to speak and she was not about to let this opportunity pass her by. She had to take the chance. Stepping away from Spencer's reassuring touch, she gathered her strength and addressed the room.

"You all know me and what I have endured at the hands of King Grayson Brock. Some of you may be aware that my motivation was to spare the lives of my parents. Innocent people that the king imprisoned simply because I disobeyed him. They were taken from me, meaning the only family I have left is the child I carry. The child whose blood gives me the right to claim that throne," Nadia called out, pointing firmly at the grand chair behind her. "King Grayson has never been challenged, and in his arrogance never thought he would be. He never imagined having to defend his actions, but today, I swear to each of you that he launched an assault on our people, the people of Iliria, for no other reason than to maintain the favour of Imperator Harlyn Rainer."

"This is ridiculous," spat the king, who had a distinctive bruise that was slowly darkening into a black eye. "We retaliated against the mage rebels that attacked our fair city. My actions were to defend my people!"

"There was no attack, I orchestrated a break-in, but it was only to rescue Queen Nadia and Spencer from the dungeon," Caitlin shouted out defensively, but while Spencer hushed her, Siljanna used Caitlin's outburst in their favour.

"I can confirm that claim," she declared. "There was no attack on Carlisse. When I served the Imperator, we not only arranged for the king's incapacitation but lured the so-called mage rebels here, in order to capture them. Our plan failed and soon after, I realised I was supporting the wrong side in this conflict, as are all of you."

"King Grayson is a cruel man who takes action only if it provides him with personal gain," Nadia continued, her voice clear and strong. "Having Imperial allies could provide us with untold perks that are years ahead of our ability to create, but to obtain them, the king sacrificed hundreds of lives, the lives of your friends and comrades for greed. Everyone that died in Iliria did so for nothing and the king will continue to risk your lives if you allow him to reclaim the throne."

Pausing for a moment, Nadia scanned the faces of every guard in the room. She couldn't be certain but believed she was winning them over.

"Guards, I command you to arrest these traitors and free me! Their claims are absurd," King Grayson shouted, only to have his restraints yanked by Siljanna. While bound, he couldn't wipe the spit from his mouth which made the once regal monarch look feral.

"A kingdom is made by its people and a ruler by their subjects. King Grayson does not deserve your loyalty, but if you support me as your queen, I will earn your trust and do what's best for this kingdom," Nadia finished as Spencer approached, noticing her body tremble even though she'd kept her voice steady.

As he reached her, Spencer took Nadia by the arm, allowing her to maintain a dignified appearance while placing his other hand over her stomach. Nadia knew his gesture was genuine, but for the first time, Caitlin seemed to pay particular attention. She was so accustomed to their love, but Nadia wondered if this small motion had revealed to her the one truth they'd hidden, that they planned to conceive a child together.

"I stand with the king," called out the gruff voice of Liam Kane, his ugly scowl and menacing tone proving that a broken hand and thorough beating was not enough to stifle his loyalty.

"Well, I stand with the queen," Finn countered.

Moments later, Finn's comrade stood beside him, showing solidarity in favour of Queen Nadia. One by one, the remaining guards slowly moved towards Nadia's side of the room, leaving a definitive empty space in front of the tyrant king. Finally, they turned and took a knee before Nadia.

"For the queen," they called out in unison.

"Traitors, you are all traitors!" King Grayson screamed, spit lashing from his mouth as he thrashed in his chains. Pulling his restraint tighter, Siljanna hauled the overweight man to his feet and removed his crown, discarding it to the floor.

"You won't be needing that anymore," she antagonised as Dylan and Finn approached, intending to escort the former king and his loyal guards to their new abode in the dungeon.

"Rotting in a dungeon is more than he deserves," Caitlin cried, her hair whipping around her face as she shook her head angrily.

"Caitlin, you're right but that decision isn't ours to make. It's Nadia's," Spencer replied calmly, and as she registered his comment, they both turned towards her. For the first time in seven years, not only was she free... she had control.

"Despite everything he's done, I can't order his death without speaking to him first," Nadia announced, collecting the fallen crown, dusting it off and then placing it on the padded seat of the throne. "His fate will be determined after that."

"Be careful," Spencer whispered, squeezing her hand with a look of deep concern in his eyes before she left.

Travelling through the castle, Nadia couldn't help but recall the last time she went to the dungeon, when she was the one in chains. If someone had told her that a mere three weeks later, Grayson would be overthrown and she would rise as the reigning monarch, she would've laughed in disbelief. The events of the day still felt surreal, but they had occurred. Pausing before the hallway that led to the dungeon, she cradled her stomach and took a deep breath.

"I don't know how little one, but I believe you are in there. Give me the strength to face my demons now, so that you never have to," she whispered, placing a hand on her stomach and silently praying that she was with child. Spencer's child.

Gathering herself, Nadia strode towards the guards outside the dungeon who bowed and permitted her access. Her heels clipped on the stone stairs as she descended, the echoing noise mirroring the speed of her heartbeat. When she reached the bottom of the stairs, she was greeted by Siljanna, Dylan and Finn.

"Your majesty," Finn announced while bowing deeply, his reverence coming with ease. Siljanna and Dylan looked at each other for a moment and then bowed too.

"May I speak with—" Nadia began but stopped herself before saying *the king*. "With my husband? Alone."

"May I speak freely first, Your Majesty?" Siljanna asked, concern evident on her face.

"You are Siljanna, the leader of the coup, correct?" Nadia asked cautiously.

"I think Caitlin can take that honour, but I did subdue the former king and his guards," Siljanna replied. Although her tone sounded modest, her words were far from it, leaving Nadia finding her difficult to read. "As she said earlier, Dylan and I are Imperial defectors."

"And for both acts, I thank you."

"Although I can't imagine the pain that man has put you through, please try to remember he is worth more to us alive than dead."

"How exactly is he useful to us?" Nadia enquired, genuinely curious why Siljanna might feel that way.

"Your majesty, keeping him alive could give us an advantage against Siranor. He was working with the Imperator and under the right pressure, could provide us with intel," Siljanna explained. "I struggled to control my own desire to do more than punch him, but his continued existence could benefit our cause."

"I will keep that in mind," Nadia replied and managed to keep her voice steady as she did so. "Although he deserves no mercy, I will not stoop to his level without just cause. Please know that no matter what happens, I am grateful to both of you for setting Spencer and myself free. I hope you will consider becoming guardians in Carlisse from this day forward."

The offer seemed to stun both Siljanna and Dylan.

"We will think on it, Your Majesty," Dylan replied, offering a proper, courtly bow. Nadia smiled in response as Finn touched her lightly on the shoulder.

"Shall I lead you to his cell, my lady?" he asked, the keys jangling in his fingers.

"Please do."

Following Finn through the dank corridor, Nadia held her head high and avoided eye contact as she passed the imprisoned guards who remained loyal to Grayson. Liam Kane spat at her feet, but Nadia refused to acknowledge the petty gesture. Arriving at a solid door, Finn stopped and faced his queen.

"My lady, before you go in there, take this," he said, handing her a dagger.

"Why?" she enquired, withholding her hand.

"I understand Siljanna's reasoning to keep that man alive, but you shouldn't go in there unarmed. He's dangerous and this cell doesn't change that," Finn replied, imploring her to take the small weapon.

After a hesitant pause, Nadia took the blade and tucked it discreetly up her right sleeve.

"Thank you," she whispered, giving Finn a soft smile to emphasise her gratitude. She could feel the cold steel against her skin but tried to ignore it as Finn pushed open the door.

"I'll be right outside," he confirmed, before letting her pass into the cell.

Leaving the door intentionally ajar, Nadia turned her attention to the single presence within the room. Sat on a wooden chair shrouded by shadow, Grayson sat with his back to her, staring at the light beyond the barred window above his head.

"Duplicitous wretch," he hissed, knowing it was her without even looking.

"Belligerent tyrant," she snapped back.

"If you think you've won, you're wrong. This is my kingdom. Even from behind these bars, I have influence far beyond your comprehension," he argued, his voice rising in both frustration and volume.

"You have no remorse, do you?" Nadia chastised, not sure why his lack of decency came as a surprise.

"Remorse, for you? Don't make me laugh," Grayson replied venomously. "I bet, deep down, you knew your parents were already dead. I admit I took a sadistic pleasure out of controlling you, but there's a part of you that enjoyed it too."

"You're sick!"

"And you're deluded. All you've achieved by imprisoning me is to seal your own fate. I don't even need to reach out to my contacts, they'll come to me. And once you bring my heir into this world, I will ensure you cease to exist."

Absorbing his threat, Nadia moved closer to her husband, the man she detested more than any other, and allowed her anger to boil to the surface. Every ounce of pain he'd caused seeped from her mind and laced her tongue as she leaned forward, allowing her lips to press lightly against his ear.

"The baby isn't yours," she whispered fiercely.

As her words registered, Grayson's expression became sheer loathing and he flung himself from the chair, attacking her in a wild rage. Grabbing her left arm with all the force he could muster, he threw Nadia backwards, forcing her to collide with the dungeon wall. Bashing her head on impact, Nadia tried to escape but couldn't reach the door before Grayson closed in, aiming to wrap his hands around her throat. He was going to choke the life out of her.

Forgetting about the concealed dagger tucked up her sleeve, she thrust both hands out to block his assault, but as she did, the blade slipped forward, landing in her palm. In her panicked state, she didn't think about whether she would hurt him or not, only about protecting her unborn child. The next thing she knew, he was staggering away from her, the dagger protruding from his throat.

Chapter Seventeen
Gambit

Finn burst through the solid cell door after hearing the commotion, only to be greeted with the sight of his former king falling to the floor with the hilt of the dagger he'd given the queen protruding from his throat. As Grayson Brock clawed at his neck and gurgled, his body desperately seeking air, Finn ignored the suffocating tyrant and turned his attention to the queen, who was shell-shocked.

"My lady, what happened?" Finn cried, grabbing her by the shoulders and pulling her away from her assailant.

"He tried to… he…" she stammered, pointing to Grayson as he writhed in pain, "he's dying."

Pivoting to look at the former king, Finn grimaced as he realised he was drowning in his own blood. Unable to let even a man as cruel as Grayson Brock suffer that way, Finn knelt beside him and twisted the dagger, ensuring the motion ended his life. He heard Queen Nadia whimper and shuffle backwards until she collided with the wall. As Finn returned to her side, he could see she was trembling.

"Are you okay?" he asked, intending to reach out to her until he noticed some of Grayson's blood was now spattered on his hand.

"I… I'm not sure," she began, her eyes fixated on Grayson's lifeless body and the pool of blood around his neck.

"Did he hurt you, my lady?" Finn asked more firmly, drawing her gaze so she focused on his steady brown eyes instead of the gruesome sight before her.

"He threatened to kill me, but I antagonised him. When he attacked, I…"

"You acted in self-defence," Finn asserted.

"I still killed him," she uttered through a heavy breath.

"No, I killed him, my lady," Finn replied, adamant to take responsibility, being the one who gave her the dagger in the first place and the one to deliver the killing blow.

"But it was my doing," Nadia pressed. Finn intended to argue further until he noticed her skin beginning to lose its pallor.

"You did what any mother would to protect her unborn child," Finn began, trying to comfort her. The mention of her baby seemed to do the trick as Nadia finally calmed her breathing, giving Finn a grateful nod. Suddenly, she wrapped her arms around herself and sunk to her knees.

"Not now," Nadia groaned, trying but failing to stand.

"My lady, what's happening?" Finn asked, his concern amplified as her fingertips blackened before his eyes.

"Please, take me to Spencer Valen. He's the only one that can help," she pleaded, her voice barely audible.

Without needing to be asked twice, Finn swept Queen Nadia into his arms and carried her out of the dungeon. Once up the main stairwell, he spotted Siljanna and Dylan deep in conversation.

"Help!" he shouted, staggering towards them as the queen clung to him.

"What happened?" Dylan called out, reaching Finn first.

"The king attacked her, but she retaliated in self-defence. I was asking if she was hurt when her skin lost all its colour and she collapsed," Finn explained, trying to shift the queen so that she was stable in his arms.

"Is Grayson Brock dead?" Siljanna asked urgently, seemingly ignorant of the queen's condition.

"Spencer... please," Nadia implored, her words hoarse.

"He wouldn't have survived his injuries... so I ended his torment," Finn answered through gritted teeth. Although the queen was light as a feather, Finn was flustered. He had expected an interrogation for the events in the dungeon but only after locating Spencer.

"The king is dead," Siljanna chided, her tone irritated as she snapped at Finn. "I can't believe you let that happen."

Queen Nadia sucked in a laboured breath as a searing pain shot through her.

"Not now," she muttered, recoiling in Finn's arms. As she repeated the words over and over, the suspicion Finn had about her health was confirmed. The queen suffered from the withering.

"She has the withering. I need to get her to Spencer Valen, he can help," Finn insisted, not even registering Siljanna's reprimand.

"Spencer went with Caitlin to the archives. Dylan, run as fast as you can and bring them to the main dining hall," Siljanna ordered, encouraging Finn to take Nadia there too.

Although she wasn't his superior, Dylan launched into action under Siljanna's command. Finn quickly realised she had an aura that made people want to obey and Dylan was responding to that. In Dylan's place, he expected that he to would've launched into action. It was a quality that would make her ideal for leadership.

A few minutes later, Spencer came crashing through the large hall doors, frantically searching for Nadia, who had been placed on a lounge chair. She looked serene, as if simply sleeping, but Spencer knew better. Crashing to his knees, he pulled open her blouse just enough to place his hands directly over her heart and then began mumbling. Everyone assumed it was some kind of spell, but it wasn't. He was praying.

After a long, tense moment, they heard Nadia take a deep breath, followed by several lighter, rhythmic ones. Spencer's relief was palpable over everyone else in the room, even Caitlin, who had entered seconds behind him. Sinking his head into the crevice of Nadia's neck, Spencer took a few seconds to collect himself before addressing Finn.

"What in the name of the gods happened?" he asked, his tone a mix of demand and desperation.

"Queen Nadia defended herself from an attack by the king. He's dead, but the trauma seemed to trigger her reaction."

"She killed the king?" Caitlin asked, her eyes widening with anticipation. "He's really dead?"

"He's dead," Finn confirmed, resulting in Caitlin clasping a hand over her mouth to contain her joy.

"How exactly did she kill the king?" Siljanna questioned. "don't understand how a person as physically weak as Queen Nadia could achieve such a feat."

"I gave her a dagger and I don't regret it," Finn confessed. "If I hadn't, I believe the queen would be the one that's dead now."

"You're right, I'm sorry," Siljanna replied glancing at Caitlin. "Although I'm disappointed that we lost the opportunity to interrogate the former king, I can't argue with that. Having Nadia safe is far more important."

Noticing her stir, Spencer supported Nadia as she sat up on the lounge chair. She placed a gentle hand under his chin and smiled. This wasn't the first time he'd saved her life and even though it wouldn't be the last, he was instantly aware of two things; the love they shared was deeper than many would ever experience and he would do anything and everything in his power to protect it.

"Are you all right Nadia… I mean, my queen?" Caitlin asked, quickly correcting her formality with the guards present.

"I will be," she replied in earnest, giving Caitlin a grateful smile. She hadn't forgotten Siljanna's admission that Caitlin was truly responsible for the coup.

Witnessing the silent conversation of thanks between the two women and long-time friends, Siljanna found herself captivated by Caitlin's vibrancy. Her russet hair had mostly fallen loose and flicked around her narrow face, which managed to simultaneously express joy and concern. Siljanna couldn't help but wonder why she was so intrigued by Caitlin, but also couldn't deny that she was.

"My lady, given the circumstances, you should address the people of the kingdom. Do you feel well enough for a public appearance?" Finn enquired, interrupting the trio's joint moment of relief.

"Give her a moment, won't you," Spencer remarked in a tone that Finn did not appreciate.

"I am merely suggesting that our monarch speaks to her people and quells the rumours that are bound to be flying around the city by now," he countered, his eyebrows furrowed as he stared Spencer down.

"He's right, Spencer. The people deserve to know what happened here and what's going to happen from now on," Nadia interjected, "I made a promise to earn the guards' loyalty and I will not break that oath. Finn, please make the necessary arrangements. I'll address the people from the courtyard balcony this afternoon."

"Of course, my lady," he replied, bowing as he left.

"This is incredible, I can't believe this is really happening!" Caitlin mused. "You're going to be a real queen and make a real difference."

"Well, I'm going to try," Nadia responded, a smile spreading across her face as Caitlin leaned forward and hugged her. "Now before Caitlin whisks me away to get ready; Siljanna, Dylan, have you thought more on my offer to join the Royal Guard?"

"We have, Your Majesty," Dylan replied, glancing over at Siljanna for confirmation that she too had decided.

"And?" Nadia asked inquisitively.

"We would be honoured to become your guardians," Siljanna confirmed, pausing momentarily as she recalled the poorly trained guards she'd encountered so far. "Although, we request the opportunity to rework the training facilities in the kingdom. Both your guards and military need to be improved."

"The remaining military you mean. I believe many were lost during the assault on Iliria," Nadia murmured.

They were all worried about the missing troops. Although the soldiers didn't know the attack on Iliria was misguided, it was strange that they hadn't all returned to the city.

"There were indeed casualties, but many more fled through the mire. The soldiers will hopefully return but I can coordinate search parties for those that don't," Dylan offered.

"Meanwhile, I'll begin training the Royal Guard properly. Anyone that wishes to join us is welcome," Siljanna added, wondering if Caitlin, with her impulsive nature, would be tempted.

"Thank you. I can tell you'll both become irreplaceable in no time," Nadia affirmed before Caitlin pulled her from the chair and rushed her away, not commenting on the training offer, to Siljanna's disappointment.

After fleeing the failed attack on Iliria, Juliette didn't find it hard to locate Noah in the dense woodland. All she had to do was follow the sound of irate screaming and trampled woodland. Dragging her hostage along after knocking the boy out, however, had proven to be the more difficult task. Finding the abandoned log cabin that Noah had claimed, she left the boy slumped against the outside wall and entered to reunite with her partner. His ruckus made it very clear they didn't need to be discreet.

"Those pathetic, useless soldiers… I almost had him!" Noah yelled, smashing everything he came into contact with.

"I'm fine thank you," Juliette replied indignantly, folding her slender arms and expecting an apology.

As he registered her annoyance, Noah turned, his deep scowl portraying just how livid he was. As he recalled it, she abandoned the fight before him.

"Did I partner a mewling child or an assassin? I'm not your babysitter, Juliette."

"Oh, get over yourself! I wasn't expecting to be rescued but I would appreciate my partner being grateful that I'm not dead," she yelled back, refusing to let his frustration intimidate her.

With an exaggerated groan, Noah found an old chopping axe and launched it across the room. He'd clearly intended for it to lodge into one of the cabin's thick wooden support beams, but it just clattered to the floor, knocking over a small stack of logs on the way. Stepping on a log before it collided against her leg, Juliette raised her eyebrows as if to ask, *Are you done now?* and silently waited for Noah to calm down.

"We can rest here but then must return to Carlisse. I want to have a word with King Grayson about his so-called military," Noah demanded, his temper slowly receding.

"Fine, but you can go fetch the boy," Juliette replied, flopping into a big armchair by the unlit fire.

"What boy?" Noah asked, looking down at her disapprovingly.

"The unconscious one. He's outside by the door," Juliette answered, emphasising how proud she was of herself. "I used him to escape Iliria, but now I have another use for him."

"Well, you're clearly not the maternal type," Noah jibed, only to receive a disgruntled look from Juliette in response. "What do you need the boy for?"

"I don't need him, but the Imperator does," Juliette explained, stretching like a cat to get comfortable. "She's been after a mage captive for a very long time. It's the real reason Dylan and I were sent after Rylie in the first place. I bet she'll also be keen to hear that Englycerol works like a poison against the Ar'encal."

As Juliette ran her fingers through her coal-black hair, Noah huffed, accepting that she was right. Heading outside, Noah found the unconscious boy.

"That's Freya's son," he chuckled aloud, lifting the boy and throwing him over his shoulder. "Maia's best friend Freya… who would've thought Juliette's desire for self-preservation would come in so handy."

Continuing to laugh to himself, Noah took Sebastian inside, barred the cabin door and made himself as comfortable as he could on the only other chair in the room.

"How did you knock the boy out?" he asked curiously, leaning towards Juliette.

"There are some rather pungent weeds that grow around the Callee River. I collected some the first time I was in Carlisse. Once dissolved and mixed with ethanol, the resulting stench is very strong. More than enough to knock out a child," Juliette explained, retrieving another vial of the same substance from her bag.

"You are insidious when you want to be," Noah commented in a tone that implied praise.

"An attractive quality no doubt," Juliette replied with absolute confidence. "It won't last long, so I recommend tying him up."

As she suggested it, Juliette pointed flippantly to a rope in the corner, expecting Noah to do the manual labour for her.

During the night, Juliette and Noah were awoken several times by Sebastian's panicked thrashing. He was young, not quite into his teenage years and very slight. His short stature added to his youthful appearance, a typical trait for the Ar'encal but not as common in mage children. As Juliette rolled over, trying to get back to sleep, Noah stood up and began pacing.

"If I remember rightly, he only has a healing touch, so poses no threat. I could punch him in the mouth to stop him screaming," Noah groaned.

"It's taking all my strength not to pour something very toxic down his throat. If I can't indulge my desires, then neither can you. Just gag him," Juliette replied, pulling the blanket she'd found over her ears to try and muffle the sound.

The only threat the kid posed was causing permanent exhaustion unless he shut up... which he didn't.

By morning, the dark circles under Juliette's eyes were prominent and matched only by her mood. Noah was equally unimpressed. He'd given up on the hope of sleeping hours before she had, and that weariness made him even more irritable than he'd been the day before. Agreeing they were too tired to make the journey to Carlisse, the pair took another day to recover. Sebastian eventually stopped thrashing and trying to call out through his gag, resulting in a blissful quiet that allowed Noah to nap for several hours.

When he awoke, Noah's matted hair was disgusting, so he got up and headed towards the river. To his surprise, Juliette was there with long oilcloth gloves on, rummaging around the river's edge.

"Looking for more pungent weeds?" he asked, unabashedly stripping before her. The water was ripe with Encia, but this was the one perk of still having the Arencian rune burned into his flesh.

"Indeed, although I find myself mildly distracted now," she muttered, taking in the sight of him as he entered the water.

Although covered with fresh bruises and scratches, he knew his muscular body was still a miraculous sight. Submerging himself beneath the water, Noah briskly rubbed his skin and hair until all the grime fell away. When he rose from the water, he turned to face Juliette and she could see his rune glowing like a hot iron.

"Care to join me?" he taunted, knowing she couldn't enter the water but enjoying her irked reaction. Grabbing a handful of weeds, Juliette stalked away, but he could just about hear her cursive mumbles as she left.

After bathing, Noah went for a quick hunt and gathered some wood. Returning to their cabin, he started a fire and cooked the wild rabbit he'd killed while Juliette garnished the basic provisions with a handful of fruit she'd found in the surrounding woods. They managed to force-feed Sebastian in between his attempts to bite them and agreed to resume their journey in the morning. It would take them several hours to reach the capital on foot so there was little point in starting until they had the strength to complete it.

Even fully rested, the journey along the winding river was a slog. Juliette had to be particularly careful as her attire, like usual, was far from suitable for trekking through a forest, but to Noah's surprise, she seldom complained. When they finally arrived back in Carlisse, the position of the winter sun told them it had passed midday, but despite that, the streets were buzzing with gossipers. It didn't take long before both Noah and Juliette heard whispers that the king had been arrested and that a public address was happening soon.

With growing concern, Juliette used her concoction to knock out Sebastian again and helped Noah to put the boy on his back. To any passer-by, it looked like a brother carrying his sleeping sibling as they mingled into the crowded courtyard. To their surprise, the gathered people included mage and Ar'encal slaves standing alongside the monarchy citizens. After a few minutes of waiting, their surprise turned to horror as Juliette and Noah witnessed Queen Nadia emerge on a balcony above them to address the amassed crowd.

"Citizens of Carlisse, I am certain in the last few days or even hours you have heard rumours that many of you may find alarming. That is why I am here before you, to alleviate your fears," she began, her voice clear and strong.

"I don't like this," Juliette whispered, but Noah's attention was fixated on the queen as she continued.

"King Grayson Brock was arrested and trialled this morning by the Royal Guards for war crimes against Iliria. His recent assault has been proven to be an unprovoked attack on innocent civilians of this kingdom. People just like you," the queen explained, pausing only to let the rising chatter amongst the people calm back down.

"What about the mage rebellion?" a voice shouted from the crowd.

"There has never been a rebellion. It was a lie, fabricated by Imperator Rainer. Furthermore, after the Royal Guard swore fealty to me, the former king made an attempt on my life. During the altercation, Grayson Brock was killed," Queen Nadia confirmed, the news causing another wave of hysteria among the people.

At the mention of his death, Noah turned his attention to Juliette, knowing that she'd formed a unique, albeit slightly disturbing bond with the king. To his surprise, she seemed more disappointed than upset.

"We can't stay here," Juliette said, turning to leave.

"Wait, let's see what else we can learn," Noah instructed, grabbing Juliette roughly by the wrist to halt her departure.

"As I carry the rightful blood heir to the throne, the duty of ruling falls to me, and under my rule, there will be changes. For too long, this kingdom has prospered from cruelty and enslavement… but no longer!" Queen Nadia declared, her voice rising above the chatter from the crowd. "Change does not happen overnight, but slavery in this kingdom will be abolished. From this day, everyone, no matter their race, religion or creed will have the same rights within the kingdom."

"She's mad!" Juliette scoffed, looking frantically at Noah whose attention was firmly back on the queen.

Bold move. Asserting your newly obtained power in this way could turn this rabble against you, he thought. *Then again, there's nothing more attractive than a powerful woman.*

"This act will sever our fragile alliance with Siranor but presents a much greater opportunity. The law will be changed to allow trade agreements with the Ar'encal, like the established relationship with our Terran neighbours as well as permitting mages to live here freely, own land and practise fair trade. We will become a great nation again but on a foundation of equality, not oppression," the queen proclaimed and as she did, a squad of Royal Guards emerged from the castle entrance and lined up beneath the balcony.

"For the queen!" they chanted, their armour clattering as they raised their spears in unison. The show of solidarity hushed the crowd for a moment before a roar of applause and cheering began.

"*Now* we need to leave," Noah confirmed, signalling for Juliette to head towards the northern gate, but not before glancing at the queen one final time.

His lingering glance caught Juliette's attention and even seemed to amuse her slightly. He wondered how she might use this knowledge but figured it wouldn't affect their arrangement. She was powerful too, in her own way and although he didn't care for her personality, he admired her tenacity.

Slipping out of the city unnoticed, they made their way to the port in Beyasil and caught a sailing that evening heading for the Western Continent town of Hale. The journey would take longer, but arriving closer to Siranor was of greater importance. They had a lot to report to the Imperator.

As the crowd cheered, Nadia realised she hadn't anticipated this reaction and found herself in a mild state of shock. It was human nature to refuse change, but the people of Carlisse seemed to welcome the idea of freedom for the mages and Ar'encal. It made Nadia realise there were more sympathisers than she'd even dared hope for in the city. With so much support, she began to believe that she really could make a difference.

When the gathered crowd started to dissipate, Nadia headed inside and was greeted by a deep, full kiss from Spencer while Caitlin, Siljanna and Dylan applauded from the sidelines.

"That was impressive, 'Your Majesty'," Siljanna announced. "I'm proud that for the first time, I can support a just ruler."

"Thank you. Your support is going to be vital in the weeks to come," Nadia replied gratefully.

"You shall have it gladly, from both of us," Dylan confirmed, his expression mirroring Siljanna's. "This is the first time I too will be following a leader with admirable morals."

"Shall we tell them?" Nadia asked, turning to Spencer with a bright look in her eyes.

"I bet Caitlin already suspects," Spencer replied, repeating the gentle, reaffirming touch he'd placed over her stomach when addressing the Royal Guards during the trial.

"I do, I do… but I still want to hear you say it," Caitlin declared, her excitement bubbling to the surface.

"It's a little too early to know for sure, but Spencer and I think we really are pregnant," Nadia confirmed, enjoying her friend's ecstatic reaction. "With Spencer as the father, the baby will have mage heritage and could be immune to the withering."

"This must remain a secret though," Spencer insisted, mostly targeting the comment to Caitlin. "Some of Nadia's support for the throne is linked to the belief her unborn child is Grayson's heir and it is his bloodline that gives Nadia a rightful claim."

"Of course, I promise," Caitlin replied gleefully. "I wouldn't jeopardise either of you but I'm just *so* happy!"

"You're not mad we didn't tell you our plan sooner?" Nadia asked, nervously biting her lower lip as she turned towards her best friend.

Caitlin exuberantly shook her head, confirming she hadn't taken their secrecy to heart and the resulting relief only boosted Nadia's joy at making the announcement.

"What makes you suspect the pregnancy at this early stage, if I may ask?" Dylan queried, not meaning to dampen the mood but also knowing it wasn't common for a woman to know with such certainty this early into a pregnancy.

"It's a feeling really," Nadia began, glancing at Spencer.

"I've been healing Nadia for several years, ever since she's been afflicted by the withering. It has always drained me to do so, but for the last few weeks, something within her body now accepts my healing touch," Spencer continued.

"It feels like my body welcomes his magic now," Nadia agreed. "I think that's why I recovered so quickly earlier, despite it being a particularly sudden onslaught of withering symptoms."

"If the baby is mine…" Spencer started to explain.

"It is, I just know it," Nadia interrupted, taking his hand with her own and making him smile.

"What does that mean?" Siljanna asked, wondering why Caitlin's reaction was so elated.

"We believe there's a much stronger chance of Nadia bringing the baby to term. A mage baby will absorb the Encia in her bloodstream rather than succumb to the withering," Spencer continued, and his words made Caitlin's eyes grow wide. "It could even cure Nadia of the withering too."

Hearing his final statement filled Caitlin with more joy than she could contain. Rushing towards them, she threw her arms around both of them and began to cry happy tears.

"It would be a miracle and while we continue to hope every day, we have more pressing matters to attend to," Nadia added, stroking Caitlin's hair as she tightened her embrace.

"Of course, I'm just a bit overwhelmed," Caitlin replied, eventually letting her friends go so she could wipe the tears of joy from her eyes.

As she did, Caitlin glanced over to Dylan and Siljanna, giving them a grateful look with the deepest of sincerity. Although Siljanna had claimed Caitlin was responsible for the coop, Nadia knew that without the skills Siljanna and Dylan possessed, she and Spencer would not be free. This wildest dream of theirs would never have come true.

"Caitlin, I need you to send a message to the leader of the Ar'encal. She and her people should be invited here to discuss the opportunities ahead," Nadia said with a smile, clearing her throat and attempting to sound regal.

"Right away, Your Majesty," Caitlin replied, chuckling softly at Nadia's formal attempt as she rushed from the room.

"Dylan, could I task you to proceed with your earlier suggestion and send out search parties for any surviving soldiers? I'm sure Finn will assist you," Nadia continued, looking to the first of her new guards.

"A wise action. I'm certain it won't be long before the Imperator discovers what's happened here so we should maximise our defences," Dylan replied, bowing slightly before leaving.

"And how may I help?" Siljanna enquired, turning towards the new monarch.

"I need you to completely overhaul the Royal Guard, from their equipment through to a full training regime. The risk of a coup worked *for* us, I don't want a similar attempt to work *against* us," Nadia explained to Siljanna's delight.

"My training days at the academy were some of the best days of my life. It'll be an honour to impart that knowledge to improve the Royal Guard," Siljanna replied. "This worthy task is something I hope my brother will be proud of me for doing, and also help to continue repairing that relationship."

"Thinking of that relationship, the guards found these while sweeping the inner courtyard," Nadia commented, collecting a pair of pistols and holding them out towards Siljanna.

"Wow, I never thought I'd see those again."

"Do you want them back?" Nadia asked, looking at Siljanna curiously.

"Not yet, but maybe one day," Siljanna answered, smiling softly before departing.

Once Siljanna had gone, Nadia and Spencer found themselves alone once again. They were quite accustomed to spending most of their time together, but things were very different now. They were free.

"And how can I best serve my queen?" Spencer asked, his tone soft and playful while his expression was pure.

"You are no longer a slave, Spencer. Are you sure you wish to continue serving the throne?" Nadia replied lightly.

"I have two very compelling reasons to stay," he answered, pushing the falling strands of dark hair away from his eyes.

"I'm glad," she replied, giving him a tender kiss. "Our priority should be changing the law and as the former archivist, you're the best person to help me bring about those changes correctly but before that, there is something I need to ask you."

"Anything," Spencer replied openly, proving there wasn't anything she could ask for that he would refuse.

"My claim to the throne is dependent on people believing this child, our child, is actually Grayson's heir. It may not feel that way now, but that'll be torture for you in the years to come," Nadia began, dipping her head in sorrow.

"I can bear the pain of this secret. Anything to keep you and our child safe," Spencer replied instantly but Nadia quickly placed her finger to his lips. She wasn't finished.

"Knowing you would endure a lifetime of pain for our family means more than I can even express but that is not what I need to ask. Although you cannot be known as this child's father, you can be their *dad*," Nadia continued, and her words piqued his curiosity.

"Are you saying I could be named a parental guardian?" Spencer asked, only to be answered with a rapidly shaking head.

"No, Spencer… my question is, will you marry me?" Nadia proposed, taking him by the hand and dropping to her knees as she spoke. The sky-blue dress Caitlin had chosen for her billowed out from the waistline as she descended, laying elegantly around her while she looked up at him with an expression of hope.

Utterly speechless, Spencer's knees quickly buckled, and he sank to Nadia's level. Her question had genuinely shocked him and she couldn't blame him. They'd dreamed about this moment for so long, it was hard to accept it was real. Several seconds passed before he realised Nadia was still waiting for him to speak.

"There is no other possible answer... *yes,*" he finally blurted out.

"That was quite possibly the longest silence of my life," she replied, sighing heavily before wrapping her arms around him. "My Prince Consort."

"I don't need a title, just you and our baby."

"We've always been yours, that title just proves it," Nadia whispered, holding him even tighter.

Chapter Eighteen
Peril

The day after the vigil faded into a sleepy blur for everyone apart from Zack, who found himself up early and spending most of his time in his father's office… the office he'd share with Parker. Despite his continued uncertainty, he had decided to accept Maia's request to become an advisor. He'd gone to her room first thing, but the healers told him she was sleeping, so instead, he left a letter for her.

Although he couldn't see the room before him, he could picture every detail. From the large maple desk to the collection of maps stowed in the far corner and the area chart on the wall, the room would always be familiar. Part of him still found it surreal that his father would never sit behind that desk again, coordinating the guard movements and liaising with their contacts across the continent while the other part of him felt it even stranger that some those duties were now his responsibility.

It was late afternoon when he decided to return to Maia. He was getting better at navigating without guidance, but it still took him some time to get from the training grounds to the infirmary. When he finally arrived, the Ar'encal healer on duty led him back to Maia's room, pulled up a chair and guided him into it.

Maia was also spending the day resting as her body continued to battle the strange poison afflicting her.

"Hello Zack, it's kind of you to visit," Maia greeted.

"How are you feeling, Maia?" Zack asked as he sat back in the chair.

"Weak... but stubborn," she replied. She sounded unimaginably tired. "I read your letter."

"Were you surprised by my decision?" he asked.

"A little, but pleasantly so. Knowing that you'll be staying here and working alongside Parker is a relief," she replied honestly.

"I'm still not certain how much help I'll be," Zack remarked, fidgeting with his cane.

"Can I ask you a favour?"

"Of course," he replied. Even though his rank had been elevated, he still spoke to her with the respect she'd earned.

"Will you gather the others in the pavilion tomorrow morning? We should prepare for what is to come," Maia requested.

"No problem. I believe Morgan intends to return to Iliria tomorrow to gather the wardens, should I ask him to remain for the meeting?" Zack asked, tilting his head inquisitively. It was a quirk he'd done for years but Maia couldn't help chuckling at the youthful familiarity of his attitude.

"Please do. He represents a valuable ally and there may be something we can do for him and the wardens before they depart," Maia replied. "I want Morgan to know how grateful I am to him and his comrades for their aid."

"That's a good point. As the entire group have basically slept through the day, I haven't spoken to anyone yet, but I'm sure they'll rouse later. When they do, I'll advise them about the meeting," Zack confirmed with pleasant nod.

"Have you not taken any time to rest, Zack?" Maia asked.

"Not really, I can't shake this restless feeling," Zack explained honestly. "Are you sure I'm the right person to act as a liaison and split the captain's responsibilities with Parker? Harrison would be a much better fit."

"Zack, the simple fact you continue to ask, tells me you are," Maia answered simply. "Did you know your father was an advisor before I asked him to take charge?"

"No... I just assumed he worked his way up through the ranks."

"He did, but his unique ability to create meaningful contacts caught my attention. Not every captain has required an advisor. Your father didn't, but his predecessor wasn't very trusting, just like Parker isn't."

"I had no idea. I must admit I was beginning to wonder if you'd made up the role to suit my limited range of abilities," Zack replied awkwardly.

"Your father doubted himself too, having been only a humble merchant at first, but he was made for the role and became a great leader through the experience. I believe you will grow from it too."

"Big boots to fill," Zack mumbled, rubbing the back of his neck anxiously. "I may stumble along the way."

"And that's okay. You'll find your feet in the end," Maia reassured, reaching out to place a weary hand on Zack's knee. "I will be forever grateful to your father, and in doing this, we both honour him."

"Part of me wishes I'd stayed in Arencia over these last few years. If I'd only known how little time I had left with him," Zack confessed, sagging forward in the chair and placing one hand on top of Maia's.

"Staying here wasn't right for you then. Your father knew that and never judged you for leaving," Maia countered. "We've all only got one life. You've spent yours honourably. Do you want to know why your acceptance was so important to me?"

"Why?" Zack questioned, taking the bait.

"Because it was your father's hope. We spoke before entering Carlisse to rescue your friends and he told me he wanted you to have a reason to stay in Arencia. He planned to train you as his potential successor, choosing you over Noah who was the expected choice at the time," Maia replied sincerely.

"Was he drunk?" Zack replied in disbelief. His natural humour caused Maia to laugh.

"I'm certain he wasn't, Zack," Maia giggled, expecting him to deflect with a joke. "Sadly, he never got the chance to train you, but he was so proud of you. Both your achievements and the man you've become. We'd all heard of the infamous *mage smuggler* and the countless people that found safety in Iliria or here thanks to his guidance… your guidance."

"Well then, I better continue to make him proud," Zack replied, sitting up straight with determination.

"Just by being the man that you are, you will. Now go and get some rest and I'll see you and the others in the morning," Maia instructed, and Zack agreed, saying goodbye before slowly making his way home.

The next morning, the entire group headed up to the pavilion. On the way, Morgan and Harrison were engrossed in a private conversation that had begun the night before. It had something to do with Noah and Tivani, but their hushed tones ensured that no one else could hear any details. When the group arrived, Maia and Alistair waiting for them. Maia was still clearly weak, sitting on a lounge chair with a blanket delicately placed over her lap, but when she noticed them, she sat upright to greet them.

"Thank you all for coming," she began and invited them to be seated. "While I still wish to speak with you all, I received some unbelievable news earlier that I want to share first."

"What's happened?" Harrison asked, hopeful it was word from Siljanna or Caitlin.

"Queen Nadia has written to us," Maia began, the smile on her face evident it was good news. "I'm delighted to inform you that not only are she and Spencer safe, but with Siljanna and Dylan's help, Carlisse has been liberated from the reign of King Grayson."

"Truly?" Lianna exclaimed. "How did they manage that?"

"The details of how are rather brief," Maia answered, glancing at Harrison as her smile grew.

"I'd put good coin on Siljanna and Dylan somehow infiltrating the castle," he suggested, knowing Dylan's particular skill set and that Siljanna would've wanted to help Caitlin in any way possible.

"Regardless of how… it's an impressive feat and has created an unrivalled opportunity," Alistair commented, piquing the curiosity of everyone around him.

"Queen Nadia goes on to explain that she gained the support of the Royal Guards and took the throne, although it cost the former king his life," Maia continued. "As Alistair just hinted, she has expressed a desire for true peace with the Ar'encal."

"Her plan sounds ambitious and includes signing a formal treaty. For that, she's requested that Maia or a spokesperson for the Ar'encal travels to Carlisse," Alistair added, sounding pleased whilst simultaneously fidgeting as if concerned.

"I may be weak but there is no force on this planet that will stop me from securing this opportunity for my people," Maia exclaimed, "but I know it is reckless to go alone."

Picking up on her unspoken question, Zack took no time at all to speak up.

"Then you should be escorted into the city," he suggested. "As your liaison in matters of alliances, I'd like to be there."

"I would too, but I've already accepted Parker's offer to join us as far as Lorvale, so I need you here to coordinate the guards in his absence and send messengers to our established contacts. This is a big shift in relations for us and will affect them greatly too," Maia explained, sounding a little disheartened.

"How about Alex, then?" Zack suggested "Would you accept the responsibility?"

"An escort mission suitable only for the finest Aegis Squire," Harrison mused cheerfully.

"I'd be honoured," Alex replied respectfully. Although he still considered Zack a friend, he was adapting quickly to his new, superior position among the Aegis Guard.

"Thank you, Alex. Lianna, would you like to accompany them?" Zack asked, turning his head in her direction. As usual, she'd walked beside him all the way from their homes and still had her arm loosely intertwined with his.

"I would," she confirmed, which surprised absolutely no one. All her friends believed that Lianna had lingering feelings for Spencer, so she wanted to prove, to them and to herself, that those feelings were gone.

"I'd like to go too," Rylie announced. "I need to have an open conversation with Siljanna."

"Is that really the best idea?" Paige asked nervously as Evie glared at her sister, shaking her head in solemn agreement with their mother.

"Siljanna did risk her life to help us save Rylie at Jumant Fort," Harrison interjected quietly, defending his twin.

"She also caused all our problems in the first place," Paige argued, her raised eyebrow revealing she remained unconvinced at Siljanna's rapid change of heart.

"I agree that Rylie should go," announced Nate, catching his wife's surprised stare. "Siljanna made mistakes, grievous ones that cost our family greatly, but without her, we wouldn't have Rylie back."

"What about Harrison's amulet? I thought that's what saved Rylie?" Evie countered.

"You're partially right. The amulet allowed Rylie to regain control but had Siljanna not been the bait, there would've been nothing to lure her to Jumant Fort and no opportunity for me to use it on her," Harrison corrected gently.

"The Aeon power fed off my rage but made me forget all logic and reason. It was like I was a passenger in my own body. Siljanna's part was crucial for the plan to succeed," Rylie acknowledged.

"Now you are back in control, Rylie, you don't have to keep wearing those suppression runes," Maia added, noticing the way she kept touching the band of the amulet.

"It's true, the suppression runes on that amulet were designed to restore your balance," Harrison explained, reaching out to take Rylie's hand. "They serve little purpose now aside from making it harder for you to continue training."

"I don't think I'm ready to take it off yet," Rylie answered gingerly. "While Maia has offered to continue training me, I'd rather wear the amulet until I have better control, especially during heightened emotional situations."

"You have an incredible power within you Rylie, but you can harness it," Maia reassured, causing her young charge to dip her head. It was a feeble attempt to hide her blushing cheeks behind her thick, wavy hair. "There is no telling how powerful you could become, but I will help you find out, and safely."

"Perhaps I could create a different amulet for you, something that enhances your clarity and control without suppressing your power," Harrison suggested, giving her hand a gentle squeeze.

"That would be great! It'd be foolish to believe I won't need to tap into my powers again, I just don't want to lose myself in the process," Rylie replied with a worried smile.

"That brings me to the original reason I called you here," Maia continued. "The threat from Siranor remains high and while I travel to Carlisse, we need to prepare for how the Imperator could respond to losing her foothold there."

"Now that Iliria is safe, I can suggest to Parker that we re-establish a guard presence along the coast," Zack began. "With Noah aiding the Imperator, that may not be enough. He knows our tactics and capabilities well, even if he cannot tell his new allies in as many words."

"When we fought, Noah gloated that Imperator Harlyn plans to attack Tivani next because she believes Siljanna is there," Harrison advised, looking over at Morgan. It was the core matter of the conversation they'd been having in private.

"But Siljanna isn't in Tivani, she's back in Carlisse, right?" Zack muttered.

"The Imperator doesn't know that," Morgan replied, sounding deeply concerned. "We were careful to hide both Siljanna and Dylan while they were in town, but someone obviously spotted them."

"Would the Imperator attack even without a recently confirmed sighting?" Maia asked, mirroring Morgan's fear.

"It's unlikely. She's not impulsive like the... *former* king," Morgan answered with a brief stutter. "She'll bide her time and strike when it causes the most impact, but while the wardens and I are here, the people in Tivani are vulnerable."

"Is there anything we can do to help?" Zack asked, and as he offered, Maia nodded in wholesome agreement.

"The wardens and I must return. While my interim commander, Téa, is a good person, she's not a warrior and has no idea about the imminent danger," Morgan admitted. "I only put her in charge because I trust her and didn't anticipate an attack on Tivani."

"I can make the necessary arrangements. The quickest way to return would be on the *Pilgrim* from Revaine. She may even still be in port," Zack replied, realising that Morgan's return with the wardens was urgent.

"Is there anything from Dawne?" Morgan asked. "We departed under the guise of training in the Sarron Islands and ideally need to return from the port in Niyati, not Yasras."

"It may technically be a shorter crossing from Dawne to Niyati, but those trade vessels make a lot more stops enroute. It'll likely be the end of the week before you get back if go that way," Zack explained.

"There's clearly a spy working for the Imperator within Tivani. We should keep up appearances," Morgan confirmed reluctantly. "If they suspect we've aided you, word of our return would be all the grounds the Imperator needs to strike."

"Understood," Zack replied assertively. "I have a couple of contacts in Dawne that should help."

"Thank you," Morgan replied, exhaling deeply as his shoulders relaxed. "I do have one more request, if I may?"

"If we can, you have my word we'll grant it," Maia expressed, and the resulting look from Morgan affirmed that their new allegiance was strong and based on mutual respect.

"Should the Imperator attack Tivani, the wardens and I will do what we can, but I would really benefit from my partner being there to fight beside us," Morgan began, shifting his body weight anxiously. "Harrison, will you return and help us?"

Deep down, Harrison wanted nothing more than to support his warden partner, but he had to accept he wasn't a warden anymore. He was an Aegis Guard and should focus his attention on aiding their cause.

"I want to Morgan, but I'm needed here too," Harrison began, dropping his head despondently. Refusing his request was incredibly difficult.

"We'll survive Harrison, you should go," Zack insisted, glancing at Maia to check she also agreed. He knew how important this would be to his friend.

Harrison couldn't deny that his unique partnership with Morgan would be an asset to the wardens but before he accepted, he turned to Rylie and took her hands in his.

"How do you feel about this?" he asked. They'd only just been reunited, and this would mean separating again.

"It feels like I've only just got you back so the thought of being apart terrifies me a little, but it's the right thing to do. You could save a lot of lives if Tivani is attacked," Rylie replied sincerely. "Just remember, you're not allowed to die."

Her final comment was accompanied by the same joyous look she'd given him during their conversation at the vigil, where she'd said those exact words.

"I'll do my best," he whispered, pulling her into his embrace.

"I'll join you as soon as I can," Rylie whispered, burying her face into his neck.

"We'd like to return too," Nate chimed in with Paige holding his hand in solidarity. "It'd be good to know what became of our home."

"But it's not safe," Evie stammered, not sharing her parents desire to leave.

"Don't worry sweetheart, we don't mean to stay. Arencia is the best place for you girls, so we'll come straight back," Nate replied, crouching down so he was level with her daughter. "With your permission, of course, Maia."

"Your entire family will always be welcome here," Maia replied, to which both Nate and Paige dipped their heads in silent thanks.

"Wouldn't you be tempted to go home one last time?" Rylie asked, encouraging her little sister to relent her concerns.

"I guess so. Perhaps we can all go," she suggested, glancing at her grandfather who had never seen the Western Continent or Tivani, where she and Rylie had both grown up.

"What a lovely idea," Nate agreed, "although, what remains of the tavern isn't quite the home we built."

"I think you might be pleasantly surprised," Morgan hinted, a playful smirk raising the corner of his lips.

"What do you mean, Morgan?" Nate asked curiously.

"You'll see when you return," he teased.

"How about this, stay in Arencia until we send word. We can let you know if it's safe before you depart," Harrison offered.

"Maybe while you are there, you could try and find out what happened to Sebastian too," Alex requested tentatively.

"That would mean the world to Freya," Maia added, knowing like any parent, her friend was desperate to find her kidnapped son.

"As your return is going to be delayed on the trade ship, should we send a warning to your colleague... Téa was it?" Zack asked. "A courier could travel on the *Pilgrim* and reach her a day or two before you."

"It feels too risky. If the missive fell into the wrong hands, the Imperator may attack sooner," Morgan replied uncertainly. "The idea that someone I trust is betraying the wardens sickens me, but I cannot ignore the possibility. There is no other way to explain how the Imperator knew Siljanna was previously in town."

"Or we can use that to our advantage," Harrison suggested.

"What do you have in mind?" Morgan asked, glancing at his partner with a glint in his eye.

"After our last confrontation, Noah will be desperate to face me again," Harrison began. "It's risky but perhaps we should reveal that I am returning to aid you."

"What will that achieve?" Rylie questioned dubiously, her eyebrows furrowing with concern.

"If he has any say in the matter, he'll insist they hold off on attacking until I'm there."

"My brother is arrogant," Zack added critically. "He'll believe he can defeat you, especially if he knows your whereabouts and can use that to his advantage."

"Exactly," Harrison agreed. "Noah's betrayal may have been spontaneous, but he gave me the impression he's far from just a sellsword. He's placed himself in a position of power."

"Of course he would," Zack remarked. "He probably influenced them to attack Iliria. His rune would've prevented him from speaking of Arencia, but it does explain why the Royal Military attacked that town. It was specifically to draw us out."

"Perhaps, but don't forget, Noah isn't a fool," Maia interjected. "Don't underestimate him based on his recent failings. Desperate and angry people can be more dangerous than those of sound mind."

"I'll be careful," Harrison replied, knowing Maia was right.

"We'll be careful," Morgan corrected. "I won't let you face this adversary alone."

With a grateful nod, Harrison thanked Morgan and the two of them headed off with Zack to compose a suitable letter to facilitate their plan. Once prepared, Morgan returned to Iliria, delivered the letter and instructed the wardens to journey back to Dawne. They had a few days before departing so once his comrades set off, Morgan returned to Arencia, comforted by the knowledge he and Harrison would soon join the wardens and catch the earliest transport ship back to Niyati.

While the guys plotted the wardens' return, Rylie, Lianna and Alex prepared to escort Maia to Carlisse for her audience with Queen Nadia, leaving Evie to have a bit of free time. It was the first time in what felt like forever that everyone she cared about was safe and well, which made the prospect of them going their separate ways even more daunting. She went to her new home, hoping she could distract herself by sketching, but the eerie quietness of the house was deafening. In the end, she decided to head over to the training grounds. Alex was practising some drills while Morgan and Harrison were also teaching Zack some self-defence techniques that he could adopt in an emergency.

Perching on a bench near the weapon racks, she dutifully became the weapons keeper, passing whatever equipment the boys requested as they trained. When Harrison approached, he asked her for a gladius short sword. It looked like the standard sword most of the Aegis Guards equipped but was an upgrade to the one Alex had now. She wondered momentarily if this was their way of telling Alex he was worthy of being more than just a squire, but as she grasped the sword, she had no time to contemplate the thought further as a vision swept over her.

Rather than fighting the images or fearing them as she once had, Evie remembered her training and embraced the vision. She was back in Tivani, at her home, which was somehow unscathed by the fire. At first, she felt a warmth inside but that quickly changed. With a rush, she was somewhere else, a familiar place but not home.

Shadows crept in around the corners of her mind, followed by a loud noise and a blinding light. She felt her mind's eye squint to see past the luminous glare, and as she did, she witnessed Harrison with his arms raised to guard his face. He was clearly disorientated. As he staggered, she saw what he did not. A blade. But it wasn't just any blade, it was a short sword, just like the one she held. As she registered the threat, the blade was thrust into Harrison's sternum. She just caught a glimpse of Noah's cruel smile as he jerked the blade free, and Harrison dropped to the floor, dead. As the horror sunk in, Evie was torn from the vision and flung back to reality.

Facing Harrison, the blade he'd requested in her hand at almost the same level as the blow she'd seen kill him, Evie venomously threw the sword to the floor with a shriek.

"No!" she cried out, wrapping her arms around herself as she started shaking.

"Evie, are you okay?"

"No…" she began, her lower lip trembling as she met his gaze. "You can't go back!"

"Evie, we've been through this," Harrison protested softly, compelling her to accept leaving was the right thing to do.

"You don't understand!"

"What don't I understand?" Harrison probed, placing his hands on her shoulders. "Did you just have a vision?"

"Yes," she sobbed. "And in it, you died!"

"What?" Harrison muttered, recoiling from her.

"You died," she said again as tears tumbled down her cheeks. "Please Harrison, don't go, I'm begging you."

For a moment, Evie wondered if her vision was giving Harrison reason to doubt. Their plan was risky and even if everything went as they intended, he would find himself facing Noah again. From what she'd heard of their last confrontation, Noah had proven he was in fact a skilled swordsman.

Glancing over his shoulder towards Morgan, who was laughing while training Zack and Alex, Harrison took a deep breath and then turned back towards her.

"Evie, I know you're worried, but I can't stay behind."

"Why not?" Evie argued, shaking her head in disbelief.

"Because I want to defend our hometown and help Morgan. He's my partner," Harrison explained, imploring her to understand.

"What about Rylie? And me? You promised you wouldn't die… you promised!" Evie countered, clinging to his impossible guarantee out of desperation.

"Evie…" Harrison whispered, a soft smile on his face as he stroked her hair. "By just telling me what you've seen, you may have changed my fate, but I promise I'll be extra vigilant."

"If anything happens to you, I don't think I could live with myself," Evie mumbled in between sobs. She knew she'd failed to convince him.

"By making me aware of the danger, you've already saved my life. Was it Noah who attacked me in your vision?"

"Yes, he killed you with a sword just like that one," Evie replied, pointing to the blade she'd discarded.

"And were we alone?" Harrison questioned.

"I'm not sure… maybe," Evie answered, clenching her hands together to try and stop them from shaking as she used her arm to wipe away the tears.

"Okay, so clearly our plan works. Noah waits until I return to strike," Harrison began, returning his hands to her shoulders. "We'll revisit the plan and do whatever is needed to ensure I don't fight Noah alone. Does that sound okay to you?"

"No… but I know there's no stopping you," Evie grumbled and as she did, Harrison just pulled her in for a hug.

"I won't tell you not to worry, but I *will* be careful," he promised.

"You better!" she replied firmly, throwing her arms around him and burying her head into his shoulder. Part of her feared this moment would be the last chance she'd ever get to hold him and so she kept her arms around him for as long as she could.

Chapter Nineteen
TIDINGS

It was the thirteenth day since his return to Tivani and Dorian Pesaro woke with a strange sense of belonging. He met with Téa for breakfast as they'd done every day, planned the warden rotations and patrolled with her. He'd even gotten to know some of the locals like poor Elijah Ashby, who was still struggling to recall his time in the capital after the tavern fire, the friendly baker in the market square and the apothecary; but out of all his new contacts, the one he valued the most was Téa.

There was something about her that was utterly captivating to him. She'd trained to become a warden because she'd been small and bullied as a child and wanted to prove she had more than just inner strength. She then spent time training in Siranor and became quite adept with scientific and political procedures before choosing to return to the general warden ranks and form close interpersonal connections with people, making them feel safe and valued. He'd never met anyone like her, ever.

Thanks in part to his fake title and the rapid rapport he'd built with Téa, Dorian found that the other wardens treated him with respect. Being quite a few years younger than most of them, he had expected it to be harder to earn the wardens trust, but it had come easily. The only issue plaguing his conscience was that the person he portrayed wasn't who he truly was. He was just a military graduate who had impressed General Owen with his observational abilities and knack for subtlety. With each passing day, Dorian felt something he never had on a mission before. Guilt.

He tried to convince himself the wardens were at fault, that this was his role and that failing the Imperator was not an option, but watching Téa speak with the locals, a warm smile on her face while fidgeting with the strands of her cropped, blonde hair made it impossible. She was a genuinely good person and the more he'd gotten to know her, the more he wanted to confess everything.

She was just about to join him when a courier came running towards her, handing over a letter. She seemed to recognise the handwriting and ripped through the seal.

"Who's that from?" Dorian asked curiously.

"Commander Foster," she exclaimed, her relief evident. "He and the wardens are on their way back!"

"Wonderful, I finally get to meet the Warden Commander with more loyalty among his peers and respect from his charges than any other I've heard of," he declared cheerfully.

"Oh no…" Téa muttered, her eyes focusing intently on the letter once more.

"Téa, is something wrong?"

"Dorian, I need you to leave," she replied hastily.

"Why, what's going on? Téa, talk to me," Dorian begged, realising just how badly he didn't want to return to Siranor. Gently taking her free hand in his own, he prayed that she wouldn't insist that he departed, or would at least give him a reason why.

"I've been lying to you," she began, grasping the letter tightly before shying away, as if ashamed.

"What do you mean Téa? Please just tell me what's on your mind and I promise we can work this out," Dorian pleaded.

"If I tell you the truth, I will betray someone very dear to me," she began but faltered as the words she wanted to say caught in her throat.

With a look of complete dejection, Téa dropped her head and tried to turn away from Dorian but her reaction made his heart throb so much that it hurt. Without a thought of professionalism or his objective, Dorian pulled her into his arms. As their lips met, Téa was initially shell-shocked but before long melted into his kiss. When he finally released her, Dorian placed his fingers under her chin and lifted her face so that their eyes met.

"There is nothing you can say that will change my opinion of you or how I have come to feel," he began with a shy smile that lit up his face. "Granted, I didn't intend to be quite so forward, but I do not regret it."

"And what if I were to tell you that Warden Commander Foster, every guardian currently abroad with him and I are traitors?" she queried, her chest rising and falling rapidly with each breath.

"Are you telling me that you're traitors?" Dorian asked gently, his gaze unwavering.

"Yes. Everything I've told you about Commander Foster's whereabouts was a lie. He's not training in the Sarron Islands, he's aiding Harrison Stone and the so-called mage rebels," Téa admitted, searching Dorian's eyes for a reaction.

"You are not the only one that's lied. I've been lying since the moment we met."

After his first visit to Tivani, when he'd spied on Commander Foster and identified that Siljanna Stone and Dylan Rose had taken shelter in town, Dorian had an annoying gut instinct that they were not bad people. While those earlier thoughts had just been a suspicion, he was utterly convinced that Téa was good. Those combined feelings were enough to break his fealty to the Imperator.

"What are you talking about?" Téa muttered, catching the determination in his eyes.

"I'm not an Imperial liaison, I've been working at the behest of the Imperator as a reconnaissance agent," he confessed. "I was sent here to spy on the Tivani wardens and identify traitors."

The look of horror on Téa's face was exactly what he'd feared. He tried to reach out for her hand again, but she pulled away sharply and began pacing before him.

"You've been spying on us," Téa repeated, not asking him to confirm but using the words to berate herself for not seeing through his deception.

"To start with, yes; but things have changed. Téa, I've truly come to care for you," he vowed, his voice reflecting the large weight that had been lifted just by telling her the truth.

"What will you do now?" she muttered quietly, the question riddled with a serious undertone.

"I... don't know."

"Do you intend on telling the Imperator?" she pressed, the piercing look in her eyes fiercer than he'd ever seen.

"No," he replied and whether it was his resolute response, the look in his eyes or simply her desire for the relationship they'd built to be true, after a moment's hesitation, she handed him the letter.

As he read the contents of Commander Foster's missive, Dorian knew parts of what was coming. He knew the wardens had betrayed the Imperator and protected the Ar'encal at Harrison Stone's request. On any other mission, having that knowledge confirmed in writing would've filled him with eagerness to report back, but not this time. He couldn't imagine anything worse than providing this evidence to Imperator Harlyn or any of his superiors in Siranor. In fact, reading the version of events from Commander Foster's perspective only increased his certainty that the Imperator was wrong. Whether she was misguided by the series of events or driven by an ulterior motive, he couldn't say, but in his heart, he knew he could no longer support her.

Some of the details were vague but the letter covered how they'd defended Iliria from the Carlisse military assault, Siljanna and Dylan's part in overthrowing King Grayson and emphasised that the Imperial military could be planning to attack Tivani, which of course he knew to be true. In the final paragraph, there was also a deliberate mention of Harrison's intention to return with the wardens. Despite the dangers, he expressed that protecting his hometown and the people there was worth the risk. After a long silence, Dorian turned to Téa and handed back the letter.

"He's right, the Imperator does want to launch an attack on Tivani," Dorian confirmed.

"Why are you telling me this?" Téa questioned, her body stiff with suspicion. "A few minutes ago, I felt like she could've trusted you with anything, but now, I can't be certain if I'm dealing with a man or a snake."

"Because it was my duty to tell her when," he admitted, wounded by her words and making sure to emphasise '*was*'.

"Why didn't you send word while Commander Foster and the others were gone… does the Imperator already know he helped Harrison and the Ar'encal?" she asked urgently.

With her hand resting just above her weapon, Téa was prepared to strike, but Dorian clung to the hope that she wouldn't if he proved himself an ally. Seeing her torn expression, Dorian closed his eyes and recalled everything, from his training encounter with the so-called traitors in Wutel Canyon, his military and covert training with General Owen, being invited into the Imperator's Shadow Council all the way upto the time he'd spent with Téa.

Helping her and the wardens in Tivani had been the first time in his life when he'd been both appreciated and happy. He knew he wanted to stay but had just one chance to convince Téa.

"I haven't reported back and I'm not going to," Dorian stated while clasping his hands together to prevent them from shaking. He so rarely spoke from the heart that he found this moment truly nerve-wracking. "Being here has changed me, Téa. You've changed me. These orders came because of my earlier report to the Imperator. I caused this issue… so now, I'm determined to fix it."

"What do you mean, you caused this?" Téa questioned, locking her gaze onto his youthful brown eyes.

"When I was here before, I located Siljanna Stone," he began. "I found her hiding in her old family home, but also overheard her and Commander Foster's plan to support the mages in Iliria. It was my last report that encouraged the Imperator and her allies to coordinate a swift, secondary attack on Tivani, but the Imperator needed a viable target to justify the assault."

"So, you were waiting for Commander Foster to return and what… just hoped one of the Imperator's targets would accompany him?" Téa pressed. She was still suspicious of him, but her posture had relaxed.

"Initially that had been my hope, but even when I reported back the first time, I had a niggling doubt," he explained, inching closer to her.

"About what?" she asked, her hand still hovering over her weapon. While awaiting his response, Dorian could tell she was studying his every nuance to decide if she could trust him.

"I've met Commander Foster before, Siljanna and Harrison too, but it was years ago. I led a team to challenge them during their final trial to become wardens. I was just a promising military trainee at the time, but they taught me a valuable lesson and Harrison was especially kind after defeating me," Dorian recalled, allowing the memories of that day and how he felt afterwards to embellish the tale. "I didn't want to believe any of them were traitors but now I realise while they have been branded at such, it's for a noble cause. A cause I also want to support."

"Commander Foster… Morgan is just trying to do the right thing and protect innocent lives, just like Harrison Stone did when he helped his mage friends escape Tivani." Téa explained, letting her hand drop from the hilt of her blade. "I don't know if you overheard everything, but Siljanna told us that the Imperator sought a fugitive mage for some kind of experiment. That was the main reason she encouraged Siljanna's misguided pursuit, but the Imperator's deception was revealed in Carlisse. Now, she too seeks redemption."

"That's where Cameron Weiss died," Dorian mumbled, the pieces finally coming together.

"Is that relevant?" Téa asked, tilting her head curiously. The Imperator declared the death of her chief advisor when she reinitiated the war, but Téa didn't understand why that fact was important, which filled Dorian with enthusiasm to explain.

"You obviously haven't heard the rumours from around the capital. It is strongly believed that Harlyn Rainer and Cameron Weiss were lovers, but they ceased any hope of a relationship when she became Imperator. Losing him and having her plans thwarted would've been more than enough to motivate her to recommence the war," he advised with certainty. Although he didn't know the Imperator well, she'd made a very distinct impression on him and he believed that with the right motivation, Harlyn Rainer would justify any means to complete her goals.

"So, this is some kind of vendetta," Téa exclaimed. "Would the Imperator endanger so many lives just for revenge? Surely that's an abuse of power to the highest degree."

"I believe so," Dorian said, reaching out for Téa's hand once again. This time, she didn't back away. "You can't believe that I would continue to support someone with such a motive, can you?"

"I don't. I could never think so little of you… but what will you do?" she asked, lacing her fingers through his as a sense of relief washed over her face.

"Use my position to help you and Commander Foster instead," he promised. "The Imperator is awaiting my report, but we can use it to mislead her and perhaps even stall the assault."

"Thank you, Dorian. When Morgan and the others return, we'll devise a plan to deal with this."

Three weeks after she had declared the war anew, Imperator Harlyn found herself heading back to the war room for an update from her Shadow Council. Located across both the first and second basement levels of the Imperial Courthouse, but only accessible to the Imperator, her chosen council and the most senior members of the military. The halls didn't need to be shrouded in darkness as they were, but as Harlyn marched towards the war room, she couldn't help but think the diminished light was fitting.

Before the end of the day, she and her advisors would deliberate on the most effective ways to paint mages and the Ar'encal as the aggressors of the conflict whilst using the Imperial military and her mage hunters to methodically detect and eliminate them. When she arrived, General Owen was hovering over the large world map but immediately stood to attention when she approached.

"General, what news do you have on the preparations?" Harlyn asked sternly. She'd waited long enough and was not about to offer any pleasantries.

"Four thousand skilled and able-bodied soldiers await your command ma'am," he replied confidently with a salute.

"Good, combined with the mage hunters, my renewed private guard and the city mercenaries, that gives us an attack force of over five thousand," Harlyn remarked, speaking loud enough for the General to hear but evidently talking to herself.

"Has there been any word from Private Pesaro in Tivani?" the General enquired, acknowledging that while he'd usually receive reports on all his subordinates' actions, she had specifically instructed Private Pesaro to report to her.

"Nothing yet, which is disappointing to say he's been there for nearly two weeks," she grumbled, answering his question without looking at him.

"What are your orders, ma'am?" General Owen asked directly.

He had recommended Private Pesaro for covert work so any failing from him would reflect badly on the General and Imperator Harlyn was not in a forgiving mood.

"Tell the troops to stand fast until we receive updates from both Tivani and Carlisse," she instructed, folding her arms as she joined General Owen beside the war room map.

It was an impressive feature, taking up nearly a third of the room and had a highly accurate scale of both the Western and Eastern Continents. In fact, the only details the map excluded were the Terran Subways and their sprawling underground cities. Although the Human and Terran races had been allies for decades, very few cartographers had ventured below ground since the early days of her father's time as Imperator.

"Where are Miss Lawrence or our newest ally?" General Owen questioned, glancing around the otherwise empty room. He knew Noah's name but the way he said *newest ally* emphasised how little he trusted him.

"They're enroute. The soldiers at the city limits sent word of their arrival earlier," Harlyn responded, just as the heavy doors to the chamber opened.

Stalking inside, Noah approached the Imperator with Juliette close behind, dragging a small child with her.

"You've arrived," the General sighed, sounding decidedly disappointed that they had.

"Did you miss me?" Juliette teased, discarding the child who quickly scurried into the corner of the room.

"We have word. It's critical enough that we came in person," Noah hissed, his furrowed brows and deep scowl as dark as his mood.

"Like we had a choice," Juliette muttered, sparing a glance towards the small child who had huddled into a ball, trying to become as small as possible.

"What happened, and who is that?" Harlyn exclaimed, her eyes darting between the child and Juliette before finally landing on Noah.

"You were supposed to organise the attack on Iliria and then send word so we could coordinate a simultaneous strike on Tivani."

"Well you know that didn't happen," Juliette began, crossing her arms in a huff as Noah silenced her.

"That foolish king had no intention of waiting for a coordinated assault. He'd all but dispatched his sloppy, so-called military when we arrived. I took command but the Carlisse soldiers were pathetic, fleeing as soon as they encountered a decent resistance," Noah explained, spitting his words with disgust.

"The Ar'encal and mages had help too. There were trained guards and a retinue of wardens aiding them," Juliette added, and latter detail caught Harlyn's attention.

"That confirms your suspicions of traitors within the wardens' ma'am," General Owen said, but quickly fell silent again with a mere gesture from the Imperator.

"Being right is a small consolation when my bloody elite guardians are betraying me!" Harlyn shouted, her usual composure faltering. Biting her lip, she tucked a stray strand of dark hair behind her ear before turning her attention to the child huddled in the corner of the room. "And who exactly is that?"

"That is a gift," Juliette informed enigmatically.

"From King Grayson?" Harlyn assumed. "Is he trying to apologise for his recklessness and maintain our alliance?"

"It'd be remarkably difficult for him to give you anything. King Grayson is dead," Juliette declared, only to receive a look of utter horror from the Imperator.

"Dead? Gods spare me this insufferable stupidity!" she cried, tilting her head upwards as if either of the gods could hear her.

"Based on my observations, it's no real loss," Noah mumbled, still sounding bitter.

"Be quiet, Noah," Harlyn demanded before turning back to Juliette and pointing harshly at the child. "Explain!"

"You wanted a mage, I've just delivered one," Juliette replied cockily. Everything about Juliette from her posture and grin to the way she flicked her hair, exuded confidence. No matter how terribly they'd failed in Iliria, she knew this delivery would absolve them.

"That child is a mage?" Harlyn questioned dubiously.

"I can assure you of that," Noah replied.

"We had another encounter with Siljanna's brother during the assault and despite the end result, we struck a hefty blow to our enemy. I killed one of their top warriors and kidnapped the boy so you can finally continue your experiments," Juliette boasted.

"Is that true?" Harlyn asked, turning to Noah for confirmation.

"It's true. Juliette killed my father," Noah replied, shocking both Imperator Harlyn and General Owen into a momentary silence.

"And what was your father to the Ar'encal?" Harlyn questioned, breaking the silence.

"You know this rune prevents me from giving you specifics, but he was vital. They will be crippled without him."

"Good," Harlyn muttered without any thought to offer her newest ally condolences. *He's not bothered by his father's demise, so why should I be?*

Turning towards the young boy, Harlyn assessed the child as he diligently pressed himself even harder into the corner, as if trying to make himself disappear. The child was small, with neatly cut blonde hair and lightly tanned skin. His hazel eyes had been rubbed raw, indicating he had been crying and Harlyn also spotted a strange red mark around his nose and mouth.

"Leave me alone," the boy whimpered.

"What's your name, child?" Harlyn asked calmly, walking towards him and crouching down just a few feet away.

"Sebastian," he stuttered. "Please don't hurt me."

"I don't want to hurt you, Sebastian… I want to fix you," Harlyn replied, sounding more like a scientist than the commanding leader she had been a moment ago.

Extending her hand towards Sebastian, the young boy had no other option than to take it. For the briefest moment, he met her intense gaze and knew that this fix was going to come at a price but had no idea what that could be. Only Harlyn knew her plans for the boy and she had no intention of sharing with all the people currently present. After all, she had only said she didn't want to hurt him, not that she wouldn't.

Rising to her feet and pulling Sebastian out of the corner, Imperator Harlyn dusted him off and inspected him more thoroughly. He was skinny but overall looked healthy and would do as an experimental specimen. Deep-down she knew Cameron would not have approved, but they were at war. In times like these, she had the power to do what was needed, even if her methods were arguably unethical. As she attempted to lead Sebastian out of the war room, she was stopped by the impertinent voice of Juliette.

"You're welcome!"

"Juliette, you truly are insufferable, but fortunately you have some uses," Harlyn hissed. "Now that King Grayson is gone, your subterfuge is no longer required in the Eastern Continent, and we'll just have to take it by force. I want a full report of what happened in Iliria sent to my laboratory. After that, get to the Tulam facility to ready the mage hunters."

"For what?" Juliette replied, her curiosity piqued.

"The Imperial citizens must believe that the mages and Ar'encal are the aggressors in this conflict, so I need the mage hunters to make that happen."

"Oh, we can do that. Are you concerned about an increase in withering case numbers?" Juliette enquired.

"Not if my plan with young Sebastian is successful," Harlyn replied, squeezing the young boy's hand slightly as she felt him try to pull away.

"Excellent, I will equip the hunters with Encia and other toxins that replicate the appearance of the magical attacks we've encountered," Juliette replied, looking very pleased with herself once more.

"Hmm, a useful tactic," Harlyn muttered, with a hint of surprise.

"Where will the attacks take place?" General Owen asked.

"Why does that matter?" Juliette questioned.

"I'm concerned about the potential impact to the morale and safety of the Imperial Citizens. Surely, we should notify the wardens or coordinate an increased military presence around each attack," General Owen explained, turning to the Imperator as he spoke.

"Noah, you will coordinate these attacks," Harlyn replied. "Unlike the now deceased King Grayson's attack plan, our assaults will be neither be rushed nor ill-conceived."

"It'll be my pleasure," Noah replied, cracking his knuckles as he turned to the war room map and focused on the area around Siranor. "General Owen, I need you to tell me all you can about the Imperial towns and regions so I can best formulate a strategy."

"Of course," General Owen began but faltered, unsure how to address Noah.

Although Noah had failed in Iliria, Harlyn felt drawn to him. He had a tenacity that she could admire and if she instructed General Owen directly, he would obey her command. That was his duty.

"Noah will take over Cameron's role as my chief of security and tactical advisor," Harlyn informed, answering the General's unspoken question.

"Of course… sir," he said, correcting himself and addressing Noah formerly as he joined him at the tactical map. "With your position, you are also entitled to inspect the Imperial Military anytime you wish. Mr Weiss frequented training regularly and selected his preferred soldiers for sensitive and urgent missions."

"Thank you, I'll do just that," Noah replied, standing taller than he had a moment ago.

He was naturally taller than General Owen, but his posturing made their size difference even more noticeable. The Imperator had just promoted him into the top echelons of her ranks and that action was enough to vindicate him and the boost Noah was apparently all he needed to get over his earlier sullen mood.

"Imperator, shall we notify you once the logistics are in place?" General Owen asked, calling out to her before she departed.

"Yes, also notify me if any word is received from Private Pesaro in Tivani," she commanded, finally reaching the door.

"It will be done," Noah assured.

"Don't fail me," Harlyn replied, swiftly leaving with the goal of taking Sebastian directly to the Institute, a goal that nothing or no-one was going to prevent.

Chapter Twenty
BREAKTHROUGH

Leading Sebastian through the glass halls of the Institute and into her private laboratory, Harlyn once again tried to reassure the youngster.

"I know you're scared. Someone as young as you shouldn't even be thinking about this type of thing, but your involvement could provide a breakthrough for my research."

"What are you going to do to me?" Sebastian asked, his voice quivering. He'd stopped trying to resist once he realised just how big Siranor was. Even if he could escape his captors, he'd never escape the city without help.

"First, I'm going to ask you some questions," Harlyn replied. "I need to have a comprehensive medical file for you before starting the clinical trial of En-glycerol."

"En-glycerol?" Sebastian repeated, breaking the word down and slowly saying each syllable as best he could.

"It's a compound I've been working on for many years. My last subject was an Ar'encal descendant but despite not giving me what I needed, I learnt a lot from those tests," Harlyn explained. "When he rather unwillingly consumed En-glycerol, his body rejected it almost instantly."

"What does that mean?" Sebastian asked, stiffening with panic.

"My best theory is that En-glycerol reacted with his stomach acids and caused a negative reaction," Harlyn continued, reaching for a small notebook in her jacket pocket and flicking through the pages of her tests on Nate Auren.

"Will it kill me?" Sebastian mewled as tears welled in his eyes.

At first, Harlyn was taken aback by his question. Although he was a mage, it was only the Encia in his blood that made him different. Without a connection to magic, he'd be normal... human. Despite that, this poor child associated losing his power as not just a bad thing, but fatal.

"I truly don't believe it will," Harlyn began, failing to comfort the youngster who now had tears dampening his cheeks. "What I meant was that you should throw up. At least that's what happened to my last subject."

"Is that all?" he asked, his lower lip wobbling. "I'll only be sick?"

"Maybe," Harlyn continued, glancing at her new subject before referring back to her notes. "I've had time to analyse my previous tests. My earlier oversight was that by making the subject consume En-glycerol, it didn't bond with the Encia in his blood. If the same happens with you, I will inject it directly into your bloodstream."

Shaking his head, Sebastian looked at her with eyes that begged her to reconsider.

"All I do is heal people. Please, I don't take my power, it's who I am!" Sebastian pleaded.

"No. Who you are is a young boy that should be playing with his friends, going to school and learning life skills; not a boy with unnatural abilities and the corresponding reclusive lifestyle forced upon you by being different," Harlyn countered, her tone becoming stern as she swiftly turned and looked straight at Sebastian.

"What's so bad about being different?" Sebastian moaned, wiping away his tears. "If you find all magic so undesirable, then why do you want to take mine?"

"Because it's power, and in the right hands, power is everything," Harlyn answered. She had her reasons to want to control magic but quickly shook her head as she realised, she was having a debate with a child. "How old are you anyway, ten?"

"Eleven… nearly twelve," Sebastian corrected with a frown.

"Oh, my apologies," Harlyn replied sarcastically. "You are still nowhere near old enough to realise how much better your life could be if you were normal."

"Who would want to be normal when they can be special?" Sebastian muttered, his question said so adamantly that Harlyn found herself unable to answer.

She'd striven to be great for her entire life, first as a scientist then as Imperator and in doing so, believed she was special but with one sentence, this boy made her question that belief. *Could a person only be special if they control magic? Is that what my uncle truly believed?*

"En-glycerol was my uncle's life work. He tried to perfect it, but suffered from significant exposure to Encia," she said hesitantly, having never told anyone but Cameron the truth about Elias Rainer's fate. "The withering would have claimed his life…"

"Would have?" Sebastian probed in only the way a child could.

"He died at the hands of the wardens," Harlyn continued tersely. "But now, I can complete his work… our work. Unlocking this power will benefit the entire human race."

"You wouldn't use it for personal gain?" he scoffed, challenging her motives. "Not at all?"

"There is only one question I seek an answer to, and only magic can help me find it, but that pursuit will cause harm to no one," Harlyn retorted before glancing across the room to where a small urn that contained her uncle's ashes, rested on a shelf.

Looking at them always made Harlyn smile. There were only two people that had told her she was special, Cameron and her uncle and she believed he was there in spirit now. She would see his life's work through and get an answer to her burning question, no matter the cost.

"So, this research was the death of him, may be the death of me and yet you claim this pursuit of knowledge will hurt no one," Sebastian argued, revealing the cracks in her story.

"Be quiet child! I've already told you it shouldn't kill you. I am doing this to better all of humanity," Harlyn snapped, forcing him into a chair. "In an ideal world, my test subject would've been a fugitive mage, like Rylie Auren, but I cannot let idealism stop me now. I'm too close."

The chair was equipped with leather straps, two that would go over his wrists, one over his thighs and two more around his ankles. After fixing the lower restraints tightly in place, Harlyn forcefully handed Sebastian a vial of En-glycerol and stood over him until he drank the contents. He was reluctant to swallow at first, but once he did, his body reacted. Pressing his arms into his stomach, Sebastian soon doubled over.

"I'm going to be sick," he groaned before ejecting what little he had eaten since being kidnapped onto the floor.

"Exactly the same as before," Harlyn muttered, avoiding the pile of vomit while scribbling the result in her notebook.

"Are you going to inject me now?" Sebastian asked, already knowing the answer and trying his best to inch away from her.

"Yes, although we should repair your body first," she explained, walking over to him only tying the restraint over one of his wrists. The buckles were awkward to reach, even from her angle, so she felt confident that he couldn't escape, even with one hand free. Handing him a bottle of water, she glared at him until he took a sip. "I'll get you some food too. You haven't eaten properly all day."

"I don't want anything," Sebastian replied.

"I don't care, you will drink all of that water and eat some food. In the meantime, I'll take some blood and hair samples for testing before we continue," Harlyn insisted. Resisting her was futile.

Once he finished drinking, she tied up his free arm and took the samples she needed for the tests. His blood revealed the small specks of glistening Encia which she still found mesmerising. *How could something so small create such power?*

She knew from her years of study that testing Encia infused water was not enough. Stagnant samples would always slowly degrade. Encia somehow managed to regenerate itself in flowing water, a process she could not recreate in her laboratory, but she assumed the same thing occurred in the bloodstream of mages. Sebastian's sample proved it.

After several hours of testing and cleaning up the earlier mess, Harlyn finally felt ready to begin the second trial of En-glycerol on Sebastian. Leaving the exhausted child bound to his chair, she left to collect one of her many batches of En-glycerol from a cooler in the secure storage room within the main research hall. Getting what she needed, Harlyn paused to lock the storeroom when she heard a nearby internal door click shut as someone entered.

"Who's there?"

"It's only me," replied the recognisable voice of Charlie Blake, one of the more competent warden scientists. "I'm just collecting some books for my research paper. You're working late, Imperator."

"Yes, I'm currently performing a clinical trial of En-glycerol," she replied, knowing he was one of the few wardens who had taken an interest in her project.

"Congratulations, does that mean a mage has turned themselves in and volunteered?" Charlie enquired brightly.

"Not exactly, he's a prisoner brought over by my mage hunters," she answered and could hear Charlie's enthusiasm wane.

Charlie wasn't the empirical scientist she was, usually letting his moral compass get in the way of obtaining evidence and making progress, but during his time at the Institute, he had contributed significantly and proven himself astute in political matters too.

"May I observe?" he asked to Harlyn's surprise.

"As long as you don't try to stop me, do as you wish," she replied, allowing him to grab the books he came for and then open the door for her.

When they reached her room, Charlie entered behind Imperator Harlyn but immediately noticed the young boy bound in a chair. The child was slumped over, his head clearly heavy from exhaustion but awake. As concern flooded his mind, Charlie panicked over two questions, *what had Harlyn done and how long had they been here?*

Snapping his attention back to the Imperator just as she carefully placed the vials of En-glycerol on a table beside the boy, he grabbed her by the shoulder.

"He's your test subject?" Charlie chided, his voice a mix of disgust and desperation, hoping to be wrong.

"Yes," she replied with a stern look, revealing she felt no shame.

"Ma'am, this is completely unethical, he's a child! He can't be more than ten years old," Charlie argued wildly as he tried to get the Imperator to see reason.

"He's nearly twelve, actually," she quipped.

"Well, that changes everything," Charlie declared, mirroring her earlier sarcasm without knowing it.

"Mr Blake, I gave you permission to observe with the condition that you wouldn't stop me. This trial is happening and if you don't like it, the door is right over there," Harlyn asserted, pointing towards the exit.

"But you don't know how a mage could react to En-glycerol, it could be fatal. Imperator Harlyn, please, you must reconsider."

"No, I won't," Harlyn replied bluntly, taking a syringe and filling it with her solution.

As she strode towards Sebastian, she could feel Charlie's rigid presence behind her. He was whole-heartedly against her methods but didn't physically stop her. With her free hand, she cupped Sebastian's drooped head, rousing him from whatever mental escape he'd gone to. His eyes were red from crying and sleep deprivation but when he saw her, he didn't flinch.

"Is it time?" he asked quietly, all his energy depleted.

"It's time. Be brave Sebastian, you could prove that En-glycerol truly is the salvation for all mages," she replied, stroking his cheek before gently sterilising a patch on his arm with clear access to a vein.

Inserting the needle, Sebastian closed his eyes tightly and whimpered. Then all three of them went utterly still as they waited to see how his body would react. The silence was paralysing until after what felt like minutes, Sebastian began to convulse. As the spasms got worse, Charlie could see the restraints marking his wrists and ankles, but he knew he couldn't loosen them, no matter how badly he wanted to. Even Harlyn showed some concern by approaching the boy and placing a hand on his knee in a feeble attempt to hold him steady.

Tracing his skin from the point of the injection, Charlie and Harlyn could see his veins going dark. As his body shook, blood began to trickle from Sebastian's nose. Just as Harlyn was about to scoop up the blood with a cotton bud, he threw his head back and started to gurgle. Grabbing the bucket she'd strategically placed by his feet, Harlyn encouraged him to lean forward while she stroked his back and he wretched up curdled blood. Looking at the contents of the bucket as if it were gold, Harlyn rushed to the side bench to take samples. While distracted, Charlie dashed over to the boy and began removing his restraints.

"Are you okay, kid?" he asked, deeply concerned for his welfare, but the child didn't answer.

As soon as the last restraint was off, the boy just slumped into Charlie's arms and sobbed once more, finding a reserve of tears he hadn't spent. While cradling him, Charlie assessed the boy for any negative side effects. Although the ordeal had been traumatic, once the convulsions stopped and he'd expelled the blood Harlyn rapidly collected, his symptoms appeared to alleviate. To Charlie's relief, the boy was pale and weak, but okay.

"Did it work?" Charlie asked harshly, looking over his shoulder towards Imperator Harlyn.

"It worked, it really worked," Harlyn exclaimed, putting a sample of blood underneath her microscope to take a closer look. "Wait... no! No, no, no, no, no!"

"What's wrong?" Charlie challenged. He was not about to let her repeat the experiment no matter what was going wrong.

"The En-glycerol isn't containing the Encia, it's neutralising it. This wasn't supposed to happen, why is this happening?" Harlyn growled to herself.

After watching the Encia that had been ripe in Sebastian's bloodstream turn black and fragment, she grabbed a knife and strode towards him. Falling to her knees, she sliced her palm and grabbed the young boy's hand.

"What are you doing?" Charlie questioned urgently, trying to get the Imperator's attention but his efforts were futile.

"Heal me, Sebastian. Do it!" Harlyn cried.

"I can't," he mewled in response, his whole body shaking.

"Can't or won't?"

"I can't heal you!" Sebastian wept, "It's gone, you've taken my power away."

Standing once more, Harlyn grabbed a towel, pressed it into her palm and began frantically pacing the room. She spoke aloud but not to either Sebastian or Charlie, their continued presence but a footnote in her mind.

"Highly effective," she muttered. "A small amount of the compound neutralised the Encia in his system, leaving the subject weak and powerless but alive. Not the result I'd intended... but still useful."

"Imperator, please... allow me to take the boy to the hospital. He needs care," Charlie requested, his tone firm as he continued to hold the boy close.

"Hm, oh fine take him. Sebastian has done all he can for me now," she replied, not giving either of them a second glance but instead, feverishly writing in her notebook.

Not hesitating for a moment longer, Charlie grabbed a blanket, wrapped it around Sebastian and rushed him out of the laboratory. The hospital was connected to the Institute by a covered walkway so it wouldn't take long to get there but the glass corridors provided minimal insulation from the chill outside. It wasn't snowing but the darkness in the clouds overhead told Charlie it would overnight.

"Your name's Sebastian, right?" Charlie asked, shifting the young boy in his arms so that he could walk as quickly as possible while holding him comfortably.

"Yeah," he replied weakly.

"I'm taking you to a hospital, Sebastian," Charlie assured.

"I just want to go home and see my mum," Sebastian whined, unable to stop Charlie but silently grateful to be away from Imperator Harlyn.

"Shall I try to find her and bring her to you?" Charlie offered.

"No, please... don't bring her here! They'll hurt her too," Sebastian begged, grabbing a fistful of Charlie's shirt and pulling. The boy had no strength, but it was all he could do to protest.

"All right, I won't bring her here but you're weak and need medical care," Charlie explained just as the main entrance to the hospital was in sight. "Let the doctors help you and then I'll do all I can to reunite you with your mother away from this place, okay?"

Sebastian nodded before letting his head rest on Charlie's shoulder. Charlie knew the lad didn't know if he could trust him, he had no reason to trust anyone after what he'd been through, but Charlie was determined to keep his promise. Exhausted, Sebastian soon lost consciousness and seeing his body go limp was all the motivation Charlie needed to march even faster towards the hospital.

Pushing through the main entrance, Charlie found a nurse and lied, saying he'd found the young boy outside the Institute, as he couldn't imagine any way to explain what had really happened. The nurse didn't question him at all and hastily escorted them into a room and encouraged Charlie to leave Sebastian in her care.

"I'll come back in a couple of days to check on him," Charlie advised compassionately.

"I'm sure he'd appreciate that. Do you have any idea who he is or where his parents are?" the nurse asked.

"No, but he mentioned his mother and I intend to find her. All I know is that his name is Sebastian," Charlie replied.

"That'll do for now, thank you," the nurse said.

"Can you make me the primary contact for him in the meantime," Charlie requested, and the nurse confirmed with a nod, handing him the patient form as she tucked Sebastian into a comfortable bed. Quickly scribbling down his details before leaving, Charlie knew that in the meantime he had to try and find Sebastian's mother. He had no idea how, but he was determined to try.

A few hours after Charlie had taken the boy away, Harlyn also departed the Institute. She'd called her driver and by the time she made it outside, he was already waiting and greeted her with the usual reverence.

"Good evening, ma'am, where to?"

"To the Imperial Palace, James," she instructed. "Do you know where Noah Harper went this afternoon?"

"Ah, your new advisor," James checked, "I believe he went with General Owen to the barracks ma'am but at this late hour, he could be at the apartment we've provided him. Would you like me to summon him for you?"

"Yes, I have a pressing assignment for him," Harlyn advised.

"Shall I bring him to you this evening or first thing in the morning, ma'am?" he asked, realising that while a summons from the Imperator was usually of the highest priority, the hour was incredibly late.

"Immediately, this matter cannot wait," Harlyn emphasised.

After dropping her at the Imperial Palace, Harlyn heard the vehicle race off, James taking her instruction with the intended urgency. It'd take a good hour to locate Noah and bring him back to the palace, so Harlyn decided to take that time to freshen up. It had been a long day, but she'd accomplished more in the last few hours than she had in weeks and that excitement prevented any desire for sleep. As she entered the palace, her stepmother, Sabine was clearly waiting for her but attempted to disguise it by reading a book.

"Oh Harlyn, you're back," she announced, feigning surprise.

"What do you want, Sabine?" Harlyn groaned.

"Why do you assume that I want something?"

"Because you don't like to read and wouldn't be sitting in the lobby unless you were waiting for someone, and that someone unfortunately seems to be me," Harlyn replied, her disdain for the woman apparent.

"Harlyn, why do you always speak to me in that way? I understand you're under some pressure," she replied only to be curtly interrupted.

"Some pressure? You don't have a clue, Sabine. You couldn't understand even if you tried," Harlyn mocked with an indignant tone. Rolling eyes she did nothing to hide just how little she cared for Joseph Rainer's beloved second wife.

"That is unnecessarily cruel, Harlyn. What would your father say if he heard you speak to me in this way?" Sabine challenged.

"Don't bring him into this," Harlyn countered, but deep down she knew that her father wouldn't have approved.

While her own feelings were that Sabine was little more than a gold-digging trollop, Joseph Rainer had loved her more than he ever loved Harlyn's mother, Miranda. She often wondered how different her life would've been if her mother and uncle's relationship had gone unnoticed and her parents' marriage not crumbled.

In her heart, Harlyn truly believed her uncle was her biological father. The discovery of his affair with her mother led to her Miranda's exile, Elias burying himself even deeper in his work and Joseph moving on with Sabine, eventually marrying her. Their story was like a tragedy one might find in a typical romance novel.

Looking back at the woman who was barely ten years her senior, Harlyn sighed heavily in defeat.

"I'm sorry, Sabine. My attitude was uncalled for," she apologised through gritted teeth. She could force herself to be polite but that didn't mean she had to mean it.

"Apology accepted," Sabine replied, a manipulative glint in her eyes. "Besides, it's only a small favour I wanted to ask of you."

"Of course it is," Harlyn said, trying to swallow the sarcasm.

"It's my quarters, they are just simply too small. I'm still in my prime and could entertain dignitaries, to serve the Imperial court of course. I am also within my rights to find a suitor, but just cannot do so in that inferior wing," she explained.

"You want me to build you a new home?" Harlyn clarified, dumbfounded by her audacity.

"Oh no, nothing that extravagant," she insisted. "An extension would suffice. An additional ensuite bedroom, dining and ballroom would be a good start... perhaps some fresh landscaping to the courtyard."

"Sabine, are you even aware we're at war?"

"Surely that won't impact us in Siranor, will it?" Sabine argued, only marginally concerned.

"I hope not, but I simply cannot prioritise your request at the moment," Harlyn replied, using all her self-control not to scream.

"All I ask is that you don't forget, my dear," Sabine accepted before lounging back in the chair and picking up the book she'd been pretending to read. Harlyn noticed the title, 'The Therapy of Horticulture' and it solidified in her mind that Sabine absolutely hadn't been reading it.

"I'll note to come back to the subject later, Sabine. Now please excuse me, I want to freshen up and review my notes before Noah arrives," Harlyn replied, attempting to pardon herself.

"Oh, is Noah visiting? Perhaps I could—"

"Don't push your luck, Sabine" Harlyn threatened before turning towards her own chambers, and Sabine thankfully let her go without another word.

After being side-tracked, Harlyn had limited time to freshen up but managed to get a quick shower while her attendant whipped up some dinner and delivered it to her study. She'd just finished the plate of food while reviewing her notes when there was a knock on the door.

"Come in," she called and was pleased to see Noah enter.

"You wanted to see me, Imperator?" he enquired, rubbing his eyes after being woken up when summoned.

"Yes, please take a seat," she replied, and he did as instructed. She swiftly ensured the solid wooden door was firmly shut so they could speak in private.

"I assume you've completed the trial of your substance," Noah commented, moderately curious.

"En-glycerol, yes," she began, feeling the pressing need to correct him. "I won't bore you with scientific jargon, but my compound doesn't absorb Encia, it neutralises it."

"So, the trial was a failure?" Noah suggested, only to be silenced by Harlyn's resulting glare.

"The trial was a success, just not in the way I imagined. Although I cannot use it to manipulate Encia and therefore control magic, we can still weaponize it."

"How do you plan to do that?" Noah asked, a sly grin forming in the corner of his mouth.

"Even a relatively small amount of En-glycerol purged all the Encia from within the subject, leaving them completely incapable of casting," she explained. "With some help, I believe it can be manufactured into blade coatings, bullets and perhaps even some of Juliette's grenades."

"And it will completely strip the mages of their power?" Noah checked, impressed by the unexpected potential of Harlyn's substance.

"It did for the boy. I cannot say for sure if it will work as effectively against all mages, but it'll give our soldiers and mage hunters an edge in the battles to come," she replied enthusiastically.

"Speaking of battles, I have devised a strategy to create the appearance of mage rebellions across the continent. We'll start with some of the smaller towns and villages, but there will have to be attacks near Siranor as well," Noah advised Harlyn wasn't fazed by the suggestion in the slightest.

"You're absolutely right and in fact, I would like you to make the first attack on the outskirts of the city," Harlyn instructed.

"That can be arranged. Is there a particular reason?"

"We need the people to believe the mages and Ar'encal are the aggressors. Attacking Siranor is a bold move and following the attack, we can ramp up the propaganda," she began. "I do have an ulterior motive too. I need another test subject."

"Another mage, why? Did the boy die during the tests?" Noah asked. "It doesn't bother me if you killed him, but I know who will be impacted if you did and I find imagining their pain amusing."

"No, he's fine. One of the wardens from the Institute took him to the hospital. But it's not a mage I need this time, I need someone suffering from the withering," Harlyn explained.

"Because your compound neutralises Encia, you want to see if it will cure the withering too," Noah realised, catching on quickly to her intention.

"Indeed," she gloated. "It's rather ironic that I used this exact reasoning to manipulate Siljanna Stone, and now it may very well come to pass."

"If it works, you'll be deigned a hero. The people would believe anything and everything you say," Noah emphasised, looking at her with a greater degree of admiration.

"Take Juliette and simulate an attack nearby," Harlyn ordered. "I suggest one of the trade outposts or the train station. It needs to look like the mages were attempting to disrupt our livelihood with little to no regard for civilian casualties."

"How many captives do you need?"

"One or two will be sufficient," she replied, completely calm as she delivered her instructions.

"Consider it done," Noah replied, standing from the chair and giving her a courtly bow as he turned towards the door. Before exiting, Noah paused and looked back to face Imperator Harlyn.

"Is there a problem?" she asked.

"Your former advisor, Cameron… would you have entrusted him with this task?" Noah asked. "I mean no offense, I'm just trying to ascertain how I fit into your evolving plan."

"The bond I had with Cameron was unique," Harlyn began, her glance shifting from Noah to her hands and back again. "He wouldn't have approved of endangering Imperial citizens in this way, but there wasn't a moment in the entire time I knew him that he failed to support me."

"If I may be so bold, you haven't really answered the question," Noah replied.

"I wouldn't have asked Cameron to do what I've just asked of you," Harlyn advised, her shoulders set back as she focused her full attention on Noah. "But you are not him, and your unique circumstances and insight make you the ideal person for this task."

Seemingly satisfied by her response, Noah nodded gracefully and departed the study.

Chapter Twenty-One
Lethal Cure

Tulam was possibly the smallest and most boring town Noah had ever been to, so when he arrived in the early hours of the morning after meeting the Imperator, he wasted no time in searching for Juliette. Finding the temple of Temu where she requested they meet, he was accosted by a group of believers that called themselves *Temurians*. Despite beseeching him as best they could, he repeatedly declined to join their weekly book club. He'd been waiting for nearly thirty minutes when suddenly, Juliette tapped him on the shoulder.

"What now?" Noah groaned, expecting it to be another religious crone trying to convert him.

"So you've met the local loons," Juliette teased.

"Where did you come from?" he asked, searching for some kind of secret passage or doorway.

"From the mage hunter base of course," Juliette replied. "Where would you least expect to find a hideout of assassins?"

"Underneath a temple," Noah said, realising he hadn't seen her approach because she'd come from inside the temple behind him.

"So, I assume the Imperator has a new task for us," Juliette commented, prying for more details.

"She does indeed, and we get to do two of your favourite things," Noah began, a wicked smile on his face.

"Do tell," Juliette replied, her eyebrows lifting as she mimicked his expression.

"First we need to simulate a mage attack on the outskirts of Siranor and then, abduct someone with the withering," Noah informed as Juliette led him down a concealed staircase just inside the main temple entrance.

"Does the Imperator care about the body count?" Juliette asked, just about able to contain her enthusiasm.

"No," Noah replied, appreciating the glint in Juliette's eyes. She was relishing this even more than he had expected.

"And what about the abductees, does he or she need to already be suffering from the withering?" she questioned, biting her lip as she awaited his reply, her whole body seeming to purr.

"Imperator Harlyn failed to be specific," Noah advised, his smile spreading as Juliette shivered with excitement.

"In that case, there isn't a moment to lose," Juliette declared, taking Noah by the hand and leading him down a dark passageway.

They arrived at a heavy door with multiple locks, but Juliette simply pressed down on a nearby tile with a grin. After hearing several loud clicks, she easily pushed open the door, revealing the true mage hunter base of operations. The hidden facility was a hive of activity that looked like an insidious hybrid of barracks and a thieves' den.

After meeting the group of mage hunters Juliette had personally selected, Noah was shown the newest collection of weapons at their disposal. Noah knew they needed to make the attacks appear as though mages were responsible, so blades and guns were being left behind. In exchange, they had an array of grenades including oil and acid bombs that could easily be set aflame or frozen, smoke grenades, flash-bangs, and Juliette's new favourite concoction that she'd nicknamed a 'halo-bomb'.

"What exactly does it do?" Noah asked, turning the new bomb in his hand.

"It's a mixture of chemicals including psilocybin that I've brewed and then synthesised into a gas. When it explodes, a cloud is released that will induce hallucinations," Juliette replied, caressing the grenade like she would a lover, or perhaps more accurately in Juliette's case, a pawn.

"Mimicking illusion magic, very clever," Noah commented, even more impressed than he let on.

"I'm sure it'll come in handy," Juliette boasted. "By disorientating people with a flash-bang or halo-bomb, we'll give ourselves enough time to capture the unfortunate souls who are about to suffer from the withering."

"Do you have raw Encia on hand too?"

"Yes, I ventured to the shoreline yesterday," she answered, her eyebrows raising as she tried to ascertain if Noah was surprised or pleased by her proactivity. "Where is our first target to be?"

"There's a trade outpost southeast of here, just on the outskirts of Siranor," Noah began.

"So close to the capital… bold," Juliette acknowledged with glee. "There's a wonderful jewellery merchant based at that outpost. She often gets precious stones from her Terran contacts for some utterly unique pieces."

"I never imagined you'd have an interest in jewellery," Noah commented as Juliette flashed a ring that was coiled around her finger.

"This is Adamite. Beautiful and toxic in large quantities due to the trace amount of arsenic within," she explained.

"Are you describing yourself or the ring?" Noah replied, cracking a charming smile.

"I think we both know the answer to that," Juliette answered, leaning in to kiss him on the cheek. Her lipstick left a mark, but Noah just smiled, wiping it off slowly as if allowing her touch to linger on his skin.

Enjoying his slow, yet purposeful actions, Noah quickly realised that Juliette was considering a quick dalliance, but he snapped her attention back to the task at hand. They spent a few minutes collecting their gear and briefing Juliette's chosen hunters on their intended target, the jewellery merchant's stand and then departed for the trade outpost.

It was late morning by the time Aaron and Georgina Blake made it to the outskirts of Siranor. Since having their son, Hugo, they didn't get much time alone, but today was their tenth wedding anniversary and Aaron had planned the entire day for them, including a babysitter. It had begun with breakfast at the cafe where they'd first met, then a stroll through the gardens where he'd proposed. The next stop was to the jeweller who created Georgina's wedding ring, where he'd also present his beloved wife with her anniversary gift.

Originally, he'd planned to get earrings or a necklace but with Hugo currently in what they called the *monkey phase,* climbing over everything and pulling at whatever caught his eye, he'd decided on a bracelet instead. They'd had their ups and downs over the years and raising a toddler was more exhausting than either of them ever expected, but Aaron adored his wife and planned to remind her of that throughout the day.

"Are we almost at mystery stop number three?" Georgina asked, a smile still warming her face.

"We are my love," Aaron replied, leading her towards the jeweller, who waved at him joyfully, but they never made it.

Terrified by a loud noise and blinding light, Aaron clutched onto his wife's hand and pulled her close. Encircled by hysterical screams, he used his body as a shield her before throwing himself to the ground with her in his arms. Colliding with something wooden, which he hoped was one of the trade stands, he pushed Georgina behind it and cradled her as they both tried to block out the cries of other, less fortunate people.

There were more bangs and breaking glass followed by the roar of fire until finally, the fading light was replaced with a cloud of heavy smoke. Aaron's gut told him they needed to keep moving but as he tried to pull Georgina away from their hiding spot, he couldn't. She was completely catatonic. Refusing to succumb to fear and leave his wife, he returned to her side and prayed that whoever was behind the attack wouldn't find them.

Each minute of chaos at the trading post felt like an eternity, but eventually it ceased. Desperately trying to snap Georgina out of her trance, he whispered pleas, but they fell on deaf ears. That concern distracted him from the figure that methodically approached.

"What do we have here? A pair of mice that found a hole to hide in," announced a sinister female voice.

Aaron struggled to make out the person before him, his eyes still sore from the blinding light and smoke. All he could be certain of was that she was slender and had short, dark hair.

"Please, don't hurt us," he begged.

"This is a rebellion buddy, and if *we mages* don't stand united, your corrupted Imperium is going to slaughter us all," replied the woman.

Watching as the woman waved her associates over and then started rummaging through her satchel, a sense of dread overcame him.

"These two will do nicely," confirmed a strong male voice. "Get the shackles."

"No, please! You won't achieve anything by taking us," Aaron pleaded, holding onto Georgina who shrank even further into her mind.

"You know what to do," the man commanded, restraining Aaron and pulling him away from his wife.

As the woman came closer, Aaron spotted a vial in her hand. She reached out, grabbing Georgina by the chin and when she offered no resistance, poured the contents down her throat. All he could do was watch helplessly as Georgina tumbled to the floor.

"What have you done to my wife?" he cried, pulling frantically at the restraints.

"Your wife is very unwell, sir," replied the woman, her face clear now the smoke was lifting. "In fact, I'm quite certain she has the withering."

"This can't be! She hasn't come into contact with—" but Aaron stopped himself, realising what was in the vial his wife had just been made to consume.

"Is there any more for him?" asked the male captor, who seemed to be the group's leader.

"Wait, you can't! Please," Aaron cried, writhing as best as he could while bound, but all it accomplished was a sharp kick to the leg, making him fall to his knees.

"No, I brought one vial," the woman answered. "What shall we do with him?"

"While I appreciate your dastardly mind, let's take them both back to the holding cells. I'm sure we'll find a suitable drink for him on our travels," the leader replied.

The last thing Aaron saw was the woman taunting him with a wave before a sharp blow struck the back of his head. Then there was nothing but darkness.

When he woke, Aaron couldn't tell if it'd been minutes, hours or even days but he recalled the events at the trading post clearly. As he pushed himself upright, he couldn't believe how weak he felt. It was as though his entire body resented him for moving. That was when he noticed the blackened tips of his fingers and began to tremble, the realisation setting in. He had the withering.

His next immediate concern was for Georgina. His addled mind made looking around the room difficult, but he was too exhausted to move. Assessing his surroundings, he quickly realised he wasn't in the type of holding cell he expected for a rebellious group of mages. The walls were mostly glass and there was a faint but distinctly clinical smell. Looking into the neighbouring room, he spotted his wife and stared, only relaxing when he saw her chest rise and fall in a steady but laboured motion. She was sick but alive.

He'd been in hospital enough times to know they weren't there, but wondered if they were in the Institute, and if so, *had they been saved?* His hope blossomed when across from him, sitting at a large desk was a woman clad in white, her raven hair and confident demeanour recognisable to anyone who called Siranor home.

"Imperator Harlyn, is that you?" Aaron asked, calling out to the slender woman before him. The woman jumped at first but then turned to face him revealing she was indeed the Imperator.

"How are you feeling?" she asked, her studious glare assessing his symptoms.

"Awful," he replied honestly. "How is my wife?"

"She's unconscious again. She woke briefly and started screaming the name 'Hugo' over and over, so I gave her a sedative," she advised rather dispassionately.

"That's our son," Aaron explained, believing that knowledge would garner some sympathy from the Imperator. "Please, can you tell me how long it's been since the attack on the trade outpost? I only arranged our babysitter for one day."

"The attack happened a few hours ago," Imperator Harlyn replied. "It's early evening now."

"Is there someone who could call my brother? He'll look after our son while we recover, I'm sure of it," Aaron pleaded.

"Of course, what's your brother's name?" Imperator Harlyn enquired, her pen and notepad at the ready.

"Charlie Blake, he's a warden here at the Institute," Aaron answered, trying not to think about both his and Georgina's fate by focusing on their son's continued care instead.

"Charlie Blake is your brother," the Imperator replied, although she didn't sound happy by the revelation. "Calling him may not be necessary. I may be able to heal you."

Aaron could feel the relief lift his spirits as a heavy breath escaped him. He fixed his gaze on the Imperator, unable to contain the tears.

"Truly... but how?" he began, the words stuttering out.

"With a formula I've been working on called En-glycerol. I've never properly tested it on a human, but in every scenario, it neutralised all Encia from the blood. It may be your only chance."

"I'll take it," he replied without hesitation, trusting the Imperator's wisdom.

Without a further word, Imperator Harlyn filled a syringe and entered Aaron's room. With his eyes firmly closed, she found a vein and injected the En-glycerol directly into his bloodstream. Feeling the alien substance travel through his body, Aaron soon felt his nose running and a lump forming in his throat. Covering his face with his hands while he coughed, Aaron was shocked to see blood spattered on his palms. Before he could worry about it further, he found himself retching over the side of the bed, thankfully into a small bedpan that he hadn't even realised was there.

"How do you feel?" she asked after he collapsed back onto the bed, his body trembling.

"Better, I think," he replied honestly. Even though his body was still wracked with pain, he felt somehow revived. Raising his hands before her, they could both see his blackened fingertips receding and the colour of his veins returning to normal.

"It's working," the Imperator exhaled. "Think of all the lives that can now be saved."

"Do you have more? Please, can you cure Georgina?" Aaron begged, reaching out and grabbing the Imperator's hand, forgetting that his own were covered in blood. Being as weak as he was, she easily pulled away, but the desperation in his eyes seemed to breach her otherwise frosty exterior.

"Yes, of course," Imperator Harlyn replied, wiping her hand on her coat and smearing the otherwise pristine garment with tendrils of blood. "We just need to wait for her to come around from the sedative."

"Can I take her home and give it to her there?" he asked.

"I don't see why not," she nodded with a smile, giving him the second dose of En-glycerol. "You are still weak though, so allow my wardens to take you home."

"Thank you, ma'am," Aaron replied, utterly grateful. His big day of romantic plans might've fallen through, but it would end with Georgina in his arms and them safely back at home.

Imperator Harlyn moved towards the external door and called for her guards. Moments later a slender, beautiful woman with short black hair entered the room. Her face was one Aaron would never forget. She was the one who poisoned Georgina and most likely him too. Panicked and ignoring every screaming muscle ache in his body, Aaron darted from his room to his wife's bedside.

"You!" he snarled, "Don't come any closer."

"What's the problem, Mr Blake?" Imperator Harlyn enquired, his reaction startling her.

"She's one of the attackers, ma'am! She cornered my wife and made her drink Encia. It's because of her we both became sick!" he cried, his voice getting louder and louder as the woman introduced to him as one of the Imperator's wardens revealed an entirely disgruntled expression.

"You let him see your face, Juliette?"

At that moment, Aaron's earlier relief was gone and was replaced by a deep-set feeling of dread. *Was the Imperator involved in the attack?*

"If he saw me, he saw Noah too," Juliette protested. "Not to worry, I can use my concoctions to induce short-term memory loss. What he remembers now, he surely won't when I'm through with him."

"No," the Imperator replied firmly.

"Why not?" Juliette asked, cocking her head towards the Imperator.

"His brother is a warden and Charlie is already suspicious of my experiments," Imperator Harlyn replied, rolling her eyes as she turned her back on Juliette. "If Charlie recognises the symptoms of your toxins or worse, of my En-glycerol then all of our efforts will be wasted."

"Your efforts?" Aaron screamed, "You mean the assault was nothing more than a ruse to implicate mages? You killed all those people for nothing!"

"Damn, this guy's smart," Juliette quipped, earning nothing more than a piercing, sidewards glance from the Imperator.

"He's a liability," she corrected harshly.

"What would you like me to do about that?" Juliette asked biting her lip with excitement.

"He's served his purpose, we know En-glycerol can cure the withering now. As far as I'm concerned, there were no survivors from this afternoon's attack."

"You can't do this!" Aaron wailed, rushing for the door but Juliette got there first, slamming the glass panel in his face.

With a sharp flick, a metal bolt secured the door and in his weakened state, no amount of thrashing helped. All Aaron could do was watch as the Imperator turned her back on him, returning to her desk while her so-called warden, who he considered little more than a murderer, searched through a satchel, finally taking out two cylindrical vials.

"Now it's my turn to use you as a test subject," Juliette declared, her sinister grin widening. "I'm sure you don't mind, seeing as you've been so helpful already."

Helplessly, Aaron watched as Juliette opened a small ventilation hatch and rolled the first object into the room he and Georgina were imprisoned within. It smashed on the floor and released a nearly imperceptible gas. Rushing to his wife's side, Aaron covered her face with his forearm while trying to mask his own mouth and nose too, but it wasn't enough. He could feel his mind begin to spin as the room became blurry. Then he was back there, at the trade post, surrounded by the loud noises of mage attacks.

"You've got one! Stop them," cried a female voice. "Don't let her escape. Kill her!"

Hearing the words, Aaron looked down and could see his arm pressed around an unfamiliar face. The woman stared back at him, malice filling her eyes. She grabbed his arm, trying to free herself but he pressed down harder as she writhed beneath him.

"I'm sorry, I can't let you go. I have to protect my wife... my son. He needs us!" Aaron cried, taking his free hand and covering the woman's nose, blocking her airways.

The woman fought and clawed at his arms, but he didn't relent until her body went still. *I've never killed anyone before, but I didn't have a choice... did I?*

"Well done," said the earlier voice that he slowly recognised as being Juliette's. "You've just killed your beloved wife."

Shaking his head and rubbing his eyes, Aaron looked down to see the suffocated form beneath him. To his horror, it wasn't an angry mage, it was his wife. The realisation hit like a ton of bricks as he fell backwards from her bedside and tumbled to the floor, beneath the ventilation hatch.

"No," he mouthed, unable to bear the thought of what he'd done. It wasn't her; it couldn't have been... he'd never hurt *her*.

He didn't have to live with the pain for long though, as Juliette rolled the second vial through the shaft. As it crashed beside him, the liquid that emerged sounded more like an acidic gas, hissing and bubbling in the open air. Realising there was no hope, nothing he could do, Aaron inhaled deeply and let whatever the vile toxin was to enter his body. Once again, his body shook but by that point, Aaron was physically and mentally numb. Within a few minutes, his throat had swollen, and tears of blood ran from his eyes. Finally, there was nothing but the welcome embrace of oblivion.

"What was that?" the Imperator asked, having briefly glanced over her shoulder during the raucous.

"My latest creation," Juliette said with a grin. "It induces short-term hallucinations. I call it a halo-bomb."

Without a word of judgment, the Imperator turned back to her desk, grabbing a sheet of headed paper.

"Get Noah and take their bodies to the hospital. Pretend that you've only just found them," Imperator Harlyn instructed. "I have to focus on announcing that En-glycerol cures the withering."

"Right away," Juliette replied, walking out of the room to fetch Noah.

After two days and several failed attempts at locating Sebastian's mother, Charlie returned to the hospital to check on him. Striding through the main entrance towards the nurse's station, his attention was briefly caught by the news headline on a nearby paper:

Guerrilla tactics! Rebel mages strike outpost, sixteen dead!

Charlie had briefly heard about the attack on the radio the day before but hadn't realised so many people died. Finding himself disappointed but unsurprised that the details in the local newspaper, the Imperial Press were sketchy at best, he made a mental note to ask the wardens on duty about it later.

He was one of the few Institute wardens who kept up with physical training even though his focus was on scientific and political advancement. In doing so, he made some valuable friends at the Siranor guardhouse. While they technically answered to General Owen at the barracks, Tutor Matthews from the academy also visited frequently to assist with the day-to-day operations and was often treated like the commander. Even though it wasn't his role, his presence was comforting.

Charlie was just about to approach the nurses' station at the hospital and ask about Sebastian when he overheard two nurses talking outside a nearby patient room.

"Did you hear the news? The Imperator has done it, she's synthesised a cure!" the first nurse exclaimed.

"I did," replied the second. "It's the miracle we all needed after a day like yesterday."

"All those innocent souls," murmured the first. "I'm still struggling to get my head around what happened yesterday. So much death… and for what?"

"Because we're at war, Jen," insisted the second nurse. "There wasn't anything we could do, don't forget that."

As the nurse named Jen nodded, she caught sight of Charlie in her peripheral vision and hurried over.

"Warden Blake, I didn't realise they'd already called you. Thank you for coming so quickly."

"I'm sorry, no one called for me, I'm just here to check on the young boy I brought in the other day, Sebastian," Charlie explained, looking at her with a perplexed expression. *Why was she expecting me if not to check on the boy?*

"Oh, I assumed you were here to collect your nephew," she gasped, covering her mouth with her hands.

"Why is Hugo here?" Charlie asked, as his eyes searched the area in a panic. "Are my brother and sister-in-law okay?"

Noticing her colleague fretting, the second nurse strode over to address him.

"Warden Blake, my name is Adele, I'm one of the senior nurses. I can only apologise if you haven't been contacted, sir," she began, in a solemn yet sympathetic way.

"Please, tell me what's going on," Charlie pressed, his concern growing with every passing second.

"Your brother Aaron and his wife were at the outpost yesterday during the mage attack. I'm terribly sorry, they didn't survive," Adele explained.

Grief stuck Charlie like a bolt through the chest, taking his breath away. *How could they be dead?* He knew Aaron had planned a romantic day for their anniversary but never imagined they would've been anywhere near the outpost.

"What, but how can this be? I… I need—" Charlie began, before realising that he had no idea what he needed.

"I can take you to them, if you'd like," offered Nurse Adele.

"Your nephew's babysitter is still with him, they'll be okay for a few more minutes," added Nurse Jen who wrapped her arms around herself, reading his devastation and trying to prevent a shiver from running over her skin.

"Thank you. Yes, please take me to them," Charlie replied, swallowing his dread.

This news was quite literally the last thing Charlie had expected to hear upon entering the hospital. While he was shocked, he couldn't believe they were gone until he saw their bodies with his own eyes. The nurse led him through the emergency department and into a large, remarkably cold room that was filled with covered bodies. Sixteen to be exact.

"We've kept all of the victims in here to be identified by their families but will need to move them to the morgue soon," Nurse Adele explained, checking the chart in her hand to find the gurneys that held Aaron and Georgina.

As she read their charts, a tear rolled down the nurse's cheek. She may have been able to give reassuring words to her colleague, but she too was deeply saddened by what had occurred. Pulling the covers away, the nurse revealed the pain-stricken face of his brother who appeared to have been brutally beaten and drained, while next to him lay his beloved wife, her skin blackened and sickly.

"What happened to them?" Charlie whispered, unsure if he wanted to know the answer.

"We believe that Mrs Blake was likely unconscious and suffocated to death. As for your poor brother, I really cannot say."

"When can I take them home?" he asked breathlessly.

"You can't I'm afraid, sir. We have strict instructions to cremate all the victims after identification, due to the potential Encia exposure," the nurse replied, shying away from Charlie, expecting him to react badly. Luckily for the nurse, he understood the dangers and was not going to argue.

"May I have a moment alone with them?" he pleaded softly. "To say goodbye."

"Of course, just please be careful and don't touch them," Nurse Adele instructed. "Although the Imperator has announced that her En-glycerol is an effective cure for the withering, we haven't received a supply yet."

Nodding to confirm he understood her warning, Charlie took some nearby oilcloth gloves and a lab coat from the wall. Smiling softly at him, the nurse left, giving him a moment with his dearly departed family. After she was gone, Charlie desperately tried to focus his mind away from who he was examining, as he began inspecting their bodies. He was a scientist and needed to be certain their causes of death were correct.

Starting with Georgina, he paid particular attention to the dark circles under her eyes and the pallor of her skin. Reaching for her hand, he noticed the same blackening around her fingertips and knew that she had clearly suffered from the withering. At the end of the gurney, he found a chart filled with doctor's reports and x-rays. Upon examining Georgina's, he discovered that her hyoid bone was broken. That implied strangulation, not just suffocation as the nurse had said.

Presuming she was just trying to be kind, he moved his attention to his brother. They'd looked so similar growing up but now, Aaron was horribly disfigured, which somehow made the examination easier. The most noticeable condition was the blood stains streaming from his eyes. It was as if the vessels had spontaneously haemorrhaged and Charlie could only hope that by the time they did, his brother was incapacitated and couldn't feel the pain that would've accompanied such a condition. The severe swelling around his throat was gruesome but led him to notice the dryness and discoloration around Aaron's mouth.

Taking his brother's medical chart, Charlie flicked through the report and noted that the doctors had also discovered a pin-prick indent on his arm, as if he'd been injected with something. That was when the memories of Sebastian and the En-glycerol clinical trial bombarded his mind. He quickly seized his brother's hand and noticed that, although milder than his wife, Aaron too had signs of the withering. With the pieces fitting together like a puzzle, it became clear that his brother hadn't been killed by some cursed magic or at the hands of rebellious mages. He and Georgina had somehow contracted the withering, been cured and finally, murdered.

An immense feeling of anger soon overwhelmed Charlie. He couldn't comprehend why the trade outpost would have been targeted by anyone other than mages but also couldn't explain why Aaron and Georgina appeared to have died in the manner they had. It didn't make any sense, but it did make Charlie realise he needed to leave Siranor. Now.

Marching from the room, Charlie headed back towards the nurse's station and found Nurse Jen.

"Please, take me to my nephew. I'm going to take him away from the city for a while," he requested firmly.

"Of course, right this way," she replied.

"Will you also discharge the boy I brought in the other day? His name is Sebastian," Charlie added, remembering his promise to the boy and not wanting to risk leaving him anywhere near the Imperator or her hunters, even if he no longer had powers.

"Oh, I think we had planned to keep him in for another few days for observation," Nurse Jen began, but stopped when she registered the resolute look in his eyes.

"I've found his mother," Charlie lied. "She's a traveller from the Scarlett Bluffs and terribly worried about him. I've promised to reunite them in Tivani. Sebastian will be safe with me, so please release him into my care."

"Of course, I'll arrange his discharge papers and you can be on your way in about an hour," she replied.

"Please hurry," Charlie said with a nod, as the nurse pointed to his nephew, Hugo in the soft play area. His babysitter, Jessie was still with him and trying her hardest not to cry in front of the toddler. When she noticed Charlie heading towards her, she darted up and gave him a big hug.

"I'm so glad you are here!"

"Thank you for staying with Hugo. I only just found out what happened," he replied.

"Of course! I couldn't just leave the little guy. What's going to happen now?" Jessie asked, her voice frantic.

"I'm going to care for Hugo," Charlie began. "I know it's what Aaron and Georgina would've wanted. Please go home and get some well-earned rest."

"Are you sure you don't want me to stay?" Jessie questioned. He knew she'd once had a crush on him, Georgina had said as much when trying to set them up on a date, but her concern for his situation seemed genuine.

"Honestly, we'll be okay. I'm going to take Hugo to Tivani for a few weeks. My good friend is the warden commander there," he explained, knowing that Jessie was a city girl and although she loved Hugo and had been very close to Aaron and Georgina, she wouldn't want to accompany him.

"Good, I'm glad to hear you are going to take some time away from your duties to be with Hugo," she replied, just as the nurse returned with Sebastian.

"Don't worry about the discharge paperwork, I can sort that out for you," she announced, her expression kind as she ushered Sebastian towards him. The young boy was still pale but looked much better than he had before.

"Who is this?" Jessie queried, confused by the boy's arrival.

"This is Sebastian, I found him the other day near the Institute. He was severely unwell and needed care but now he's a bit better, I'm going to return him to his family in Tivani," Charlie replied, continuing the lie he'd spun for the nurse moments ago.

"My mum's in Tivani?" Sebastian called out, equally excited and nervous. Noticing the look in Charlie's eyes, Sebastian rapidly spoke again. "Still… Oh, I'm so glad you found her."

"No problem, Sebastian. Now come on, you're with us," Charlie replied, picking up his two-year-old nephew who giggled, pleased to see him. "I'll need to pop to my brother's place to grab some things for this strapping young man and to my house for supplies. We should then be able to catch the overnight train to Tivani."

Chapter Twenty-Two
Atonement

The day after the wardens left marked the day that Alex, Lianna and Rylie would travel to Carlisse with Maia to secure peace between the monarchy and the Ar'encal. It was a vital opportunity, the first of its kind since before the war and Rylie could tell the prospect of success was driving Maia, despite her continuing affliction.

Maia wasn't the only one filled with nervous anticipation though. Lianna would soon see Spencer and confront her earlier mistaken feelings for him, and Rylie was going to have a conversation with Siljanna for the first time since the tavern fire.

"Are you almost ready to go?" Rylie asked, popping her head into Lianna's room. "I think Alex and Maia are already waiting for us by the Crescent Falls."

"My bag is ready, I'm not sure about me though," Lianna replied, anxiously biting her nail.

"Nervous?" Rylie asked, tilting her head with a kind smile.

"Aren't you?" Lianna questioned, her distress apparent. "Do you know what you're going to say when you see Siljanna?"

"I know *something* needs to be said, but I don't know what that something is yet," Rylie answered honestly, admitting to herself she hadn't given the actual conversation much thought. A lot of what could happen depended on Siljanna's reaction, something she couldn't plan for.

"I know I'm overthinking things, but I just can't stop worrying about seeing Spencer again," Lianna fretted, roughly tugging her hands through her hair. "I was such an idiot before and if Caitlin told him that I almost stayed in the hopes of getting romantically involved…"

"Even if she did, this is why you wanted to go back, remember? To make sure this whole situation is behind you. Would you rather be in my shoes?" Rylie quipped with a shrug and a smile. "How do you tell someone that you're hurt and angry but sorry and grateful to them?"

Those were the emotions she somehow had to convey to Siljanna, and she had no idea how she was going to get there. She just knew that she had to.

"Yes, I'd much rather be you," Lianna retorted playfully.

"Come on, let's go. We're only torturing ourselves by dawdling!" Rylie asserted, grabbing Lianna by the hand and pulling her towards the door. She just about managed to grab her bag on the way.

The two of them headed up the pathways to the falls and when they arrived, they spotted Alex and Maia who were indeed already waiting and deep in conversation.

"Are you sure you have everything you need?" Alex asked, checking through Maia's bag, clearly not for the first time.

"There is no need to fret, young squire," Maia replied kindly, trying to stifle her laughter. "We're stopping in Lorvale enroute and I'm sure they have both an apothecary and sundry shops if I have forgotten anything."

"Yes, but, what if…"

"Alex, I'm not sending another Ar'encal in my place," Maia interjected, her empathic abilities revealing his primary concern was for her health. "This condition may be draining but I am strong enough to keep it at bay."

"As long as you're sure," he grumbled, returning his attention to her bag, checking the contents again while mumbling something about where to store her cane.

"Is he being a pain, Maia?" Lianna called out, alerting them to her and Rylie's arrival.

"Quite the opposite, he's being over-cautious," Maia replied, her warm smile briefly disguising her discomfort from the toxin in her system.

"Alex, the rambunctious pick-pocket… are you sure we are talking about the same person?" Rylie teased.

"Oh, they grow up so fast," Lianna joined in playfully.

With a groan, Alex moved away from the bags and ushered the women onto the waterfall platform. With a subtle wave of her hand, Maia triggered the rune that would elevate them to the top.

"Parker is going to meet us with the horses and travel as far as Lorvale," Alex explained. "Caitlin and Dylan should be there when we arrive and will take us onwards to Carlisse to enter the castle via the eastern entrance… to avoid the crowd."

"Crowd?" Lianna enquired.

"Yes, Queen Nadia has already announced to her subjects about the impending change to their laws. That led to the Royal Guard anticipating large crowds in the castle grounds to see the treaty being signed," Alex confirmed.

"Was there much opposition to the peace accord?" Rylie asked, not having even thought about the reaction of the Carlisse citizens until that moment.

"Not that the queen has mentioned in her letter," Alex advised. "A few noble houses refused to give up their slaves, but they apparently changed their tune when the alternative was being stripped of their titles and land."

"Wow, I can't believe the noble resistance was so easily toppled," Lianna commented, the glee she felt portrayed in her glistening eyes.

"She hasn't gone into explicit detail, but it sounds like Queen Nadia has truly followed the procedures set out in the Royal Archive when changing the laws. She's been very clever in her approach and only used threats when justified," Alex replied, mirroring his sister's joy.

"How are you feeling, Maia? Tomorrow is going to be a tremendous day," Rylie asked, turning to her teacher.

"Nervous, excited but most of all, fortunate," Maia replied, placing a hand softly over her heart as she spoke. "When the Uprising began, the Ar'encal leader at the time could do little but fight back and when he died, the best I could offer my people was survival. Tomorrow, that will change, and I'll be able to give them something precious: freedom."

"I can't imagine what it was like living through the war," Lianna whimpered. "To be targeted so mercilessly and witness so much devastation. I think my powers would have driven me insane."

"There were a lot of empaths here and across the Eastern Continent that crumbled under the strain, especially in the early stages of the war," Maia admitted. "I tried but failed to save many of them. In fact, it was your grandmother, Rylie, who had the willpower to overcome the emotions and she helped countless other mages to channel their abilities too. Thanks to her, many more of us were able physically survive the emotional burden."

"Really?" Rylie remarked, wishing with all her heart that she could've met her grandmother.

"Yes, she was a remarkable person," Maia replied. "When we get back from Carlisse and resume your training, I'll show you some of her old diaries. She used to love drawing, just like your sister and I know if she was still with us, she'd be immensely proud of you both."

"I'm not certain about that," Rylie doubted, a guilty grimace twisting her face momentarily. "I'd still be an unchained, fiery mess if it wasn't for all of you and this amulet."

"You were overcome with a power that no mage has confronted in my lifetime," Maia countered. "Coming back from that was no small feat, Rylie."

"I've got a long way to go before I'll consider taking this thing off though," she replied, closing her eyes briefly as she touched the amulet, grateful for its presence.

"When he returns from Tivani, Harrison and I will create that new amulet for you, something focused on clarity instead of suppression," Maia advised. "That should allow you to retain control while tapping into more of your Aeon power."

Unable to help still feeling concerned, Rylie just smiled weakly at Maia, who placed a reassuring hand on her shoulder as they ascended and passed through the fall's illusion. Just as Alex had advised, Parker was waiting for them with the horses and before long they were enroute to Lorvale.

They took their time riding to town and when they arrived, Maia made the mistake of teasing Alex by saying she'd forgotten her supply of Encia, the one thing she was currently dependent on, but no apothecary would stock. She soon regretted the joke, however, as he removed every item in her bag onto the street until he located the precious vials. While he was scrabbling on the floor, Parker arrived and greeted them with a confused smile.

"Is everything okay?" he asked.

"Don't ask," Maia replied, hiding her face in her hands as she tried not to laugh.

Parker was originally from Lorvale and knew the town like the back of his hand. After helping Maia to put her belongings back in the saddle bags, he led the group on the quickest route to their meeting point at Delancy Park with Caitlin and Dylan. Also on horseback, the pair waved them over and once closer, the girls spotted another familiar face.

"Oh look, it's Zack's buddy, Cruise!" Rylie exclaimed with delight, the gentle creature reminding her of their absent friend.

"Our original steed," Lianna chimed.

"Is it just me or does it feel right that he's the one leading us on this journey?" Rylie asked happily.

"It's not just you," Lianna agreed, leaning over to stroke the horse affectionately.

After they'd finished fussing over the docile creature who was nibbling on the grass on a nearby hedge, Caitlin looked around the group and noticed that Maia's saddle bag looked hastily packed.

"Do any of you need supplies before we head off to Carlisse?"

At that moment, Alex's attention shot straight to Maia, then to her bag and back again.

"We're all fine," Maia commented, giving her squire a warm smile. "Perhaps we could stop for a short rest, just so I can take my tinctures, though. I won't be long."

"There's no need to hurry, we've allowed all day for the journey," Caitlin assured with a chuckle. "With me leading the way, we won't get lost like Dylan and Siljanna did."

"Thank you," Maia replied graciously. "Rylie, perhaps you could assist me? It'll be good practice for you to handle Encia again."

"Of course," Rylie agreed, dismounting her horse before helping Maia to do the same.

Parker indicated a small rural enclosure inside the park and offered to take them there, but Maia politely declined. She wanted a moment alone with Rylie but despite her wishes, Alex insisted to stand guard nearby. Although the accord was going to change the lives of the Ar'encal on the continent, it would take time before the locals, especially in towns like Lorvale and Revaine would get used to seeing mages and Ar'encal walking freely among them.

Tucked safely out of sight, Maia pulled out the vial of Encia from her bag, discarded the cork and held it before Rylie.

"What do you need me to do?" Rylie asked.

"Encia naturally forms in water, and as an Elementalist, you can control that. In order to drink the purified Encia, I can extract the essence in the water from the vial, but I'd like you to do it."

"I never realised you were such an opportunistic teacher, Maia," Rylie chuckled, taking the vial from her. "You have more, right? In case this goes wrong."

"I do, but you'll be fine," Maia encouraged. "Although your power is currently suppressed, you can still cast, and your emotional state will still impact your ability. Focus on the water, just as you did that day on the lake. Draw it from the vial to your hand."

"Okay, I'll try," Rylie nodded, focusing intently on the vial.

As the elemental rune on her amulet softly glowed, Rylie tried to move the water, but the substance didn't react. Sensing her frustration, Maia also noticed the suppression rune flicker into life and knew her pupil needed additional motivation.

"Remember, I need that tincture to help control this affliction. Use that urgency to your advantage. It doesn't have to be a handicap."

It would take much more concentration with her amulet on but after a few moments, Maia could feel the wind swirling around the bottle, towards Rylie's hand, as if encouraging the water to elevate itself from within the vial. At first, there were just a few droplets but slowly the rest followed.

"The Encia is within the water Rylie," Maia informed. "I don't need the water, just the Encia. What will separate them?"

"Encia doesn't evaporate," Rylie answered, keeping her gaze focused on the levitating liquid.

"So, tap into your inner fire," Maia instructed, urging Rylie to proceed. With the magical water still flowing around her hand and between her fingers, Rylie closed her eyes, coiled the water in her palm and focused on the heat that once consumed her. "You only need a small flame. One flame."

Like an eager child, the fire leapt to her fingertips and the heat that enveloped her hand soon evaporated the water. Opening her eyes just as the crystalline granules of Encia dropped into her hand, Rylie gasped.

"I did it."

"Well done," Maia announced as Rylie tipped the salt-like essence back into the vial and handed it to Maia.

"But wait, when you gave me Encia to take before, I drank it in water form," Rylie realised. "Did you really need me to do that?"

"No, I could've drunk the Encia in the water," Maia admitted with a cheeky grin. "But whatever has poisoned me makes me urge whenever I have too much fluid in my system so taking Encia like this is much better. That wasn't the point though."

"You wanted to prove what I could do, even though I didn't need to," Rylie realised.

"Exactly," Maia confirmed, swallowing the pure Encia and relishing in the relief her body felt in the moments after.

"Are you both okay?" Alex called from beyond the bushes.

"We're fine!" Rylie called back, glancing quickly at Maia to ensure that she was.

"On our way, Alex," Maia added, breathing deeply as she stood without the need for her cane. "This strength won't last long so let's get moving."

It was early evening when the group reached the eastern gate and even though the larger crowd had gathered at the main gate, there were still hundreds of people milling around, hoping to catch a glimpse of the Ar'encal leader. Ahead of all the people was a regiment of Royal Guard, led by Siljanna.

"Welcome to Carlisse," she greeted.

Rylie couldn't help but embrace the irony. The last time they'd met in Carlisse, the encounter had been an ambush that led to several repercussions; Noah's betrayal, Zack's blindness, Harrison being shot, her transformation and the discovery of Imperator Harlyn's deception.

"Thank you," Maia replied, dismounting first and striding towards Siljanna, extending her hand. The Ar'encal didn't typically shake hands by way of greeting, but it was a human custom and Siljanna gratefully accepted the gesture before waving over another guard.

"This is Finn, he and Dylan will take you to your rooms," she explained as Alex strode over with the bags and dutifully passed them over.

"Be careful with those," he instructed, speaking to the older guard who quickly assumed he was Maia's squire.

"Of course," Finn replied, indicating with his head for Dylan to help. "Caitlin will take the horses to the stables and ensure they are tended to."

"If everyone is ready, please follow us," Dylan added, grabbing the remaining bags.

"I'll catch up," Rylie called out before turning back to Siljanna. "Can I speak with you for a moment?"

"Yes, of course," Siljanna replied with a nervous nod.

As the rest of the group headed inside, Siljanna led Rylie to a quiet alcove where they could talk.

"There is so much I need to say to you, but I'm not really sure how to begin," Rylie admitted.

Taking a seat on a nearby bench, for the briefest moment Rylie found herself seated while Siljanna was standing over her. That positioning was all it took for the memories of the tavern fire to come flooding back. The last time Rylie had been this close to Siljanna, she had thrown her to the floor and accused her of starting the fire which led to Sampson Stone's death. After that night, Rylie never imagined they would speak again. Siljanna had caused so much pain and hardship, it was difficult to trust her, even though they'd once been the closest of friends.

With the memories flooding Rylie's mind, the suppression rune on her amulet began flare and as Siljanna took a seat beside her, she noticed immediately. Although she didn't know what the rune symbolised, Siljanna did know the power within Rylie was both immense and terrifying. Cautiously inching away, her free hand hovering over the combat knife tucked into her bracer, Siljanna looked at Rylie and for the first time, Rylie acknowledged that Siljanna feared her.

Smirking at just how much the tables had turned, Rylie relaxed and as she did, the rune on her amulet faded. Glancing sideways at her former friend, Rylie laughed softly, which in turn made Siljanna breathe a sigh of relief. Communicating without words, both girls knew this was their chance to make amends.

"You deserve an apology," Siljanna said, sounding ashamed of all she'd done. "After everything I put you through, *I'm sorry* feels rather pathetic."

"You tried to kill me and then I tried to kill you… how about we call it even on that subject?" Rylie jested, although her comment fell flat as both women knew it wasn't that simple.

"Your reaction was terrifying, but not intentional," Siljanna countered. "I allowed my grief to justify attacking you and your family in ways no decent person, let alone a friend, ever should. For that I am truly sorry."

"My dad put aside his anger towards you, the least I can do is the same," Rylie replied softly.

"It's more than I deserve," Siljanna whispered.

"That's not entirely true. I found out about Evie's abilities over a year ago, when your mother was murdered," Rylie confessed. "I could've told you and Harrison back then that we had Ar'encal heritage, but instead I kept silent. If you had known that there was a chance I could trigger powers but hadn't, you may not have reacted so angrily during the tavern fire."

"We were taught at the academy that mage abilities trigger during stressful situations. I cannot honestly say if that hindsight would've changed anything, but I wasn't thinking rationally that night, but I truly appreciate that you told me," Siljanna replied. "If we'd both made better choices prior to and during that night, our current situation could be very different."

"Exactly, and for that, I'm sorry too, Sil," Rylie added, reaching out to touch her former friend's hand.

"Shooting Harrison was a mistake, but it turned out to be the best mistake I made during those weeks of insanity," Siljanna remarked, a shiver running down her spine. "If that hadn't happened, I may not have discovered how the Imperator manipulated me or realised the error of my ways."

"It's a shame you didn't find out before I transformed," Rylie agreed, taking in a deep breath as she relived the moment in her mind.

"Do you remember what happened?" Siljanna enquired curiously. "I mean, were you aware of what was going on after you transformed?"

"I remember bits, although mostly I just remember being enraged. When I thought you'd taken my parents and killed Harrison, I couldn't bear it."

"It's called an Aeon form, right?" Siljanna asked.

"How do you know that?" Rylie replied, tilting her head at the surprising insight Siljanna had.

"Some guy grabbed me from behind and saved me from your attack," Siljanna began. "He said you'd become an Aeon. I didn't get to ask him any more questions though as we stumbled across Harrison's group who had pinned down the Imperator, which is when I heard her confession."

"I wonder who your mystery hero was," Rylie pondered. It could've been Lucas or one of the guards, but she also couldn't help but wonder if it was Noah.

"I wouldn't call him a hero. Moments later he proved his cowardice by leaving me and I never saw him again."

"Well your cowardly saviour sounds like it may have been Noah Harper, a former guardian of the Ar'encal. He's a rotten human being, but he told you the truth, I became an Aeon. It meant I was infused with near god-like power, although explaining how will take more time than we have," Rylie began, mindlessly touching the centre rune on her amulet, which represented the mark of the elemental goddess. "Maia Uriel, the Ar'encal leader is also my teacher but hadn't seen or heard of a mage transforming the way I did in her entire life."

"She looks pretty young so it may not be that rare," Siljanna suggested, trying to sound reassuring.

"Maia is nearly ninety years old," Rylie informed, only to chuckle at Siljanna's resulting shock.

"Seriously?" Siljanna questioned, her eyes wide.

"The gift of the Ar'encal is more than just immunity to Encia, it apparently also gives them long, youthful lives," Rylie replied to which Siljanna just raised her eyebrows and nodded gently, her expression saying what her words did not, *lucky bastards*.

"How is Harrison? I had hoped he would travel with you for the signing of the accord," Siljanna continued after processing that latest piece of information about the Ar'encal.

"He's gone back to Tivani with Morgan to aid the wardens," Rylie explained. "They fear the Imperator plans to strike soon."

"And Morgan wanted his partner back," Siljanna added, finishing Rylie's sentence.

"Exactly," Rylie replied with a smile. "And although we've only just gotten each other back, I knew he'd never forgive himself if he didn't help."

"I'm glad you're finally together," Siljanna admitted. "Harrison's crush on you started in our second or third year at the academy!"

"You knew?" Rylie asked with a mirthfully surprised chuckle. Siljanna's admission was just further proof of how oblivious Rylie had been over the years.

"Of course." Siljanna laughed. "What I should've said is that it's about bloody time the two of you got together."

"Did everyone know accept me? Why didn't you tell me sooner?"

"Because he should've told you sooner," Siljanna replied lightly. "And I enjoyed watching my brother squirm."

With a deep laugh, the tension dissipated from both Rylie and Siljanna. It wasn't quite the near sisterly bond they used to have, but the conversation had put them in a much better place.

"He told me he loves me," Rylie expressed fondly. "And I love him too."

"All right, this is getting a bit too soppy for me now," Siljanna quipped, although her smile gave away the fact she was happy for them.

"Hey, I know you have a softer side in there. It's underneath the sarcastic, ultra-competitive tactician," Rylie teased. "That little place in your heart where Charlie Blake resides."

"Ha!" Siljanna spurted out, "Oh, poor Charlie, I was wretched to him too."

"Have you seen him recently?"

"When I was in Siranor, he came to see if he could help me, but when he discovered what I was planning, he tried to get me to calm down and reconsider," Siljanna began. "Our conversation didn't end well. Charlie is a good man and I'll always care for him, but I'm not sure if it's in *that* way anymore."

"Is there someone else?" Rylie probed, her eyes alight with excitement. It had been the longest time since she and Siljanna had chatted like this and deep down, Rylie was grateful. She was beginning to understand why Harrison had been so willing to forgive her after the events at Jumant Fort.

"I'm not sure yet," Siljanna replied, glancing over her shoulder in the direction of the stables. Rylie noticed the gesture and peered over too, before remembering who had just gone to the stables.

"You like Caitlin?" she announced a little too loudly.

"I don't know!" Siljanna whispered, quickly placing her hand over Rylie's mouth.

When neither Rylie nor Siljanna feared each other's touch, they both realised it was another sign that their friendship could be repaired.

"You'll be in for a lifetime of trickery with that one," Rylie chimed, amazed that after everything, Siljanna had feelings for a mage. She also couldn't help but wonder if she fully understood the extent of Caitlin's abilities, but it didn't matter at that moment.

"I get a distinct feeling that'll be the case even if we just remain friends," Siljanna countered, burying her face into her hands to hide her blushes.

"You're not wrong," Rylie chuckled.

"Besides, I need to have a similar conversation to this one with Charlie. He deserves that much. And now that I'm not being a total bitch, old flames may yet rekindle," Siljanna continued, implying that she and Charlie had never truly ended their romance. "For the time being though, I'm going to remain in Carlisse and support Queen Nadia. It feels like this is where I'm meant to be."

"That's how I feel about being with the Maia and the Ar'encal. With them, I have the chance to learn how to control my power, and hopefully one day, without this suppression amulet," Rylie advised, agreeing with Siljanna's sentiment as she slowly removed her fingers from the item around her neck.

"Well, I suggest we get you settled into the guest rooms with your friends. Tomorrow is going to be a day to remember and I'm going to ensure that it's for all the right reasons," Siljanna resolved as the pair stood and headed towards the guest rooms.

The following morning came like a whirlwind, with attendants, guards and advisors rushing from pillar to post to prepare everything for the signing. Not wanting to cause any fuss, Lianna made her way to the dining hall with Alex and Maia only to find Rylie, Siljanna and Dylan already there.

"Good morning," Alex chirped, seeming a lot more at ease among their allies in the castle than he had on the road.

"Hey!" Rylie called out, waving as they entered. "Did you all sleep well?"

"The beds here are strange," Maia commented, still in a sleepy haze. Her random remark made the others laugh but focus on her as she sat down. She bypassed the food on offer in exchange for another dose of her Encia tincture.

"Are you sure we can't get you anything to eat?" Dylan asked. "It was my former partner that caused your current condition, so please let me know if there is anything I can do to ease your burden."

"I'll be okay, thank you," Maia replied. She was just about to ask him a question when they were joined by Queen Nadia and Spencer.

"Great, you're all here," Nadia greeted, her usual cool features replaced with a warm glow. "Welcome to the new and improved Carlisse kingdom."

"Thank you, Your Majesty," Maia replied sincerely.

"Please, call me Nadia. I consider everyone in this room a friend and do not require any formality from you," Nadia replied with a genuine smile. "This kingdom has much to atone for, but today we will make a good start."

"The accord you've created is going to bring peace and freedom to my people, that is all we could ever ask for," Maia insisted.

"Oh, but we intend to do more," Spencer hinted, his hand firmly held by Nadia. The two of them shared a joyous smile at the news he was about to share. "I was reading through some of Alistair's old journals. He noted that the land on the southern city limit, between Carlisse and Lorvale, used to be shared with the Ar'encal. We intend to gift that land back to your people."

"In exchange, we hope the Ar'encal might consider creating a trading village, allowing the kingdom citizens to establish and benefit from commercial networks with your people," Nadia added.

"I will discuss the prospect with Zack Harper. I've appointed him as liaison for the Ar'encal with all our allies. I believe you've met," Maia replied, seemingly overwhelmed by their generosity.

"We have indeed, it'll be wonderful to work with him," Nadia confirmed fondly.

"He'll be thrilled to create another safe place for both mages and Ar'encal too, thank you," Lianna added, her cheeks glowing at just the thought of Zack and how he'd feel learning of this opportunity.

"If I recall correctly, he was your guide when you first came to Carlisse, right?" Nadia asked.

"Yes, he used to operate under the guise of the mage smuggler," Lianna answered.

Turning away from them for a moment, Queen Nadia approached the guards at the door who both bowed before her.

"I am amongst trusted friends in this room and have no need for guard attention. Please go and assist Finn with the preparations for the accord signing," she instructed. The guards nodded respectfully and instantly departed, doing as she requested.

Turning back towards the group, Lianna watched as Queen Nadia slipped her hand into Spencer's and then gently placed the other over her belly.

"There may even be a royal mage that will come and visit… once they're old enough to walk that is."

As Lianna and Rylie realised her meaning, knowing more about the troubles she had faced previously than the others did, they rushed to their feet to congratulate the couple.

"This is fantastic news," Rylie exclaimed, embracing Nadia without any consideration for her regal position.

"Congratulations," Lianna added, gently hugging Spencer.

With a lingering glance, she noticed the look Spencer gave Nadia. He was totally in love and Lianna recognised how deep his feelings were instantly.

"When is the baby due?" Rylie asked, "Is there still a chance that something could go wrong?"

"There's always a chance and I'm only about a month in but this pregnancy feels different. It's almost as if the baby is absorbing the Encia in my system as my withering symptoms recede every day," Nadia explained, and her words explained the glow in her skin.

"It was a risk, us trying to conceive without the former king becoming aware of our duplicity but the risk seems to have paid off," Spencer admitted.

"If all goes well, the baby is due next year, in late autumn," Nadia added.

"Well, in that case, your child may very well be blessed," Maia announced, getting the undivided attention of both Nadia and Spencer. "By Ar'encal tradition, next year is 340-Viritus, the year of our healer deity and it sounds like your child could be born with healing powers."

"Just like their father," Nadia mused.

"Is there a chance the baby could completely heal Nadia of the withering?" Spencer asked, turning his full attention to Maia.

"I couldn't say as I never imagined encountering a pre-natal healer... but Rylie has certainly taught me not to underestimate the capabilities of mages," Maia replied, her expression pure delight.

"This day just keeps getting better!" Nadia exclaimed, washed with a sense of relief and anticipation.

As the rest of the group rose to give their congratulations to Spencer and Nadia, Lianna grabbed Rylie by the hand and pulled her to one side.

"I felt it!" she whispered excitedly.

"Felt what?" Rylie replied, mirroring her friend's hushed tone.

"How much he loves her. How much Spencer loves Nadia."
"And?" Rylie probed, hoping that her friend's reaction was a precursor to good news.

"And I couldn't be happier for them!" Lianna continued, a massive smile spreading across her face as her eyes twinkled. "His adoration is encompassing but I don't want to be the focus, I want him and Nadia to be happy together."

"Because..." Rylie added, pressing her friend to say what she really wanted to say,

"Because I love Zack and want to be with him. Gods, I wish I could see him right now."

Hearing her finally come to terms with her feelings made Rylie laugh and throw her arms around Lianna, giving her a big hug. The scene in the dining room was joyous, with everyone in the room smiling. It took a knocking on the main door to draw the groups attention away from celebrating.

"I apologise for the interruption but the crowd in the courtyard is getting larger and rather eager," Caitlin said as she popped her head into the room.

"Let us not keep them waiting then. Maia, are you ready?" Nadia asked.

"Absolutely," she replied in earnest.

Standing side by side, Queen Nadia and Maia Uriel, both leaders having endured unimaginable hardships, emerged onto the castle balcony before the amassed crowd. With the kingdom subjects and the recently freed mage and Ar'encal slaves below as well as Lianna and all their friends gathered behind, the peace accord was signed. A roar of applause followed.

Chapter Twenty-Three
Serendipity

Heading back to Tivani was a surreal experience but Harrison and Morgan enjoyed the journey, even though it took slightly longer going through Niyati on the trade vessel. There was a sense of sadness among the wardens, who all mourned Quinn Ashby in their own ways. They hadn't witnessed the vigil in Arencia, but Morgan had collected the young man's ashes after the service and knew the Ashby family would hold a memorial service too.

Once the ship docked in Niyati, Harrison joined Morgan on a brief diversion to visit his parents, but they quickly pressed on to Tivani. Approaching the southern bridge, Morgan noticed Téa waiting for them and greeted her with an energetic wave, happy to see that things seemed calm in town.

"It's good to see you!" she called out as they drew nearer.

"You too, Téa. Has everything been okay here?" Morgan asked, allowing another warden to take his bag while they spoke.

"We had an unexpected visitor," she began, stepping aside so that Morgan could see Dorian. He was vaguely familiar, but Morgan couldn't pinpoint why. Wearing Siranor military garb he somehow managed to look official yet present himself in an informal manner. Morgan decided to play it safe and greeted the young man with a salute.

"Good to meet you, Commander Foster, I've heard many great things about you," Dorian began, bowing politely in front of Morgan, who's rank would've made him Dorian's superior. "My name is Dorian Pesaro, a *former* military liaison from Siranor."

"Former?" Morgan queried, signalling with a subtle hand gesture for Harrison to remain back with the other wardens for a moment.

Harrison partially did as instructed, turning so that Morgan's company would only see his back, but he was close enough to hear what they were saying.

"Yes, I came here at the behest of the Imperator but have my reasons for deferring that loyalty to you instead," Dorian advised, speaking so plainly that it took Morgan by surprise.

Why would this young liaison think that he was deferring his loyalty by supporting him and the Tivani wardens... unless he knew more than he should?

"That's a rather bold statement," Morgan commented, eyeing Dorian suspiciously after shooting a quick sideward glance at Téa.

"What I need to say should be discussed in private," Dorian replied, his implication clear.

"I trust him, Morgan. Please hear him out," Téa implored.

Uncertainty struck Morgan. This Dorian fellow could well have been the informant who had reported Siljanna's presence in Tivani to the Imperator. *But if he's the spy, why does Téa trust him?*

Disregarding his earlier warning, Harrison turned around and joined them, standing solidly beside Morgan.

"Is everything all right?" he asked, looking squarely at Dorian.

"Harrison Stone," Dorian said, extending his hand and needing no introduction. "Good to see you again."

"Again?" Harrison questioned, shaking the young man's hand. "There is something familiar about you, but I can't place when or where we might've met."

"In the Wutel Canyon during your graduation trial," Dorian advised and instantly, the hint of recognition he'd felt made sense.

Dorian was the leader of the military group they'd fought outside the old temple. Harrison had battled and subdued Dorian while Siljanna, Morgan and Aiden defeated the rest of his team.

"Of course, now I remember you," Harrison replied. "Perhaps we should move this conversation to your office, Morgan."

Heading swiftly for the guardhouse, Téa readily gave Morgan back his keys and they each took a seat in his office. Shutting the door behind them, Morgan returned to the matter at hand with trepidation.

"Why exactly did you come here?" he asked, analysing every word Dorian said, searching for signs of duplicity.

"You clearly made your way up through the military ranks to become a formal advisor at a fairly young age," Harrison added, folding his arms and mirroring his partner's suspicion.

"You taught me a valuable lesson that day," Dorian began, a humble smile warming his face. "Humility. Ever since our encounter, I've ensured that I learn all I can about the situations I face, combat or otherwise and adapt accordingly. That aptitude worked in my favour, opening doors that were closed to many others."

"So, you became a spy and have been reporting our actions to the Imperator," Morgan accused, reading between the lines to support his prediction.

"That was originally my charge, yes," Dorian confirmed honestly, his tone quiet but steady. "I have since found out more than my superiors intended and find myself questioning those orders."

"Did learning of my imminent arrival keep you here?" Harrison asked, wondering if Dorian's duty included reporting to Noah. "Last time I checked, I'm still a wanted fugitive."

"I only discovered that thanks to Téa," Dorian admitted.

"You would think me a fool, Morgan but when I received your communication, I told Dorian the truth and showed him your letter," Téa explained but was quickly silenced by Morgan's irate glare.

"What do you mean, you told him?" he challenged, unable to fathom any reason why she would do such a thing and hoping that somehow, he'd misheard her. "We anticipated the informant would discover the contents of the letter, but I never imagined you'd betray me, Téa."

"But he helped me, Morgan. Please, try to understand… Dorian came clean too. He was meant to report back to the Imperator, but never did," she stammered, her voice shrinking until it was barely audible.

"And what if he was lying? He could've told you that and then sent a secret report to the Imperator. She could know everything," Morgan countered, shocked at her naivety.

"He wouldn't lie to me. He wouldn't," she mumbled, shaking her head fervently.

"You don't know that! Can't you see that your actions may have signed all our death warrants, Téa?" Morgan argued.

"But I trust him," she replied, looking up at Morgan with a doe-eyed expression that jolted him to the core. "You have to believe me, Morgan. I know him. He wouldn't betray us. He and I… we care about each other."

"What? That's ridiculous! You've only known this man for two weeks," Morgan growled, bashing a fist into his desk with such force that the solid structure shook. The person before him now wasn't the friend he knew. The person before him was a lovestruck woman so desperate for acceptance that she'd allowed herself to be brainwashed. "Are you telling me you were willing to risk my life and the lives of every warden here, people you have called friends for years… because you have a crush on this man?"

Téa couldn't speak as Morgan's words sunk in. All she could muster was the strength to turn away as a distraught look washed over her face.

"I have not reported anything back to the Imperator!" Dorian swore, attempting to defend Téa. "If she hadn't been so easy to care for, Commander Foster, I may never have told her anything and could've still discovered the truth by stealing your letter."

"Keep quiet before I silence you myself," Morgan threatened, scowling menacingly at Dorian before shifting the entire weight of his glare back to Téa.

"You cannot silence me with idle threats, Commander. The people and wardens here seem to covet you as the best leader they've ever had, but I'm struggling to see why," Dorian chided, attempting to stand beside Téa but with a hand motion, she told him to stay back.

Harrison tried placing a hand on his friend's shoulder, knowing it took a lot to trigger this kind of reaction. Morgan had struggled to trust people since Harrison's mother's death but becoming this irate was unusual.

Their intention had been to flush out the informant but discovering Téa had been so careless was an unwelcome shock; so much so that he violently brushed off Harrison's hand and ignored his calming attempt, focusing all his frustration back on Téa. She'd never learn how reckless her actions were unless he told her.

"I trusted you!" Morgan cried, his voice intensifying. "With my affairs, my concerns, my secrets… and you just gave them to a stranger without a second thought!"

"I was prepared to strike him down, Morgan. For you!" Téa yelled, her whole body trembling. "You left me alone and in charge of the wardens all while knowing I doubted my ability to handle that kind of pressure. I was drowning until Dorian came and helped me. Even then, I would've chosen to protect you if he betrayed us."

"You… you've never killed anyone," Morgan realised, his anger quickly receding.

"I wanted to trust Dorian, so I had to find out if we could," Téa continued, her entire body quivering as she spoke.

"And you believe we can?" Harrison asked, shifting his gaze to Dorian and then back to his partner, who was still recoiling from the revelation that Téa had been prepared to kill Dorian.

"I swear myself to your cause and command," Dorian confirmed, once again addressing Morgan. He could only hope that the commander was listening, but Morgan didn't make it easy for the young man to tell as he refused take his eyes off Téa. "The Imperator intends to commit atrocities just to progress this war. At first, I believed her cause to be noble, but now I know that's not true. She's hiding something."

"Do you have any idea what it could be?" Harrison questioned. "Any insight you have could really help. It never made any sense why she supported Siljanna's hunt for us to begin with."

"Sadly, I don't know her reasons," Dorian admitted. "From what I've heard, her father, the former Imperator, Joseph Rainer was driven by power. His motivation was to conquer the Eastern Continent while her uncle, Elias Rainer wanted nothing more than to control Encia so that all humanity could wield powers akin to the Ar'encal. Imperator Harlyn seems to have continued both pursuits... but I do not know to what end."

Before any of them had the chance to ponder what the Imperator's motivation could be, they heard a ruckus coming from the front of the guardhouse and raised voices calling for Commander Foster.

"I'd better go and see what that's about. Do not leave this room until I return," Morgan commanded, his second comment aimed directly at Dorian.

"I won't," he replied, raising his hands in submission as Morgan left the room.

Turning towards Téa, Dorian attempted to mutter *nice fellow* but her and Harrison's attention was locked on the commotion. From within the office, they could hear raised voices that started off frantic but soon eased. After a few minutes, heavy footsteps told them Morgan was on his way back, and he wasn't alone.

"Come in, come in," Morgan said, his tone exuding his usual calm demeanour as he ushered the new arrivals into his office. "You'll never believe who else is here."

Knowing that Morgan would never invite in a person that would be a threat to Harrison, he relaxed against the desk but Téa and Dorian didn't share his certainty. Harrison assumed it might be one of their old academy tutors or maybe even Elijah Ashby, but he was wrong and pleasantly surprised to be so.

"Charlie, is that you?" Harrison called out, striding towards the door to embrace his old friend, only pausing when he spotted the sleeping toddler in one arm and another young boy sticking as closely as he could to the back of Charlie's legs.

Clearly not used to having the children, Charlie fumbled slightly, attempting to accept Harrison's embrace but instead just smiled awkwardly at him.

"Harrison, it's good to see you well," he replied, his usual politeness radiating through his words and emphasised by his smart attire, despite his dishevelled hair.

Assuming the toddler was the nephew he'd mentioned while they were at the academy, Harrison crouched down and turned his attention to greet the child. For the second time since returning to Tivani, he felt a pang of recognition when looking at the boy's face. While the child didn't recognise him, his eyes widened as he caught sight of the partially exposed rune over his collarbone.

"You're an Aegis Guard!" he cried, rushing towards Harrison and crashing into his arms. "You came for me!"

"Sebastian?" Harrison breathed, barely able to speak through the surprise. He embraced the youngster, unable to believe he was truly there, but it had to be him. Freya's kidnapped son would be the only person on the Western Continent to know what his rune signified.

The young boy just sobbed, nodding as he pressed his face deeper into Harrison's shoulder.

"This is the boy that was kidnapped from Iliria?" Morgan asked, almost as stunned as Harrison. "Charlie, how did you find him... how did you know to bring him here?"

"It's a long story but that part is just a happy accident," Charlie advised, taking a seat and moving his nephew so that the little one was cradled more comfortably across both of his arms. As he took stock of the others in the room, Dorian also recognised him.

"Hello Warden Blake," he greeted politely.

"Private Pesaro, if I'm not mistaken," Charlie responded graciously. "Please excuse me, I don't seem to have a free hand to offer you. Can I assume you aren't here on official business?"

"I was, but my circumstances have somewhat changed," Dorian replied, looking towards Téa affectionately.

"That makes two of us with altered situations then," Charlie confessed, turning his attention back to Harrison and Morgan.

"What's happened, Charlie?" Harrison asked, suddenly realising that not only was Charlie's visit unannounced but he also looked deeply shaken.

"You are safe here, that I can promise you," Morgan reassured, even though he remained uncertain of Dorian's true intentions.

Looking down at his nephew, Charlie took a deep breath to steady his nerves before responding.

"There was an attack on the outskirts of Siranor," he began. "My brother, Aaron and his wife were murdered, leaving me as the only person capable of caring for Hugo."

"Good gods, Charlie… I'm so sorry!" Téa exclaimed, pressing her hands against her heart as if preventing it from leaping out of her chest.

"The Imperator has claimed it was a strike by rebel mages, but I have my reasons for believing otherwise," Charlie continued, swallowing his dread.

"What kind of reasons?" Morgan asked gravely.

"I was able to examine their bodies at the hospital," Charlie explained. "While I cannot say with certainty, they definitely did not appear to be the victims of malicious magic."

"So that's how they plan to bolster support for the war," Dorian commented, his expression resolute.

"How do you mean?" Charlie probed, hoping to understand what possible motive could've led to his brother's death.

"The Imperator and her Shadow Council made it very clear they want to defeat the mages and Ar'encal as swiftly as possible. Creating the façade that mages are the aggressors would justify swift and brutal countermeasures."

"If they create enough panic, the Imperator could issue strikes anywhere, not just in Tivani," Harrison realised, speaking his concerns aloud to the group.

"Could we deploy some of the guards from Tivani to warn other wardens?" Dorian suggested.

"That might be exactly what the Imperator wants us to do," Morgan muttered, refusing to let go of his earlier suspicion. "Spread our forces thin so that less of us are here to defend Tivani."

"I didn't mean to imply that," Dorian promised, his tone slightly panicked. "I was only trying to help."

"It was an innocent suggestion, Morgan," Harrison commented, not wanting to aggravate his partner further but also sympathising with anyone being falsely accused. "Besides, if we sent messengers to the other wardens, we could gain support without weakening our defences."

"If the Imperator succeeds in creating mass hysteria, she'll follow up with damning propaganda. We'll need all the help we can get," Charlie added.

Unaware of their earlier confrontation, Charlie had no reason to judge anyone in the room and quickly became the voice of reason, just as he had been during training. Finally, Morgan glanced at both of his academy friends, then took a moment to register Téa's pleading expression before slowly approaching Dorian.

"I've sworn my loyalty to you and committed treason to reinforce your friend's suspicions. What else must I do to convince you?" he questioned, desperate to gain Morgan's trust.

Harrison couldn't say anything but knew that no matter how much intel Dorian received before being sent to spy on them, there was no way he could've known how greatly the recent events impacted Morgan, or his ability to trust strangers. He and Morgan had spoken a lot in the year after his mother died, and Morgan firmly believed it was underestimating the danger of a stranger that led to his mother's death.

He'd admitted back then that some nights, he still wondered if he'd said or done things differently, would Anora still be alive? Their lives would be so different now if she hadn't died but Harrison had always tried to reassure him that he did everything he could. No matter how much they wished for the past to be different, they couldn't change it. Recalling the person Morgan had been just over a year ago, Harrison couldn't help but draw similarities between himself and Dorian. He was just trying to help them through an awful situation, and he hoped his partner had realised that.

"You're right," Morgan replied, extending a hand towards Dorian. "I apologise."

Morgan's response had clearly been unexpected to Dorian, but was gratefully received and a huge relief to Téa.

"Allies are hard to find in wartime," Dorian began, "but I promise I am an ally, and I will continue to prove it."

"If you were privy to the Imperator's Shadow Council, do you know anything more of a substance called En-glycerol?" Harrison asked and as soon as he mentioned it, Sebastian pulled away from him, his eyes glistening with unshed tears.

"That's what she used on me," he mumbled, clasping his hands together and chewing on his thumb nail as the memories came flooding back.

"The Imperator has been working on En-glycerol for years, but the project was highly confidential" Charlie responded, believing he'd know more about it than Dorian possibly could. "How have you heard of En-glycerol?"

"It's some kind of weapon," Harrison explained. "One of the mage hunters used it against an Ar'encal, and she reacted just like a person with the withering."

"That is a cruel twist of fate," Charlie began, putting together the pieces and realising the full potential of the Imperator's creation. "The Imperator tested that same substance on Sebastian, and it stripped him of his power. She now also claims it can cure the withering."

As Charlie explained, Sebastian crumbled to the floor and lowered his head, distraught at the part of him that was now missing. Harrison quickly moved to sit beside him and placed a protective arm around the young boy.

"We theorised as much," Harrison commented without taking his arm away from Sebastian, who had started to sob,

After detailing what he knew of the Imperator's experiments and recent claims, Charlie quickly moved on to ask about Harrison's situation.

"Are Rylie and Evie safe?" he asked gently, noticing Harrison's tired expression. "Does Siljanna still hunt you?"

"Oh Charlie, I'll share that story with you once we find a bed for your nephew and have strong drinks in hand," Harrison jested with an exhausted chuckle.

"Well, you're alive so I'll take it there's a happy ending," Charlie replied playfully, fully expecting to be in for quite the tale before the day was done.

"It's getting happier by the day," Harrison confirmed. "Rylie and some of our allies should be in Carlisse as we speak, sealing a peace treaty with the new queen. Then to top it off, you rescued Sebastian for us."

"Do you think my mum will come and get me?" Sebastian asked fearfully, looking down at his hands again.

"I pity anyone that stands in her way once she discovers you are here and safe with us," Harrison replied, cheering the youngster up immensely.

As the mood in the room lifted, Charlie's nephew began to fuss. They'd travelled a significant distance and while he was too little to understand what was being said, he was acutely aware that neither of his parents were nearby.

"Perhaps we should relocate this conversation to somewhere more comfortable… and familiar," Morgan suggested, looking over to Téa, an unspoken question in the air between them.

"Familiar?" Harrison enquired, his eyebrows raising with curiosity.

"Oh yes, it's ready," she replied with a bright smile, reaching into the desk and pulling out another set of keys. "They finished moving in the new furniture the day before last."

"New furniture?" Harrison probed, hoping for an explanation.

"Since you've been gone, the wardens rebuilt the Hawk Eye tavern," Téa replied, the joyful news and Harrison's reaction illuminating her face.

"Seriously?" Harrison gasped, utterly lost for words that would convey his gratitude. "Nate and Paige will be so touched when they find out."

"Although we didn't know when they'd return, the tavern was like the heart of town. We couldn't leave it as little more than charred rubble," Téa asserted, much happier to share this news than she'd been earlier.

Agreeing they would all benefit from the respite, Téa and Morgan handed over to the senior guards on duty and then helped Charlie, Dorian and Harrison to take their bags to the tavern. Making his way through the streets of his hometown was more comforting to Harrison than he imagined possible. The sight of the fountain that still stood proudly in the centre of the square made him pause but passing it and laying his eyes on the rebuilt tavern filled him with solace.

"Now I'm home," Harrison muttered under his breath.

"I'm looking forward to hearing this tale of yours and to that strong drink, my friend," Charlie teased, catching his comment.

"Let me warn you, some parts are rather gritty," Harrison replied with a smile.

"Can I assume that it'll include an explanation for that fetching new tattoo and reveal what or who the Aegis Guard are?" Charlie asked.

"Some things are better left unsaid," Harrison replied, knowing in actual fact there were details he couldn't tell his friend, no matter how much he wanted to.

As they settled in, Charlie spent a bit of time with his nephew, keeping Hugo entertained until he was ready for another nap while Harrison wrote a letter for Freya, explaining that Sebastian was safe and a second note detailing the reconstruction of the Hawk Eye tavern for the Auren family.

Eager to get the letter posted, Téa offered to escort Sebastian to the courier and suggested they also collect some provisions for dinner. After they'd gone, Harrison, Morgan, Charlie and Dorian met by the bar to continue their conversation. After recounting his journey so far, evading specific mentions of Arencia or anything that would trigger his rune and allowing Morgan to fill in some of the gaps, Harrison encouraged Charlie and Dorian to delve into their own experiences and suspicions.

"I witnessed how En-glycerol stripped Sebastian of his power and now you say it reacted like a toxin to the Ar'encal leader," Charlie pondered, his inquisitive mind reeling. "Imperator Harlyn may be calling it a cure but as you said earlier, it's also a weapon."

"I'd be willing to bet she'll utilise it in every possible way," Harrison added, and Morgan nodded firmly in agreement.

"Her leading mage hunter is a toxins expert, so I'd be inclined to agree too," Dorian said supportively. "I recall meeting Juliette, she is an instantly dislikeable person."

"Do you know who her new advisor is, the one that replaced Cameron Weiss?" Charlie asked.

"I know his name is Noah and he's slithered into the top ranks of the Imperator's council because of his unique insight into the Ar'encal," Dorian replied. "Although it's strange, sometimes he seems eager to destroy them then moments later he's reluctant to share key information that would aid General Owen and the military."

"It's not reluctance, he's incapable of saying some details," Harrison explained. "Noah was a guardian and part of the same group I have now joined."

"The Aegis Guard," Morgan confirmed, answering Charlie's questioning glance. "Any mage sympathisers that join their ranks are given a powerful rune."

"That's the tattoo I can see on your collarbone," Charlie remarked and Harrison looked in his direction with a smile, giving his friend a subtle nod.

"If I understand correctly, it protects Harrison and others like him from the effects of Encia but in return, silences them from speaking the secrets of the Ar'encal," Morgan outlined, not wanting to overstep and reveal more than Harrison or the others would've wanted.

"It cannot cure the withering though," Harrison added. It was a sad fact that the Ar'encal had several, powerful runes, but no variation or combination could cure someone already afflicted by the disease.

"How intriguing," Charlie muttered, his academic mind aroused. "It's funny, many of the wardens at the Institute believed Elias Rainer, and to an extent, Harlyn herself, were obsessive over magical studies but when you mention things like that, I begin to understand why. Is there any way to remove the rune?"

"That I don't know," Harrison admitted. "Do you think that could be Noah's aim, to remove his rune?"

"If he truly intends to betray the Ar'encal and your Aegis Guard, that's what I'd do," Charlie replied.

"He's already betrayed us," Harrison confirmed, the venom in his response audible as they spoke of Noah. "He led the recent attack on Iliria and mercilessly commanded the death of our captain, who was also his father. He deeply despises me, and the feeling is mutual."

"You appear to be opposite sides of the same coin," Charlie mused. "Both sons of warriors now passed, both skilled in combat and both willing to take extreme risks to achieve your goals."

"I'd really rather not be compared to Noah, if you don't mind," Harrison quipped, taking a long swig of his drink.

"He did say opposite sides," Morgan added jovially, giving his friend a cheeky wink. "Good and evil one might say."

"Ah the blissful black-and-white version of events where our roles are interchangeable depending on your perspective," Harrison replied, having always believed that no person can be purely good or purely evil, even though both Noah and Juliette were inching closer to the latter with every action.

"I don't think the Imperator intended for Noah to lead that assault though," Dorian advised. "He and Juliette were meant to coordinate the attack with King Grayson and time it with an assault here. A two-pronged assault to flush out you and the Ar'encal defenders as well as your sister, who we assumed would be here."

"But you never gave them the signal to attack Tivani," Morgan acknowledged, making Dorian smile.

"I hope by failing to report back that I prevented an attack on Tivani, but I won't take that credit until we know for sure," Dorian replied with a soft smile.

"Perhaps Noah's hubris changed their plan," Harrison retorted. "The assault was ruthless, and with their numbers we should've been easily defeated, but we prevailed."

"Sometimes it's the quality of your ranks rather than the number of soldiers that makes all the difference," Dorian mused, his eyes shutting momentarily as he stifled a laugh. "Just recall our training battle at the Wutel Canyon."

"Ha! Very true," Harrison replied, remembering how Siljanna dominated the bulk of Dorian's group while Morgan and Aiden had defeated the gunners.

"Was she there in Iliria… did Siljanna help to defend you?" Dorian asked curiously.

"Yes, my sister was with us."

"Your sister is truly terrifying in combat," Dorian smirked.

"Indeed. I was grateful to have her on our side rather than against us," Harrison replied.

"Where is she now?" Dorian asked, clearly hoping Siljanna would be enroute to aid the wardens.

"I believe she's staying in Carlisse for now but will support us when needed," Harrison advised, the confidence he had in her almost surprising him. Just a few weeks ago, she was the greatest threat to everyone he held dear. Now, she was defending them, and he believed she'd do so.

"That takes us back to the valid point made earlier; we should garner more support from the wardens," Charlie suggested.

"Agreed," Harrison added quickly. "That way, we can do more than just defend Tivani, we could counter these false mage strikes and take the fight to the Imperator's front door."

"Let's not get too far ahead of ourselves," Charlie replied, a hint of caution in his tone. "Dorian and I know first-hand what the true might of the Imperial Military is. If the Imperator launched an attack with even a quarter of the troops at her disposal, we'd be decimated."

"I will address the wardens here in the morning and reveal the truth to those that don't yet know," Morgan offered.

"You're certain they'll side with us?" Charlie checked. He didn't seem to doubt Morgan but equally, didn't know many of the wardens in Tivani or how deeply they respected their commander.

"The Imperator has declared war and is falsifying mage attacks on civilians to justify it," Morgan replied. "I don't believe there's a warden alive that wouldn't."

"Perhaps that's the answer," Harrison pondered. "We shouldn't just reach out to the wardens in Tivani, we should reach out across the continent. Would our old tutors help us?"

"It's worth a shot but that wasn't our original plan," Morgan began. "We intended for the spy to leak Harrison's presence in Tivani and encourage Noah to react impulsively.

"Now that Dorian is on our side, however, we need a new way to influence when and where they'll strike," Harrison concluded.

"The Imperator and Noah have no reason to suspect I'd betray them and still await my instruction on when to attack so leave that task to me," Dorian offered. "As your friend will be coming here to collect her son, should I try to divert the attack away from Tivani initially?"

"It'll take over a week for word to reach our friends and for them to travel here," Harrison calculated, assuming they'd take the faster route via Yasras. "We should try to encourage the attack to happen before they arrive. I'd rather clear the threat than have it looming."

"If we can drive them back or away from Tivani in that time, it'll be much safer for the others to visit," Morgan suggested, taking his original communication to Téa and handing it to Dorian. "Do you think you can convince them you stole this?"

"I almost convinced you," Dorian assured. His particular skill set would come in very handy, but now it was working in their favour.

"Then make your way back to Siranor and we'll prepare for the assault," Morgan instructed.

Consenting to their plan, Dorian took the letter to his room with the intention of storing it safely among his belongings. To his surprise, Téa was waiting beside his bedroom door, staring at him as he approached.

"You're back," he greeted warmly, intending to take her by the hands and kiss her cheek.

"You're leaving," she replied, her eyes filled with a mix of fear and sadness.

"You overheard us. I didn't even realise you and Sebastian had returned," Dorian admitted.

"Must you go? Surely you can report back to the Imperator in another way."

She wanted to wrap her arms around him and make him stay, but she couldn't bring herself to look him in the eye. The idea of losing him now was too much.

"She will expect my report in person, but I'll be fine. As soon as I can, I will return here… to be with you," he insisted, reaching for her hand and imploring her to look at him.

"That's not making the idea of your departure any easier," she countered but she couldn't resist his determination. They both knew she would relent to their plan.

"I must go but I promise to be cautious," Dorian reassured. "After presenting them with this evidence, they'll have no need for me. Once dismissed, I can come back to you."

"What train will you depart on?" she asked sombrely.

"The quickest train is the mid-morning service," Dorian replied.

"Then I'll escort you," Téa insisted. While she'd given in to their plan, she didn't have to like it.

Chapter Twenty-Four
Revealed

Time was of the essence. Dorian knew he had to coerce the Imperator and Noah to either attack Tivani quickly or not at all. He was determined to help Commander Foster as he'd promised. Rushing from the train station to the Imperial Courthouse, he asked the bored receptionist to contact them urgently, giving her a jolt of excitement. Waiting for what felt like an eternity in the marble foyer, he began fidgeting with the ring on his finger. He earned the ring when passing out with the military, but nothing could distract him from the irritating clock. Each tick indicated precious time slipping away. Seventeen minutes passed before Imperator Harlyn and Noah found him.

"Private Pesaro, you're late," Imperator Harlyn greeted harshly. "However, I'm informed you have pressing news so am willing to forgive your tardiness."

"I do ma'am. Can we take this discussion to the council chamber?" he replied, hoping his energy appeared sincere.

Descending swiftly into the dark halls of the Shadow Council, Imperator Harlyn ushered Dorian and Noah to the war room where they could talk in private.

"Tell me, is Siljanna Stone finally back in Tivani?" Harlyn enquired, a hint of spite evident as she spoke.

"Not Siljanna, but perhaps someone of even greater interest. I stole this communication and then came back here as quickly as I could," Dorian explained, swallowing hard before handing over the letter and praying the Imperator would believe his tale.

Imperator Harlyn quickly read the contents of the letter before flippantly handing it to Noah, whose eyes lit up at the mention of Harrison Stone's imminent arrival.

"We have to capitalise on this opportunity, Imperator," Noah insisted, throwing the letter over the map marker for Tivani on the war table and decisively stabbing it in place with a knife. "We now have evidence that a fugitive and mage protector is in Tivani."

"But why would he risk returning?" Harlyn wondered aloud, folding her arms with suspicion. "Did you reveal our plan to attack?"

"I may have hinted at such a thing," Noah admitted, ducking his head in shame. "I taunted him, but that was all. I was hoping to rattle him, so he'd make a mistake and I could finally end him. I failed to consider that our original plan would be altered by other recent events."

"While I'd usually punish such an oversight, the result has still proven advantageous," Harlyn grumbled, turning her attention back to Dorian.

"The letter implies that Harrison wishes to repay the wardens for their help at the battle in Iliria," Dorian continued.

Although he'd tried to prepare for every eventuality, Dorian was now personally motivated to protect Tivani. He wanted to prove his loyalty to Morgan and ensure Téa's safety. Those motivators made him anxious at the prospect of failure and in turn, trying to decipher the Imperator's reaction became difficult.

"I thought those were wardens on the battlefield in Iliria," Noah hissed, recalling the ill-fated battle. "My newly acquired knowledge of the Imperial Military made me suspicious. The warden garb is rather distinctive, as was their ability to tear apart those useless soldiers from Carlisse."

"Do you know how many wardens have betrayed us, Dorian?" Harlyn asked sternly.

"There were eighteen missing from the roster, but I must admit... all the guards in Tivani seem devoted to their commander. Should he lead a call to arms, I believe they would all follow Morgan Foster," Dorian replied.

"Tivani can't have more than thirty-five wardens..." Harlyn began, thoughtfully pacing the room.

"It matters not, I'll lead one hundred of our men against them," Noah countered, his desire to face off with Harrison once again overpowering every other thought or mission. "Please, Imperator, we cannot ignore this opportunity."

"I'm not saying to ignore it, I'm saying to play it smart," she corrected, turning swiftly towards him with an insidious look. "The letter said they will arrive at the dock in Niyati, so I propose you take a large group of mage hunters and catch them on the main road between Saint's Bay and Fenian. Make it look like another mage strike, a devastating one. We can accuse Harrison of leading the assault."

"Then he'll be a target. Every mage hunter on the continent will want to track him down, but he's mine. I will ask nothing from you apart from this. Let me be the one to destroy him," Noah requested, turning sharply towards the Imperator.

"Of course, and when you do, you'll become a hero," Harlyn replied with a look of absolute confidence. "If there is one thing I don't doubt, it's your desire to kill Harrison Stone."

Noah quickly expressed his approval of her plan with a deep, menacing laugh but before he could leave the room, Dorian glanced at the map, searching for any reason to divert the assault to Tivani, where the warden defence would be waiting.

"But all the main roads across the river go through Tivani. How will the hunters get by undetected?" he queried hastily, giving Noah a reason to pause. "Wouldn't a precision strike by a smaller group be the smarter approach?"

"They can travel west, through the Imperial farmlands to Galnor and then take the road through Fenian," Harlyn advised, pointing out the route on the map. "It'll take longer, and you must remain discreet, but it is possible to make it in time."

"The interim commander in Tivani received that letter two days ago," Dorian replied, spinning what he hoped would be a believable tale. "I wasn't able to get my hands on it straight away, but as soon as I did, I came here."

"In that case, I'll send scouts ahead to survey the main bridges in and out of Tivani, just in case Harrison makes it there before we can intercept him," Noah added, and his strategic deduction was approved by Harlyn.

"What if the scouts get caught?" Dorian countered, knowing that the plan was to draw Noah into the heavily defended town, rather than a few random scouts.

"Then they die," Noah answered bluntly.

"We need an excuse to deploy more forces should the need for backup arise," Harlyn suggested, completely ignoring Dorian's comment and focusing her attention back on her newest advisor.

"How many guards would you usually travel with if visiting the neighbouring towns?" Noah asked, a plan clearly formulating in his mind.

"Usually six, maybe ten at a push," Harlyn replied. "Even during wartime, it'd be difficult to explain a larger escort without causing a panic."

"It's better than nothing. We can announce an Imperial visit to Galnor as the first stop on a tour of the southern towns," Noah began.

"To what end?" Harlyn questioned, looking at Noah with the expectation that he had a good reason to justify such a notion.

"Supplying them with your cure for the withering, of course," he advised confidently.

"Make it happen," Harlyn asserted, beyond pleased. "Even if we have missed Harrison and the traitorous wardens on the road, we can facilitate the attack on Saint's Bay and accuse them of orchestrating it, which should draw them out."

"Let me return to Tivani then. I can be your eyes and ears from inside the town," Dorian offered, very aware that this was not the outcome he and the others had hoped for.

"Don't be ridiculous," Harlyn retorted, scoffing at his idea to return. "If they didn't know it before, they'll certainly be aware you've betrayed them now. Stay in Siranor and lay low for a while."

"As you command, ma'am," Dorian replied, knowing that he couldn't insist further without raising suspicion.

Although Téa would be worried about him and he couldn't warn the wardens of the Imperator's plan, he had to believe they'd find a way to overcome the challenge and that he'd reunite with Téa soon.

Enacting their plan with cold efficiency, Noah had mobilised the scouts, coordinated the Imperial entourage to escort Harlyn and departed for Galnor with Juliette and the mage hunters by mid-afternoon, leaving the Imperator to announce the purpose of the tour and begin travelling a few hours later.

When Noah and the mage hunters drew closer to Galnor, he disbanded them, convinced that a group of their size would attract unwanted attention. Instructing them to mingle in town until the Imperator's entourage arrived and then regroup by the bridge to Fenian, he and Juliette decided to kill the time at the inn, getting intimately reacquainted.

An hour later, they were rudely interrupted by a hesitant knocking on the room door.

"What?" Noah answered abruptly, frustrated at being disturbed.

"Mr Harper?" asked the nervous innkeeper.

"Do you expect there to be another man in the room under my name?" he barked in response.

"There is someone in the lobby asking for you, an Imperial scout," the innkeeper replied, quickly departing to avoid irritating him further.

"For the love of the gods. I better head downstairs," Noah announced, pushing Juliette off him and reaching for his trousers.

"Oh, can't it wait? Just five more minutes," she groaned, wrapping her body around him so that it was hard for him to move.

"It's never just five minutes with you," Noah muttered, to which she replied with a grin filled with pride. "Get dressed, you're coming with me."

Once downstairs, Noah and Juliette were quickly approached by the scout, who saluted at the sight of them.

"Sir, there's a development I must advise you of."

"It better be a lot more important than the Imperator's arrival, which I am aware is imminent," Noah replied, as Juliette wriggled under his free arm and pressed against him, mindlessly playing with one of the buckles on his jacket.

"I've just returned from scouting the southern bridge in Tivani, sir," the scout began, stammering nervously. "The wardens there are preparing heavy defences on all of the bridges, and I overheard that Harrison Stone is already there."

"Godsdammit," Noah spat. They should've been atleast a day ahead of his arrival but were already too late.

"Sir, that's not all; I overheard some of the wardens talking. Harrison Stone arrived yesterday, before Private Pesaro would've left town."

"What!" Noah yelled, his frustration quickly resurfacing.

"Dorian lied to you," Juliette chirped, seemingly amused by the prospect.

"That bastard has sided with them," Noah accused, utterly enraged. "We need to alert the Imperator and deal with this."

"She'll be here soon, we don't have to leave straight away," Juliette remarked, still largely disinterested in the situation.

Noah shot her a glare that told her to start caring, but that only resulted in her rolling her eyes and faking a modicum of interest while motioning with her hand towards the door, allowing Noah to lead the way. Marching to the main road he knew the Imperator would be travelling on, Noah waited for Harlyn to arrive while Juliette searched for any reason to complain about being forced to follow.

"I don't want to wait out here," she moaned, placing her hands defiantly on her hips. "We could be using this time in a number of more pleasurable ways."

"Just shut up, Juliette. I can already hear her vehicle on approach," Noah scolded, turning away from Juliette like she was a petulant child.

With no other motorised vehicles in the outlying towns, it was easy to differentiate the Imperator's transport from any other. She was in one of the military vehicles rather than her usual car, but that was purely for security. When the vehicle came into view, Noah waved them down and the driver stopped so that he was standing before the Imperator's window. Noticing him, she rolled down the glass to address him.

"What's the problem? You and the hunters should be departing now if you intend to ambush Harrison," she questioned.

"The *problem* is Dorian Pesaro," Noah began. "He lied, Harrison Stone arrived in Tivani yesterday, before he left."

"Intriguing. I wonder what else he's lied about?" Harlyn considered, mildly annoyed at the deception.

"I couldn't say, but can think of someone who could find out," Noah replied, glancing over his shoulder at Juliette.

"On that matter, I agree," Harlyn said, catching on to his unspoken suggestion.

"At the very least, our scouts report the wardens are anticipating an attack. Dorian was probably sent to encourage us to do so with reduced numbers," Noah growled, realising how he'd tried to manipulate their choices.

"Well, we won't be giving them that satisfaction," Harlyn announced, picking up on Noah's anger and quickly sedating it. "Juliette, you're rather effective at interrogations if I recall. Return to Siranor and find Dorian Pesaro, find out all he knows by any means necessary."

"Ha! The last time someone gave me that order, things got a little bit *messy*," Juliette replied, lingering on the last word with an exaggerated smile.

"Do I look concerned?" Harlyn asked bluntly, her gaze unwavering. "I don't care how you get the answers, just get them and report back to Noah. Before we left, I told Private Pesaro to lay low, so he probably won't be at the barracks or anywhere obvious."

"Don't you worry, I'll find him," Juliette purred.

"My tour must continue as planned now, so I leave this situation with the two of you," Harlyn said. "Don't disappoint me."

Rolling the window back up as she instructed the escort driver to continue into town, Imperator Harlyn left Noah and Juliette on the road, standing in a cloud of grit and dust. After muttering a few choice curse words, Juliette who had spent much of her youth in Galnor led Noah to the nearby stables and had him rent her a horse. Riding would shave hours off the journey and even if time wasn't of the essence, she didn't want to walk.

As she mounted the steed, Noah placed a hand on her thigh to capture her attention.

"I'll hold off on staging the mage strike until you find out what Dorian knows," Noah announced. "Be sure to contact me as soon as you do."

"Well then, stay at the inn, somewhere with a phone. I know you aren't a fan of our technology and left the pager we provided you with in Siranor, but if you want a quick answer, that is how I'll get it to you," she mocked, knowing that he cared little for any of their technological advancements.

Noah had spent his whole life on the Eastern Continent and never needed a device for instant communication. As a matter of fact, he rather despised the idea of these telephones. Having to be readily available to another person who was miles away when some small device buzzed or rang, which everything in the Western Continent seemed to do. It was infuriating.

"Fine. Be hasty," he insisted to which Juliette responded with a wicked grin, seizing the reins and digging her heels into the horse's side so that the creature charged forward. It'd be nightfall by the time she reached Siranor, so her search for Dorian would begin in the morning.

Rising early, Juliette spent most of the day searching for any trace of Dorian Pesaro. He had gone to ground and was better than she expected at covering his tracks. She needed him to make a mistake, just one. The mage hunters had informants dotted around the city and if he was seen by or spoke to any of them, she'd learn about it; and eventually he did. *Who would've thought buying a newspaper from a downtown street urchin could be so dangerous?* The reward for Dorian's location was ten crowns, more than enough to encourage the kid to ditch his stand, follow Dorian to his hideout and report back to Juliette.

"You're a difficult man to find, Dorian Pesaro," she announced, waiting outside until he exited the small hideout in the northern sector of the city.

Before Dorian even had a chance to respond, Juliette wrapped herself around him, covering his face with a larger dose of the concoction she used to knock out Sebastian. Instantly robbed of his consciousness, Dorian dropped to the floor at her feet. Dragging him into her vehicle, Juliette took him to the prison on the third basement level of the Imperial Courthouse, where she and Dylan used to keep Imperial captives and other persons of interest.

Although the thought of her former partner somewhat irritated her, Juliette had always enjoyed interrogating prisoners at the prison, especially when utilising the sound-proofed cell, which she fully intended to do now. Only a handful of people knew the way to the underground entrance and by the time she got there, it was late, meaning she was able to get Dorian inside and chained without anyone seeing her. Once ready, Juliette cracked open a jar of smelling salts and thrust them under Dorian's nose, shocking his body awake.

"Where am I?" he asked, still dazed.

"That doesn't matter," Juliette began, prowling around the shadows of the room like a cat. "I need to know what you know."

"Who are you?" he barked, trying to make sense of what was going on while she skulked out of view. When he tried to wipe his blurry eyes, he quickly became aware that he was restrained.

"I'll be the one asking the questions, traitor," Juliette snarled, striding forward so that Dorian could clearly see her face.

"Traitor? I'm a loyal informant of the Imperator, I swear," he promised, aware of her affinity for using poison in interrogations.

"You're renowned for being a good liar, Dorian Pesaro, yet so far I find your attempt severely lacking," Juliette taunted. "While I'd usually enjoy nothing more than drawing this out over several days, I find myself under pressure to expedite this line of enquiry. Either tell me what you know of the traitorous wardens and the nature of Harrison Stone's presence in Tivani, or I will have to resort to more unpleasant tactics."

"I cannot tell you what I do not know!" Dorian cried, thrashing against the heavy chains. "I stole that letter from the warden commander and brought it straight to Siranor for the benefit of the Imperator."

"Unpleasant tactics it is then," Juliette replied, reaching into her satchel and searching through the various options at her fingertips.

By the early hours of the following morning, Dorian's body had been brutally assaulted by poisons that made him sick, itch, cry, shake and convulse. He was beyond exhausted and any resolve he once had was gone.

"Harrison Stone is here to help defeat Noah and the Imperator," he whimpered, just a Juliette threatened him with yet another concoction. "To repay the wardens for helping him defend the mages and Ar'encal in Iliria."

"And why did you decide to support their cause?" Juliette pressed, running her fingers up his bare chest, ensuring that each nail dug ever so slightly into his flesh.

"Leave me be. I've told you all you need to know," Dorian mumbled as sweat trickled from his brow into his eyes.

"And I thought you had special skills. You were meant to be the ideal choice for that mission. What changed you, or more precisely, who?" Juliette probed, enjoying this chance to torment him further.

"Leave her alone!" Dorian cried, the plea shaking from his lips as his body shuddered under Juliette's touch.

"Her... and who might this sweetheart of yours be?" Juliette asked, but Dorian just squeezed his eyes shut, refusing to answer.

Rubbing her body against Dorian's, Juliette lowered herself until her elbow connected with his gut. Striking him as hard as she could, Juliette smirked as he doubled over in pain. Sputtering what little fluids were left in his system, Dorian's legs finally gave way. Only the chains kept him from crashing to the floor.

"She's no threat to the Imperator, unlike Charlie Blake," he coughed, sounding desperate to distract her, but she'd happily take the bait if it was a juicy titbit.

Recalling Charlie's name and the Imperator's reaction to Juliette's earlier capture of his brother for the experimental use of En-glycerol, Juliette pressed her prisoner to explain.

"How exactly is Charlie a threat?" she demanded, wrapping her hand around his throat and pushing him back against the wall.

"He took a mage child from the Imperator and is working with Harrison to reunite him with his mother," Dorian spluttered, barely able to speak with the pressure she'd applied to his throat. "Charlie also sussed out that his brother was murdered and believes the Imperator was responsible."

"Well, now I am insulted, I was most certainly the one responsible for killing his brother," Juliette retorted, releasing her grip slightly. "When will Harrison be departing to take the child home?"

"He's not, they are planning for the mother to travel to Tivani. Others may also join her," Dorian explained, closing his eyes with shame as the words tumbled from his mouth.

"Other mages are travelling to Tivani?"

"Yes, but some were former locals too," Dorian continued. It was too late to deflect from the truth, and he was too weak to try.

"Oh, I wonder if that's Rylie Auren then," Juliette mused, a playful look adorning her face. "She used to live in Tivani with her precious family. If so, the Imperator will want to know. She no longer needs Siljanna Stone as a motive for apprehending that particular mage."

"Why does the Imperator want her?" Dorian asked as a deep sense of foreboding swept over him.

"She killed Cameron Weiss," Juliette answered, her voice upbeat and pleased to reveal that nugget of information before walking away from Dorian towards the heavy door.

"You can't leave me like this," Dorian cried.

"Can't I?" Juliette asked theatrically, exiting the room and relishing in the way the heavy door sealed Dorian and his raspy pleas for freedom.

Making her way up into the main Imperial Courthouse, she was initially surprised to see all the desks unmanned before recalling the time. She thought about waiting until a more reasonable hour but then remembered Noah's insistence that she advise him as soon as she had useful information, so decided to pick up the phone and call the Galnor Inn, despite the time.

A male night manager for the inn answered the phone but was startled at her insistence to speak with a guest and initially refused.

"I know what hour it is, and that Mr Harper will be asleep," Juliette snarled. "Wake him."

"Ma'am, I—" the man stuttered.

"Wake. Him," she instructed firmly, tapping her fingers on the desk impatiently.

After a momentary static, Juliette heard the night manager scuttle up the stairs, presumably towards Noah's room. Another few minutes passed until she heard a loud slam followed by heavy footsteps crashing down the stairs. Finally there was a muffling sound as someone picked up the receiver.

"This had better be good," Noah growled.

"More allies of Harrison Stone will soon be descending on Tivani, including that little brat, Sebastian's mother and Rylie Auren," Juliette replied, knowing that whatever mood he was in, that knowledge would garner his full attention.

Spitting at the mention of Rylie's name, Noah started to accuse Juliette of having nothing worthy of waking him, until the haze cleared from his sleepy mind.

"Wait... I could use Rylie's arrival to my advantage. Harrison would do anything to protect her, making his actions rather predictable."

"I wonder what he would do if there was a devastating mage strike just down the road from Tivani?" Juliette pondered wickedly.

"Rush her and anyone else dear to him to Yasras, most likely. To catch the next available ship back to the safety of the Eastern Continent," Noah replied, quickly catching on to Juliette's train of thought and piecing it together with Imperator's backup plan of instigating a fake mage strike near Fenian and accusing Harrison of being the organiser behind it.

"But Yasras may not be the safe haven they'll be expecting," Juliette hinted.

"Precisely," Noah chuckled menacingly. "Stay in Siranor and have fun with Dorian. I'll find you next week."

Chapter Twenty-Five
Incursion

The days following the signing of the peace treaty had been incredible, with hundreds of former slaves giving thanks to their new queen as she offered them homes, paid work or granted them the freedom to leave. Just having a choice meant so much to those people, and Nadia found their relief strangely relatable. Although privileged in some ways, she too was a former captive of King Grayson and had spent many nights longing for freedom. Now she had the power of a true queen, she gladly liberated everyone who had suffered at the hands of Carlisse's tyrannical former king.

Maia and the others stayed for a few days, meeting the mages that wanted to learn more about their powers, but by the sixth day, they were all keen to return home. While Maia's priority was to discuss the prospect of the gifted land and new Ar'encal trading village with Zack, her desire to see him paled in comparison to Lianna. Gathering their things, Alex loaded the saddle bags while the girls tacked up the horses.

Riding beneath the portcullis of the western city gate, the group were surprised to see Freya Ewor come charging up, a letter held tightly within her grasp and the entire Auren family close behind.

"What are you guys doing here?" Rylie asked curiously.

"We've just received word from Harrison," Nate began. "The contents of his letter has caused quite a stir."

"They found my son! Sebastian's safe and in Tivani!" Freya announced, her joy contagious. "Your family has offered to take me there. They assumed you'd like to join us."

"They're not wrong!" Rylie exclaimed, her delight for Freya and the prospect of going home with her family visible.

"Grandad is coming too. He wants to see where we grew up," Evie explained, able to squeeze her arms around Alistair's waist as they shared a horse.

Looking over at Maia with hopeful eyes, Rylie checked it was okay to leave with the others. She wanted to continue training but the chance to see her old home again, even briefly, and check in on Harrison and Morgan was too tempting.

"You can go," Maia confirmed with a laugh, knowing exactly what she was going to ask. "I'm sure Alex and Lianna can escort me safely home."

Rylie had been riding Cruise, but knowing his saddlebags were filled with Maia's possessions, she dismounted, helped Alex to switch mounts and hopped on the back of her father's horse. Waving as the trio departed, the others made haste to Revaine, leaving their horses with the Driftwood Ranch stable hand and reaching the dock just in time to board the *Pilgrim*.

A few members of the crew recognised Rylie and Evie from their first journey and once they purchased tickets, welcomed them back on board. Crossing the Ensen Sea was smooth, despite the changing season bringing wintery showers almost every day. As the ship carried them towards Tivani, the Auren family went over every detail of Harrison's letter, especially the mention of the Hawk Eye tavern's restoration. The anticipation made the family more excited with each passing day.

Arriving in Yasras by early afternoon on the fourth day, the first thing they noticed was the temperature difference. Although it felt much colder on the Western Continent, patches of frost on the cobbled streets were beginning to melt, indicating it had been colder in the weeks prior. With the road conditions challenging, Rylie expected the journey to Tivani would take longer but nothing slowed Freya's pace. She couldn't wait to hold her son in her arms.

Travelling up the steep hill out of Yasras was a slog but Rylie knew once they reached the top, the trek would be a lot easier. They were all cautious for Imperial scouts, keeping their hoods up but were relieved to discover the roads were quiet.

"It'll be good to see Tivani again," Nate admitted, looking at his wife lovingly.

"I still cannot believe the wardens have rebuilt our tavern," Paige added, holding his hand.

"Do you think it looks the same, will it still feel like our home?" Evie wondered, just a few paces ahead of her parents.

"I'm not sure sweetheart, but we'll find out together," Nate replied, giving his youngest daughter a warm smile.

"How much longer until we get there?" Freya asked impatiently.

"We should reach the eastern bridge in a couple of hours," Evie replied, giggling at Freya's reaction and immediate burst of speed.

The main road would be significantly quicker than the forest tracks Evie, Rylie and Harrison had used when first fleeing the continent and Rylie was especially glad that they'd be able to stick to it all the way.

"I don't know if I'll be able to keep up at this rate," Alistair commented playfully in between heavy breaths. "My old bones aren't made for this pace, incline or chill."

"Don't worry, Grandad, the road flattens out soon," Rylie assured.

"It feels a lot colder than I remember," Evie expressed, pulling her coat closer. The temperature rise as Winter Thaw kicked in usually felt significant, but she'd acclimatised to the milder temperature of Arencia quickly.

"Really? It barely feels cold to me," Rylie replied.

"As an Elementalist, you don't get a say in this conversation unless you can do something about the weather," Alistair teased.

"I'll let nature stay in control, thank you," she replied with a soft laugh. Although she was feeling a bit more confident about her powers, Rylie didn't want to push her boundaries yet, especially without Maia to guide her.

"It's just the coastal winds. It'll feel warmer in Tivani," Nate promised, pulling Evie into his arms, allowing her to benefit from his natural body heat.

When they arrived at the eastern bridge, they noticed the increased defences but amidst the large warden presence was a familiar face.

"Morgan!" Rylie called out, waving to him from across the bridge. Realising who it was, he signalled for the other wardens to stand down as he jogged over to them.

"You're here already, that was fast!" Morgan greeted, his tone welcoming.

"Where's my son? Please, take me to Sebastian," Freya begged, wasting no time with pleasantries.

"Of course, Freya, follow me," Morgan replied and led her into town with the Auren family following close behind.

As they traversed the cobbled streets, memories flooded each member of the Auren family but when they laid their eyes on the Hawk Eye tavern, it was as if they were living a dream. The last time Rylie and Evie had stood facing the exterior of their home, it was on fire, but before them now was the same building, its original exterior shape and styling preserved, just renewed. For Nate and Paige, their last experience had been from within as the building collapsed around them. Instead they now saw a sturdy, welcoming structure, just like the one they had built all those years ago.

"Is this where you grew up girls?" Alistair asked, leaning forward and poking his head between Rylie and Evie.

"It really is," Evie began, a beaming smile spreading across her face. "It's tidier than I remember, but it really is our home!"

"Will you show me inside?" he asked and without responding, Evie grabbed him by the hand and marched towards the front door. Rushing ahead of them, Freya burst inside and began calling for her son.

"Sebastian? Sebastian!"

"Mum!" Sebastian shouted, clattering down the stairs from the upper floor and rushing across the room, colliding into her embrace. Holding each other so tightly, only they could hear the muttered words they said to each other, but their reunion made everyone in the room smile.

Watching Nate standing with his family inside the home they all thought was gone, Morgan couldn't help but smile inwardly. It had been his idea to rebuild the Hawk Eye tavern but Téa and the wardens had done most of the hard work to make it happen.

With a beaming smile, Evie began to give Alistair a tour while Nate just wrapped his arms around his wife and Rylie introduced herself to Téa, who was standing behind the bar, cleaning glasses, just as Rylie used to do.

"What do you think, Nate?" Morgan asked from behind him.

"It's incredible," Nate replied, exuding gratitude as he turned and shook Morgan's hand.

"Do you think you'll move back once the war is over, run the tavern again?" Morgan wondered, having a good hunch on how Nate would respond.

Nate looked to his wife who nodded. They'd already decided what they wanted to do, knew what was truly important.

"Although what you and the wardens have done is incredibly kind, we're going to move back to the Eastern Continent and stay closer to the girls," Nate answered, raising his eyebrows as he looked at Morgan, hoping he and the wardens wouldn't take any offence.

Seeing his tavern home rebuilt obviously meant a lot to Nate, but his daughters would always be the most important thing in his life.

Morgan knew he'd give anything to see them happy and know they were safe.

"I thought you might say that," Morgan admitted cheerfully, clapping Nate on the shoulder and telling him without words that there were no hard feelings.

"We'll need someone to manage this place for us though, do you know of anyone that might be interested?" Nate enquired.

"I'd be interested," Téa called out, rushing from behind the bar to join them with Rylie not far behind.

"You would?" Morgan questioned, not realising she'd considered leaving the warden ranks.

"These past few weeks have proven that while I can be a warden, the pressure of leadership is not for me," Téa explained, avoiding eye contact with him at first.

"Téa, is this because of my outburst—" he said apologetically but she hushed him.

"No, Morgan, I promise. That was just the icing on the cake."

"Running a tavern does come with its fair share of ups and downs," Nate advised, looking to Téa as if ensuring the young woman knew it wasn't going to be without difficulties.

"I'm certain of it, but I believe this is the type of challenge I will thrive on," she replied whole-heartedly. "I'd like to make this a safe place for mages, Ar'encal and potentially even an informant hub for the wardens."

"That's very warden-like behaviour," Morgan added proudly, "Still protecting people, just in a slightly different way."

"A way that doesn't require organising guard rotations and stabbing people," Téa jested, making the others around her laugh.

"Did I just hear that a vacancy may have opened up in Tivani for a warden?" Charlie called out, jogging down the stairs to join his friends.

"Are you considering a transfer, my friend?" Morgan asked, his eyes brightened by the prospect.

"Well, I have it under good authority that the commander here is pretty great, so yes, I think I am," Charlie replied humorously. "Do you think I'll be accepted?"

"I'll put in a good word," Morgan laughed, striding over to embrace his friend. Having Charlie in his ranks filled Morgan with a huge sense of relief. "Do you remember how to use a sword?"

"I'm sure I can work it out," Charlie replied with a cheeky wink. "It's going to be quite a transition for Hugo, but I think growing up in Tivani will be good for him."

"Hugo, is that your nephew?" Rylie asked, walking over to Charlie and receiving a friendly hug.

"Yes, but that's a long and tragic story I'll share with you later. For now, I'd much rather focus on this very happy reunion," Charlie replied, glancing over at Sebastian and his mother. Noticing that he'd joined the group, Sebastian took his mother's hand and dragged her towards Charlie.

"Mum, this is Charlie. He's the one that got me away from the Imperator after she stripped my powers," Sebastian explained, looking up at his saviour with a bright smile. "He made sure I was looked after and then brought me here. Bumping into Harrison was just good luck, so if it hadn't been for Charlie, I'd still be trapped in that awful Institute."

"I can't thank you enough," Freya said, throwing her arms around Charlie's neck with gratitude.

With a soft chuckle, Charlie placed a hand around Sebastian's mother, accepting her unexpected embrace.

As she pulled away, he was shocked to see how young she looked but Morgan subtly touched the bridge of his nose, which encouraged Charlie to notice the ridges on Freya's. It didn't take long for him to realise she wasn't just a mage, she was Ar'encal. He'd learned just as much about their race as Morgan had during their academy days, but seeing how youthful they were with his own eyes left him momentarily speechless.

"Charlie, this is my mum, Freya," Sebastian added, nudging him to encourage some kind of response.

"Nice to meet you," he stammered, brushing his messy hair with his fingers.

Knowing that Charlie was trying to make himself look more presentable made Morgan chuckle. If he didn't know better, he'd think that his friend was developing a bit of a crush. Wiping the tears from her eyes, Freya smiled impishly at Charlie before turning to Morgan to ask about the missing member of their group.

"Where's Harrison, will he be joining us later?"

"He's with the wardens at the southern bridge," Morgan replied. "I'm sure he'll return any minute."

Morgan wasn't far wrong. In the time it took for Evie and Alistair to return from the house tour and Téa to offer a round of drinks, Harrison entered the room. He spotted Freya with her arm wrapped around Sebastian next to the Auren family, who were all gathered in the lounge with Morgan and Charlie in the armchairs by the fireplace.

"Hello stranger," Rylie called out cheerfully, rising from her seat to greet him.

"Hey you!" Harrison replied, pulling her into his arms and kissing her affectionately. He didn't want to make a big, romantic scene in front of the group but that didn't stop Rylie from tucking herself into his side.

"They rebuilt our home!" Evie exclaimed, waving joyfully at Harrison as he approached. Her sheer enthusiasm made him smile. She'd been so worried about returning but couldn't have looked any happier now.

"The wardens really have done an incredible job," Rylie said, looking around the room happily. "It's almost a shame we don't plan to stay."

"I had wondered if you'd return… to our new sanctuary," Harrison commented, unable to say 'Arencia' with Charlie and Téa within range.

"This will always be our home, but bricks and mortar aren't as important as keeping our family together," Rylie replied, squeezing his hand. He knew that they all considered him part of their family.

"Téa is going to take partial ownership of the tavern from now on and manage it for me," Nate added, looking over his shoulder and greeting Harrison with a tip of his drink bottle.

"Ha, are you thinking of investing in that tavern we spotted in Dawne?" Harrison enquired, intending for it to be a joke but Nate seemed to genuinely consider it.

"I am now," he replied, glancing at Paige who just rolled her eyes and laughed.

"Harrison, look what you've started!" she scolded playfully as Harrison mouthed an apology through a cheesy grin.

After dinner and more banter, Charlie heard Hugo crying upstairs and went to attend to his nephew. He was joined by Freya and Sebastian who seemed to be enjoying his company. As they departed, Evie, Nate and Paige took Alistair over to the bar and began detailing how Nate's old display used to look and the subtle differences in the building now.

With her sister out of earshot, Rylie turned to Harrison and Morgan with a worried expression. Something was on her mind.

"Have there been any problems since you returned?" she asked. "Any threat from Noah or the Imperial Military?"

"Not yet," Harrison began. "We were hoping they would strike before you arrived. We even have a man on the inside feeding them information that should've enticed them."

"But it appears he may have failed," Morgan inserted. "That's why we've been bolstering the warden defences at each bridge and throughout town."

"If they come here, they'll be in for a fight," Harrison concluded, nodding confidently towards his trusted partner while also hoping to reassure Rylie.

"It does mean you and your family shouldn't linger, however," Morgan admitted, not wanting to cut their time short, but equally concerned for their safety, almost as much as Harrison was.

"We'll be ready to leave in a hurry if needed," Rylie replied. "We packed lightly. I can't help but wonder though, what are Noah and the Imperator are waiting for?"

"It may be because she's just announced a tour of the southern towns," Morgan said thoughtfully. "While outside Siranor, the Imperator is vulnerable. It'd be a brash move to send troops to attack us before she returns to the safety of her palace, and Imperator Harlyn isn't a brash woman."

"Why would she leave Siranor?" Rylie questioned.

"To deliver her cure for the withering," Morgan answered, having caught the announcement on the radio a few days ago.

"She really did create cure for the withering," Rylie mumbled, trying her best to speak through the shock. "Does it work?"

"It's the same stuff that made Maia sick and stripped Sebastian of his powers, as we theorised. I can't imagine how she made it, but whatever En-glycerol is, it reacts to Encia and destroys it. We have no reason to believe it doesn't work though," Harrison admitted, his furrowed brows hinting at an underlying concern. *Could the Imperial tour be a rouse to disguise a more sinister agenda?*

"Well, luckily, we don't need a cure anymore," Rylie announced, assuming the basis of Harrison's concern was for Queen Nadia. "When we met with Nadia in Carlisse, she had good news to share. She really is pregnant with Spencer's child, and as the descendant of a mage, the baby seems to be curing her condition."

"That's great," Harrison replied, genuinely pleased for their friend. She truly deserved a little happiness after everything she'd endured. "How did the signing of the peace treaty go?"

"It was incredible," Rylie explained, going into detail about the day itself and the following time she and the others had spent in the kingdom.

"Did you get a chance to speak with Sil?" Harrison enquired after she finished, tilting his head curiously. He hadn't even thought to ask until now but as the idea sprung to mind, he couldn't wait to know what had happened.

"I did…" Rylie teased, letting Harrison stew for a moment over what the outcome of their chat may have been.

"And?" he probed, encouraging her to elaborate.

"It'll take time, but we are both keen to repair our friendship."

"I'm glad."

Although Siljanna had put them through a lot, she'd also taken great risks to earn their forgiveness. This was another positive step towards having a healthy relationship with his sister again.

"Maia also managed to squeeze in some more training while we were together," Rylie continued, explaining how she could conjure and control small amounts of water, air and fire even with her suppression amulet on.

"Are you considering removing that amulet then, or do you still want Maia and I to create a new one?"

"Oh, I still want a new amulet. Although it's harder to cast with this on, it's preferable to Aeonic flame-girl," Rylie jested. "In an ideal world, I'd like to tap into my power gradually."

"You were pretty hot," Harrison quipped, causing Rylie to frown playfully, a look that said, *really?*

"More like terrifying," Morgan interjected while stifling a laugh. "Maybe Noah found out you're here and that's why they haven't attacked… because he's afraid."

"If only," Rylie laughed. "I can't imagine any circumstance whereby Noah would admit to feeling fear. He's too cocky. Plus, I'm fairly sure he hates me almost as much as he hates Harrison."

"What exactly did you do to earn so much hatred from him?" Morgan asked, turning towards his partner with raised eyebrow and giving him a look that encouraged him to explain.

"Wound his ego," Harrison replied. "Noah Harper is little more than a spoilt brat that is used to dominating everyone around him. None of the guards in Arencia ever truly liked him, but before we arrived, he was considered their best warrior and next in line to become captain."

"You just said *Arencia* without your rune cutting you off," Morgan interjected, a puzzled look on his face.

"That's because everyone in earshot already knows of its existence, so I can speak freely," Harrison replied, placing a hand on his rune which was cool beneath his fingertips.

"It's incredible how that thing works. You've learnt so much, like crafting similar runes into clothing and items," Rylie added, reaching for her amulet without thinking. "The effect is permanent on flesh, but not on other items. Why is that and how did you make the power last in my amulet?"

"I can't say with certainty but the belief among the Ar'encal is that Encia thrives off the oxygen in our blood. That's why the Aegis Guard are branded," Harrison began.

"Why is the branding process important?" Morgan probed, genuinely curious to understand.

"Well, the heat liquifies the Encia, which is then absorbed by our skin. This allows it to join with our blood," Harrison continued, finding it helpful to apply scientific theory to the spiritual explanation he'd heard. "The power is then revitalised with every heartbeat."

"That's probably why the placement of the rune is so important. Being close to the heart ensures the infusion with oxygen," Rylie added, her mind recalling the medical training she once treasured.

"It's also more difficult to destroy, unless the goal is to also kill the host," Morgan commented, hinting that against iron or steel, the Arencian rune would not provide any kind of protection.

"True, but that's why I believe the effects are permanent when placed directly on the skin," Harrison concluded. "As for your amulet, the stone in the centre is crystallised Encia, allowing the runes to draw from it as a source of power."

"So will it deplete over time?" Rylie asked.

"Eventually, but the stone should only dissipate when a rune activates," Harrison replied hopefully.

"I didn't realise, I wonder how much energy I've already depleted," Rylie muttered, worrying at her lower lip.

"Try not to overthink it. Maia seemed genuinely impressed with the craftmanship. We both believe it should last a while."

"A man of many talents, not unlike myself," Morgan proclaimed jovially, aiming to lighten the tone of their conversation.

"Being handy with a shiny sword doesn't mean you're talented," Harrison retorted with a wink.

"That sounds like a challenge! If I didn't have duties to attend to, I'd remind you how talented I can be," Morgan teased.

"Thinking of training, you were getting into the spirit, Rylie. Would you like another combat lesson in the morning?" Harrison offered, hoping to spend a little time alone with her.

"That'd be great. Think you can beat me again?" Rylie challenged playfully, making both Harrison and Morgan laugh.

"I reckon I stand a good chance," Harrison asserted.

"It took me a few years but trust me, he's beatable," Morgan encouraged, impressed by Rylie's enthusiasm.

"Well, if we are going to be up early for training, I better head to my room and get to bed," Rylie admitted, waving goodnight to the rest of her family who were gleefully recalling stories for Alistair.

"I'll walk you up," Harrison offered as she reached the stairs.
"I do know the way," she giggled, bounding upwards and towards the rebuilt version of the room she'd grown up in.

Opening the door, Rylie paused as she looked around the room.

"Without my things and Evie's artwork hanging from the walls, it really just looks like any other lodge room, rather than my room," she said without sounding sad. "This is the first time since we arrived that this place hasn't felt like home. Don't get me wrong, I'm thrilled to see the tavern rebuilt, but I know now that returning to Arencia really is the right thing for us."

Turning in the doorway to face Harrison, she rested against the frame, and he instinctively leant forward to kiss her.

"I'm staying just down the hall if you need anything," he began, only to be interrupted by a kiss from her in return.

Caressing his face and neck as their lips were locked, he could feel the warmth rising through her skin. He had wanted her for so long, and now as his hands held her firmly around the waist, nothing felt better than knowing she wanted him too. As their kiss ended, Rylie ran her hand across his chest, caressing his rune until she felt his elevated heart rate and paused.

"This is another reason why I want to keep my amulet on," she whispered. "So I can't hurt you."

"You've never hurt me," he replied, cupping her face in his hand.

"I never imagined a love like this," she muttered softly, her hand gliding down his arm until their fingers intertwined.

"I could never image loving anyone but you," he confessed, leaning down to kiss her neck.

Shivering under his touch, Rylie coiled herself around him and Harrison quickly melted into her embrace. As her body heat intensified, his rune tingled to life, as did the runes on her amulet but neither of them cared. Their focus was purely on being as close as two people can be.

Slipping into the bedroom and softly closing the door, they shared one passionate night with no thoughts or fears of what tomorrow might bring. Entangled in each other's arms and reassured by the fact that most of the people dearest to them were resting in one of the rooms down the hall, Rylie and Harrison allowed themselves to embrace their feelings and then rest until morning.

By the time Evie woke, Rylie and Harrison had already headed to Elijah Ashby's blacksmith to check in on the gentle giant and utilise the open space of the blacksmith for a training session. Making her way into the kitchen, she overheard her mum fussing over Hugo and assumed she'd offered to care for him, allowing Charlie to go with Morgan to the guardhouse and meet his new colleagues.

Grabbing a bite to eat, she spotted Freya and Sebastian also having breakfast at the bar.

"Good morning," she greeted sweetly.

"Hello Evie, did you sleep well?" Freya asked, knowing all too well how turbulent sleep could be for mages with precognition.

"I did thank you," she replied, unsurprised but grateful that Freya was just as kind as all the other Ar'encal she'd met so far.

"I'm glad to hear that," Freya replied compassionately.

"Have you had any luck getting your powers back, Sebastian?" Evie enquired, encouraging him to chat. He was quite reserved but would engage when included in a conversation.

"No, nothing yet," he admitted, "I'm hoping when we return to Arencia the other Ar'encal might be able to help me."

"It's worth a try," Evie replied, trying to sound supportive.

She couldn't help but wonder if her power had been stripped, whether she would want it back. While she loved being able to use her power to let Zack see the vigil, that and seeing Harrison and Rylie's first kiss were the only good things she'd experienced through her visions.

Hearing them talk about the Ar'encal caught Alistair's attention. He'd been sitting in one of the armchairs with steaming cup of coffee in hand but pottered over to join them.

"You've settled in quickly, Alistair," Freya chuckled. "If I recall, after you sided with the Ar'encal during the first Uprising, it took months for you to feel at home within our hidden sanctuary, even with your wife by your side, yet it's taken only one evening here."

"Well, it is rather cosy here," he declared, clearly proud of what his son's family had achieved.

"Do you know where Dad and Téa are?" Evie wondered aloud, having not seen either of them since waking up.

"He said something about popping to the town hall to sign off on some ownership paperwork," Alistair explained, looking down into his coffee cup and saddened by how little liquid remained. "He's making Téa a partial owner of the tavern as well as asking her to manage it. I think he's planning on using the money she's offered to buy another tavern in Dawne."

"That's great!" Evie cheered, noticing her grandfather's reaction to the dwindling coffee in his cup and deciding that she'd head into the kitchen after breakfast to brew up another pot for him.

"Do you have any plans today, sweetheart?" Alistair asked.

"Well, after making you some more coffee, would you all like me to show you around town? The market and park near the southern bridge are some of my favourite places in Tivani," Evie offered, knowing both locations would be well within the warden's defensive perimeter. "We may not be here for long, but I'd love to show you around in whatever time we have."

"That'd be lovely," Alistair answered in thanks, with both Sebastian and Freya nodding in agreement.

After finishing their breakfast with another pot of coffee, Evie, Alistair, Freya and Sebastian spent the day meandering through the cobbled streets of Tivani, letting Evie recall stories of her childhood as they went shopping in the market, where Evie bought herself a new sketchbook and then relaxed in the park. As they sat beside the small pond, feeding the ducks, Evie drew a few outlines of Freya and Sebastian. She'd almost forgotten how much she loved to draw. One sketch looked particularly sweet, so she gave it to Freya as they headed back to the tavern.

When they entered, Paige came rushing up to her daughter and pulled her into a tight embrace. Something had clearly panicked her.

"There you are!" she yelped. "I've been so worried."

"Why, has something happened?" Evie asked, her voice muffled while her face was squashed into her mother's chest.

"Didn't you hear the news alert on the radio?" Paige asked, her pitch elevated with distress. "There's been an attack just outside Fenian!"

Hearing Paige's raised voice alerted Harrison, Nate and Rylie to the fact that Evie and the others had returned. Rushing over to join them, Harrison thrust their bags towards them.

"You all need to go upstairs and pack, now," he instructed and none of them were about to disobey him.

"Forty people were caught up in the attack and they're all dead," Nate explained, bounding up the stairs with his family in tow.

"They're claiming it's another rebel mage strike, aiming to hit the Imperator's escort," Harrison added, rapidly placing water bottles and other supplies in each bag.

"It's more likely meant to draw the wardens out of town," Rylie theorised, looking over her shoulder to Harrison who had likely come to the same conclusion.

"The wardens will be expected to offer support, but Morgan and I are going to get you guys out of town first," Harrison concluded, without revealing what he thought the purpose of the falsified strike was.

Had the wardens left immediately, Tivani and the Auren family would've been largely unguarded, something Harrison would never allow. They would've been prime targets for Noah. Since the radio announcement was broadcast, Morgan called and said that he'd dash from the guardhouse to Elijah's and arrange horses. Riding to Yasras rather than walking would ensure they reached the harbour town before nightfall.

In the time it took for the group to pack, Elijah and Morgan arrived outside the tavern with the horses. Although Harrison had been able to chat with his former mentor a few times and give his condolences for the loss of his nephew, once again he needed the older man's help to get through a crisis. Long gone were the days when they ambled down the winding path from the blacksmith to the tavern for a friendly pint.

"Be safe, Harrison. And look after my horses," Elijah instructed as a shudder ran down his back. He hadn't been directly involved when Harrison, Rylie and Evie fled before, but this situation was still too close for comfort.

"Thank you, Elijah. Morgan and I will bring them back by morning," Harrison promised, packing his weapon just in case.

"Don't try to be a hero," Elijah pleaded, locking his gaze on his former apprentice. "Although I hope that you can see the Auren family to safety again, you need to watch your back. You're being targeted too this time."

"I won't let him do anything stupid," Morgan swore.

Travelling as fast as the horses could take them meant the group arrived in Yasras just as the sun was setting. Relief filled each of them when they registered the sight of the *Pilgrim* still in port. Their window to escape had waited for them. Tethering the horses and saying a quick goodbye to Morgan, the group hurried towards the dock. Realising the crew were nowhere to be seen, Harrison went to find the captain and negotiate their passage.

Expecting to find him in the port-side office, Evie watched him briskly walk away until a vision suddenly swept over her. Not just any vision, *that vision*. Reliving the terrifying images, she realised the truth. Alerting Harrison hadn't been enough and unless she did something, he was going to die, right now at Noah's hand. Without a word, she spun on her heels and ran as fast as her legs could carry her towards the office, reaching Harrison just in time to see the flash of blinding light and the blade.

Struck by both the brightness and noise of what must've been a grenade, Harrison was disoriented. Then he felt something spatter on his face. Blinking rapidly, he wiped his hand across his cheek only to see droplets of blood. *Is it mine? Who attacked me?*

As his vision slowly cleared, he searched his body for a wound but found nothing. Realising he was unharmed didn't put his mind at ease. If anything, it increased the panic in his heart.

His fears were soon confirmed as standing across from him was Noah, a sickening grin on his face. The reason for his expression was also the cause of the blood. Evie had gotten between them and now, the tip of Noah's blade was protruding from her lifeless torso. Wrenching the sword back, Noah threw Evie at Harrison. As her body collided with him, they both crashed to the floor.

"Evie... Evie!" Harrison screamed, rolling to his knees and pressing desperately against her wound.

He knew it was hopeless. He'd held his mother's body shortly after she died; he'd seen the blood escape and felt how still her body had gone. This was the same... and it broke him. Hearing a guttural cry, he assumed it had escaped his own throat as he gave up on applying pressure and just cradled Evie in his arms. After a moment he realised the cry actually came from Nate, who had fallen to his knees and slumped over his youngest daughter.

Hot tears flowed down Harrison's face, stinging his cheeks and making his eyes raw, but as he heard the rest of the group approach, another fear came to mind. *Where's Noah now?*

"No!" Rylie cried, her voice cracking as she stumbled towards them, her mother inches behind. They fell to the ground by Evie's side as Harrison stood, searching desperately for Noah.

"This can't be happening," Paige sobbed, tears flooding down her cheeks.

"Come back little sis, come back," Rylie pleaded as she wept, squeezing her sister's hand just as she used to when Evie would lose consciousness after a seizure. It was clear she hadn't accepted the truth... yet.

"You have to get out of here, now!" Harrison demanded, but his order fell on deaf ears.

Picking Evie up from the floor as gently as he could, Harrison rushed towards the *Pilgrim*. Her long hair was matted from the dirt and chilled water on the path, but the way Evie's slender limbs hung down, offering no resistance to his motion confirmed that she was gone.

Reaching Alistair, Sebastian and Freya who were still beside the gangplank of the ship, Harrison carefully placed Evie in her grandfather's arms. Giving both him and Freya a look of pure desperation, he urged them to board.

"What happened?" Sebastian cried as the horror registered as reality, but Harrison ignored him.

"Get them on the ship," Harrison commanded, pointing at Paige and Rylie while turning to Freya. "Now!"

Silently understanding why he'd given her the instruction, Freya grabbed Paige and Rylie whilst muttering a chant. She somehow managed to calm them and simultaneously ushered both women and Sebastian on board. Harrison knew it was some kind of channelling ability but in all honesty, he didn't care exactly what she'd done. All he wanted was for them to get away from Yasras.

Hearing the commotion, Morgan rushed down the pier just as the sun sunk below the horizon, his katana raised as he searched for his friends.

"What happened?" he called out, trying to process the scene before him, stopping only when he realised that Alistair had paused on the gangplank and was cradling Evie's body.

"We're under attack," Harrison answered abruptly.

"Where's Nate?" Alistair cried, his voice trembling.

Turning back to where he'd last seen Nate, Harrison witnessed the man, who had been more of a father to him than any other, rise, an aura of darkness surrounding him. Shifting his gaze from the dead form of his daughter to Harrison, their sight locked on each other. At that moment, Harrison realised Nate's eyes, which were usually a warm shade of brown like his own, were now as black as coal. With a simple nod, Nate vanished, consumed by the shadows.

"Where did he go?"

"He's become a shade," Alistair stuttered.

"What does that mean?!" Harrison barked, drawing his broadsword while continuing to search for any sign of Nate or Noah.

"It's a curse," Alistair answered, still frozen on the gangplank. "It'll consume him until the trigger emotion is sated."

Even though his attention was divided, Harrison registered Alistair's warning. If he didn't want the ship to depart so badly, he would've asked more questions.

"We'll find him, just go!" he pleaded, glaring at Alistair. As soon as the older man turned and was on board the ship, Evie still held tightly in his arms, Harrison kicked the gangplank away.

Seconds later, the captain of the vessel appeared on deck and looked down at him, a dumbfounded sailor alongside. Neither of them understood what they were seeing, but neither were going to risk asking. Hearing the captain instruct the sailor to set off, Harrison waited until the ship set sail before stalking up the dock, letting his anger take over.

"I'll make you pay for this, Noah! Do you hear me?" he screamed, brandishing his weapon wildly.

Epilogue

Marching away from the dock, Noah couldn't help but smile. What occurred may not have been his plan, but the result was even better than he could've hoped for.

"Well that was fun," he muttered to himself, looking over his shoulder in the direction of Harrison's screaming.

Noah always knew that protecting his pathetic friends would contribute to Harrison's demise, but until his blade pierced that little girl's heart, Noah hadn't considered how satisfying it'd be to cause that damage himself. That was the reason he didn't strike Harrison down—because he realised that he could do worse. Much worse. He could kill everyone Harrison cared about first. Then, once his soul was utterly crushed, Harrison would beg him to take his life, and Noah would gladly oblige.

Revelling in his own genius, Noah continued walking briskly towards the town gate, making sure to avoid the shadows. Although he'd never seen a mage with shadow powers, he remembered his studies. The Ar'encal claimed to despise shadow magic but in truth, they feared it, calling the mages that succumbed to such dark powers a 'shade'.

Noah was certain that the other man who cried for the girl had triggered shadow magic. A dark aura had enveloped him before he disappeared, and it was enough to warrant caution. A shade could supposedly move invisibly through shadows and bend negative energies to their will, but Noah had never been taught what that meant and had no desire to experience such potentially dangerous abilities first-hand.

It was also rare for such a mature adult to trigger magical abilities, so Noah made the safe assumption that the man was related to the girl… probably her father.

"Garnering the hatred of a father with newly triggered powers isn't ideal, but I'll adapt. Even a shade can't get through Siranor without alerting suspicions and if he causes some chaos while trying to find me, it'll just support the Imperator's propaganda about the rebel mage strikes."

As he departed Yasras and started heading up the steep hill, Noah wondered if En-glycerol would strip this type of magic as easily as it had the healer powers. Resolving that he'd only test the theory once equipped with some, Noah focused on reaching his destination, Siranor.

Wielding his broadsword defensively, Harrison continued searching for Noah as Morgan reached him. Mirroring his guarded stance, even though he was still unsure what happened, Morgan accepted that his partners reaction was justified.

"Harrison, tell me what happened," Morgan asked, trying to speak as calmly as possible. He'd never seen his best friend this way.

"He killed her," Harrison roared. "Noah killed Evie!"

"That's what I feared," Morgan admitted, trying to match Harrison's energy but counteract his anger with reason. "I saw her in Alistair's arms and knew something terrible had happened.

"I won't let him get away with this. He must be nearby just waiting to strike again."

"Then let's find him, together," Morgan replied. He'd promised to help Harrison stop Noah, and this seemed to be their best chance.

Instantly, Harrison began crashing through Yasras, destroying anything that could've provided enough cover to conceal Noah. As his rage intensified, Harrison soon started targeting the front doors of people's homes, kicking them free from their hinges and searching the homes while the residents inside wailed with fear.

As his friend continued on a war path, Morgan's concern grew. There was absolutely no sign of Noah or of Harrison calming down. With one final check to confirm their surroundings, Morgan sheathed his weapon and placed both his hands securely on Harrison's shoulders, blocking his path.

"Harrison, stop. I think he's gone."

"Get out of my way, Morgan!" Harrison growled, his entire body rigid, every muscle primed and ready to attack.

"No," Morgan argued, pushing his outstretched arms into Harrison's chest, forcing his enraged friend to stop. "All you're doing is scaring innocent people and damaging their homes."

"I don't care! One of these *innocent people* as you call them could be hiding Noah! If I have to, I will ransack every house to find him."

"Harrison, listen to yourself. You sound insane!" Morgan yelled, frowning deeply and pushing back as Harrison tried to get passed him. "Although I can't imagine why Noah didn't kill you when he had the chance, he's gone. He's probably halfway to Siranor by now."

"Then I'll hunt him down there," Harrison spat, glancing towards the hill out of town, knowing the exact route to take.

"And once again, you've landed in the realm of insanity," Morgan replied, grabbing Harrison's weapon hand. "Just take a breath. Shouldn't we focus on finding Nate instead?"

"He'll be hunting Noah too, so we are already doing both," Harrison insisted.

"What do you think happened to him?"

"Alistair thinks he's become a shade. I don't know much about it, but it's a dark power," Harrison answered, reluctantly lowering his blade.

"Power... so Nate's triggered magical abilities?" Morgan surmised. "It can't be like Rylie's recent transformation though, can it? Please tell me he isn't an Aeon."

"No. I think he's just a mage, but the darkness around him looked different. This power is different," Harrison said, sorrow building inside him to accompany the anger.

"What do you mean, could you sense Nate's emotional state?" Morgan questioned, wondering if that was some other ability of the Aegis Guard.

"I don't need to sense how he's feeling. I know how he's feeling."

"What do you mean?" Morgan questioned, his brows furrowing.

"Anguish. And that won't change until Noah's dead," Harrison answered, his tone hollow. "So I'm going to kill him."

"Harrison, you know that won't take the pain away!" Morgan insisted, trying to make his friend see sense. He wasn't raging anymore but the look on his face was ferociously determined. "Don't let Noah change who you are. Don't let him turn you into a mindless killer."

"You credit me with too much goodness, Morgan. You think of me as someone above reproach, but I'm far from it."

"Harrison, you know I'll help you stop Noah. If that means killing him, so be it," Morgan began, trying to use the words his friend would listen to. "But right now, we should focus on what matters. Saving Nate and keeping innocent people safe."

"Between us, Morgan, you're the good one… the hero. I'll leave protecting the people to you. I fight to protect the people I love, and for the second time in as many years, I failed!"

"You're grieving, Harrison," Morgan countered, trying his utmost to console his friend. "What happened here is not your fault."

"Isn't it? She begged me not to come!" Harrison said, his voice breaking. "Evie told me that Noah would attack, and I still couldn't stop him from getting an advantage over me. It should be me that's dead right now, not her!"

"You'd wish that on them?" Morgan challenged, refusing to back down. He knew this feeling, had felt it when Anora died. The healing process was not easy, but he couldn't let his friend blame himself.

"Think of Rylie and all of the people that rely on you in Arencia… your new friends."

As much as he didn't want to, Harrison had to concede to Morgan's point. If he'd died, Nate may have still succumbed to whatever cursed state he was now in and there would be no one alive as motivated to protect his friends or see the one responsible brought before a blade. The only fate he deserved.

Finally accepting that Morgan was right and that Noah was gone, Harrison stalked towards the horses with Morgan following close behind.

"He's like a rat, returning to his hole after killing a weaker mammal," Harrison hissed, and Morgan found the comparison fitting.

Mounting one of the horses, Harrison had to settle the wilful creature which reacted instantly to his rage by snorting and stomping its hooves. Quickly grabbing the reins, Morgan once again used his body to block Harrison's advance.

"Where are you going?" he asked firmly.

"Back to Tivani… for now," Harrison answered, his voice flat but the anger within still pulsing through his veins.

"What are you planning to do?" Morgan added cautiously, moving aside but only to mount his own horse.

"I'm going to show Noah and the Imperator a true *uprising*," Harrison swore.